Agonizomai Series

Book 1

***

Frosted Fire

***

Maegan M. Simpson

DEDICATION

To my brother, Levi.
You may be taller, but I'll always be your big sister

Explore the
Archives of Tyrethia

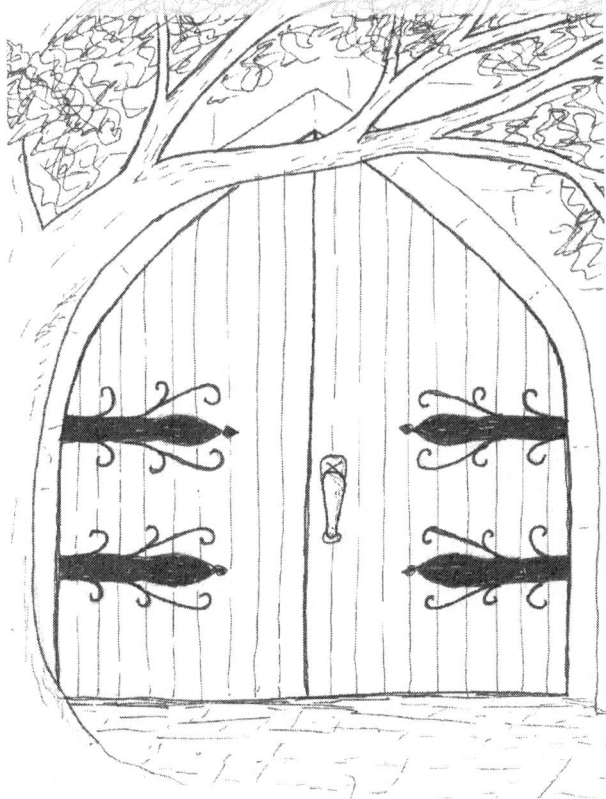

Visit Maegan's Website at:
https://maeganmsimpson.com/

CONTENTS

ACKNOWLEDGMENTS

I would first like to thank my Heavenly Father for the talent and love for writing that He has given me, and the time and freedom to pursue that talent. The credit and glory for this story goes to Him.

Thank you to all my friends who encourage and support me in many ways. I especially want to thank Sarah, for sticking with me since the beginning of this whole writing thing, and Lexi, for listening to all my crazy ideas and encouraging me that they're worth something. And thank you all for being so willing to read my writing and for not laughing at my crazy ideas and moments of inspiration.

Thank you to my professors at Colorado Christian University for teaching me so much and helping me grow, in soul and faith as well as in knowledge. Throughout my time at CCU, you've challenged me to think deeply, to always be learning, and to pursue God with all I am. Thank you for pouring into me, and I pray that the lessons I learned from you are visible in my life and my writing.

And finally, thank you to Mom, Dad, and Levi. Your support allows me to pursue these stories as more than a hobby, and your work behind the scenes is why my books are legible and I am still sane. You help me more than you know, and I continually thank God that He gave me *you* as a family. I love you!

Frosted Fire

Forward:

II Timothy 1:7

For God has not given us a spirit of fear, but of power and of love and of a sound mind.

Author's Note:

This book is the first of The Agonizomai Series. Agonizomai in Greek means to contend with an adversary or to strive earnestly. In our world we are all contestants in the constant spiritual battle between God's people and evil, but so often that battle is unseen and therefore disregarded. The stories of Agon and the visible battles the characters fight are meant to reflect the struggles we face in the spiritual realm every day.

Frosted Fire

Chapter I

Iyanka strolled down the pathway, running her hand down the wet leaves to collect their dewdrop tears in her hand. A breeze caressed her face, free from the stifling summer heat she'd suffered through for months. And free from the baking warmth she constantly endured in the kitchens. It had been too long, far too long, since she'd tasted that refreshing chill in the air.

At least the rains have come, she thought. And with them, a whisper of fall.

Blast this land, and its blistering summer! Why would anyone settle in a land where summers brought heat shimmering across the ground?

I want my home. Home, where even in the depths of summer the nights were cool, the hills green with vibrant life. Home, in the shadows of mountains which always bore a reminder of winter's glittering chill. Where Iyanka knew every sight, and scent, and sound like her own mind.

Home, where her nightmares dwelt.

Images, unbidden, flooded Iyanka's mind. Statues shattered upon the floor, covered in a frost that failed to save its masters. Empty halls, blood-stained stones, walls that held onto the screams that had echoed across them as Iyanka's life crumbled to dust. All that would be left to Iyanka at home was memory, memory that ached and burned…memory that turned to horror, of ice tinged red and numbing terror.

Iyanka stopped, her hand outstretched toward the currant bush beside her, and squeezed her eyes shut. She wasn't there. Those memories weren't here. *Breathe.*

She hadn't come to dwell on what she'd lost, or to spend her scant minutes of freedom chasing ghosts. She'd come for fresh air, to wander under the shadows of the trees that she could trust to protect her secrets as well as they guarded their own. She'd come for a stolen moment of joy. Now, she was afraid it would take more than strolling along a few paths to regain the shards of peace she held onto these days.

But she wouldn't let memories ruin this taste of freedom. She came out determined to enjoy herself, to celebrate the wet air, and she would. She *would.*

She squinted up at the cloudy sky. Cook would expect her to be back in an hour. It didn't leave time to reach the deep forest…unless, of course, she ran. She might make it to that hidden glen. Just a glimpse, just enough to help her hold on until tonight, when she could sneak away.

Iyanka twisted on her heel and took off running through the forest, the cool ground soft under her bare feet. Maybe if she ran fast enough, she'd have a few minutes to spend at the feet of those ancient trees.

The scenery was a blur of greens and browns as she ran. She saw rocks and trees just in time to avoid colliding with them, ignoring the smaller branches that reached out to brush her hair, her arms… Her legs *burned*, her lungs gulping in the cool air as her light red hair streamed out behind her. Slowly, the memories of gray stone stained red blurred with the rest, fading away to be replaced by the here and now: gasping lungs, pounding feet, skin chilled from the wind. She wasn't free from them, but the chains loosened.

Nearing a meadow she'd spent many moonlit hours in, Iyanka slowed to navigate the thicket of trees at its edge. Jumping stumps, weaving between the closely grouped branches, took all of her concentration. So she was caught off-guard by the hand that took hold of her arm, yanking her to the side. Her scream cut off before it really began, muffled by a second hand clasped over her mouth.

Heart pounding, Iyanka looked up into dark, flickering eyes staring out of a soot-covered face. A familiar face. *Andrin.* He was one of the new weaponsmiths Baron Malchomy had brought in over the past few months. He seemed to never leave the fires at the smithy. *Why is he here? Why did he stop me?*

He put a finger to his lips and pointed to the meadow, shifting his grip on her so that she could turn. She did, heart stuttering when she spotted a dozen soldiers filling that friendly space. They wore the dark, stained armor and silver crossbow crest of the wielder hunters. *What are they doing here? Who are they looking for?* She would've run straight into them.

Iyanka turned to Andrin, questions in her eyes. He again motioned for silence and, when Iyanka nodded, removed his hand from her mouth. But the grip on her arm didn't loosen, pulling her down to join him in a crouch. Iyanka tensed at the warmth radiating from his skin, unused to being so close to another person in the open air, but didn't move away. Her focus needed to be on the meadow, on whatever the hunters were doing in her forest.

They both looked out where the hunters trampled the grass. One knight rode at their center, his shield bearing the image of a severed wolf head. Iyanka didn't recognize the coat of arms, but decided his choice of image told her enough. She fervently hoped she never had to meet him, even to serve his dinner.

As she watched, two more hunters emerged from the trees, dragging a prisoner between them: a man clothed in rags and covered in dirt. Iyanka watched with dread as flame licked up the ropes he was tied with, only to die out when they neared the hunters' queer weapons…blocked by the enchantment that had allowed the hunters to conquer the wielders in the first place, the enchantment that made wielders defenseless against them even now.

Small fires in the grass followed the man's progress, quickly snuffed out in the rainy weather. Those fires only increased as the knight dismounted and strode toward the prisoner, flames leaping far into the air only to suddenly die as the knight walked by. The hunter unsheathed his sword.

Iyanka didn't want to see what came next, but she couldn't look away. She couldn't help but watch as this man, this stranger, was murdered for a gift he didn't ask for. Murdered with the help of an enchantment that was far darker and more dangerous than the natural gifts the hunters condemned. The last of the fires flickered to nothing as his blood poured onto the ground, staining it the same red as Iyanka's memories. The same red she'd been trying so hard to escape…

She hardly noticed as the cold slid through her veins, leaking out into the air to freeze any water within its reach. Until she felt a hand on her arm, scalding hot compared to her icy skin.

Andrin hissed in her ear, "Watch yourself, ice princess. You'll get us killed."

Her panicked gasp formed a cloud of steam in the chilled air. *What have I done?* He knew. *He knew.* And how could he not, when Iyanka looked around to see ice coating every surface within arm's reach of her body? Ice princess indeed.

Could she convince him to keep her secret? Could she beg for mercy? *Four years of hiding in a castle of murderers, all for nothing.*

Terror only made it worse. Iyanka's ice kept leaking out of her, extending the bubble of winter surrounding her. If it reached the edge of the trees, it would all be over, no matter what Andrin did. She stumbled back a step, tripping over a root. Andrin caught her, his hand again wrapped around her arm, scalding her skin. She tried, unsuccessfully, to pull away. *Why won't he let go?* Her skin must feel like ice. *Why isn't he calling them to kill me?*

"Hold still," he hissed again, his face so close to hers that his breath tickled her ear. The heat of it melted the frost in her hair, making water drip down the back of her neck. But she obeyed. Closing her eyes, she reined in her cold, beckoning her power to return to her heart where it belonged. But she could do nothing about the ice surrounding her, nothing but pray it melted before the hunters saw it.

She opened her eyes to check its progress, confused when her eyes met bare grass at her feet. She whipped her head up, seeing the ice still clinging to the leaves and branches around her. She took another breath, and realized how warm the air was. Much too warm for the rain-soaked day, too warm for the ice still surrounding them...

Iyanka turned to stare at Andrin, eyes wide and face numb with terror. Small flames shone in his eyes and licked up his arms. They stopped before they touched her skin, but his scalding touch suddenly made far too much sense. *Fire wielder.*

Should she be relieved, that it was a fellow wielder who found out her secret? Or more terrified? Because the wielders of fire and ice had been at war for centuries, and any progress her mother had made toward peace had been destroyed with their kingdoms. Would Andrin decide to continue the war? Would he throw her to the hunters?

While Iyanka's mind twisted, searching for a way to come out of this day alive, Andrin had been pulling them back into the trees, out of sight of the hideous scene they'd just witnessed. Now, he turned and ran, his grip on her wrist forcing her to keep up. His pace was slower than Iyanka's run earlier, but still she struggled. And the entire way, her eyes saw red. Red on stone, red on grass, ice and fire dying away before those wicked blades...

Andrin halted, and Iyanka nearly ran into him. Only after he steadied her did she realize they were at the edge of the forest, near the fortress. She turned to face him and saw his dark eyes lit with flames watching her. She flinched, and he frowned.

"Meet me here tonight," he said.

Iyanka nodded, turning to go back to the oppressive kitchens that right now sounded like a blessed haven. But she stopped when his overheated hand touched her arm, looking over her shoulder to see what he wanted.

His gaze pinned her in place. "If you're not standing here when the moon reaches the top of the trees, I will come in and get you. Understood?"

"Clear as ice," she whispered.

His frown deepened, but he nodded. "Good."

He released his grip on her arm, and that was all the signal she needed to start running. The dark stone shouldn't have looked like sanctuary, but she was so relieved to be out of Andrin's grip, and *not* in the grip of those hunters, that she didn't care. A few words, and he could condemn her to death. And yet instead he asked, *demanded*, that she meet him in the forest. Why? To ask why she was here, of all places? She intended to ask him the same thing.

Andrin's strange request distracted her enough that she was nearly trampled when a dozen horses cantered through the fortress gates. She was left leaning, breathless, against the wall to avoid them. They didn't spare her a second glance. Grateful, but still nervous, she followed them at a slower pace into the courtyard, sticking close to the walls as she made for the entrance closest to the kitchens. But she didn't go in, morbid curiosity causing her to pause and watch the hunters.

They'd stopped in front of the steps leading to the keep, where Baron Malchomy stood and watched with a kind of cold pride. The knight dismounted his horse and climbed the stairs to bow to the baron, while two of the others lifted a long form wrapped in cloth from the back of one of the horses.

A lump formed in her throat as the ice welled up in Iyanka's heart, begging to be released. She forced her eyes away, shutting out the congratulations Baron Malchomy showered on his praised hunters. Her eyes searched the courtyard instead, freezing when they found Andrin leaning casually against the wall near the smithy. He stood there easily: like he'd never been outside, like the whole proceeding meant nothing to him. But his eyes...his eyes burned with fury. Iyanka fled toward the kitchen.

0O0

That evening she quietly slipped from the kitchen, holding her breath until she was sure the often-irritable cook wouldn't demand to know where she was going. Cook had been slightly appeased when Iyanka returned early from her break, but sneaking out when the work wasn't finished would erase any good will Iyanka had accumulated.

As she walked through the courtyard, she noticed the dim glow of the forges to her right, but she resisted the urge to turn and search for his burning gaze among those working there. She would have those disconcerting eyes on her soon enough. There was no good reason for her to seek them out.

It wasn't that long after twilight, but the guards at the gate were already so full of drink that Iyanka stuck to the shadows and walked past them. Once outside, she kept her eyes trained on the dark shadows that marked the trees. She didn't see anyone at their edge. Was he hiding? Was he behind her, following her out into the open? When she reached the shelter of the trees she allowed herself to look back over her shoulder, but no one was there. The open field between her and the fortress contained nothing but moonlight and swaying grass.

"What are you watching for?"

Iyanka squeaked in fear as she turned toward the voice. A tall figure leaned against one of the trees, nearly invisible in the night's shadows. Iyanka met his dark gaze. His flames were hidden, but somehow his eyes still burned. Her mouth opened…and closed when she couldn't remember what words she'd been about to speak. Instead, she just stared at Andrin with fear, and maybe a little admiration.

He pushed away from the tree, stretching his hand out to her. She stared at his hand, breathing deep, before she dared to take it. Her freckled hand looked pale and fragile there, in his calloused palm. But his grasp was gentle in its warmth, nothing like his scalding grip from that morning. He turned toward the trees and strode confidently into their depths, pulling Iyanka along.

Iyanka followed behind more easily than she would've predicted. She visited the forest often under cover of darkness, when the work was finally done and her fears wouldn't let her sleep, but never like this. Following Andrin was strangely simple. She felt in tune with him, like they were connected in some way beyond her hand in his. And Iyanka savored that feeling, even daring to close her eyes. It had been a long time since she'd felt that secure, that close to freedom.

Too soon, Andrin slowed to a stop and dropped her hand. Iyanka tried to ignore the wave of disappointment at the loss of warmth, confused. It should've scared her, the heat of his hand. She opened her eyes, realizing as she turned that she was in her glen.

"How do you know about this place?"

Andrin took a step away from her. The moonlight shone into the clearing with enough strength that Iyanka could see the details of his face. She stared at him, suddenly feeling like she'd never *seen* him before…or maybe that she *had.*

He had smudges of black from the smoke in the smithy, barely visible against the warm brown of his skin, and his dark hair fell in unruly waves across his forehead. His cheekbones were high and well defined, his jaw was square and covered with dark stubble. His eyebrows were lowered over eyes that shone like burning coals even in the dark. He was altogether too handsome for Iyanka's comfort, and that strange familiarity wouldn't go away. It brushed against the edges of her mind, refusing to be captured. His dark eyes locked on her ice blue ones.

"You think you're the only one who seeks the trees' protection? They have more power here than most other places in the forest."

"So, it really is safe," she breathed, looking up at the branches.

"Not safe," he said. "Never safe. The trees can only do so much."

She returned her gaze to Andrin, taking his words to heart. *Never safe.* He still hadn't explained why he'd brought her here.

"Will you turn me in?" she asked.

"No," Andrin answered. His gaze still bored into her, but she couldn't decipher what he was thinking. She thought she saw flames flicker in his eyes.

"Why?" Iyanka asked. "There was no love lost between your people and mine, even when we were at peace."

"That was never true of everyone," he said, his eyes flashing. "You of all people should know that, Princess Iyanka."

Iyanka felt the blood drain from her face, and for once the cold wasn't pleasant.

"How do you know that name?" she gasped.

She hadn't been called Iyanka since her home was attacked. For the second time that day she lost control of her power, and frost crawled across the surface of the ground. When it neared Andrin it halted. The fragile frost was no match for the heat pouring off him.

They stared at each other, neither seeming to notice the obvious power leaking out of them.

"You look far too much like your mother for me to mistake you for anyone else," Andrin said. When he saw her look of confusion he smiled. "I am Prince Victorin."

Iyanka's breath caught. She didn't know if she wanted to scream, cry, laugh, or run away. Prince Victorin, son of King Ignacio, the fire wielder Mother had been negotiating with to become allies. The prince who had agreed to marry a frost princess to seal the treaty...Iyanka's betrothed.

The power they would control if the marriage had taken place was the reason the hunter ranks were formed in the first place. The hunters tore down two kingdoms to keep them apart, and now here they were: hiding as workers in the same castle, threatened by the same enemy.

Was there a possibility they could work together? Could that be why he brought her here, to propose an alliance? Iyanka was so tired of being alone, never able to trust anyone, knowing if anyone found out who she was they would turn her over to the hunters without a second thought.

But how do I know I can trust him? How can I be sure...?

"How long have you known?" she asked.

"The moment I set eyes on you," he said. "It's why I've stayed these months. It's dangerous...too dangerous to leave you here alone."

24

Iyanka blinked. He'd been in the castle for months. If he really wanted to protect her, if he didn't want to leave her behind…

"Why didn't you tell me?"

He raised his eyebrows. "You didn't recognize me. And I wasn't sure you'd believe me if I tried to explain. We only met a handful of times."

Iyanka frowned, turning her eyes to the ground. It was true that they hadn't spent much time together…but she'd always felt safe in his presence. She'd considered him trustworthy. *And yet I'm questioning him now, after he's already protected me…this isn't how mother would've wanted me to act.*

"I apologize," Iyanka said. "Thank you for protecting me today."

Iyanka performed a deep curtsy, spreading her thin skirts around her as best she could. The effect was somewhat ruined by her drab clothes and messy hair, but she could add a flourish to make up for it. She tapped into the ice swirling in her heart and channeled it through her bare feet and into the ground, sending a new layer of frost winding over the dead leaves in the shape of a curling lily. It glittered in the moonlight like silver and diamonds. Iyanka shivered in delight. It felt wonderful to channel her power into something other than making the dish water bearable.

She hadn't dared to do something like this in years, but she felt oddly safe performing for Victorin. She didn't need to hide from him…so why not? It gave her a flash of pride when his face shown with amazement for the briefest second.

"There is no apology necessary," he said.

He snapped his fingers and flames licked across the surface of the ground, melting the frost without even singing the leaves. Iyanka could have sworn the flames were shaped like dragons. She wasn't the only one who enjoyed showing off.

She frowned as the last of the flames disappeared, her mind returning to darker matters. "Why were you at the meadow this morning? Were you following the hunters?"

Victorin's expression darkened, any semblance of amusement disappearing. "No. I was supposed to meet with one of my men, but the hunters found him first."

The fire wielder in the meadow… Victorin knew him. And he'd watched his death. *How did he stand it?* And she'd been selfish enough to fear for *herself…*

Victorin kept his eyes locked on hers as he continued. "If the hunters found him so quickly, it means they suspect I'm in the area. If they find me, chances are they'll find you as well."

His words should have terrified Iyanka, but she understood what he was saying without the accompanying fear. The terror would come later, she was sure, when she was least expecting it. She'd been living with the constant fear of being found for nearly four years…this was no different.

"What do you want me to do?"

"Allow me to protect you," he said. "And…train with me."

Iyanka cocked her head to the side. "Train how?"

Fire and ice could only destroy each other, so what would be the point? Unless he meant fighting *without* using her ice. So she could defend herself. It would make sense…there'd never been a reason for her to learn to fight until it was too late.

While Iyanka thought, Victorin had stepped forward. Now he stood just within reach, and even from that distance she could feel his warmth spilling into the air.

"There was something about us that terrified the barons of the south. Something beyond political power, or else they wouldn't have attacked our kingdoms so fiercely." He paused, inching even closer. "I believe I've discovered what it is."

Iyanka's heart pounded against her ribcage, her breathing shallow. She was intensely aware of Victorin's proximity. At the same time, she couldn't stand the idea of moving away.

"I don't understand," she whispered.

"Let me show you?"

His eyes searched hers, until Iyanka nodded. He took her hand again, this time raising their joined hands, twisting his own hand so their palms pressed against each other. All the while his eyes didn't release hers.

"Send ice into my hand."

Iyanka's lips parted, on the edge of a protest. The look in his eyes stopped her. He was serious…and he knew what he was asking. Gently, she reached into the well in her heart, dipping out a handful of ice to send racing toward her palm. She waited for him to gasp, to pull back. But he didn't. And when her frost reached his skin pressed against her own, it didn't *stop*. The frost continued to spread, leaving her body to crawl up his arm. Still he didn't flinch back. He didn't take his eyes from her.

Iyanka knew when he sparked his fire. But instead of evaporating her frost, like it *should* have, it danced along the ice. As Iyanka stared, the fire took on a bluish hue, racing down Victorin's arm toward her own. She tried to flinch back, but Victorin interlocked his fingers with hers, keeping their hands together. And then the fire was dancing across her own skin.

Iyanka couldn't help the gasp, in fear or maybe wonder, as those flames licked her flesh…and didn't burn. Wherever fire touched her skin, ice appeared to trace its path. She looked back to Victorin. *What's happening?* He didn't speak, but his eyes said enough. Calm, steady…reassuring. And even though what was happening was *impossible*, even though adrenaline raced through her veins to follow the ice, she held still.

Ice and fire continued to spread, until it reached her chest. There, flame enveloped her heart, frolicking around the edges of her well without really touching the ice within. Frost reached out to meet it, and a shiver spread through her body as those elements touched. Again, she gasped.

The fire retreated, as did her frost, until it twined only around their hands in a wreath of blue flame. But Iyanka didn't notice. Her focus was inward, where the smallest flame flickered within her heart. Weak, dwarfed by the snowstorm that dwelt there…but flame nonetheless.

"How?" she breathed, staring at the frost-bitten flames across her fingertips, marveling at that tiny fire in her chest. She looked up.

"Victorin," she said, his name wonderfully foreign on her tongue. "What just happened?"

He was smiling, his eyes lit with hope.

"We just became what the barons fear most."

"I still don't understand."

Iyanka sounded desperate even to her own ears, but she was past caring. Everything she knew, everything she'd been taught about the wielders…all of it was called into question by the sight before her. Fire and ice didn't coexist. Except here they were. And she had no idea what to do with that.

"Iyanka," he said in a calming voice, his eyes capturing her gaze again. "Think back to before the hunters attacked. The southern barons had been supportive of your mother and my father seeking peace. They rejoiced, even. Why would they so suddenly see us as a threat?"

"Hadn't they been planning the attack for years?"

"They had explored weapons capable of defeating us, but from what I can tell they hadn't planned to attack so soon. They attacked Queen Visha in the dead of winter, when she was at her strongest and they at their weakest. My father was in the middle of a war council with his generals and half the army gathered around him. Why would they plan for years and risk it all in the actual attack?"

"They were worried about our kingdoms being united," Iyanka said.

"Think deeper than that," Victorin said.

Deeper… Memories of darkness and confusion rose in her mind. People screaming, ice cracking, men in dark armor killing…no. That was not what he meant. She went further back to the days before the attack that remained as clear as the finest ice in her memories. Most clear was the strange mix of excitement and fear regarding her betrothal, and most painful of all the fierce hope she'd had. The hope of peace for everyone, and of a happy life with the prince her mother esteemed so highly…

"It was a few weeks after our betrothal ceremony," Iyanka said.

Victorin stepped closer. "Just after they learned a prince from the fire kingdom was going to *marry* the daughter of the ice queen."

Iyanka glanced again at their firelit hands. "*This*? This is what they feared?"

"I'm convinced of it." Victorin lowered his hand but didn't release Iyanka. "They knew something we didn't, how we can combine our elements and make them even stronger."

"And how does it work?" Iyanka asked, gently tugging on her hand. He didn't release it, but she realized that she didn't mind.

"I haven't learned that," he admitted. "It's taken me four years to learn this much. Once the alliance of elements is made, it's supposed to bring the power of a dozen wielders. But while we were at war, there wasn't much chance of us rediscovering it."

"But the barons knew," she clarified.

It didn't surprise her that the barons withheld information for their own gain; she'd ceased being astonished at their greediness after a few months of cooking food for them. What she wouldn't have guessed was that their secrets were somewhere Victorin could access.

Then again, she'd heard rumors that fire wielders had spies stationed in every land and fortress across Elnar. How else would an assassin have been able to infiltrate the ice palace itself? Iyanka shook her head, pushing away the dark thoughts. Victorin continued.

"And they know that the information has been shared, as well. The man who guarded the fortress where the records are kept was killed shortly after he gave me access to the text."

"And now they suspect that you're here," Iyanka said, horrified. Watching the fire wielder die at the hand of that knight was heartbreaking, terrifying, *wrong*...but what if something like that happened to Victorin?

"Not yet," Victorin said. "They might suspect that I'm in the area, but they don't know I am in Baron Malchomy's castle. If they even suspected I'd be dead. But that is why we need to leave this place as soon as possible."

"But wouldn't leaving make them suspect us?"

Victorin smirked, which made her heart flutter. "I don't think they would suspect the ice princess and the fire prince were within their walls in the first place, but

I have an idea to make our disappearance less suspicious." He winced. "It would be asking a lot of you, though."

"Tell me," she said, hoping her nerves didn't show. She wouldn't be a fragile princess...she would help.

"We could buy time if we have a reason to be seen together." He met her eyes again. "If, for instance, we were a couple."

Chapter II

Iyanka's breath caught. That…that was not what she had expected. Victorin continued before she could find her voice.

"We can court long enough for all of the servants to realize what's going on, then when we disappear they'll assume we've eloped. It's…unfair to use you in such a way, but it *would* erase any suspicion."

And like that, Iyanka's hopes were dashed. For the briefest moment, she had thought his request was genuine, that he actually wanted to court her. That, maybe, he wanted to pick up where they left off four years ago.

She was *so* foolish! Of course Victorin wouldn't want to tie himself to her after all that had happened, and certainly not the first day they'd spoken in over four years. She should *not* be disappointed. *And yet I am.* She closed her eyes so her hurt wouldn't show, fighting to keep her voice steady.

"Victorin," she said. "We were betrothed. The idea of you pretending to court me is not offensive."

Her voice wavered, but she'd have to live with it. When she opened her eyes, she was shocked to meet Victorin's gaze, suddenly intense. She quickly looked away, but not before she caught a glimpse of *something* in his eyes, some strong emotion she couldn't name. Hopefully it wasn't contempt.

Victorin cleared his throat. He stepped back and finally released Iyanka's hand, to her disappointment. She hadn't realized how oddly *comforting* it was to feel his fire blending with her frost until it flickered out. Her hand suddenly felt bare, incomplete.

"We should return," he said. "You need to rest."

Iyanka doubted there would be much rest for her tonight, but she refrained from saying so. If she did, he'd ask for an explanation, and that was something she didn't want to get into at the moment. There was nothing he could do about it, anyway.

Iyanka was silently glad when Victorin offered his hand to her again, to lead her back through the darkened forest. She knew where they were. She didn't *need* guidance to get back. But she wasn't going to tell Victorin that…she wanted to feel his calloused fingers around her hand. Tangible proof that she wasn't alone…for the first time in four years, she wasn't alone.

But even that didn't erase the foolish disappointment in her heart. But why? Why would she be disappointed? He was protecting her, he'd shown her a secret he'd spent *years* searching for, trusting her with a melding of powers she'd never guessed was possible. And he was going to get her *out* of this place. There was so much for her to be grateful for, to thank the Creator for. Did she really expect him to regard her betrothal as still binding, even after all that had happened to nullify it? What would she even feel if he *had*? *I shouldn't wish for more. This is enough…more than enough.*

Frosted Fire

Victorin released her hand as soon as they met the edge of the trees, turning to face her.

"We should enter separately. Even with the guards so unaware, I don't want to risk being seen together yet."

"Alright," Iyanka said, though she'd rather he walked her to the door. *This is enough.* She dipped into a shallow curtsey. "Goodnight, *Andrin.*"

"Goodnight, *Glafira,*" he said, calling her by the name she was known by in the fortress. She thought she saw him smile, but it was too dark here to be sure. She turned and jogged to the castle gate, resisting the urge to turn and see if he was watching her. But at the gate she slowed, not wanting to wake the guards. They never even stirred.

Iyanka made her way up to the room she shared with the other kitchen maids and laid on her thin cot. The fear didn't strike that night; she was too busy marveling at the new feeling in her heart. As weak as the fire was in Iyanka's heart, it was there, and she didn't think it was going away. She wondered if she could conjure a flame. She didn't dare try at that moment, but the curiosity burned within her. What were she and Victorin capable of now that they shared each other's power?

The power of a wielder was a part of who they were, a part of their very being. Wielders were *created* with the ability to manipulate ice, or fire, or wind, within their hearts. If that power was taken away, they would die. That was why the enchantments the hunters used were so dark and dangerous: it stole the

35

wielders' element from their very blood. If she now had a piece of Victorin's element within her heart, and hers in his, it meant they were connected in ways Iyanka hadn't thought possible. She couldn't begin to guess the implications of what they'd done.

But more than that was her wonder, her *joy*, that Victorin was *alive.* Alive and *here*, sleeping under the same roof. Iyanka had spent the past four years believing everyone she ever knew to be dead. She'd learned to live with the loneliness, but now…now she didn't have to. Victorin: the prince who fought for peace, the prince her mother had trusted so completely…the prince she'd dreamed of having a life with. He was *here*. He wanted to protect her. That warmed Iyanka's heart more than the fire, more than the mystery of what had occurred that night. She had someone here who *knew* her, knew her and wasn't afraid or disgusted. She had someone she could confide in.

Iyanka sighed in contentment as she rested her head on her pillow. She fell asleep looking back on memories of Prince Victorin in the ice palace, and comparing them to the ash-smudged man she saw today. His burning gaze shone in all of her memories, making her feel protected and cared for.

OOO

Iyanka awoke to Elsie's poking and prodding. Iyanka groaned, but obediently sat up and pried her eyes open. Elsie stood beside her bed, already dressed, as she tied off the end of her braid. She grinned as Iyanka slowly blinked up at her.

"Time to wake up, lazy bones."

Iyanka rolled her eyes as she stood. "I'm no more lazy than you, Elsie."

Elsie raised her eyebrows. "Is that so? Well at least I didn't sneak away early for who-knows-what purpose."

She winced. "Was I missed?"

Elsie put a dramatic hand to her chest. "Only by yours truly. Gretta was the only other one to realize you were gone, and she would never tell."

"Don't count on it," Gretta called across the room. "If I have to wash caramel off one more bowl I'll be as insane as the wielders."

Elsie tipped her head back and laughed, so she didn't see Iyanka flinch. "We have all had our time washing. Be thankful it wasn't that fancy dish Baron Leon demands whenever he comes a-calling. Now *that* is a nightmare to wash off."

There was a chorus of agreement from the other girls in the room. Iyanka quickly pulled on her dress and started finger combing her hair. Most of the other girls were already dressed and were fixing their hair, or straightening their beds. She must have slept in.

Elsie plopped down on the pad next to Iyanka. "So where *did* you go last night?"

"The forest," Iyanka answered, hoping they wouldn't ask anything else. She didn't know how much she could tell without giving something away.

"That creepy place?" Gretta scrunched up her nose. "Why would you go there?"

"Gretta," Lynn said, shaking her head. "Don't sound so reproachful. There are plenty of things she could've been doing in the forest..." her smile turned mischievous, though her eyes weren't as bright as usual. "Like meeting a special someone."

Iyanka rolled her eyes. They were closer to the truth than she liked, and she didn't want to encourage any rumors. Although, if Victorin was going to pretend to court her...

Elsie bounced in her seat. "Is that it, Glafira? Did you sneak away to meet with your true love?"

Iyanka giggled at Elsie's dramatic words. "Something like that."

That gained all of the girls' attention. They crowded around Iyanka, all asking questions about the man Iyanka went to meet. She answered all of them as vaguely as possible, or not at all. Gretta stood at the door with her hands on her hips.

"It's time to get to the kitchen before Cook comes up here to get us. I don't fancy attracting her ire today of all days."

The girls complained as they stood and finished readying themselves, but there was an urgency in their movements now. No one wanted to raise Cook's ire. Iyanka braided her hair and tied off the end, then strode out the door. But her joy had dimmed at the reminder of what today signified: the fourth anniversary of the hunters' attack on Eisadel and Siersh. Cook was bound to be in a foul mood because of it; her son was one of the soldiers killed during the attack on Siersh, the fire kingdom. Iyanka also dreaded this day, and all the memories it held: the day her world collapsed in blood and ash.

That night would be the barons' grand feast celebrating the slaughter of Iyanka and Victorin's peoples. Iyanka only hoped she wasn't chosen to serve. She did *not* want to be in that room as the hunters and barons painted the wielders as bloodthirsty barbarians and bragged of the women and children they'd killed. She didn't want to risk losing control and frosting them all.

Iyanka entered the kitchen and went about her work as usual. Cook was in a bad mood as expected, but Iyanka kept her head down and didn't draw any attention to herself. The day went along like normal, besides the extra preparations for the feast. Iyanka did her best to concentrate on her work, but during the monotonous tasks she couldn't help but daydream.

Throughout the day she felt the fire in her heart flare at seemingly random moments. After a while she realized it was Victorin using his fire in the smithy. How lucky he was to have a trade that allowed him to *use* the power within him, even if it was just for heating forges. Iyanka had to make do with cooling scalding pans when no one was looking. Still, feeling that he was near was comforting.

At one point near the middle of the day, Iyanka tried to summon a flame on her fingertip. No matter how she tried, though, she couldn't channel the fire in her heart. It was there, but it wasn't hers to control. Her ice came as readily as ever, and when she tried it she had to plunge the pot she was holding into the dishwater so no one would see the frost coating its surface.

With all of the busyness in the kitchen, and her focus on the pulsing fire in her heart, she could almost forget the barons in the halls above. When the time came for taking the food to the great hall and serving, Iyanka hung back and continued washing the never-ending pile of dishes. The other girls were chosen, leaving only Cook and Lynn in the kitchen with her. On her way out, Elsie glided past and embraced Iyanka from behind.

"You're an angel," she said.

"Have fun," Iyanka answered, her cheeks burning with shame. They all thought she stayed behind as a sacrifice. But the truth was she would rather wash dishes for the rest of her life than go serve wine to the barons. She cooked their food and worked in their halls, but she didn't want to have to face them, or their favored hunters.

Lynn and Iyanka cleaned the kitchen and washed the dishes the girls brought down from the great hall. They worked in silence and pretended not to notice Cook's red rimmed eyes. The work was hot and exhausting, but it was no different from usual. The feast would last all night, but Cook allowed Lynn and Iyanka to leave once the kitchen was clean.

Lynn went straight up to bed, but Iyanka ducked into the courtyard. It had occurred to her earlier that Victorin hadn't specified when he wanted to meet again. She hoped he would still be in the smithy so she could talk to him. The pulsing of Victorin calling upon his fire had stopped a while ago, but maybe he was still around.

Iyanka was in the middle of the courtyard when she heard raucous laughter. She turned and saw a group of five or six men sitting on the stairs together. They didn't wear their armor, but the swords still at their hips marked them as hunters. No other weapon emitted such dark emptiness. She ducked her head and continued her trek across the courtyard, but one of them saw her and called out. Iyanka tried to ignore them and keep walking, but one of them stood and strode toward her.

"What's a pretty girl like you doing out so late?" he asked, smiling in a way that made Iyanka's skin crawl. Her fingertips cooled, but she clenched her hands into fists.

"Looking for someone," she answered.

"I'm someone," another of the men called.

Dread churned in Iyanka's stomach, and ice spread to join it. The man stepped closer.

"I need to go," Iyanka said, turning toward the smithy and praying Victorin was there.

The man called out asking her to wait, but he didn't follow her. Iyanka ducked into the smithy so she was out of sight and looked around. She was grateful to see Victorin's tall frame outlined in the glow of the forges, and even more grateful to see that he was alone.

"Glafira?" he asked. "What are you doing here?"

His tone was disapproving, and protective. It made the dread melt away. The ice was more reluctant to fade, but that was alright.

Iyanka edged away from the door. "I wanted to talk to you. We didn't set up another time to meet."

Victorin stepped away from the forges, which caused the glow to light up one side of his face. His expression was grim.

"Now isn't a good time."

"Why not?"

Victorin stepped closer and bent down to whisper in Iyanka's ear. "The barons aren't just here to celebrate. They are here for a council to decide how to counter wielder resistance."

Iyanka's breath caught. Victorin stepped back and looked down at her.

"You don't have to be frightened. They'll be watching the gates closely, but if they suspected us we would already be dead."

The thought struck her that his words weren't very comforting, but that wasn't why her heart was pounding.

"Resistance?" she whispered. "There are enough wielders left that they're fighting back?"

Victorin's eyebrows lowered in concern. "You didn't know?"

Iyanka shook her head, silently reeling. *Resistance.* Why hadn't she heard?

"The only news I've heard about wielders is the hunters bragging of their conquests. I...I thought I was alone."

Victorin frowned and looked around. "This isn't a good time," he muttered, obviously conflicted. Iyanka placed her hand on his arm to get his attention.

"What is it?" she asked.

Victorin met her gaze and his face smoothed, his eyes warm and soft. He glanced around again.

"Do you know of any place in the castle where we can be sure we won't be overheard?"

"The store rooms, but Cook is still up…" Iyanka bit her lip as she mentally paged through the places that would be abandoned at this time of night. "We could go to one of the towers."

Victorin frowned again. "There aren't guards in them?"

She shook her head. "No one is ever in the towers. I don't know why."

Victorin hesitated. "Alright," he said. "Which is the easiest to reach without anyone seeing us?"

Iyanka bit her lip again. "Normally, the one to the east, nearest the kitchens, but…"

"But what?"

"There are hunters in the courtyard," she admitted.

Victorin's expression darkened. "And you walked over here by yourself?"

"Yes," Iyanka admitted, looking down to avoid his gaze.

Victorin sighed. "Let's just go, then. They probably won't even remember seeing us, come morning."

Victorin strode into the courtyard, gaze on their destination, and Iyanka trailed close behind him. She tried not to look at the soldiers still sprawled across the stairs, tried to resist the urge to grab onto the back of Victorin's shirt, just to reassure herself that he was close. They only made it ten steps into the courtyard before one of the soldiers whistled.

"So that's who you were looking for," he called.

Iyanka hunched her shoulders and kept walking. Victorin fell back so he was between her and the men, but that just incited more comments. Iyanka was content to ignore them and get through the courtyard as quickly as possible, but when one of the men commented on Iyanka's purity Victorin stopped. He turned to face the hunters, ignoring Iyanka's tugs on his arm.

Dread and ice flooded through Iyanka again. If Victorin used his fire, there was no way it could end well. Heat surged in her chest, and Iyanka watched in horror as Victorin's face darkened. She could see flames in his eyes, but could they? The hunters were nudging each other and joking around, so apparently not.

"Victorin," Iyanka whispered, forgetting to use his alias in her panic. "Don't."

The fire surged again, and Iyanka panicked. She tried the first thing that came to mind, which was covering the fire with her ice. Not enough to smother it...just enough to cool the flames. It worked, and Victorin looked down at Iyanka with alarm.

"Let's go," she mouthed.

After an eternal moment, he nodded. But he wrapped a protective arm around her shoulders before continuing, this time ignoring the comments the hunters still lobbed at them.

Iyanka breathed a sigh of relief when they made it inside. Victorin didn't pause or even slow, but kept moving through the halls and into the tower. When they climbed through the trap door that led to the top of the tower, Victorin carefully lowered the wooden door and turned to Iyanka. She stood with her back to the wall and waited for him to speak.

"How did you do that?"

Iyanka shrugged, worried that he was angry. "I didn't think. I was scared, and I did the first thing I could think of to get your attention."

He kept staring at her, and Iyanka shifted nervously. "I hope I didn't hurt you. I just didn't want you to do anything that would reveal you."

He shook his head. "I was going to blast those wretched..." he trailed off and shook his head. "But just when I was reaching for my fire, your ice rose up and cooled it. It didn't *hurt*, it was just...strange."

"So, we can prevent each other from using our elements?" Iyanka asked with dismay. She didn't want that kind of power over anyone.

"No," Victorin said. "If I'd needed to, I could've reached my fire, but your ice slowed me down long enough to realize what I was doing."

Iyanka relaxed. That was alright, then. "What else do you think we can do?"

He shook his head. "I don't know. We'll have to discover our capabilities as we go."

"Is there no way to find more information about mixing elements?"

Victorin frowned, and there was a trace of fury in his eyes. "I'd sent Crevan to search for just that, but whatever he found is now lost."

Crevan must have been the fire wielder in the meadow. Iyanka's heart ached, but she didn't know anything she could do to help him. She settled for resting a comforting hand on his arm.

He smiled wanly and shook his head. "That isn't what we came up here to discuss."

Iyanka shrugged and stared up at Victorin, waiting for him to speak. He stared back at her.

"You know nothing of what's happened to the wielders since the attack?"

"I know that the hunters have never stopped searching for wielders in hiding," Iyanka said, shivering. "Even Frieda's Refuge isn't safe anymore."

"The city isn't," Victorin said. "The forest in the north of Frieda's Refuge has become a haven of sorts for Wielders revolting against the barons. The thick trees and steep ravines make it difficult for the hunters to pursue them."

"Have you been there?" Iyanka asked. "How many wielders are there?"

"I have been there," Victorin answered. "When last I visited there were a few thousand hidden in villages throughout the forest, but more wielders keep traveling there. They have a leader who organizes raids for supplies and keeps the hunters busy so they can't search for the villages."

Over a thousand wielders in hiding...that was beyond anything Iyanka could have hoped for. "Are there wielders in other places too? Are they evading the capture more successfully than the hunters claim?"

"Yes," Victorin said slowly. "There are others. Some are successful at hiding, but the hunters are still lethal. It is dangerous trying to hide in plain sight, and it has resulted in more lost lives than any of the resistance attacks."

His voice was reproachful now, and Iyanka closed her eyes. "I know it's dangerous. But I didn't know what else to do. I didn't think I had anyone to turn to."

"You could've turned to your family."

Iyanka opened her eyes. Victorin was watching her with caution. "What do you mean?"

"The resistance in Frieda's Refuge is led by Prince Milek."

Iyanka stared at him, her mouth open but no words coming out. Her heart thundered in her ears. Milek was *alive*? Her little brother was alive? She reached out and put a hand on the stone to steady herself, frost spreading across the stone in response to her touch. Victorin took her hand in his, halting the spread of frost, and swept his hand over the stone to melt the ice.

Iyanka watched with a strange detachment. Milek, her little brother, was leading the wielder resistance? The boy who squeaked when he was frustrated and loved to play pranks on the servants was responsible for hundreds of lives? *Milek is alive!* She didn't realize she was crying until the tears froze on her cheeks, falling only to shatter on the stone.

"How?" Iyanka choked out, her eyes desperately searching Victorin's. "How did he survive the attack?"

"I don't know," Victorin admitted. He watched her closely, worriedly. "As soon as I could, I travelled to the ice palace, but it was days after the attack. The hunters were pursuing the wielders to Frieda's Refuge. Milek was leading a group in a search for survivors when I arrived…he wasn't in a state to explain how he escaped."

"Oh, Milek," Iyanka whispered. He was only fifteen when the barons attacked…only fifteen! She should have been there for him. She should have stayed instead of running.

"Does he know I'm here?" Iyanka asked. She stared out at the tops of the trees, not really seeing anything.

"Yes," Victorin answered. "I sent word to him as soon as I knew it was you. He almost came to see you, but the consequences would be too great. Milek would be easily recognized, and he didn't want to put you in any more danger."

Iyanka nodded, though more tears slipped down her frozen cheeks. Milek didn't want to put *her* in danger? He should be worrying about putting himself in danger! She knew danger, she'd been living with danger for four years.

It sounded like her little brother was all grown up. Would she ever see him?

"When we leave," Iyanka said, turning to Victorin. "Where will we go?"

"Creator willing, we'll go to Frieda's Refuge to reunite you with Milek. But the journey will take weeks, longer if we have hunters on our trail."

"When can we leave?"

Victorin looked out on the forest with a thoughtful look. "It's hard to say. Much of it depends on what the barons decide at this council."

"What do we do until then?" Iyanka asked, bouncing on her feet.

"We keep our heads down and begin our plan," he said. "We need to cement our excuse for disappearing without drawing the attention of the soldiers or the barons."

Iyanka nodded, suddenly very aware of Victorin's warm grasp on her hand. "How do we begin?" she asked, not meeting his eyes.

"When do you next have liberty?"

"Not for several days, maybe longer with all of the guests here," she admitted. What she didn't add was that she might have to stay in the kitchen even then to make up for the times she sneaked away. Iyanka didn't enjoy leaving all the others to the work she was supposed to do, but there were times when she couldn't *bear* to be in the kitchens.

"Can you meet after your work is complete?"

"Yes," Iyanka said without hesitation. She got little sleep no matter when she retired, so why not use the time for something that mattered?

"Good. Meet me at the forest's edge tomorrow night once you leave the kitchens."

"That may not be until late," Iyanka warned.

"It doesn't matter," he said. "I'll be waiting."

"Alright," she whispered.

He turned and tugged her toward the stairs, seeming to forget that he was holding her hand. She followed without complaint. He led her down the stairs and through the halls, only stopping when they reached the stairwell that went up to the servants' quarters. Victorin turned to face her, releasing her hand.

"Sleep well," he said.

"I'll see you tomorrow," she said, smiling.

Victorin nodded and tucked a strand of her hair behind her ear. He met her gaze and smirked. "Try not to ice over the castle between now and then."

Iyanka's breath caught, and before she could respond he was out of sight. She waited there for a few seconds before turning to climb the stairs, a smile still on her lips. She opened the door slowly and closed it behind her as silently as she could in case Lynn was already asleep, jumping when she turned and found Elsie standing next to her cot. She looked over at Iyanka and smiled in a mischievous way she recognized all too well.

"Look at that smile," Elsie whispered, walking over to Iyanka. "You were with your secret love."

Iyanka rolled her eyes, heart pounding and face heating. "Not everything has to do with romance, Elsie."

She tried to walk over to her cot, but Elsie slipped in front of her.

"Oh no," she said. "You're not brushing me off that easily. He has to be really special to put that sweet smile on your face."

He turned and tugged her toward the stairs, seeming to forget that he was holding her hand. She followed without complaint. He led her down the stairs and through the halls, only stopping when they reached the stairwell that went up to the servants' quarters. Victorin turned to face her, releasing her hand.

"Sleep well," he said.

"I'll see you tomorrow," she said, smiling.

Victorin nodded and tucked a strand of her hair behind her ear. He met her gaze and smirked. "Try not to ice over the castle between now and then."

Iyanka's breath caught, and before she could respond he was out of sight. She waited there for a few seconds before turning to climb the stairs, a smile still on her lips. She opened the door slowly and closed it behind her as silently as she could in case Lynn was already asleep, jumping when she turned and found Elsie standing next to her cot. She looked over at Iyanka and smiled in a mischievous way she recognized all too well.

"Look at that smile," Elsie whispered, walking over to Iyanka. "You were with your secret love."

Iyanka rolled her eyes, heart pounding and face heating. "Not everything has to do with romance, Elsie."

She tried to walk over to her cot, but Elsie slipped in front of her.

"Oh no," she said. "You're not brushing me off that easily. He has to be really special to put that sweet smile on your face."

"When can we leave?"

Victorin looked out on the forest with a thoughtful look. "It's hard to say. Much of it depends on what the barons decide at this council."

"What do we do until then?" Iyanka asked, bouncing on her feet.

"We keep our heads down and begin our plan," he said. "We need to cement our excuse for disappearing without drawing the attention of the soldiers or the barons."

Iyanka nodded, suddenly very aware of Victorin's warm grasp on her hand. "How do we begin?" she asked, not meeting his eyes.

"When do you next have liberty?"

"Not for several days, maybe longer with all of the guests here," she admitted. What she didn't add was that she might have to stay in the kitchen even then to make up for the times she sneaked away. Iyanka didn't enjoy leaving all the others to the work she was supposed to do, but there were times when she couldn't *bear* to be in the kitchens.

"Can you meet after your work is complete?"

"Yes," Iyanka said without hesitation. She got little sleep no matter when she retired, so why not use the time for something that mattered?

"Good. Meet me at the forest's edge tomorrow night once you leave the kitchens."

"That may not be until late," Iyanka warned.

"It doesn't matter," he said. "I'll be waiting."

"Alright," she whispered.

Chapter III

Rising the next morning seemed like an impossible task. Every part of Iyanka begged to go back to sleep, and if it wasn't for Elsie and Lynn's prodding she would've given in. On a normal night, kitchen workers got few hours of sleep, and Iyanka was used to less than most. This time was worse, though. She'd only gotten snatches of sleep, and even that wasn't restful.

Iyanka rose and dressed under Lynn's watchful gaze. She went downstairs with all the other girls, but she felt strangely detached. Everything was the same routine she'd gone through for years, and yet not. She saw it through a different lens knowing that Milek was alive. Her time at the castle, working in the hot kitchen and joking with the other girls, was all unnecessary. Her fear and pain and loneliness all could've been prevented. If only she'd had the courage to stay in the north. She could've spent those four years surrounded by people who loved and needed her. She could've helped her brother.

Elsie and Lynn tried to tease Iyanka out of her mood, but after a while they gave up. She felt a little guilty, but she was also grateful. With all that was spiraling around in her head, she didn't have the energy for interacting with anyone. It was hard enough concentrating on her work and not frosting everything she touched in her emotional angst.

She couldn't wrap her head around the idea that Milek was alive. It was more than she could've hoped for, and yet it filled her with sorrow. All the time she'd spent in Baron Malchomy's castle, her little brother had been providing safety to wielders and *leading* them. How was he leading over a thousand wielders at nineteen years old? How was he keeping the hunters away and solving the problems of so many all on his own? Milek shouldn't have all that responsibility on his shoulders.

Her thoughts of Milek continued in a swirling mess of indescribable joy and crippling guilt until that afternoon, when a hunter entered the kitchen and banished it all with an ocean of familiar dread. His presence brought unusual silence as everyone went about their work as unobtrusively as possible. They may have held up the hunters as their protectors, but Iyanka had learned that few people in Baron Malchomy's fortress felt comfortable interacting with them.

The thought struck her that hunters must've been lonely, when even the people they supposedly protected shunned them. But she shook her head and did her best to banish the thought. Hunters were evil; they used evil enchantments and hunted down innocent people. They didn't deserve her pity.

The soldier walked around a bit, until Cook came in and saw him. She put her hands on her hips and stared him down.

"What are you doing in my kitchen?"

He bowed his head to her, but his eyes still darted around the kitchen. Iyanka's fingertips grew cold as her ice ran through her veins. *Why is he here?*

He looked around at everyone, his boring gaze causing every girl to lower her eyes except Gretta. He looked back to Cook and spoke. "I'm here on the orders of Captain Wulfguard. For the safety of everyone present, the castle is to be searched and the inhabitants examined."

"For the safety of…posh," Cook said. "You're doing nothing except disturbing our work."

"I have orders," he said, unintimidated by Cook's tone.

"And I have mine," she countered. "There's plenty of work to be done without you coming in and stealing my workers for some nonsense. There are no fugitives in here, you can be sure of it."

"You do not want to resist," the soldier warned.

"I'm not resisting, I'm refusing. Now pick up an apron and start cooking, or get out."

Cook and the hunter glared at each other as everyone in the kitchen held their breath. Iyanka had never seen anyone speak so boldly to a hunter. Then again, she'd never seen anyone stand up to Cook, either. The tension was as thick as winter frost as they waited to see what would happen.

After a minute the soldier broke eye contact with Cook and strode to the wall where the aprons hung. He grabbed one off its hook and quickly tied it over his uniform. Despite the danger he emanated, the flour-spattered apron covering the dark uniform was an amusing picture. He turned back to Cook, his chin lifted in defiance.

"I have my orders," he said.

Cook shook her head and muttered something about stubborn boys.

"Fine," she said, tossing a hand in the air. "Have it your way. Now start peeling potatoes."

He nodded and turned toward the sack of potatoes on the wooden table. The girl there nervously edged out of his way as he picked up a potato and a knife.

"One more thing, hunter," Cook said. "If you touch one of my girls, you'll find yourself tossed out faster than you can say feast day. No matter your blasted orders, understood?"

The hunter nodded. Cook huffed and turned, glaring at everyone until each girl returned to her work. The kitchen was more silent than Iyanka had ever heard it, and everyone kept sneaking glances at the hunter calmly peeling potatoes at the table. He worked with his hands while his eyes roved the kitchen, his gaze intense and probing. Occasionally he'd meet the gaze of a girl watching him, and the girl would quickly duck her head.

Iyanka resisted the urge to look at him, worried that he'd see the ice in her eyes and recognize what she was. Like the others, though, eventually she fell to temptation and looked his way. His head was lowered, but as soon as Iyanka looked at him he looked up, his gaze locking on hers. He straightened in his chair and continued staring at her, almost as if he was daring her to look away. His eyes were dark; sad, but hard and challenging. Nothing like Victorin's warm gaze. Iyanka ripped her eyes away and stared down at the spoon in her hands. She needed to concentrate on her work.

Iyanka continued with her task and kept her gaze firmly on what was in front of her. A part of her screamed to glance over, just once, just to make sure that he wasn't watching her. She resisted and tried turning her mind to other things. If she kept looking at him, it might raise suspicion. The other girls had practically forgotten his presence already. The only sign they remembered was how they skirted around him in a wide circle. Except bold Gretta. She walked right past him without a glance or bat of the eye. Iyanka would've thought she couldn't care less about the hunter's presence if it weren't for the way her hands shook the slightest bit.

The rest of the day passed too slowly. Iyanka was counting the seconds until she could escape the kitchens to see Victorin, and the hunter's presence was making the day drag on far too slowly. To be fair, he did work hard at whatever task Cook assigned him. Iyanka didn't think he'd said a single word since the end of his standoff with Cook. He just worked and watched.

He watched all the girls work and interact with each other. He watched Cook bustle about, setting tasks for everyone and completing her own work. He watched the clamor of girls wanting to serve supper. Iyanka managed to not look straight at him again, but she knew that he still watched. She knew he watched as she, Elsie, and another girl stayed behind to finish the day's work and prepare for the next day.

Cook walked up and handed him a small loaf of bread with meat stuffed in the middle, standard fare for the kitchen girls as it could be eaten quickly and didn't require utensils. Still, he didn't move from his seat at the table. Iyanka went about her work, trying to go at the same pace as Elsie even though she wanted to rush through everything.

"You may go," Cook said to the hunter. Her voice wasn't friendly, but Iyanka couldn't tell if it had any more crankiness than usual.

"The work isn't finished," the hunter protested in a silky voice.

"Close enough to finished," she said. "I don't have any more work for you, and I want you out of my kitchen."

"*My* work isn't finished," he said. "Since the work here is almost done, I'm sure you wouldn't mind if I ask your workers some questions."

"Yes," Cook said, crossing her arms over her chest, "I would mind. You have no reason to question my girls. The Baron knows I'm no wielder sympathizer, and I know these girls like my own children."

The hunter's eyes glittered as he stood. "Then you shouldn't mind if I question them."

"You'll scare them silly looming over them, asking them foolish questions with that dark weapon of yours at your belt."

"I'd advise you to watch your words," the hunter said. "This *dark weapon* is why you're in this kitchen and not enslaved to those monsters."

"They're tools of darkness, and that's plain for any to see. I won't have a lad like you near my girls. Now get out."

"Fine," the hunter said. "But think long and hard about who you're really loyal to. I expect more cooperation when I return tomorrow."

Cook sputtered about not having him in her kitchen again, but he was already gone. Iyanka felt like she could finally breathe again. The kitchen suddenly seemed warmer and brighter with the hunter gone, which worried Iyanka as much as anything. If the hunter's enchantment affected her that much just being in the same room, what would it do if a hunter actually held her at the point of his sword? Would it begin to steal her ice even without touching her blood, or would it merely block her ability to use it?

Cook stopped glaring at the doorway to turn toward Iyanka and the other two girls standing near the washtubs.

"That's enough for tonight," she said. "But wait a few minutes before you leave. Make sure he gets back to whatever hole he sleeps in at night."

Elsie and Iyanka exchanged glances. No one talked about the hunters in that way…no one. Even those who believed the enchantments they used were evil didn't say anything disrespectful where others could *hear*. Why did Cook dislike this hunter so much? She thought wielders were monsters, so she should've seen the hunters as heroes. Why was she so bent on protecting her workers from him? The hunter was a danger only to Iyanka, and Cook couldn't have even known that.

Iyanka worked alongside the other two girls for a few more minutes, cleaning up while they waited for the hunter to be long gone. Assuming he wasn't waiting for them to come out so he could question them without Cook's interference. Iyanka shivered.

Finally Cook shooed them out of the kitchen, and the girls called goodnight as they fled to escape the towel she snapped at them. Elsie and the other girl, Liesel, giggled, but it was all Iyanka could do to force a smile. She only bothered with the effort to prevent their questions. She wasn't sure she could withstand them tonight, not without giving something away.

They reached the stairs that led to the servants' rooms and Iyanka stopped.

"Are you coming?" Liesel asked.

Iyanka shook her head. "I need some fresh air. I'll be up in a while."

Liesel pursed her lips and started to protest, but Elsie grabbed her hand and pulled her up the stairs.

"If Glafira wants to sit out in the cold, let her. We'll be in our warm beds getting well-earned rest."

Liesel turned and climbed the stairs, not seeing Elsie turn back and wink at Iyanka. Iyanka sighed in relief, for once grateful for Elsie's obsession with all things romantic. She turned away from the stairs and toward the exit. The courtyard was abandoned and silent, but Iyanka was cautious as she edged toward the gate. She didn't trust the silence, not tonight. The guards weren't as unaware as they were most nights, but they still weren't hard to sneak past. They were so involved with their own conversation they didn't even see her.

Honestly, she thought as she walked toward the forest. *I don't understand why they keep these sentries. Anyone could get in or out and no one would know until it was too late.* She supposed she should be grateful—their lax behavior was the reason she could come and go so freely—but the lack of security bothered her. Even in the fortress of her enemy, she couldn't shake the feeling that having such horrible sentries was dangerous. The sentries at the ice palace were wonderful men who took their charge seriously, and yet assassins were still able to kill her father in his own study. What could happen to the baron and his guests if even a kitchen girl could sneak past his guards? More importantly, what could happen to his people? He claimed the blood he'd shed was to protect his people, and yet he didn't care enough to train better sentries to protect them.

Iyanka shook her head and picked up her pace. Here she was dawdling and thinking about Baron Malchomy's negligence when she should already be with Victorin. She looked up at the trees and thought she saw his shape in the deep shadows. She started running, grinning when he stepped into the moonlight as she drew closer.

She stopped in front of him, trying to school her expression so her smile wasn't quite so wide. To her shock, he took a step to close the distance between them and grabbed her in a tight embrace. Iyanka was stiff for a single heartbeat, unsure how to respond, before she let herself relax. She felt so safe in his warm arms...

"Don't turn around," he whispered. "Someone is watching us from the tower."

And just like that, all thoughts of safety and warmth drained away, fear flowing in to take its place. *The hunter from the kitchens?* Had he seen her leave? Did he want to know where she was going? The ground seemed to quake beneath her, and it took her a moment to realize it was her own body trembling, her legs threatening to give out. Victorin tightened his hold on her.

"Don't be afraid," he said. "He won't see us once we're in the trees."

Iyanka nodded, not trusting her voice. Victorin changed his grip on her so they were side by side, but he didn't let go of her waist. She kept her arm wrapped around him, leaning on him. Maybe he'd think it was so she didn't fall, but really Iyanka wanted his nearness, his warmth. She wanted to hide in his arms, to be sure he was really *beside* her. She imagined from the tower they would look like a couple in a sweet embrace, and even in the midst of her terror she wished it was more than an illusion.

"Can you run?"

"Yes," Iyanka whispered, her voice almost nonexistent. She just wanted to get away: into the forest with Victorin and away from whoever was watching them.

Victorin watched her for a moment, almost like he didn't believe her, but then he slipped his hand into hers and started running. He didn't run fast, hardly more than a walk, and Iyanka knew he was taking it easy on her. She didn't want him to think she was weak, but at the same time she was grateful for the slow pace. Her legs were still shaking, and if Victorin hadn't been guiding her she was sure she would've tripped. She hated that she was being so weak, but she couldn't push back the terror. She never could.

They made it to the glade before they stopped. Victorin turned to face Iyanka and they stared at each other as they caught their breath.

"Do you know who was watching us?" Iyanka asked.

Victorin shook his head. "He looked like a hunter, but it was too far to tell for sure."

"I might know," Iyanka said. "A hunter came to the kitchen today. He said he had orders from someone named Wulfguard to question everyone in the castle."

Victorin's expression was grim as he stepped closer to her. "Did he?"

Iyanka shook her head. "Cook wouldn't let him. But he stayed for the rest of the day and watched us, and he said he'd return tomorrow."

Victorin lifted his hand to his head and grabbed his hair, whispering something that sounded like a curse word.

"They suspect there are wielders inside the fortress," he said. "Or else they wouldn't be questioning the servants *now*, of all times."

"What do we do?" Iyanka asked.

Victorin turned and stared up at the trees, muttering to himself. Iyanka watched and waited for him to speak.

"We can't leave tonight," Victorin decided. "We aren't well enough prepared and it's too suspicious. They'd be on our trail as soon as you were missed in the kitchen."

"What do I do if he questions me?" Iyanka asked.

Victorin turned and met her gaze. "Hopefully that won't happen. If it does just try to act like every other girl in there. They're scared of him, yes?"

Iyanka nodded.

"That means he won't be suspicious if you're nervous. Keep your ice hidden and try to answer his questions as honestly as you can without giving away your identity."

"What if he realizes who I am, anyway?"

"Then he'll take you before the barons to confirm you are a wielder. If that happens, try to stay calm and trust me." Victorin put his hands on her shoulders and looked her in the eyes. "I promised your brother I would keep you safe. I will not let them hurt you."

Iyanka nodded, her throat tightening. "And what if they discover you?"

Victorin's face softened, his thumbs ghosting across her shoulders. "Then you get out and wait for me in the forest. My men will come for you if I can't."

Iyanka didn't want to think about that, about what would happen to stop him from coming to her. But the scene in the meadow played over in her head without her permission, and her eyes burned with unshed tears.

"That isn't good enough, Victorin," she whispered.

He frowned, his brow wrinkled in concentration. He didn't look away from Iyanka, but she could tell his mind was elsewhere.

"I want to try something," he said. "Try sending your ice into my heart."

"What will that do?" Iyanka asked.

"I don't know yet," Victorin admitted.

"What if it hurts you?"

"Then you'll stop."

Iyanka wasn't satisfied with that answer, but she'd already run out of questions. Frowning, she tapped into the ice in her heart and watched Victorin closely. She wasn't sure how to send her ice into him without touching him. Until Iyanka found that solitary flame in the midst of her blizzard, and remembered the heat that pulsed in her heart whenever Victorin used his fire. *His fire is still his own, even when it's in* me: *it must be the same with my ice.*

She felt the fire in her heart and tried to imagine the ice in Victorin's. She tried sending her power into that little flame, coaxing the ice to grow and frost to spread. She heard Victorin's sharp intake of breath and jerked her head up to look at him.

"Don't stop," he said. "It's working."

She was confused until she saw his hand was covered in thin frost. Iyanka continued sending ice into Victorin and watched as the frost on his palm spread slowly up his arm. *He doesn't* look *like he's in pain.*

"Keep at it. I'm going to add fire."

Iyanka watched as Victorin fashioned a flame in the palm of his hand. When it touched the frost it doubled in size, taking on a bluish hue as it licked at the ice. Victorin kept it isolated to his palm, but it looked like it took effort to keep the fire from spreading to cover the ice. Iyanka kept sending her ice, but instead of spreading across his skin it seemed to fuel the fire, making the flame leap and dance.

"Now stop," Victorin said. Iyanka cut off her frost, and the fire in Victorin's hand slowly returned to normal and melted the frost coating his arm. He snuffed out the flame and looked up at Iyanka.

"If either of us is caught, we'll try to activate our element. We might be able to feel something despite the enchantment. If I am captured, get to safety and try sending me your ice. Your element might not be blocked by the enchantment if you aren't directly exposed to it."

"But can you control it?" Iyanka asked. She didn't want to accidentally freeze him.

"I don't know," he admitted. "But if it comes to that your ice might be my only chance."

Iyanka still wasn't satisfied with his answer, with the kind of risk he'd be taking, but it successfully refuted any other arguments she might come up with. Victorin smirked when he saw her frustrated expression.

"It'll be fine, Iyanka," he said. "We'll be careful, and by tomorrow night I'll have everything prepared for our departure."

"Will we leave tomorrow, then?"

"Yes," Victorin said. "If the barons are already suspicious, waiting until the end of the council won't gain us anything. Better to get a head start and try to reach safety before they pursue us."

"Do you want me to get anything from the kitchens?" Iyanka asked.

Victorin shook his head. "I have enough supplies to last a week at least. Gathering food might raise the hunter's suspicions, not to mention the Cook's."

Iyanka nodded, glancing up at the moon through the gap in the trees. Tomorrow was her last day in the castle. She was surprised to realize that she would miss it: the other girls in the kitchen and her escapes to the forest. But she would not miss the fear.

"We should return," Victorin announced. "I need to set a few things in order before tomorrow, and you should get some sleep."

Iyanka was disappointed they didn't get to spend more time together, but she understood. She turned away from Victorin so he wouldn't see.

"Do you think he's still watching?"

"Probably," Victorin answered, coming to stand by her side. "It doesn't matter though. It's probably better that he sees us return, anyway."

Victorin held out his hand and Iyanka took it without hesitation. They ran through the forest again. This time Victorin kept the pace faster, and Iyanka enjoyed the wind that pushed her hair away from her face. Faster also meant less time with Victorin, but she tried not to focus on that.

When they reached the edge of the forest, Victorin spun so he was facing Iyanka and raised her hand to his lips. She knew it was just for show for the watcher on the tower, but her face still heated in a blush. Victorin smirked.

"The flames have traveled to your face, I see," he said.

Iyanka looked away in embarrassment, but Victorin turned her face back to him. He watched her for a moment. For some reason his scrutiny made her blush again, and she fought the urge to look away. He opened his mouth as if to say something, but he just sighed.

"Don't look to the tower," he whispered. "I don't want our watcher to know he's been discovered."

Iyanka nodded, but wasn't sure what she should do before she left. Just walking away felt wrong, but he'd already kissed her hand in goodbye... She gave in and stepped forward, wrapping her arms around Victorin and resting her head against his chest.

"Goodnight, Victorin," she whispered.

Victorin wrapped his arms around her in a warm embrace. "Goodnight, Iyanka. Stay safe."

They stayed like that for a few more moments. Victorin was the first to step back. Iyanka looked up at him and nodded, making an effort to smile. As she turned to walk back to the castle, she wished she knew what Victorin was thinking. Embracing him was a bold move on her part, something she would probably regret by morning, but she wished she knew what his reaction was. Had he returned the embrace unwillingly, just to keep up the show? Did he need that connection as much as she did? Was he regretting now that he'd ever launched this plan? Everything was so confusing, and Iyanka feared there were some answers she'd never find. She pondered everything as she crossed the fields to return to the fortress.

Iyanka could feel eyes watching her as she approached. She itched to know if she was right, but she followed Victorin's instructions and didn't look up. Walking past the sentries was as easy as leaving had been, but she made an effort not to let down her guard. It would be all too easy for the hunter to corner her at this time of night. *I can't take any chances.*

She didn't see anyone in the courtyard or the halls leading to the servants' quarters. When she tried to open the door, though, it was locked. Iyanka jostled the door a little, praying it was just stuck. It didn't budge. The door was never locked, though. Why now? What had happened?

Something knocked and the door swung open, making Iyanka jump back with a squeak of fear. When she saw Gretta's round face she started breathing again. Gretta reached out and grasped Iyanka's wrist, pulling her into the room before she shut the door. Iyanka watched as Gretta lifted a cross bar into place across the door, effectively preventing anyone from opening it from the outside.

"What were you doing out there?" Gretta whispered, turning to face her.

"I was out in the forest," Iyanka responded. "Why is the door barred?"

"So that hunter can't get in. Why do you think?" Gretta hugged herself. "I saw him hanging around earlier."

"Why won't he leave us alone?" Iyanka breathed, her fingers tingling with fear and ice.

Gretta shook her head. "He wants something, or the barons more like. And I don't think they'll leave us alone until they get it."

With that uplifting note Gretta returned to her bed, leaving Iyanka to undress and climb into her bed as quickly as she could manage in the dark. It would've been easier if she hadn't accidentally frosted the laces of her dress as she tried to untie them.

The hunter watching them from the tower was bad enough, but hanging around her room? What did the hunter hope to accomplish? She didn't understand why they would suspect her now; she was doing exactly what she had for the past four years.

Iyanka shivered as she tried to fall asleep. The thin covers surrounding her seemed like too little protection. She tried to convince herself there was no danger, at least not that night, but she still searched the dark for unfamiliar shapes and strange movement. *The door is barred, and he has no way of knowing which bed is mine. I am safe. I am safe.* She repeated the words in her mind until her eyes closed on their own accord, and she slipped into sleep.

Chapter IV

"Who'd like to be questioned first?" The hunter, Iyanka now knew his name was Ald, stood in the door to the kitchen while Cook silently fumed nearby. His eyes roved the kitchen, and Iyanka barely resisted the urge to hide behind something.

Gretta stepped forward, her chin lifted in defiance. "I do."

Ald nodded and motioned for her to exit ahead of him. Gretta walked past him as she left the kitchen, her shoulders stiff and her hands clenched into fists at her sides. Whether from fear or from anger Iyanka wasn't sure. The hunter nodded to Cook and left the kitchen.

Cook muttered angrily, her face red with anger. "Back to work," she barked.

Though her anger wasn't directed at them, everyone in the kitchen was *very* prompt to follow her order. Iyanka set about kneading dough as the others returned to their assigned tasks. Cook was still furious, but she took it out on the cookware instead of her workers. Pots and pans clanked as she put together the stew Gretta was assigned to. All of the girls worked silently, and Iyanka was sure they were all wondering the same thing: when would Gretta return? What was the hunter asking her? Who would he question next?

Iyanka ran through the instructions Victorin had given her for if she was questioned as she worked, repeating them over and over in her head. She wished she could simply sneak away and hide in the forest until night, when Victorin would come and she'd never have to see the castle again. But she couldn't. She couldn't raise his suspicions any more than she already had.

When Gretta reentered the kitchen, all the girls dropped their work and gathered around her. They peppered her with questions about what had happened until Cook pushed her way to the front and ordered them to return to their work. Every girl withdrew to her workspace, but no one was actually focused on whatever was in front of them. They all were watching Cook and Gretta as Cook put her arm around the girl and began asking her if she was hurt or upset.

Iyanka saw Gretta's red eyes and wished herself a thousand miles away. If this hunter, Ald, could make strong Gretta cry, he would surely cause Iyanka to slip up in some way. She didn't stand a chance.

"I'm fine," Gretta snarled, pulling out of Cook's grasp. "He didn't hurt me, he just...he isn't a gentleman."

Cook pursed her lips, but let Gretta return to her work without another word. A few seconds later the hunter entered and looked around the room. Cook crossed her arms over her large chest and glared at him like her gaze could turn him to ash...but she didn't say anything. What had Ald done that stopped Cook from raging at him?

"Who's next?" he asked. His eyes locked on Iyanka, but Liesel stepped up.

"I'll go," she said, her hands visibly shaking. The hunter nodded and gestured for her to go before him.

The pattern continued for several hours. Ald would question one of them, she would come back shaking or red-eyed, and he'd ask who would be questioned next. With each time Iyanka's dread and fear grew. There were fewer and fewer girls between her and the hunter, and at some point she would have to step up. It was a miracle that she hadn't yet, but whenever the silence stretched on another girl stepped up just before the hunter selected someone. While he was away the kitchen was much too quiet; none of the girls who had been questioned were willing to talk about what he'd asked.

Iyanka was washing pots beside Elsie as she waited for the bread to rise, but she was so on edge she could barely concentrate on what she was doing. Someone across the kitchen dropped a spoon, and Iyanka jumped. She looked around, hoping no one saw, before hunching her shoulders and returning to her work. The terror, that creeping, edging terror, was digging its silent claws into every nerve in her body. Every sound around her only made it worse.

She felt a touch on her arm and flinched, flushing with embarrassment when she realized it was just Elsie. She looked down at Iyanka with a look of concern.

"It's happening again, isn't it?" she whispered.

Iyanka nodded, biting her lip when someone set a pan on the counter a little too loudly. Elsie patted

Iyanka's arm in sympathy, not realizing that even that small touch made Iyanka want to scream.

"Go to one of the towers," Elsie whispered. "If you're missed, I'll tell them that you're sick."

Iyanka knew she shouldn't, it was too suspicious, but she wasn't sure how much longer she could stand the kitchens before she lost it. She closed her eyes and tried to push back the terror, but she could feel it slowly taking over. She needed to get out, feel the sun and taste the wind. She opened her eyes.

"I'll come back soon," she said.

Elsie nodded and gently squeezed her arm. "Don't worry about it. I'll take over the bread."

Iyanka didn't argue. She turned and practically ran to the door, nearly colliding with Valia, the girl the hunter had last taken to question. Iyanka didn't stop to think about what that meant: she was too focused on escape. She made it all the way to the top of the eastern tower without seeing anyone, but she still was careful to close the trap door. Iyanka stood with her eyes closed, trying to focus on nothing except the cool wind on her face. She was free, she was safe…so why did the panic still gnaw at her?

Iyanka retreated to the wall of the tower and sat down, leaning her back against the cool stone and taking comfort in its sturdiness. The anxiety ate away at her, sapping her strength and causing the tears she'd been holding back to fill her eyes and stream down her face. She hated this. Iyanka drew her knees to her chest and wrapped her arms around her legs, trying to make herself as small as possible. She hated all of this. Iyanka noticed Victorin's fire pulsing and began focusing on that. It helped calm her and keep her mind off Ald, off what was awaiting her when she went back down.

Iyanka wasn't sure how long she sat there, feeling Victorin's fire rise and retreat. At some point she heard a creak as the trap door was lifted. She looked up, thinking it was Elsie or Victorin, but the figure who climbed through the door had brown hair, and an all-too-familiar uniform…

Iyanka scrambled to her feet, ready to flee, but there was nowhere to run. No choice but to stand and wait. Ald stepped up to the tower and turned to face Iyanka. When his gaze met hers, he smiled in friendly way that made goosebumps rise on her arms.

"There you are," he said. "They said you were sick, but you look fine to me. Why did you leave?"

Iyanka stood with her hands pressed against the wall at her back, trying to keep them from shaking. The fear that had driven her to the tower was back in full force, pressing on her chest and nearly suffocating her. She wasn't convinced she could speak even if she tried.

Ald stepped toward her, and Iyanka pushed herself against the wall until the edge of a rock was digging into her back with a sharp pain. Ald looked her up and down and stepped back again.

"There's no need to be scared. I just want to know why you left."

His tone was soothing, kind…dangerous. *What did Victorin say to do?* Iyanka panicked, wracking her brain for what he'd told her. She'd been repeating it over and over that morning, so why couldn't see remember it?

She felt another surge of Victorin's fire. She concentrated on the comforting warmth and tried to clear her head. *Be honest…be as honest as I can.*

"I needed to get out," she said, her voice trembling.

"Out of the kitchen?"

Iyanka nodded, her eyes darting down to his hand on his sword hilt. He must have noticed because he shifted his hand to his belt. His eyes still bored into her, and she was worried if he looked too closely he would see the ice swirling in her veins. It was awakened by her fear, and now it begged to be used. It took everything within her to keep her hands from leaking frost onto the tower rock.

"Why did you need to be out of the kitchen?" he asked.

"I…I couldn't stand it anymore," Iyanka answered. "It was too hot, too loud…I just needed to be out."

Ald inched to the side, so he was the smallest bit closer to her. "Did it have something to do with being questioned?"

Honesty. "Partly," Iyanka admitted.

Ald nodded and rocked back on his heels. "Well, since we're up here I'll question you next. Ready?"

Iyanka watched him and didn't say anything. He chuckled and shook his head.

"Alright then. Your name is Glafira?"

"Yes," Iyanka said. Her voice cracked, and she could only hope it sounded like fear instead of dishonesty.

"How long have you worked in Baron Mal-chomy's kitchens?"

"Almost four years," she answered. How far could she go before the truth would reveal her?

"What brought you here?"

What could she say? What brought her to Baron Malchomy's fortress was desperation, a last effort to save her life. The attacks, the hunters, the death…the loss of all she had ever known. What could she say? She closed her eyes and shook her head.

"It's hard to explain," she whispered.

"I'm a patient listener."

Iyanka bit her lip. *This isn't working.* "I thought I had no other choice."

"Glafira," he said. "Vague answers will not help you. It will be easiest if you just tell the truth."

His voice sounded closer than before, and when she opened her eyes he was standing right in front of her. His hand was on the hilt of his sword again, and his gaze was hard.

"Please don't," she whispered.

"Don't what?" When she didn't answer he tilted his head and inched closer. "I'd be most glad if you proved my suspicions wrong, but to do that you'll have to answer my questions."

He already knew. He knew what she was, that's why he'd come to find her. Iyanka didn't know a way to convince him he was wrong, and she didn't think for a second that begging would get her anywhere. What could she do?

"I can't," Iyanka said.

"Why not?" Ald furrowed his brows, his gaze still on her face.

Because you're right, she silently screamed. Iyanka concentrated on the cold stone beneath her palms, and realized with horror that ice was leaking out of her and on to the tower. She felt the frost begin to spread, but not yet where Ald could see.

"I just can't," she said, her voice thick with desperation. She couldn't move, or he would see the tell-tale frost. Iyanka tried to stop the flow of cold, tried to keep her ice inside her, but her raw emotions were making it volatile and nearly impossible to hold back.

The hunter slipped a hand behind his back. "Answer the question, Glafira."

Tears started spilling over and running down her face. She didn't want this to be happening. She didn't want this to be her. *Victorin, please save me.* She couldn't hold the ice in anymore, and when she finally gave in swirling ice crawled across the surface of the whole tower, cracking in the warm air. Ald stumbled back, shock lighting up his features. Maybe she could run.

No sooner had the thought occurred to her than Ald jumped forward and held a dark knife to her throat. Her ice immediately cut off, halting the spread of frost across the tower. Iyanka could feel something oppressive and dark pressing against her throat, threatening to choke her, even though the knife wasn't touching her skin. It was unbearable...her ice swirled within her, still at her command but sealed inside. Her sense of it was dulled somehow, like she was feeling it through a thick curtain. It made her ache in a way she'd never known.

Ald glared at her, but not in triumph as Iyanka would've expected. He looked almost sorry, but entirely resolute. She didn't have the thought or energy to ponder why; it took all of her concentration to keep breathing with the darkness bearing down on her.

He jerked his head toward the open trap door. "Climb down. I'm taking you to the barons, ice wielder."

Iyanka obeyed, climbing down the steps as tears filled her eyes, blurring her vision. She tried to stay silent, but every so often a sob would escape. Ald didn't bring the knife any closer to her skin, but he didn't move it away, either. He walked behind and to the side of her so that Iyanka could only see glimpses of him unless she turned her head. She couldn't see his expression, but she didn't want to. Iyanka didn't want him to see her pain, either, but she wasn't strong enough to keep it hidden.

All of it was unbearable: the fear, the evil cutting off her ice, the pain of failure... After four years, four years of fear and caution, she was facing the fate she'd avoided from the beginning. Why? Why was this happening? She was *so* close to freedom; a few more hours of avoiding detection and she would've escaped with Victorin.

Iyanka tripped on a crack. She stumbled forward, and Ald jerked the knife away so it didn't cut her. He let out a curse as ice quickly spread beneath their feet, pressing the knife against her side and grabbing her arm.

"Be careful," he growled.

"…Glafira," a voice nearby whispered.

Iyanka turned to face the speaker and wished she hadn't. Elsie was standing in the doorway leading to one of the storerooms, her hand against the doorframe as if she needed the support. She looked back and forth between Iyanka and the ice coating the floor, then up to Ald's knife against Iyanka's side.

"Get back to work," Ald ordered.

Elsie looked back up at Iyanka, her eyes wide with horror, and slowly backed down the hall toward the kitchen, and another pain gouged Iyanka's frantic heart. Ald prodded Iyanka forward so she had to turn away, so she didn't see Elsie turn and start sprinting toward the kitchen.

Iyanka walked willingly enough for most of the way, being careful not to trip again, but when they reached the hall leading to the great study the barons were in, she halted.

"Please don't make me do this," she whispered, the tears starting anew. "Please don't make me go in there."

Ald's grip on her arm tightened. "You will face the barons, Glafira. Do not resist."

Ald began the walk down the hall. Iyanka tried to resist, but his grip was like iron. She ended up being half led, half dragged down the hall, the knife still at her side.

"Please," she cried, "please don't."

The hunters guarding the door looked up at her cries, putting their hands on the hilts of their swords. They nodded to Ald when he stopped before them. Iyanka pulled as far away as she could and didn't meet their eyes.

"Sir Wulfguard is expecting me," Ald said.

One of the hunters jerked his chin toward Iyanka. "What's with the kitchen girl?"

"She's an ice wielder who's been hiding in Baron Malchomy's kitchens. They'll want to question her before she's disposed of."

Iyanka whimpered at the casual mention of her impending execution, but the men paid her no attention. They both stared at Ald for a few seconds before moving to open the doors. Ald stepped toward the room, but Iyanka couldn't force her feet to move. She wouldn't, couldn't, walk to her own doom.

Ald leaned over and whispered in her ear. "Walk, or this knife will cut you."

That spurred her into motion, but her feet still felt like blocks of ice as she moved forward. Iyanka flinched when the hunters slammed the doors behind her. Ald slowed their pace once they were inside, which was more than fine for her. The Baron's voices created a steady hum in the room, with a voice occasionally rising above the rest to restore order.

The room they were in was more similar to a ballroom than a study: the walls were plastered a light yellow, with tapestries and shields making up the decorations. The room had no windows, but was well lit by hundreds of candles and lanterns hung from the ceiling and displayed in tall stands. The center of the room was dominated by a large table, where all sixteen barons were sitting. The table was covered with maps and forgotten refreshments.

Baron Malchomy sat at the head of the table and watched the other barons squabble with each other. The knight from the meadow, Iyanka guessed it was Wulfguard, stood just behind and to the right of Malchomy, surveying the room with boredom. When he saw Ald and Iyanka he bent down and whispered in Baron Malchomy's ear, which caused the Baron to look up. Iyanka shuddered as the barons' pale eyes surveyed her and Ald. He slowly stood and pressed his hands against the surface of the table.

"My lords, there is an urgent matter for us to discuss."

The knight beckoned Ald closer, and he prodded Iyanka into motion. She tried dragging her feet, but the pressure of the knife against her side prevented her from stopping completely. Baron Malchomy and the knight watched her as she approached, and as she drew closer one by one the barons turned to stare at her as well.

"Who is this?" Baron Richard asked. "What does one of your kitchen girls have to do with the wielders?"

"Simple really," Baron Malchomy said, straightening and clasping his hands behind his back. "She is one."

If Iyanka had thought their gazes were hard to bear before, it was nothing compared to the way they stared at her now. All of the barons watched her with slack jawed disbelief, except for two or three who looked…pained. Iyanka glanced back and forth between them and tried to keep her breathing even. The closest Iyanka saw to sympathy among them were the few who looked troubled. What had she expected? These were the men who authorized and launched the slaughtering of her people and Victorin's. These were the men who continued to hunt them down…why would they ever feel sympathetic toward her?

"Baron Malchomy."

The man who spoke was a thin man Iyanka had only glimpsed once or twice. He steepled his fingers and pointed at Iyanka. "You expect us to believe this girl is a wielder who infiltrated your fortress as a kitchen girl? How could she accomplish such a thing?"

"That is precisely what I want to know," Baron Malchomy answered. "I believe the information she has will be valuable to all of us."

"Wouldn't it be more prudent to have her interrogated by one of your hunters?" Baron Leon asked.

"She was discovered just this afternoon," Wulfguard said, his voice low and menacing.

Iyanka saw a few barons begin to say something, but Baron Malchomy held up his hands to forestall other questions.

"Let us question the prisoner before we squabble among ourselves. It's rude to keep her waiting."

This caused a dark chuckle out of a couple of the barons, and murderous glares from another few. Several barons still looked uncomfortable, which Iyanka thought was strange. Any pondering on the subject, however, was made impossible when the knight stalked up to her and drew his sword. Iyanka tried to back up, but Ald was an immobile wall behind her.

"Wait," Malchomy said, holding up a hand. "Before we begin the questioning, let's verify that she is indeed a wielder and not an innocent kitchen girl at the wrong place in the wrong time."

"My lord, that's not the best idea," Ald began, but Wulfguard interrupted.

"Do not question."

Wulfguard glared at Ald behind her, then jerked his head at the knife at Iyanka's side. She heard Ald sigh before he slowly removed the dagger. Both men backed up a step, and Iyanka felt the oppressive feeling of their weapons fade. She was nearly overcome by the intensity of freedom, and then of powerlessness. The cold that had built up inside her suddenly had an escape, and nothing Iyanka could do was going to stop it. As soon as the weapon's influence was gone the winter inside burst out of her, coating the floor in crystalline ice that shimmered like diamonds. The temperature around her dropped so drastically that Wulfguard's breath hung in the air like fog. The cold comforted Iyanka, twisting and surrounding her like an old friend.

Wulfguard lifted his sword to rest next to Iyanka's neck, cutting off the ice so quickly that it's absence ripped through her like a knife. She gasped, and Ald's quick grip on her arm was the only thing that kept her from collapsing to her knees. Iyanka breathed heavily and watched the ice slowly begin to melt in the warm room. She looked up and saw all of the barons on their feet and staring at her with varying mixtures of disgust and terror. Baron Malchomy was by far the most terrifying in the crowd: his expression was closer to triumph.

"Who are you?" one of the barons asked. Iyanka couldn't tell which one. She lowered her gaze to the floor and stayed silent.

"You heard his question, girl," Wulfguard snarled, moving his sword closer to her skin. "Answer."

"Princess Iyanka," Iyanka whispered, her voice barely audible even to herself.

"Louder," Wulfguard ordered.

Iyanka leaned away from the knight, but Ald again prevented her from moving too far. Her knees shook, but she licked her lips and tried to make her voice louder.

"I am Princess Iyanka." She closed her eyes, the words reverberating in her mind. She heard the barons stirring and talking among themselves, but it seemed so far away. The last time she had spoken her name was so many years ago… She was *not* Glafira, servant of the barons. Despite the fear that clouded her mind, a small part of her, a part that sounded suspiciously like her father, was defiant. She had hidden for four years. She could not imagine anything worse than what was happening right then. She was not going to hide any-more, and she would *not* keep lying.

Her throat was dry, but she continued speaking, her voice quivering and raspy. She kept her eyes trained on the table, refusing to meet anyone's gaze but still watching them out of the corner of her eyes.

"Princess Iyanka of Eisadel, the Northern King-dom of Winter." Everyone fell silent, but she was too far in to stop now. "Lily of the North, Daughter of King Dane and Queen Visha, Sister of Crown Prince Milek, Betrothed to Crown Prince Victorin of Siersh, an Ice Wielder of Elnar, friend…" Her voice trialed off. There was one more…one other title kept by royalty of Siersh and Eisadel for generations, ever since the events that formed Frieda's refuge. Could she really? Could she speak the title wielders kept that most infuriated the barons? She stared at the ground. If she didn't she would be forgetting everything that ancient girl had given for peace. "And friend of Frieda Hearthnen."

There was no shouting, no infuriated uproar. Iyanka heard a silence more painful than any audible fury she could imagine. She dared to look up, but the moment she saw the barons she wished she hadn't. All of them were facing Baron Malchomy…who was glar-ing at her with hate and fury radiating off him. But his fury wasn't fire, it wasn't ice…it was an abyss of dark-ness. She flinched and looked down, wishing she could disappear with the ice that was melting all-too quickly.

"Do not," he snarled, "say that name. It is far too pure to come from the lips of an abomination like you."

"She's not the one who broke the trust and sanctuary of Frieda's Refuge." The voice ran out clear, and strong, and so much braver than Iyanka's.

Everyone else turned to see who spoke, but Iyanka turned to see his face. Victorin stood near the entrance to the room, the door guards holding their swords to his back and chest. He glared at Baron Malchomy, but if there were flames in his eyes Iyanka couldn't see them. *He must be burning on the inside.* Iyanka searched for the feeling of his fire amid her raging blizzard. When she found that flame she felt ashamed that she hadn't felt it before: it felt like a wildfire was blazing in her chest. How had she not noticed before? Could he feel her ice?

Victorin kept his gaze locked on Baron Malchomy in challenge. Iyanka glanced at Malchomy and saw him watching Victorin warily.

"What do you have to do with this, weaponsmith?" he asked, his voice choked with disdain. "Are you fond of the little ice witch?"

The flame in Iyanka's chest doubled with Victorin's fury, making her let out a small gasp. No one paid attention except Ald, who's grip on her arm loosened the slightest bit.

"I would refrain from calling her names if I were you," Victorin said, his voice low and menacing. "Especially if you have so little knowledge of your servants to think I am only a weaponsmith."

Malchomy's lips pulled back in a snarl. "You must be arrogant indeed to threaten me when my warriors have their weapons against your flesh."

"Not arrogant," he said. "Furious. Furious that you would call her an abomination when the true monsters in this room are those holding her against her will."

"Baron Malchomy," one of the other barons said. "Who is this man? If he is your servant as you claim, then force him to bridle his tongue!"

Those words started an argument amongst the barons. Iyanka kept her gaze on Victorin and ignored the barons as much as she could. Victorin finally turned his gaze to her, and even without visible flames his eyes burned. The flame in her chest dimmed for the briefest second before roaring again. He watched and waited for the significance to sink in, which took several seconds. *He's still in control. Which means so am I. The enchantment only blocks our power from coming out…it doesn't steal our control.* Iyanka thought back to the night before, trying to remember what she did to control her ice in Victorin. Would it work, though? They were both under the suffocating influence of the enchantment.

Suffocating… Iyanka remembered in the courtyard, when she'd cooled Victorin's fire with her ice. What if she could do that, only in reverse? If she could use her ice to fuel his fire, would it be strong enough to break through the enchantment?

Iyanka closed her eyes to try out her theory, but a large crash interrupted her concentration. She opened her eyes to see Baron Malchomy with a fist on the table, glaring at each Baron in turn.

"If you would like to question my handling of the servants in my fortress, I suggest you wait until this is resolved." He turned his gaze to Victorin, his expression hard. "Who are you?"

"A suggestion from one ruler to another: when you set out to kill someone, ensure that you know what they look like." Victorin inclined his head without breaking eye contact, his eyes hard. "Prince Victorin, at your service."

Chapter V

Iyanka was again faced with Malchomy's fury as he alternated his glare between her and Victorin. She again wished she was invisible, but Victorin…he stood strong and didn't show any sign that the Baron's fury intimidated him. Iyanka was a little surprised none of the other barons said anything, but maybe they found Malchomy's anger as terrifying as she did. Wulfguard, however, didn't seem to have such qualms.

"Your orders, sir?" he asked, his sword inching closer to Iyanka's neck. Baron Malchomy ignored him and sat down at the table, still glaring at everyone in the room.

Iyanka tried leaning back into Ald, but he was still keeping her in place. She looked over at Victorin and saw that the hunters guarding him had moved their swords to a more threatening position as well. She had to try something, before they hurt him.

Iyanka closed her eyes and delved into the winter and flame within her. The ice swirled through every inch of her being, except the area Victorin's fire occupied. What if she brought them together? She harnessed some of the elusive cold and plunged it into the fire. The flames leaped in her heart. She opened her eyes and glanced at Victorin; he was watching her with surprise, and then with triumph. He nodded, giving Iyanka the courage to continue. Trying to block out everything else, Iyanka grabbed threads of ice and wove them into the fire. She felt the flame leap as Victorin did the same.

Flame leaped in her heart and spread through her body, fueled by the ice coating her veins. She felt the oppression and darkness begin to recede, replaced by a sensation too intense to describe. Fire and ice spread along her veins, flooding her being until Iyanka didn't know if she stood in the midst of a blizzard or a wildfire. But whatever it was it was better than the numb darkness. Her palms tingled as frost began blooming on her skin.

Ald jerked his hand off her arm, and she could hear his footsteps as he backed away.

"What are you doing?" Wulfguard snarled at him.

If Ald answered, Iyanka didn't hear him. She was too busy concentrating on the frost coating her hands, frost covered in tiny blue flames. She didn't need to look at Victorin to know that it was happening to him too, but she looked anyway. He winked at her, then turned his attention to the barons. His hand twitched, and Iyanka felt the frozen flame leap.

"It seems you have been negligent, Baron Malchomy," Victorin said. "The very people you set out to destroy, here in your fortress, and you didn't have a clue."

Iyanka heard the barons murmuring among themselves. She turned to see how Baron Malchomy would react. In turning she almost brushed against the sword and leaned back automatically. Remembering that Ald wasn't blocking the way anymore, she took a tiny step back, praying Wulfguard wouldn't notice. Iyanka jumped when the room filled with deep, booming laughter. She looked up and saw Baron Malchomy with his head thrown back.

"Threats will avail you nothing, fire princeling. You and your precious betrothed are at my mercy."

Victorin raised his eyebrow, but didn't say anything. Iyanka watched him and saw him curl his hands into fists, causing the frost and flame to leak through his fingers and begin creeping up his arms. He looked over at her and dipped his head. What did that mean? Fire leaped, and Iyanka poured in more ice to fuel it. She looked down and saw the frost and flame was growing and spreading along her sleeves and onto the floor beneath her feet. They were going to see. Iyanka took another cautious step away from Wulfguard and his dark sword.

Iyanka heard a thump and a shout. She whipped her head around and saw Victorin taking out the hunters surrounding him, knocking them to the ground and kicking their swords out of their reach. Another hunter ran toward him. Victorin side stepped and grabbed the man's wrist, causing him to bellow and drop his sword. The ice spread from Victorin's hand onto the hunter's sleeve, the fire not far behind. Victorin pushed him back so he collided with another hunter running toward him. Victorin drew a knife from behind his back and faced the other hunters. By now the ice and flame had grown and spread so that white-blue flames blazed all along his arms and along the blade of his dagger. It seemed like all but the hunters were frozen in shock, because none of the barons sounded an alarm. Iyanka stood and watched Victorin fight with fascination.

Someone grabbed Iyanka's arm and yanked her backwards. She yelped and automatically reached a hand behind her to latch onto whoever had grabbed her. There was a cry of pain and the hand released her. She whipped around to see Ald clutching his face with one hand, his other hand an angry red from touching her.

"Iyanka," Victorin called.

She looked up and saw Victorin gesturing her to him. Iyanka sprinted toward him, feeling something barely graze her back. Wulfguard bellowed in fury behind her, pushing Iyanka to run faster until she leaped into Victorin's arms. He wrapped one arm around her and leaned down just long enough to press his lips against her hair. Overwhelmed, but relieved to be in his arms, she didn't question the gesture.

"Turn around and take my hand," he whispered. Iyanka did what he said, feeling their power concentrate on their intertwined hands. She pressed against his side as she surveyed the room before them.

Half a dozen hunters were scattered before them, on the ground or clutching injuries. Wulfguard stood behind them, his chest heaving and his eyes dark with rage. His sword was lowered, but Iyanka knew better than to think his guard was down. When she dared look beyond him to the barons she was surprised to see that most of them looked frightened. Even Malchomy looked taken aback, albeit more in outrage than fear.

"If you value your men's lives you will let us leave in peace," Victorin said.

"Never," Malchomy snarled. He turned to the Baron on his left and ordered, "Sound the alarm."

"But…"

"Now!" Malchomy said, shoving the man back. The Baron's eyes were wide, but he turned and jogged toward the other door.

Victorin leaned down and whispered in Iyanka's ear. "Can you sustain ice without being in contact with it?"

"I can make it last longer, but that's all," she replied.

"How long?"

"Only a few minutes."

Victorin frowned and glanced up at Wulfguard, who was slowly advancing on them. "Do it," he said, dropped her hand and holding up his flame-covered knife at Wulfguard.

Iyanka frowned down at her booted feet, wishing she could just kick them off and be done with it. Being barefoot on the run wouldn't be a good idea, though, so she'd just have to deal with it. She crouched and pressed her fingertips to the stone floor, channeling frost to spread in a wall of sorts between her and the barons. Crystalline ice ripped across the room in a path over three feet wide, layer after layer until it was four inches thick and covered with glittering hoar-frost. It cracked in the warmth in the room, but the air around it quickly plummeted in temperature.

Wulfguard stepped back, but then sneered and kept coming. Victorin took a step closer to Iyanka. She felt his fire ignite as he set the ice ablaze. Within seconds six feet of raging fire divided the room. The barons' shouts of shock were barely audible over the roar of flame.

Victorin grabbed her arm and pulled her to her feet. Iyanka went along with him, staring at the flames as they held steady, feeding off the ice. She could barely make out Wulfguard's form on the other side. He was trying to get through, but his sword didn't seem to work on the ice-flame.

Iyanka turned and slipped her hand into Victorin's, following as he pushed through the doors. They skidded into the hall, nearly colliding with Gretta. The girl took a step back, barely glancing at Iyanka and Victorin's blazing hands.

"I thought I was going to have to come in after you," she said. "What took so long?"

"Never mind that," Victorin said. "Let's go."

They started running down the hall as Iyanka struggled to process what was happening. Gretta knew Victorin? What could she have done if she'd come in after them, and why would she want to? Gretta hated wielders.

"Is everything ready?" Victorin asked.

"Yes," Gretta said. "Everyone's waiting outside the walls, except Cook. She insisted on waiting for you."

Cook? What did she have to do with this? There was a shout behind them. Iyanka looked back over her shoulder and saw hunters at the other end of the hall running toward them.

"This way," Gretta called, turning into a narrow servant passage. Victorin and Iyanka ducked into the hall.

"Can you make an ice wall again?" Victorin asked.

"Yes," Iyanka panted. She bent down and covered the passageway entrance with ice that inched out into the hall and climbed up the doorframe. Victorin supplied the fire that set it ablaze, effectively blocking off the passageway.

Gretta whistled, staring back and forth between Victorin and Iyanka. She shook her head and turned to start running again. Victorin and Iyanka followed. They ran through dark halls and down narrow steps until Iyanka was thoroughly turned around. She was starting to wonder where Gretta was taking them when they emerged in a room filled with hay and grain. Gretta stepped aside to let them pass. Victorin forged ahead, but Iyanka paused, effectively stopping Victorin as he wouldn't let go of her hand.

"Gretta?" Iyanka asked. The girl looked at her, but Iyanka couldn't think of what to say. Gretta grinned.

"What?" she asked. "You thought you were the only wielder who thought to hide where least expected?"

Flames glittered in her eyes, and Iyanka stared in shock. Gretta shook her head with a chuckle.

"Go on," she said. "We don't exactly have time to waste."

Iyanka turned and ran with Victorin into the main part of the stable, where two horses were standing in the aisle. They stamped their hooves, but Cook was holding their bridles and trying to sooth them.

"There you are," she said. "Come get on these beasts before they break loose."

Iyanka was more confused than ever, but she followed Victorin and watched as he vaulted onto the creature's back. The stallion snorted, but Cook pulled his head down and glared at him until he quieted down.

"Take the other horse," Victorin said, pulling Iyanka onto the horse behind him. "We need to reach the forest as soon as possible."

Cook grumbled as she mounted the other horse and held a hand out to Gretta. Gretta ignored the offer of help and heaved herself up behind Cook.

"Stubborn girl," Cook muttered.

"Come, Aunt," Gretta said. "You can scold me later. I don't think the hunters are coming to bid us farewell."

Cook's reply was lost in the clatter of hooves as Victorin urged the stallion into motion. They trotted into the courtyard, scattering villagers and leaving shouts of fear and outrage in their wake. Iyanka heard someone shouting to close the gate, but they were past the guards before the soldiers could do anything.

And then they were out of the fortress and galloping across the surrounding meadow. Wind whipped past Iyanka's ears and blocked out all sound except the horse's hooves pounding against the ground. She tightened her grip on Victorin and leaned her head on his back, closing her eyes and focusing on his solid warmth. She was out. Better or worse, she was gone from the fortress. Iyanka hoped she never stepped foot within those evil walls again. She refused to be sorry. Glafira the servant was gone…she was Iyanka, Ice Princess of Elnar.

Chapter VI

They were forced to slow their pace when they reached the forest, but Victorin didn't stop. Iyanka searched for Cook and Gretta and found them riding behind, talking in hushed whispers. But as she turned back, her eyes caught movement in the trees beside them. She whipped her head around, ready to call out a warning, stopping when she saw it was Elsie and Lynn. Elsie waved, but didn't say anything. Iyanka looked around and saw two other horses around them carrying people from the fortress. The horse nearest Iyanka and Victorin carried another weaponsmith and a young page with a gap-toothed smile who continuously sneaked into the kitchen for snacks, and the other carried one of the fortress guards.

"Why is everybody here?" she whispered to Victorin. "Are they all wielders?"

"No," he replied, steering the horse around a stump. "Not all of them are wielders, but they all want to stop the barons."

"But…I had no idea," Iyanka said. She looked around at Cook and three of the girls from the kitchen, not to mention the page, and one of the guards…

"Your idea was a popular one, it seems," Victorin said. "It's no wonder they weren't discovered…most came forward when they heard you were taken, otherwise I never would've known."

Iyanka looked at the people surrounding them. So many faces she recognized. She'd never considered any of them of hiding a secret like hers. How could she have missed it?

Iyanka heard leaves rustling, even though there was barely a breeze. She looked up and saw branches swaying back and forth like they were being tossed by a great wind. The leaves twisted and waved. There was a strange purposefulness to their movements...

"What are they doing?" she asked.

Victorin looked up. "I don't know," he admitted. "Hopefully they're helping us."

Iyanka continued to watch the trees, but they didn't show any other sign that anything was out of ordinary. She noticed, though, that they rode away from the glen. She'd assumed they would go there, though she wasn't sure why.

"Where are we going?" Iyanka asked.

"The northeastern edge of the forest," Victorin answered. "It adds time to our journey, but the hunters usually stick close to the roads."

"So if we cut through the heart of the forest they won't follow us?" she guessed.

"That's what I'm hoping," he said. "They should ride around the edge and pick up our trail where we exit."

"Yeah, they should," the weaponsmith said. "But the hunters haven't been predictable as of late."

"That's true, Egan," Victorin replied. "But I'm hoping old habits will reign in this case."

"Are you talking about the trees?" the page piped up, glancing up furtively at the forest surrounding them.

"That's exactly what he's talking about," Egan, said. "The barons are scared to venture too far into the forest, on account of all the ghost stories they've made up to explain why the deep trees are never cut down for firewood."

The boy nodded. "I heard that the trees don't like that we cut them down, and if you bring an ax too close, they'll come alive and strangle you with their roots."

Egan chuckled. "Those're nothing but old wives' tales, lad."

"Then why *don't* we cut down the trees?" he asked, his face turning a pinkish hue.

"Because they're wielders," Iyanka explained, her voice barely above a whisper.

The boy turned to face her, his eyes wide. "They're what?"

Iyanka smiled. "Wielders. We would call them plant wielders, but they called themselves gardeners. They controlled plants: vines and flowers and trees, all at their command."

"But…" the page leaned toward Iyanka and whispered, as if he didn't want the trees to hear. "What happened to them? Why are they trees?"

"They let their power go to their head," Iyanka sighed. "They revered nature more than the Creator, and so the Creator let them taste what nature was really like."

"The Creator turned them into trees?" the boy whispered.

"Not for forever," Iyanka added. "Only until they changed their hearts and were willing to serve Him and Him alone. But few of them have ever turned back."

"But they could?"

Iyanka looked up at the branches above her. "I hope so."

"It's ironic," Victorin said, "that after all that's happened the barons still regard the ancient law to never cut the trees at the center of the forest, when this forest would've been razed long ago if they only remembered the truth."

"They disregard the ancient customs they *do* remember," Gretta grumbled from behind them.

The painful reminder of Frieda's Refuge silenced the conversation. For a while they all rode in silence, the only sound that of the horses and the trees. It was strange…such peace and quiet so soon after terror and chaos. It felt wrong to ride through the forest as if nothing was out of the ordinary, as if they didn't have soldiers hunting them. She wanted to run, to hide, to do something other than leisurely ride through the forest like they were on a picnic. She didn't understand how Victorin could be so relaxed when barely an hour before he'd been held at the point of two swords.

Come to think of it, Iyanka didn't understand how she was so calm. They'd nearly *died*, but the edge of unease, that strange sense that everything was *wrong*, that had plagued her all morning was missing. Why was that? She would have expected it to be the opposite…

"Miss Glafira," the page whispered.

Iyanka turned toward him and saw him staring up in wide eyed wonder. He briefly turned to make sure she was paying attention, then looked back to whatever had caught his attention. Iyanka followed his gaze and gasped. The trees were interlocking branches above them, twisting around each other as if holding hands. Their movements were creating a sort of tunnel.

"Victorin," Iyanka whispered. "Look at what they're doing."

Victorin looked up and stopped his horse. He held up a hand for everyone else to halt as well; the forest was filled with whispers as everyone saw the trees' movements and wondered at the purpose.

"I don't like this," Egan said. His hand strayed to the hilt of his knife, as if it could somehow defeat the entire forest. "They've never done this as far as I've heard."

Iyanka looked around and saw the trees swaying and shifting, roots pulling out of the ground and digging into the earth in new places. She glanced behind them and then ahead, noticing a pattern.

"I think…" she paused, looking again. "I think they're protecting us. Look."

She pointed behind them and waited for Victorin to turn. "They're blocking off where we've been. Wouldn't that stop the hunters from following us?"

"And they're clearing a path ahead of us," the page added excitedly. "So we can ride faster."

"They're forcing us to go where they want," Gretta said. She scowled. "You better not be leading us to an ambush or something," she shouted into the forest.

A thin branch broke away from the rest and reached down to gently touch the top of Gretta's head. She stiffened, but the branch receded soon enough. Elsie chuckled as Gretta glared at the trees with her lips pressed in a thin line.

"I think that was meant to be comforting," Elsie said.

"It wasn't," Gretta growled.

Iyanka turned away from the two women and looked around at the trees. Without a word, she slipped to the ground and walked up to the edge of the trees. She heard someone ask what she was doing, but she ignored them and lightly touched her hand to the bark of one of the trees. She was grateful they were helping, but she was also...heartbroken. Mourning lives she never knew. These trees weren't plants: they were people. They knew who they were and where they'd come from. They *knew* what was going on, well enough that they were helping them escape...and yet they were still trees. Even knowing the fate the wielders were facing and wanting to help, they remained in their leafy prisons.

"It's your choice, you know," she whispered. "You don't have to be trapped here."

A small branch pulled away from the rest and caressed her cheek. Iyanka smiled at the gesture, but slowly backed away. She couldn't force them to turn back: she could only remind them that the choice was theirs.

Iyanka took Victorin's offered hand and climbed back onto the horse. She sighed and rested her head on Victorin's shoulder. He didn't say anything, but he gently squeezed her hand before letting go.

"We need to keep moving," he said.

"You trust them?" Egan asked.

"Yes," Victorin said, urging their mount into a walk. "They're wielders just like us."

Everyone slowly continued forward, though they all stayed in a tighter group now. Iyanka looked around at the others occasionally, but mostly she watched the trees. They formed a narrow road a few dozen yards ahead of them, trees slowly shifting to the side and roots pulling out of the way. She even saw one tree use its roots to pull a small boulder out of the way. Behind them the trees returned to their normal positions, except with their branches held too low for a horse and rider to pass beneath. Any hunter who wanted to journey through the forest after them would have to go on foot, dodging roots and low hanging branches along the way.

They rode for several hours, at a much faster pace thanks to the trees. The light was quickly fading when Victorin halted his horse.

"We'll rest here tonight," he called out.

"Will the hunters camp for the night?" Iyanka asked in a whisper.

Victorin dismounted the horse and turned to help Iyanka down. "It depends on whether they tried following us through the forest or stayed along the edge. If they stuck to the road they might be able to continue through part of the night, but they won't make much progress."

"If they continue on?"

"Then we search for a place to leave the forest where the hunters aren't watching."

Iyanka frowned. "It's sounds so simple, but is it really?"

Victorin sighed and turned to face her. "I don't know. Normally hunters are fairly predictable, but lately their actions have been more volatile. When they found Crevan..." Victorin swallowed and turned to loosen the girth on the saddle. "They never should've been that deep in the forest."

"How long will we be in the forest?" she asked, deciding to change the subject.

"It depends on where the trees take us. If I'm correct in my guess, they'll let us out near Truestone Lake. That would keep us in the forest for at least two weeks, and we could escape north through the hills and into Frieda's Refuge near the river."

"But won't they just follow us?"

"Yes, but the people there are sympathetic to our plight. They'll help us if they can."

"Do we risk a fire?" Egan called.

Victorin deliberated for a moment. "Not tonight," he decided.

"Now why not?" Cook asked. "With the trees protecting us I don't see any harm in a little warmth."

"Because the trees cannot stop the hunters if they're determined, only delay them," Victorin said. "We're not far enough into the forest to know that they won't see the smoke and follow it."

Cook opened her mouth to protest more, but Egan didn't give her the chance.

"You would argue against our prince?" he asked, stepping toward Cook and glaring at her.

Cook puffed up. "I don't recognize titles as an invitation to boss people around, especially when we've been doing just fine on our own."

Iyanka glanced between Cook and Egan. If they were already fighting, how would their party ever make it to Frieda's refuge? She looked up at Victorin to see how he'd handle the situation.

He held up a hand to stall Egan's retort, then switched his gaze to Cook.

"I don't ask you to bow to me as prince, or respect me for my lineage. But I do ask you to trust me to keep us safe."

"Like your father kept us safe?" Cook spat back. "Like you kept Claude safe? We revealed ourselves to save Glafira, but don't deceive yourself. I have no respect for your family or their idea of safety."

"Claude's death wasn't his fault," Elsie added, her voice quiet.

"No," Cook agreed, her voice softening as she glanced at Elsie. Her voice hardened as she looked back at Victorin. "But it was his family trying to turn us into what we're not and doing all that warmongering that got us into this mess."

"No, it's not," Iyanka said without thinking. When a dozen pairs of eyes turned to look at her, some of them spitting anger, she regretted saying anything. She couldn't leave it like that, though. They couldn't blame Victorin for everything when his only part in bringing the barons' wrath was seeking *peace*.

"Victorin's family might've been part of it, but it was my family's fault too." Iyanka looked around, meeting eyes to see if they understood. "It was our fighting *each other* that made the Barons see us as monsters."

Gretta snorted. "And they don't like feeling threatened."

"Which they currently do. They will put every effort into stopping us," Egan said. "We need someone to lead us who knows how to evade them, and Prince Victorin does."

Cook didn't say anything, but she put her hands on her hips in the way she did whenever someone was out of line in the kitchen. Egan nodded like the matter was over and turned away, but Victorin didn't move. Iyanka looked up and saw his mouth in a frown and his eyebrows furrowed. He was watching Cook with troubled eyes, though she didn't even glance at him.

"I knew my father's vices and flaws more than anyone," he said. "I lived out the consequences the same as your son and all of our soldiers."

"What's your point?" Cook asked.

"I do not blame you for not trusting my family, but I will not allow anyone to keep me from protecting these people." Victorin bowed his head to her, then turned around and strode away.

0O0

Victorin disappeared among the trees, and he stayed away longer than Iyanka was comfortable with. She wanted to follow him, so he wasn't alone, but Egan stopped her when she tried. He said he needed time to think. So instead, Iyanka helped the other girls set up rustic sleeping areas, clearing areas of rocks and branches. She couldn't help but glance up often, to search for him. *What about Cook's words unnerved him?*

Iyanka was still pondering that question when a breeze whipped across the ground where the girls were kneeling, bringing leaves from all around and depositing them in their freshly cleared area. Iyanka watched with wide eyes and turned, searching for the source of such a sudden wind. Lynn was staring at the ground, her face red.

"It's to make the ground softer," she explained.

"Fine by me," Gretta said, carefully standing and going over to the horses.

The page ran up to Lynn's side and put his hand on her shoulder.

"That was amazing! Can I try?"

Lynn smiled indulgently at the boy. "We still have to be careful, even if we aren't at the fortress. Maybe tomorrow."

The boy looked crestfallen, and Lynn frowned, her eyes pained as she watched him. But she glanced at Iyanka and her face cleared, a smile taking its place.

"Gla...Iyanka. I don't think you've officially met my little brother, Zefyr."

"Just Zef," the boy corrected, pushing sandy-blond hair out of his eyes, interest overtaking his disappointment. "Aren't you the reason we left the castle? Are you a wielder? Will you tell me more about the trees sometime? Why do you have two names?"

"Slow down," Lynn laughed. "You can't speak like the wind and expect people to keep up."

"Sorry," he said, ducking his head.

"I'd love to answer your questions," Iyanka offered, her heart swelling for this enthusiastic child. He was so young, surely no older than twelve...but how much heartache had he felt in his short life?

"You're sure?" Zef asked.

Iyanka nodded, and Zef practically bounced in place. Lynn put a hand on his arm.

"Just remember your manners," she warned, turning in Iyanka's direction. "Iyanka is royalty, after all."

Zef looked Iyanka over with wide eyes that made her want to sink into the ground. Was it really that big of a deal? Sure, when Siersh and Eisadel were at their zenith being royalty meant something, but now? Now she was the princess of a broken and lost people.

"Does everyone know?" Iyanka asked, sighing.

"Just everyone from the kitchen," Lynn assured her, though her answer wasn't reassuring at all. "We tried helping you the best we could, but we didn't know how to tell you…how you'd react…"

Iyanka looked down at her hands. "All that terror and hiding for nothing," she muttered.

"Not nothing," Lynn said, standing and dusting off her skirts. "It kept you safe *outside* the kitchen, after all."

With that, Lynn followed Gretta toward the horses, leaving Zef looking torn between following his sister and staying beside Iyanka. Apparently, the promise of sated curiosity won out, because he turned toward Iyanka and sat down, looking up at her with big eyes.

"What do you want to know?" Iyanka asked, leaning back on her heels.

"You're the ice princess?" he asked. "What were you doing in Baron Malchomy's castle? How did you survive the hunters' attack?"

"I am the ice princess," Iyanka said. "And I was in the fortress for the same reason you were: to hide from the hunters."

He nodded, letting the third question drop away, to Iyanka's relief. "Your real name is Iyanka? Is Glafira made up?"

"Yes. My name is too unique…I had to come up with something else while I hid."

"I guess that makes sense," he conceded. "Though I've never heard of anyone named *Glafira*, either."

Iyanka shrugged one shoulder. *I never said I was good at this.* Zef was quiet for a moment before looking back to Iyanka, tilting his head.

"Are you and Prince Victorin in love?"

A fierce heat flooded Iyanka's face even as ice crawled along her fingertips. She cleared her throat and looked away, searching for Victorin, to reassure herself that he hadn't heard. He still wasn't in sight. When she looked back, Zef's wide eyes didn't look quite so innocent as she'd first thought.

"What makes you think that?" she asked, trying to keep her voice steady.

"Well…the whole reason we left the castle was to rescue you. Lynn and Cook and the rest did it because you're their friend, but Prince Victorin doesn't act like just your friend. And you're different when you're with him…you smile when you look at him."

This boy is far more observant than I'll ever be. Iyanka cleared her throat and tried, unsuccessfully, to brush the frost from her skirts. How was she supposed to respond to Zef's pointed query?

"I'd hardly spoken to Victorin until a few days ago."

"You call him by his first name."

Iyanka bit her lip, looking for escape. She stood, brushing leaves off her knees so she didn't have to meet those bright eyes still watching her.

"I'm going to see if Lynn and Gretta need help."

"They're not doing anything," Zef muttered, but he didn't stop her or follow her.

Zef was right, they *weren't* doing much except talking. Iyanka turned, going toward Elsie instead. A mistake, since as Iyanka stepped up to her side Elsie gave Iyanka a knowing smile.

"What has you blushing like a cherry?" she asked.

"Nothing," Iyanka said, feeling her face heat up again.

"And there it is again," Elsie crowed, crowding closer. "Ho, it must be good. Come on, spill."

"It was just one of Zef's questions," Iyanka muttered. Why had she thought coming over here was a good idea? She should've stayed with Zef.

"Zef's question about what? The handsome weaponsmith turned prince, perhaps?"

Iyanka glanced at Elsie, aiming for a withering look. Elsie's eyes glinted with humor as she waggled her eyebrows.

"Stop it," Iyanka groaned, raising her hand to her forehead. "You're as bad as Zef."

"I like to think Zef is as good as me. And I'm right, aren't I?"

Iyanka held out for one, maybe two seconds under Elsie's stare.

"Yes," she admitted, staring at the trees.

Ha!" Elsie tugged on her arm. "Sit down."

"Why?" Iyanka asked, allowing Elsie to drag her to the ground.

"You are going to tell me about you and Victorin, and start from the beginning 'cause there's a whole lot you did *not* tell me."

"I didn't know I *could* tell you," Iyanka protested.

"No," Elsie said, shaking her head so fiercely her braid flew over her shoulder. "No excuses, no stalling: get talking."

A smile pulled at Iyanka's lips as she obediently began her tale: starting with the first time she'd glimpsed the tall fire prince at her father's funeral, all the way to his rescuing her from the barons. Elsie sat enthralled, her eyes wide and expressive throughout. Iyanka spent a lot of time talking with her eyes on her hands to avoid that gaze.

But when she reached the tragedy of her almost-happily-ever-after, the barons' attack, the story stopped being about her relationship with Victorin. She talked about the chaos, the carnage of that horrid day in Eisadel that still haunted her nightmares. She'd never had anyone to tell, she'd never been able to describe what she *saw* that day, how it tormented her. She talked about her fear, her heartbreak, the desperation that led her to flee south to the home of the *last* man she ever wanted to see. She admitted her regrets, her mistakes…not all of it. Some was too painful…too painful to tell. But enough to choke up her voice, to send tears sliding down her cheeks, freezing into crystal droplets that landed in her hands.

Elsie listened to it all with patience, with sympathy. Sometimes she'd gasp, or reach out to squeeze Iyanka's knee in silent comfort. And as over four years of Iyanka's story spilled from her lips, a foreign sort of relief slipped over her. Like chains falling away from her chest, letting her finally take a breath. She'd never guessed that having someone to *listen* would bring so much…release.

It was dark by the time Iyanka finished her story, ending with how Ald had found her out, and her confrontation with the barons earlier…could it really be the same day? Already it felt like a lifetime ago. Silence engulfed the clearing when she finished. Iyanka didn't know what to say, now…it seemed neither did Elsie.

The first sound was footsteps, and someone knelt and wrapped their arms around Iyanka's shoulders. *Lynn.* Gretta did the same, embracing her other side, and Elsie took Iyanka's hands from her lap to hold them. Iyanka didn't look up, worried she'd see Cook and the men standing near too, listening to her bared heart. But even with the creeping embarrassment at having an audience for her tears, she leaned into those warm arms. She let more tears gather, eyes closed as she sat for a moment in that comfort, that *companionship*.

"You're not alone," Elsie said. "You never were. The Creator was and *is* with you. And so are we."

Iyanka gave a wet laugh, more frozen tears slipping from her skin. "I wish I'd realized that sooner."

"You know now," Gretta said. "We're your *friends* Iyanka. Don't forget it."

"Thank you," Iyanka whispered, her heart swelling. Oh, if only she'd trusted these girls sooner. Everything would've been so different.

Iyanka shifted, suddenly uncomfortable with the heavy atmosphere. What could lighten the mood after her tearful confession?

"Hey Gretta?"

"Yeah?"

"Since you're a fire wielder, all your jokes about wielders…"

"Extreme sarcasm with a touch of irony," Gretta replied. "My coping method so I wouldn't dump a pot of soup over every flabby baron who called us abominations."

That comment earned a few chuckles, breaking through the ice. Soon, Gretta and Lynn stood, wandering toward their makeshift beds. Iyanka and Elsie stood together, using each other for support, but when Elsie moved to follow the others, Iyanka stayed.

"Coming?" Elsie asked.

"In a minute," Iyanka said, her eyes on a shadowed figure leaning against one of the trees. Elsie followed her gaze.

"Ah. Don't want to skip your nightly visit?"

"Something like that."

"Alright. Have fun talking."

Elsie squeezed Iyanka's hand one last time before drifting across the clearing. And Iyanka stood still, taking a fortifying breath before creeping toward Victorin. All she could make out in the darkness were his ember eyes, watching her approach. She lowered her gaze as she stopped in front of him.

"Are you alright?" Iyanka asked.

Victorin placed his hands on her shoulders, a steady, comforting weight, and pinned her with his eyes. They pierced straight through to her soul.

"I should be asking you that."

Iyanka tilted her head. "What?"

"I had no idea...no idea what you went through since the attacks."

"Oh," Iyanka said, voice tiny as she looked down. "That. I didn't know anyone was listening other than Elsie."

"Don't be ashamed," he murmured, hands curling tighter around her shoulders. "Some stories need to be told. I'm just...frustrated."

"I made a lot of mistakes," Iyanka admitted, shrinking in on herself.

"No, not..." Victorin sighed. "At *myself*, Iya."

Iyanka's heart skipped a beat at the nickname, but she tried to push it aside to ponder later. "Why? No part of my story was *your* fault."

"I could've prevented it."

"What...why do you say that?"

He wasn't meeting her eyes anymore. His hands flexed, his grip tightening on her shoulders, as he sighed.

"I should have been in Eisadel when the assault happened. I meant to...but I let myself get distracted by a few...fire wielder matters in Frieda's Refuge. I was still there when the hunters attacked."

Iyanka couldn't help the small sigh of relief. The way he was acting, for a moment she was worried...but no.

"That doesn't make it your fault," she whispered. "You had responsibilities. Your first duty wasn't to my kingdom."

"But my first duty *should* have been to you. I should have been there. I should have searched when you weren't found in Eisadel…"

He trailed off in another heavy, broken sigh. Iyanka's eyes were on his shadowed face, his lowered gaze, and her heart ached. Guilt…she knew guilt. And she knew that convincing Victorin that he wasn't at fault wouldn't be a simple task.

Unsure what to say, unsure that there was anything she *could* say, Iyanka leaned toward him instead. She wrapped her arms around Victorin's waist, resting her head on his chest, mere inches from his heartbeat. And she held her breath, tense until his arms snaked around her in return, until she felt his breath in her hair. They stayed like that who-knows-how-long, not saying anything.

Victorin was the first to pull back.

"You should rest," he said

Iyanka would have argued, knowing it was still too early for sleep to find her, but she doubted Victorin would rest if she stayed up. And he needed sleep more than she did.

"Goodnight," she whispered, stepping back toward where Elsie and the other girls slept in the darkness.

She found an open spot on the edge of the line of girls, where the night air would keep her cool, and sank to the ground. And she listened closely, making sure Victorin was resting too. And she drifted to sleep listening to the groaning of the forest around her, remembering the comfort of Victorin's arms enfolding her.

Chapter VII

They rode through the forest for days, long enough to make the trees feel endless. Iyanka wasn't worried by this, mostly because Victorin wasn't concerned. But after a week in the forest with no sign of it ending, others, mostly Gretta, started making comments about the "blasted trees."

With the provisions the others took from Malchomy's stores and what the forest offered, they didn't have to worry about food. Water was another matter, and there was one tense day where Iyanka had to freeze blocks of ice to melt into their waterskins. But that was only one day. The rest of the time, they came across enough streams to satisfy them.

After the second day, Iyanka and Victorin decided that their time in the forest provided an excellent opportunity to work with their mingled elements. Each night, while the others set up camp and made food, Iyanka and Victorin experimented with their mingled fire and ice.

For the first few days, the others watched in fascination as Victorin and Iyanka twined together frost and flame, teasing out the boundaries of what their peculiar power was capable of. They even joined their experiments, when Victorin wanted to test how other wielders' powers would interact with their joined ones. But their nightly practice soon became as repetitive as the trees, simply another aspect of the long days. Everyone, except Zef, seemed to lose interest in Victorin and Iyanka's exercises.

It was only then that Iyanka began to relax, began to enjoy her nightly routine. With her friends watching her, she was a spectacle. An oddity, even if they didn't mean it. When they ignored her, looking over only when she and Victorin found something new, she could pretend it was just her and Victorin. She could revel in the feeling of their entwined powers.

Tired as she was at the end of each day, she grew to look forward to their practice. She grew to love her time spent with Victorin, holding his hand, the feeling of that candle flame blazing within her chest amid the ice and snow. It was strange, foreign...but *right*. The blue flame dancing across frost no longer startled her. The little flame in her heart didn't feel out of place. Soon, it seemed ages ago that Victorin first asked her to send ice across his skin; surely months, not days.

The practice made a more tangible difference, too. After years of hiding her existence, constantly suppressing her ice, using it freely was...difficult. She found she had to ease back into it, using it a little more each day, pushing past the strain.

And, of course, she'd never used her ice as a weapon before, never used it in tandem with another's power. In Eisadel, she'd been encouraged to use her ice for art: carved statues and intricate murals of frost. She and Milek would dare each other to use it for other things, just to see what they were capable of, but she had no formal training in using her ice for combat. Just as she had no training in physical combat, attack or defense.

When her lack of ability was made perfectly clear, Victorin also took up teaching Iyanka to fight, with and without her ice. This progressed more slowly, as Iyanka discovered, to her shame, just how weak she was. Victorin was nothing but patient with her limits, but that only made her work harder. She wouldn't disappoint him...she wouldn't fail him. Each night she curled up in her blanket sore and utterly spent, but it was worth it. Never again would she be defenseless.

And never again would she cower and hide. Here, among these people, she was known. Accepted. She had friends, people to confide in, people to lean on. And she vowed beneath those trees that she would stand by them. No matter what came, no matter what she faced, she wouldn't leave Victorin's side. No matter what the barons threw at them, she wouldn't run again.

OOo

Fifteen days on the trees' path, and they neared the edge. The road disappeared as they left the wielder trees behind, and they found a little more sunlight filtering down to meet them. It lightened moods considerably.

Iyanka basked in the quiet laughter around her, as everyone took turns impersonating someone from Malchomy's fortress. This time it was Kale, the guard, who's impersonations were often so spot on that even Cook couldn't help but chuckle.

Iyanka smiled to herself as she listened to their antics, tightening her arms around Victorin's waist as they rode slowly through the trees. Kale was impersonating Malchomy's steward, a self-important man with an unfortunately high-pitched voice. Laughter bubbled up in Iyanka's throat, but she swallowed it back, unwilling to disturb Victorin's pensive mood.

"You don't have to do that," he murmured, glancing back over his shoulder.

"Do what?" she asked.

"You know what I mean. Join in with them. Laugh. Don't let my mood stop you from enjoying the day."

Iyanka rested the side of her face against his shoulder blades, squinting at the trees as she formulated her reply.

"I know what it feels like to be left behind," she said softly, "while everyone else is laughing. I don't want to do that to you."

"I can handle being left behind."

There was laughter in his voice, but it didn't convince her. No, those words only twisted the crack in her heart a little wider, made her wonder what he *wasn't* saying. She tightened her arms around his waist, resting her chin on his shoulder, near his ear.

"But you shouldn't have to."

They rode in silence after that, surrounded by the swaying of the trees and the voices of their companions. Iyanka returned to pressing her cheek to Victorin's back, watching the dappled shadows twist as the wind shifted the branches above. It was tranquil, quiet.

Iyanka was confused when Victorin tensed, pulling their horse to a stop.

"Zef, Lynn," he called in a tone with an edge too sharp to be merely conversational.

Iyanka turned, searching for an explanation. Had they disappeared? But no, they rode just behind, near the center of the group. She found Zef's wide grin just as a gale-force wind swept past them all.

Tree branches groaned and cracked, knocking against each other. And a camouflaged form fell to the ground.

Kale was at the man's side with a knife to his throat before Iyanka had a chance to process the scene. Victorin slipped off their horse, wordlessly passing the reins to Iyanka. Everyone else dismounted, drawing weapons, and Iyanka slipped from the horse's back, edging toward Victorin even though it meant being closer to the caught-out scout as well.

"If you kill me, they'll be on you in an instant," the scout warned. His eyes were wide with fear, and he pressed back against the tree, as far from Kale's knife as he could. Kale's snort was derisive.

"You're just trying to save your own skin," Egan said, his eyes on the dappled shadows around them.

Victorin didn't waste breath responding to the man's threat. "How many scouts are there?"

The man glared in silence. Victorin met his gaze for a few heartbeats, then unsheathed a dagger. The scout flinched, but it was Iyanka Victorin turned to.

"Cover this in ice for me?"

She wordlessly took the dagger, sending a thin veneer of ice across its whole surface, and adding hoarfrost across the length of the blade. She handed it back, not needing to ask why he wanted a frozen blade. Flames erupted across the frozen knife as soon as Victorin took it: blue tinged, jagged and dancing where it touched the ragged frost.

The scout gasped in panic, struggling against Kale, who now wrestled the man's arms behind his back. Victorin soon had the blade near his throat, flames almost grazing his skin.

"How many scouts are there, and what are their positions?"

This new threat proved more than the man could take.

"Two layers, alternating positions a quarter mile apart."

"And who waits for us should you sound the alarm?"

He hesitated, and the flames on the dagger leaped. He gasped and said, "A company of hunters, on the forest's edge."

Victorin regarded the man for another moment. The flames on the dagger flickered out, and Victorin nodded to Kale. Iyanka didn't see what Kale did, but the scout collapsed like a sack of flour. Victorin turned to Egan.

"Scout ahead, see if he was telling the truth."

"Yes, Your Highness," Egan replied, disappearing among the trees in moments.

Elsie came close enough to hand Kale a length of rope she'd dug from the saddlebags, and Iyanka edged closer to Victorin.

"Any orders for us, fearless leader?" Gretta asked, her voice light but her eyes sharp.

"We backtrack," Victorin announced in a whisper. "Lead the horses on foot, and stay close."

Everyone followed his instructions without argument, a nice change. Kale grunted as he swung the unconscious scout over one of the horses. Iyanka sidled up to Victorin, keeping a tight hold of their horse's reins.

"What do we do now?" Iyanka asked.

"It depends on what Egan finds," he replied in a low whisper. "Regardless, we'll have to release the horses: in the hills, they'd slow us down. The scout we'll leave near the forest's edge for his friends to find."

Iyanka nodded, keeping her eyes ahead. Trying not to think about what was waiting for them, what they almost walked into. She suddenly felt far too exposed, the safety she'd enjoyed thinning with the forest. She trusted Victorin, she *knew* he'd do anything to keep everyone safe. And he knew what he was doing. But that didn't erase her fear, not completely. Not walking silently there, searching the shadows for more hidden men waiting to give them away.

Victorin snatched up her hand, enveloping it in his familiar, warm grasp. Some of the tension eased as she stepped just a little closer to him. *He knows what he's doing.*

They stopped in a thick part of the woods and waited for Egan. The scout woke up, but was tied to a tree that was within sight, where Kale kept close watch over him. They waited several long hours for Egan to return, which meant the adrenaline from the scout's sudden appearance had ample time to fade into restlessness and boredom. For most, at least: Kale simply leaned against a tree and watched the scout, occasionally glancing up to where the rest paced and fussed. Iyanka took to playing with her frost: making designs on the trees, coating individual grass blades, forming snowflakes in her palm…anything that kept her distracted.

When Egan *did* return, he ghosted in so quietly Iyanka didn't realize he was there until she spotted him whispering with Victorin. She stood only a few steps away, craving the sense of safety that came with Victorin's nearness, but she couldn't hear what they said. Which meant neither did the scout, of course.

Whatever was said, it left a grim look on Victorin's features. Iyanka watched, waited, making an effort to smile when Victorin met her eyes. He returned the gesture, but it was empty. When he and Egan were finished, they turned toward the group.

"The scout told the truth," Victorin announced, with a glance at that sad form tied to the tree. His next words were spoken quietly, barely loud enough for the now tightly gathered group to hear. "But he failed to mention a few things."

Egan broke in, his voice just as quiet. "Like the hunters camped at regular intervals for miles 'round the edge of the forest. Four or five to a fire, all within sight of each other."

That announcement was enough that Victorin's grim look was now mirrored around the circle.

"Can't we just go around?" Zef asked.

Lynn shushed him, glancing nervously at the scout. But if he'd heard, he didn't react. With a gesture, they all stepped further away, leaving Kale alone to watch the scout. When Egan spoke, though, his voice was still quiet.

"Easier said than done," Egan whispered. "Go to the west and we're on the wrong side of Truestone Lake. Go to the east and we'll be boxed in ravines for days. We'll be easy targets."

"I'd rather take our chances in the ravines than travel so close to Joktan's fortress," Cook said.

"Or risk getting skewered trying to make it through the hunters," Gretta added.

"It's not just the ravines," Victorin said. "There are falls we have to climb further north. Last time I tried that path, I barely made it through. I doubt it's any better now."

"What about a distraction?" Iyanka asked. Everyone's eyes turned to her, and she hunched her shoulders. "Do something to make the hunters think we're leaving the forest in one place, when really we're on the other side. Make them think we're trying the ravines when really we're escaping into the hills."

Gretta nodded. "That could work."

Kale appeared at Gretta's shoulder. "It would alert the hunters to our presence."

"Is there a good option where we *don't*?" Elsie asked.

Kale shrugged. "Just pointing out that we won't have trees protecting us from here on out. It's going to be hard to make it through the hills if the hunters know where to look."

"They already suspect," Egan said. "They wouldn't waste hunters on guard duty if they didn't."

Victorin watched Iyanka all through this exchange. Iyanka met his gaze more easily, curious what he was thinking. As the rest were discussing the dangers and advantages of each route, Victorin seemed caught in indecision. But eventually he nodded, his eyes never leaving Iyanka.

"What did you have in mind?"

0O0

Four hunters sat around their fire, watching small strips of meat sizzle as they cooked above the flames. Only one of them had their concentration elsewhere, scanning the forest behind them for any movement.

"Jain," one of the hunters said. "Relax."

"Yeah," another agreed. "No one's coming out. It's a waste even being here."

The fourth hunter snorted in agreement, not bothering to lift his eyes from the fire.

"If you three want to chat around the fire like old friends, I won't stop you," Jain grumbled. "But I'd prefer to do my job."

"We are doing our job," the first hunter protested. "Malchomy's wolf pup said not to let them through. We're doing that, aren't we?"

"These wielders would have to have a death wish to try getting through us," the second added.

"These aren't just any wielders," Jain spat. "This is the *fire prince* we're talking about. He was trained in this sort of thing since he could *walk*, and he's smarter than all *you* lads put together."

Protests and insults were interrupted by shouts to the west. They turned toward the commotion to meet flames: campfires blazing out of control, setting men on fire, spreading out across the grass, never nearing the trees... Men scattered and shouted, some trying to put out the flames while others searched for an enemy to fight.

"They're here," Jain said, managing to sound simultaneously shocked and smug.

"We have to help them!" The quiet hunter shouted. He drew his weapon as he rose, running toward the wildfire before Jain could stop him. The other two merely stood, eyes wide and jaws slack.

"*Don't* run off," Jain ordered. "It might be a distraction."

The two soldiers obeyed without argument, drawing weapons and watching. Their own fire now lay forgotten, meat charred. Its flames lay flat under the fierce winds that ripped through the trees, slamming into the hunters without warning. Jain squinted, fighting to see through the gale, and noticed the fires to the east burning normally, no wind tossing the trees.

"Let's go," Jain shouted, marching toward the east. "They're trying to reach the gorges!"

The other two followed Jain quickly, not wanting to be left behind and all too happy to escape the wind. As they marched off, they didn't see the dark figures leave the trees, silhouetted by the fire as they crept toward the nearby hills.

0O0

Iyanka walked beside Victorin near the back of the group, her hand gripping his as they walked through the night. Hunters were shouting and running on their left, and she could just see the glint of swords as the hunters on their right watched the forest. Lynn and Zef's wind covered any sound they made, but Iyanka still stepped carefully and took shallow breaths. Her heart hammered painfully in her chest, ice crawling up her throat.

They had to get out of sight. They had to reach new shelter before the hunters calmed enough to pay attention to their surroundings. Those dealing with the fire didn't worry her all that much: their eyes wouldn't see anything in the night after staring at the flames. The hunters to the east, though…their inward focus was all that protected Iyanka and the rest from their notice.

Egan led the group across the grassy field separating the trees from the rising hills. Iyanka couldn't help but wish for the horses, but they were happily grazing in the forest. Surely half the night passed by before they finally reached a narrow canyon, slipping between its banks and out of sight.

The tension left Victorin's shoulders as he let the fires behind them fade to normal, the blaze in Iyanka's chest returning to that solitary flame. He'd maintained the blaze longer than Iyanka had expected, working alone once they passed the last of the trees.

They continued up the canyon, anxious to put more distance between them and the chaos they left behind. But it wasn't long before Victorin's steps slowed. Iyanka looked up in time to see him close his eyes, lips twisting as if in pain. Every movement was slow, labored.

"You need to rest," she whispered.

He shook his head, eyes focused ahead. "I'll rest when we're further in."

"You're exhausted."

"That doesn't change anything."

Iyanka stopped, staring up at him with furrowed brow, worry plaguing her. Victorin, unwilling to release her hand, stopped as well. He stared down at her with tired eyes, forcing a small smile to his lips as he reached out and touched her cheek.

"Don't worry about me, Iya. I'll be fine. But we need to get further into the hills before sunrise."

Iyanka shifted. She knew he was right; they needed to get as far from the hunters as they could. But that didn't mean she liked it.

"Can I help you at all?"

He shook his head. "It's fine. Let's catch up to the others."

The group had stopped, waiting for Victorin and Iyanka to rejoin them before trudging on. Hours passed in the darkness before they finally stopped,

Egan leading them to a rock overhang that offered a measure of shelter.

Victorin stumbled to the back, sinking to the ground in silence. Iyanka knelt beside him, pressing a waterskin into his hands and making sure he drank. He didn't even open his eyes when he was finished, just set the waterskin on the rock and leaned his head back. Iyanka watched, wishing she could offer some measure of comfort, as his breathing slowed in sleep. Then she crept from his side, not wanting to disturb him.

"He'll be fine, lass," Cook said, handing her a piece of bread as she joined their circle. "He's just worn out."

"But…I've never seen him *this* exhausted…why?"

"Not many fire wielders could've done what Victorin accomplished tonight," Egan said. He sat at the edge of the overhang, keeping watch. He didn't bother to turn as he spoke. "Let alone walk this far afterwards."

"Fire doesn't work the same as ice," Gretta explained. "Ice can exist without a source sustaining it. Fire can't."

When Gretta paused, Iyanka nodded, showing she understood.

"If there's fuel available, no problem: start the fire and it'll do fine. But if there isn't anything to burn, or you want the fire to go beyond what it would do normally, it uses *us* as fuel. Most wielders could only sustain a fire like *that* for a few seconds."

Iyanka glanced back at Victorin's sleeping form with new awe.

"How many others could've done what Victorin did tonight?" she asked.

"Before the attacks, maybe four dozen," Egan said. "Now? Ten, maybe twelve. On Elnar, at least."

Cook snorted. "Of course, that number is thanks to Ignacio's 'training'."

The bitterness in her voice made Iyanka turn toward her. Cook was staring at the rock, Gretta rubbing her shoulder. Elsie sat close to them, her eyes turned to the darkness.

"What did he do?" Iyanka asked, dreading the answer. *What kind of father did Victorin grow up with?*

"Whenever a fire wielder showed promise," Gretta began, voice somber, "they'd be taken to Siersh, drafted into the king's army. There, Ignacio put them through a training regimen that bordered on torture: conjuring fire in midair and sustaining it until they collapsed from exhaustion, beating them if they let it go out before…every night, after they'd already trained all day. And eventually, their fire became the weapon Ignacio wanted."

"Victorin was stronger than his father," Egan added. "Much stronger. The queen died when Victorin was seven years old, and after that the king trained him personally. Forced him through training that had broken boys twice his age."

"Seemed to handle it well enough," Cook said. And although her voice was bitter, Iyanka could've sworn there was a strange glint of pride to her words.

"Always standing beside his father with those sharp eyes, seeing everything."

"Don't kid yourself, Martha," Egan said. "He nearly died from it. It's a miracle he didn't break."

Iyanka turned from those faces in the darkness, turning instead to Victorin. *And he feels guilt for what I've been through?* Her heart went out to him, watching as he slept, even as shame creeped in. *My troubles, my pain…it's nothing. How can he stand my weakness?*

"You all should get some sleep," Egan said. "We'll start walking again as soon as it's light, before the hunters can find our trail."

The group dispersed, the women retreating to the far edge of their little shelter while Kale stayed by Egan on the edge. Iyanka curled into a huddled ball, using her blanket as a pillow. The stone was wonderfully cold, and despite her lingering troubles she was asleep within minutes.

0O0

A hand on her shoulder pulled Iyanka from her dreams far too early. She opened bleary eyes to see Victorin's dark gaze fixed on her, and she smiled groggily. He retreated, and she slowly sat up, realizing as she did that their shelter was filled with the gray light of pre-dawn. Her companions were already awake, chewing on the dry bread that resembled rocks more every day. Iyanka turned back to Victorin, where he sat an arm's length away. Relief slipped through her heart: he looked stronger. But his eyes were still tired.

"You look better," she said, voice rough with sleep. She cleared her throat, ducking her head.

"I am."

He reached out, tucking a wild strand of red hair behind her ear. And she returned her gaze to his face.

"I'm sorry I worried you," he said.

"It's alright," she breathed. "I understand now…why you were exhausted."

He suddenly looked wary. "Did Egan explain it to you?"

"Egan and Cook," Iyanka replied, confused by the sudden change of tone.

"I'm assuming they discussed my childhood as well."

"Egan mentioned a few things."

Her attempt at being vague didn't work. Victorin frowned, his gaze turned to the rock behind Iyanka's head. *Is he angry?* But he sighed, and when he met her eyes again, there was no anger there. Just an old sorrow.

"My father was…not a good man. I wasn't the only one to suffer under his reign."

"I know," Iyanka whispered.

He rested his hand on the rock, closing his eyes. "Iya, I'm not a martyr. I fared better than most of the boys he…trained. They should be remembered before me."

"I understand."

Victorin nodded and started to pull back, but Iyanka stopped him with a hand on his shoulder. Warmth radiated from him even in that chill morning. He opened his eyes, a question in his eyes.

"I understand you don't want anyone to be forgotten," Iyanka said. She bit her lip, fighting for the words for what she wanted, *needed*, to explain. "But he was your father. He was supposed to be your *protector*, not forge you into a weapon. Recognizing the wrong of what he did to you doesn't mean you've forgotten the others who suffered."

For a few quiet moments, Victorin stared at her, unmoving. The light in his eyes threatened to melt her from the inside out, but she couldn't tell if that terrified her or not. She was about to turn away, unnerved, when he shook his head and sighed again.

"I don't know how you do it," he murmured.

"Do what?"

"Find the right words to completely disarm me."

Iyanka tilted her head, about to ask how she'd *disarmed* him, but he stood.

"We need to get moving," he said, offering her his hand.

Iyanka took it, blushing when she stumbled and he had to steady her. He said nothing about her lack of balance. Thankfully everyone else was already picking their way down the hillside outside, and by the time she and Victorin joined them her face had cooled.

The sky in the east was blooming with light, but the sun hadn't yet crested the horizon. Iyanka looked around in the gray-blue light at the hills around them, covered in brush and grass with rock outcroppings taking their own place in the landscape. The canyon they had escaped through was little more than a gully, with a gravel bottom. Even with her untrained eyes, Iyanka could see the trail they'd left.

Egan stepped up beside Victorin, startling Iyanka with his sudden appearance.

"No sign of pursuit yet, but I don't think our ruse will work for long."

"Agreed," Victorin said. He turned toward the group. "Time to move."

Zef leaped off the rock he'd been climbing, running over to Lynn, who snatched his hand. Zef was the only one in the group who seemed energized, though everyone's eyes were brighter than they'd been the night before. Iyanka smiled when Kale helped Gretta stand despite her protests. Her face was tomato red, and she refused to meet anyone's eyes when Kale was slow to release her hand.

"Come on," Egan grumbled. "We don't have all day."

He led the way up the hillside, following a deer trail a little below the horizon line. Everyone seemed to wake up a little more as they walked, as their muscles warmed and they pressed deeper into the hills.

When they reached an especially rocky section of hillside, Egan instructed everyone to step only on the rocks. Everyone complied without question, recognizing the purpose, but Elsie and Egan were the only ones remotely graceful about it. Victorin might have matched their assured leaps, if he hadn't been hindered keeping Iyanka from falling. After a few minutes of her struggling, Victorin scooped Iyanka into his arms and began leaping from rock to rock as if she weighed nothing.

"Don't you dare," Gretta snarled behind them. Kale replied, but his words were drowned out by Elsie's laughter.

Iyanka's face burned, and she buried her head in Victorin's shoulder so no one would see. He smelled like smoke from pine-wood fires, a comforting homey scent. And as embarrassed as she was, she couldn't help but enjoy his arms wrapped around her, his heartbeat sounding in her ear…not that any of those thoughts helped cool her face.

Victorin's perch wobbled, and Iyanka tensed. But he leaped to a more stable rock without issue.

"You might feel more secure if you put your arms around my neck," he whispered, taking the next leap.

Iyanka complied, dearly hoping her thoughts weren't written on her face. Victorin chuckled, and when she looked up to search out the cause he was gently shaking his head.

"What is it?" she asked.

"Nothing."

"I don't believe you."

Victorin navigated several more rocks before answering.

"I'm…weaker than usual this morning."

"You can set me down," Iyanka said. "I don't want to tire you more."

He laughed. "Not…that kind of weakness."

"Oh."

She was tempted to make him explain, but her creeping anxiety over the answer won out. She stayed silent.

They finally reached the end of the steppingstones, and Victorin carefully set Iyanka on her feet. One side felt chilled with the sudden air against it, rather than Victorin's solid warmth. Somehow it wasn't pleasant. She tried not to ponder that.

"Will they find our trail again?" she asked, watching as the rest of their group painstakingly caught up. Egan was already ahead of them, plotting their path.

"Probably," Victorin said. "But this will slow them down."

That was a sobering thought. They stood together but waited in silence for the rest of their companions to join them. When the whole group was on steady ground again, with sighs of relief and smiles of victory, they continued on.

Once again, Egan was the one who led them. And as they picked their way toward another of the endless hills, she pondered that: the strange dynamic between Egan and Victorin. Victorin was the leader, as shown by how Egan reported to him in decisions. Yet Victorin obviously trusted Egan's judgement and let him choose their path. Iyanka couldn't imagine most of the leaders she'd met deferring in such a way, especially not the barons.

By midday, Iyanka missed the horses dearly. Yes, the first few days had been torture, and the horses were no doubt faring better in the forest than they would among the rocks and steep hillsides, but that didn't stop her wishing. She didn't mind walking, but the activity quickly grew more tiring than it should be, watching every step to avoid a broken ankle. In the few times she dared glance up from her feet, no one else seemed to be enjoying it either. Not that they had a choice.

She winced when her boots pinched her toes. *Stupid shoes.* Walking barefoot was so much more comfortable, not that it would work out well with so many rocks. And no one else was voicing complaints, so she kept her lips sealed. *I won't be the weak one.*

They reached a small stream, barely a trickle, and stopped for a rest. They filled their waterskins and sat under a scraggly tree near the creek bed. Most of the group seemed to be doing alright with the pace, but Cook was struggling. No one complained about the chance for rest, though. The air had had a chill to it during the morning, but now the sun beat down mercilessly. Iyanka longed for the shade of the forest.

"How long are we going to be in these hills?" Lynn asked, stroking Zef's hair as he used her lap for a pillow.

"A week if we make good progress," Egan said, glancing at Victorin. "But the terrain changes halfway to the river. More bluffs, less grass, trees in the canyons.

"Better cover, but slower traveling," Victorin added. "We have to be careful about choosing our path so we don't come across cliffs or steep ravines."

"I thought we came this way to avoid all that," Gretta argued, sitting up to glare at Victorin and Egan.

"We did," Egan agreed. "And we're circumventing the worst of it. But to avoid all of the bluffs would require another day, maybe even two, and more open ground to cover. It's best to stick to the hills."

"If we can make it across the river we should be in the clear," Victorin said. "The barons control that area, but their outposts are few and badly equipped. And most of the people north of the river are wielder sympathizers, so we won't have trouble with them."

Sympathizers? There was so much Iyanka knew nothing of...so much about their homeland she *should* have known. *If only I'd stayed.*

"We should get going again," Egan said, groaning as he stood.

A few more groans and sighs marked their group as the rest stood, brushing off clothes and stretching out legs grown stiff. Their pace was faster, now, rejuvenated by the short rest, but they were quieter. Victorin stayed at Iyanka's side even when she fell to the back of the group, but neither of them spoke for a long time. Iyanka was too focused on putting one foot in front of the other, but Victorin seemed deep in thought.

"Is something wrong?" Iyanka asked, taking Victorin's hand as he helped her jumped down from a short outcropping of rock. They reached the bottom of the wash and started climbing back out, the others already halfway up the hill. *So much for not being the weak one.*

"I don't know yet," Victorin said.

"You think it's too easy?" She glanced up at him, quickly meeting his dark eyes.

"What makes you say that?"

"Well…" she edged around a bush. "They had scouts and hunters all along the forest…but they obviously weren't as observant or experienced as the hunters in Malchomy's service."

"Most of the hunters at the forest's edge bore Baron Joktan's crest. He isn't as…enthusiastic about hunting down wielders."

Iyanka nodded, eschewing a response as they climbed the steepest part of the next hill. They'd reached the next deer trail Egan had selected before either spoke again.

"I'm right, though, aren't I?" Iyanka asked.

"Yes, you're right."

Chapter VIII

"Horrid rain," Gretta growled from where she huddled close to the tree in an effort to stay dry. The effort didn't afford her much, and she continued muttering. Most of their group seemed to agree with her, as they crowded together under the scant shelter of their lone tree, high on the hill face. They were stuck there, waiting for Egan and Kale to return.

Iyanka stood a little apart, within arms length from Victorin but far enough that she wasn't smothered by the heat of the group. Gretta and Cook's response to the rain was to bring enough of their fire to the surface to keep themselves and everyone around them warm. Lynn, Zef, and Elsie gathered close to the heat with gratitude, but for Iyanka the warmth was a heavy blanket stealing her breath. She'd quickly separated herself to embrace the cool rain. Victorin had followed her, despite her insistence that she was fine. He watched her closely as she enjoyed the mist on her face.

They'd been in the hills seven days, but the rain had slowed their progress significantly and Egan estimated they had another day's journey to the river. As the rain worsened the group had decided to take shelter, giving Egan and Kale the opportunity to scout behind. It seemed like hours since the men had left, and it seemed everyone's patience was running short. All the more reason for Iyanka to step away a little.

"Milek and I used to play a game whenever it rained," Iyanka whispered to Victorin.

"What was it?"

In response, Iyanka turned to face him and held her hand up between them, allowing a drop of water to collect on the end of her finger. Sending a tendril of swirling ice through her arm, she froze that drop. It fell from her hand, disappearing in the mud at her feet. Continuing from there, she allowed the cold to rise toward her skin, freezing the rain gathered there into swirling patterns of frost. Ice coated each strand of her soaked hair, and frost turned her already light eyelashes a glistening white. Moisture pulled from the fabric of her dress curled and solidified into thorny hoarfrost and diamond droplets in dizzying patterns, until she was a masterpiece of ice and snow.

Iyanka grinned and looked up into Victorin's eyes. "Milek can turn a few clouds into a blizzard, but he never could match me at this."

"I can see why," he replied, carefully stroking her ice-encrusted hair where it hung stiff beside her face.

His touch melted some of the frost, but there was none of the blistering heat she was expecting. She reached up and very slowly touched his jaw, frowning when his skin was barely warmer than hers.

"Why aren't you keeping yourself warm?" she asked.

"I'm not cold."

"I don't believe you."

He sighed. "Conserving energy."

"I still don't believe you."

Iyanka lowered her hand and reeled her power back into her chest, allowing the frost to melt with the raindrops. Meanwhile Victorin smiled and brushed a raindrop from her cheek.

"Do you remember the first time we met?"

Iyanka allowed the subject change, her mind spinning through her memories. She remembered the first time she'd seen him, when he'd come to Eisadel. But they hadn't officially met that day. And she remembered when her mother had introduced her to Victorin, but she didn't think that was the first time...

A memory emerged, a few hours before she'd been *officially* introduced to Victorin. Iyanka remembered it now: the slight sense of fear soon overcome with curiosity, the butterflies in the pit of her stomach, how dark he looked compared to the ivory and porcelain skin she was used to...the fierce heat in her face when he'd bowed to her and spoke her name...

"We were in the gardens," Iyanka said. "I'd fought with Milek over something silly and had gone out to get some peace. You were in one of the far courtyards, watching the birds on the lake below."

"I wondered why you seemed so flustered," he replied, one side of his mouth curling in a crooked smile.

Iyanka glanced down, remembering all too clearly how little it had to with sibling bickering. Before she could think of what else to say, Egan appeared beside them. Iyanka blushed and stepped back, putting a more proper distance between herself and Victorin. Egan didn't even spare her a glance.

"The hunters have our trail. They've taken shelter from the storm, but they'll catch us quickly once they start moving."

All lightness disappeared from Victorin's expression. "Where's Kale?"

"Scouting a few hills ahead so we don't get into a tight spot."

"Good."

Victorin turned and told the others, but Iyanka only half listened. Suddenly, the rain felt sodden, unyielding. *We were so close.* The threat of the hunters had once again drifted to the back of her mind, a danger that seemed so far away here, even as they'd raced to reach the river. Now, dread and fear crashed around her head, leaving her shivering at Victorin's side. She reached out and fumbled for his hand, relaxing when her fingers were clasped within his warm grip.

Kale came jogging under the tree, panting as he stopped in front of everyone.

"Hill turns to a shale slope and bluffs about half a mile up. Only way I can see is to take the canyon: it looks like it branches off to the north and shallows out pretty quickly."

"The canyon it is," Victorin said. "Now let's try to put some distance between us and the hunters."

Zef huddled at Lynn's side, his eyes wide as he silently watched. Iyanka's heart went out to him, hating that he had to suffer this with them. He was so young, and already running for his life. Pursued by men who would kill him without a second thought. Despite all of that, Iyanka watched as Zef looked up at his sister, saw her worry, and immediately straightened with a look of resolve.

How could brothers do that? How could they be absolutely terrified, and so suddenly gain courage to be strong for their siblings? Milek had always done that...Iyanka had never understood how.

Will I see my brother again? If the hunters caught them, Iyanka doubted she'd ever get the chance.

Egan and Kale led the way down the hillside and everyone followed. Their pace was painfully slow: the rain had turned the hillside to slick mud that was treacherous, and resulted in everyone half walking half *sliding* down. All of them were coated in mud from the knees down by the time the reached the bottom of the hill.

Egan led them along the canyon a few dozen steps above the bottom, which churned with muddy water. Trees grew along the bottom of the canyon, great cottonwoods with broad green leaves and branches that creaked and groaned in the wind. They shielded the rain-soaked band from sight, and kept most of the rain off, but Iyanka didn't like walking beneath them. They sounded ominous.

She tried quickening her pace to better keep up with the others, Victorin speeding up beside her. Now they traveled in a tight group, following the path of the canyon. No one spoke, but Iyanka couldn't tell if the silence was caused by dread or the misery of the rain.

By the time they reached the north-reaching canyon Kale had seen, the rain had slowed to a slight drizzle. It made walking more pleasant, but it also meant the hunters would likely be moving again.

"How far are we from the river?" Iyanka asked.

"Might be a few miles, might be twenty," Egan said. "I'll have a better idea when we reach that hill."

He pointed to a mount that stood taller than the others about half a mile away.

"Egan," Victorin said. "Can you scout ahead?"

"I can do it," Kale volunteered. "I still have energy to work off."

Victorin and Egan glanced at each other.

"Alright," Victorin said. "Circle around to the other side before leaving cover, and don't stand at the top. Meet us at the base on the other side."

"I won't be seen."

With a nod from Victorin, Kale spun and started jogging down the canyon. Within moments he was out of sight, his footsteps nearly silent on the wet leaves.

"That one knows what he's doing," Egan commented, nodding to where Kale disappeared.

"He was trained for battle and guarding a fortress, not espionage," Victorin said.

"Still, he shows promise."

Victorin's voice was tight, *harsh*, as he said, "So did Oric."

"Aye...so did Oric."

And though Iyanka's curiosity burned at that name, at the pain in Victorin's voice, she kept silent. Now was not the time to dredge up sore subjects.

The canyon changed as they walked, and they lost the trees as they veered uphill. Soon they'd be out in the open again. Iyanka prayed they were behind the larger hill when that happened.

The ground was wet, but not as slick as it had been further up the canyon. They were able to walk faster without the risk of falling on their faces, and the mud didn't clump on the bottom of Iyanka's boots anymore. They were halfway around the base of the hill when Kale skidded up to them, face red.

"Once we leave this canyon the land flattens out for about half a mile before the river," he panted. "But we're trapped. There are twelve hunters patrolling the edge of the hills, and these aren't the incompetent helmets we faced at the forest."

"Wulfguard?" Gretta asked, face scrunched with worry.

Kale shook his head. "Ald."

"He's not much better," Cook grumbled.

Iyanka saw another emotion pass over Gretta's face, something close to panic, before she schooled her expression again.

"Are they mounted?" Victorin asked.

Kale nodded. Egan let out a low curse, prompting Cook to shoot him a disapproving glare. Iyanka looked to Victorin, taking in his look of internal debate, waiting for him to speak the plan he was obviously forming.

"That could work to our advantage," he said, slowly. "If we can unseat them and steal their horses, we'll have a better chance of reaching the river."

"How do you expect to do that?" Cook asked, pushing a strand of wet hair from her eyes with impatience. "You and the princess are the only ones who can fight them."

"That's not exactly true," Victorin said. "Their enchantment can't stop Lynn and Zef completely, and hailstones to their heads should knock them out of the saddle."

"Let's do it," Zef said, grinning. "We can take 'em out."

Lynn's face was a solemn contrast to Zef's as she placed her hands on her brother's shoulders, but she nodded. "We can do it."

"Did you see the hunters following us?" Elsie asked, wrapping her arms around herself.

Kale shook his head. "I think they took to the trees like we did."

"Then let's get moving," Egan said, starting the march to the mouth of the canyon.

Once again, everyone fell in line behind him. But now their pace was a stunted run, the air thick with apprehension as they neared the open land. They slowed near the edge, behind a rock outcropping that caused a twist in the canyon, where the hunters wouldn't see them. Everyone gathered close together, eyes watchful.

"What do you need from us?" Victorin asked Lynn.

"It'll be easier for us to knock them over if someone throws the hailstones first," she answered, her normally soft face grim.

Meanwhile Iyanka formed a rounded chunk of ice the size of Victorin's fist, and held it up for the group to inspect.

"Will this work?"

"That's perfect," Victorin said, taking the ice and tossing it into the air a few times.

"How many?" Iyanka asked, forming two more.

"Two dozen?" Kale proposed, taking the new ice stones from Iyanka's hands. "We don't want to take chances."

Zef scoffed. "We won't miss."

Victorin smiled at the boy, as Iyanka handed more ice to Egan, and then to Cook.

"All the same," Victorin said. "It's best to have extras."

Iyanka was still forming the hunks of ice, passing them out to all their companions and storing extras in a sack Elsie held for her. Victorin and Egan went to scout the best position to attack from.

Within minutes, they were all huddled behind the rocks that hid them from the hunters beyond. Zef and Lynn perched higher up, to better capture the wind and see what they were doing. Iyanka held her breath, clutching tight to her own ice stones as everyone waited for Victorin's signal. He nodded, and the chaos began.

Kale and Egan leaped into the canyon bed, launching their ice toward the hunters that waited beyond. Others followed close behind, as a howling wind whipped at Iyanka's hand, practically ripping the hunk of ice from her grasp as she launched it into the open air.

From their now-vulnerable position, Iyanka could see the hunters that waited for them. A few were already hitting the ground, while others drew weapons and circled, searching for the source of such an unnatural wind.

Two turned toward their exposed group, but were quickly knocked into the mud when Kale and Victorin launched more ice. Another volley from the rest of the group left only two hunters still mounted, swords drawn.

Their group surged forward, grasping at the dragging reins of the horses, Kale and Egan pausing to make sure the hunters stayed down. Iyanka kept close to Victorin's back, their hands lit with blue flame as Victorin launched a *flaming* ice ball at one of the still-mounted hunters. This projectile didn't knock the hunter from his horse, Zef and Lynn too busy skidding down toward them to lend their wind, but it spooked his horse, preventing the hunter from getting in their way as they ran past. Shouting and the neighs of frightened horses filled her head, making it hard to stay calm, to keep her attention where it needed to be.

Soon Victorin was handing a set of reins to Iyanka, helping her into the saddle of a stolen mount. She kept her eyes on her hands, adjusting the reins, waiting for Victorin to mount his own horse. As soon as he was in the saddle, he kicked his horse into motion. Iyanka's followed without prompting, and Iyanka turned her attention to staying in the saddle and not pulling on the horse's mouth.

Other riders surrounded her, but every face she saw was a welcome one. And thankfully Iyanka's horse seemed content to follow Victorin's lead as they thundered across the plain.

Zef shouted, "They're following us!"

Iyanka glanced over her shoulder, wind whipping her hair into her face, and saw three hunters back on their horses thundering across the plain after them. Leading them was a man with a badly dented helmet Iyanka was pretty sure was Ald.

Ice flooded her being, leaking onto the saddle, and Iyanka urged her mount to run faster. The horse grunted and complied, quickly catching up to Lynn and Zef's horse, and then to Kale's. The steed seemed to reach top speed when they were just behind Gretta's horse, in a wild gallop that would have terrified Iyanka on any other day. Now, it seemed too slow.

An eternity passed before they neared the river, the hunters slowly gaining on them. Iyanka wasn't the first to reach the bank, but when she did the others were still on this side of the water. Iyanka pulled her horse to a stop beside Egan.

"Why aren't we crossing?" she asked, eyes wide.

"Current is too fast," Egan said. "We wouldn't make it across here, especially with *them* on our trail."

Victorin and his stolen horse thundered up to the group, his mount's hooves kicking up clods of mud from their abrupt stop.

"Iyanka," he called, leaping from the horse.

Iyanka's winter blizzard swirled, pushing against the confines of her flesh, begging to be used. She looked between the swollen river and the oncoming hunters. Her heart pounded in her ears as a wind only she could hear blustered and shrieked. Were they trapped? Were they really?

"We can cross," Iyanka said, slipping from her horse's back, nearly falling on the ground. The beast snorted and sidestepped, but Iyanka ignored him. She yanked her boots from her feet, jumping around so she didn't fall in the mud, and ran to Victorin. He snatched her hand as she skidded to a stop beside him. The muddy ground was cool beneath her feet.

"I can make a way across," she said.

Victorin squeezed her hand. "First we need to slow them down."

Their hands began to glow as Iyanka fed frost into the fire already lit across his skin, winter and flame entwining with their clasped hands. By now the feeling was familiar, and it helped tame her fear as she put her power to use.

Ice pulsated out from her bare feet, freezing the ground and spreading in a wide arc around their group, adding layer after layer to the barrier. Victorin ignited the ice as soon as the arc was complete, raising a wall of flame leaping above Iyanka's head. She added one more layer to the barrier before pulling her hand from Victorin's grasp.

She dodged frantic horses, Kale fighting to keep them under control, and skidded down the bank to the edge of the river. Roaring water filled her ears. The

river was at least three horse length's across, frothing
as it ripped down its path.

Hearing shouts, Iyanka glanced over her shoulder
to find that the hunters had arrived. Two soldiers unsuccessfully prodded at the flames with their weapons.
The third was staring through the fire. Iyanka's blood
slowed as she accidentally met Ald's gaze, her panic
rising with a fury to rival the chaos surrounding her. *I
can't be caught by him again.*

She ripped her gaze away, back to the river. Her
frantic heartbeat was a lone anchor in swirling white
fear, threatening to override all other senses. She
looked out over the water and took a deep, shaking
breath. She exhaled slowly, lifting the veil separating
her ice from the air around her. The air left her mouth
in a cloud of white, snowflakes dancing on the breeze.

Ice exploded out from her feet. Deafening cracks
rung through the air as water froze, only to make way
for louder roaring as the still rushing water beat
against the ice bridge Iyanka had just formed. Iyanka
stepped onto the ice, and with another breath she
pulsed more cold into that bridge. Glittering frost
spread from her footsteps, a thrill racing through her
veins at the sense of that great mass of ice beneath her
feet. Water sloshed over the edge, running across the
top of the bridge and turning it slick. Iyanka froze the
water as it washed over, forming a wall to force the
water underneath. And she sent more ice across, etch-
ing patterns into the surface to give more traction.

She turned toward her companions. They all
stared at her, eyes wide, a look in their eyes that made

her feel like an oddity on display. She took a step back toward them, beckoning.

"It's ready," she shouted. "Bring the horses, too."

Elsie was the first to step onto the ice. Her steps were small and cautious, but she managed to coax her mount onto the frozen river with her. Lynn and Zef followed, Zef's young face pursed with concentration as he grasped the cheek piece of their horse's bridle. Cook and Egan followed, their horses giving little trouble. Iyanka backed toward the edge, giving everyone room to pass as she fed and rebuilt the ice beneath the fire wielders' feet. They made it across without mishap, leaving Victorin, Kale, and Gretta to go.

Kale was holding the reins of three horses and trying to lead them onto the ice. Gretta was watching the soldiers on the other side of the fire, still pacing and prodding at the slowly dying flames. But one of the horses broke free, and she ran to Kale's aid. They passed Iyanka on the frozen bridge, as Iyanka kept her eyes on Victorin. He still wasn't on the ice.

"Victorin!" she shouted.

He backed away from the barrier, his gaze locked on Ald, then spun on his heel and ran toward the river. The flames flickered out, and the hunters lunged forward. Victorin leaped toward the river, a hunter's blade following his path too closely… Iyanka screamed his name, thinking the sword had met its target. But Victorin's fire still raged as he landed, slipping, on the river. Heat blazed as he set the river on fire, forcing the hunters back as tall flames licked the shore.

Iyanka stood frozen, surrounded by flames that caressed her as if they were no more harmful than snowflakes, her eyes still locked on Victorin. He stood, stumbling toward her, struggling on the melting ice beneath the flames. He stretched his hand out toward her, nearing her side, but Iyanka ignored it. Instead, she threw her arms around his neck, going on her toes to draw close. Tremors wracked her body, and it took her a moment to realize it wasn't the river or the fire causing it. Victorin wrapped his arms around her, stroking her hair and pulling her even closer.

Ice cracked beneath them as the frozen fire consumed the ice bridge. Victorin released her enough for them to run to shore, barely keeping their balance, but he never let go of her hand. Iyanka held onto him tightly, even when they reached solid ground. The river behind them still roared with water and flame.

Victorin turned toward the sound, and Iyanka followed. Partly to keep hold of his hand, partly to avoid whatever looks her companions might be aiming at her. And to see if the hunters would try to cross.

Two hunters paced the width of the ice, prodding the flames with their swords as they went. Instead of extinguishing, the fire leaped and nearly engulfed the swords. One of the hunters cursed, his sleeve caught on fire, and rolled in the mud to put out the unnatural flames.

Once again, Ald stood a step back from this, sword lowered as he stared at them. His gaze rested on her for a moment, then flicked up to Victorin. Iyanka glanced between the two men, but they did nothing but stare at each other. And after a tense moment, Ald nodded and called a sharp order to retreat. Neither man resisted, chasing after the horses that had refused to get anywhere near the blue flame.

Behind her, Iyanka heard the others mounting their horses. But she and Victorin watched the hunters another moment, making sure they were truly leaving before turning away.

As Victorin helped Iyanka onto her new horse, she remembered a small detail that made her groan. *That makes things more complicated.*

Victorin was already mounting his own horse, and he glanced over at her warily.

"What's wrong?"

"My boots," she said. "They're on the other side of the river."

He stared at her for a heartbeat before chuckling. Iyanka ducked her head, face heating, but she couldn't help the smile that spread across her face. Victorin's quiet laugh made her heart…flutter. And she couldn't deny that she enjoyed the freedom of toes bare to the cool air.

"Let's get moving," Victorin said, hints of laughter still in his voice. "Before they find a place to cross."

Already mounted, the rest of their group turned their steeds toward the low rise to the north, Egan guiding them. Iyanka waited for Victorin, who was slow to turn away from the river. When he finally steered his horse toward the others, Iyanka maneuvered her horse so they rode side by side.

"Ald was the one who discovered you?" Victorin asked.

"Yes," Iyanka replied, with an involuntary shiver at the memory of that horrid day.

"How did he act then?"

"He…" Iyanka forced herself to dredge up the memory of the tower, and her humiliating walk to the barons' meeting. "He was shocked and…sad, almost. I didn't understand why. He already suspected me, but…it was like he wanted me to prove him wrong."

Iyanka glanced at Victorin, but his gaze was focused ahead of them. His jaw was tight, a habit of his when he was deep in thought. She listened to the horse's steps rattling against the ground for a few heartbeats before giving into curiosity.

"What are you thinking?"

"That there might be more to him than we see." He finally looked at her, though only for a moment. "He either doesn't have the bloodlust Wulfguard possesses, or he has his own agenda. I'm tempted to believe the latter."

"Would that be good or bad?"

"Depends on what he's hiding."

"Oi," Cook shouted, turning in the saddle to glare at Iyanka and Victorin. "Are you coming any time this week?"

Her gaze was more impatient than angry, causing Egan to heave a loud sigh that made her switch her glare to his back. But Iyanka still straightened, urgency racing through her. She never enjoyed being the recipient of Cook's glare, in the kitchen or in the wilds.

Urging their mounts into a jarring trot, Iyanka and Victorin caught up to the rest of their band in a few moments. Egan pulled his mount around to face Victorin.

"Are we risking the road?"

"Yes," Victorin said. "At this point, we want speed over secrecy."

Someone, Gretta probably, asked a question, but Iyanka wasn't listening. Her attention was stolen by a cool breeze, a taste of their surroundings that made her cast her gaze around them. To the east snowcapped peaks broke up the horizon, stretching beyond sight to meet the barrier of the Valkis mountains along Elnar's northern shore. The grass covering the hills around them was tall and lush, the perfect hiding place for rabbits and fox and birds that were still singing despite the rain. Trees dotted the landscape, tall pine replacing the scrubby oak they'd found the past few days. The wind twining around her carried the scent of rain and ice, of fir and soil. The river border might have been only a few hundred yards away, but already the land was so different, so wild and beautiful and familiar…Iyanka was home.

Chapter IX

The band located the road in under an hour. Though everyone was tired, including their stolen mounts, they pressed on. Iyanka could see that she wasn't the only one grateful for the steadier pace the road allowed. After so many days of trusting the trees for a path and weaving through the hills, the well-traveled road was a relief. If only Iyanka didn't have to watch over her shoulder for the hunters, running them down. With no river to give them escape, would they survive? How many faces would be lost in a head-on confrontation, if they found Iyanka and her companions in the open like this? Would Victorin…no. *He's here, he's safe. He'll find us shelter.*

Near sunset, when the sun finally broke through the clouds and painted everything in gold, the road entered a small valley covered in lush fields of grain and vibrant pasture. The road wound around the edge, but a narrow track cut between the fields and led to a small homestead surrounded in trees. Egan turned off on this path, but Cook refused to follow, blocking the road with her horse.

"Where are you taking us?" Cook asked.

"Martha," Egan sighed, turning his horse toward her. "How many times must I save your hide before you soften up a little?"

"Egan," Victorin said, his voice holding a warning. "All our tempers are short. Insults won't help."

Egan's annoyed expression shifted to remorse as he faced Victorin. He bowed his head. "Forgive me, my prince."

Iyanka felt off-balance watching the scene play out. She was so used to Victorin giving Egan the lead, deferring to Egan's judgment. She'd almost forgotten, until that instant, that Egan wasn't just Victorin's elder; he was also Victorin's *soldier*. And Egan was quick to back down as Victorin turned to Cook, whose fierce glare wasn't softened by her road-worn look.

"The family that lives here are friends. They've helped us many times in the past."

"Why should we trust them?" she challenged. "What would stop them from leading the hunters to our beds?"

Victorin stared at her for a heartbeat, firm and regal, before answering.

"Their son is a gardener. They won't risk hunters discovering him."

Iyanka looked around at the vibrant fields with new appreciation. Gardeners has been rare in Elnar ever since the imprisonment of their society centuries ago, and a wielder with two ordinary parents was rarer still.

Victorin shifted in the saddle, still holding Cook's gaze. "If you won't trust their goodwill, trust that."

A tense silence followed Victorin's statement, until Gretta urged her horse forward.

"Come on, Aunt. They've protected us this far."

Cook pursed her lips, but her eyes said that she'd already given in.

"And if the hunters come upon us while we sleep?"

"We'll set a watch."

Victorin's voice held steady, and soon Cook broke away.

"Fine," she growled, turning her horse down the path without looking at anyone.

Iyanka watched with confusion. Cook hadn't disguised her distrust, her *dislike*, for Victorin and Egan. What she didn't understand was *why*. And why did her protests now feel more like stubbornness and bitterness than a true distrust?

Glancing around at the rest of the group, she noted Gretta rolling her eyes, and Elsie watching with a muted sorrow. After a moment of indecision, she slowed her horse to wait for Elsie, who rode at the back of the group. She smiled at Iyanka in greeting.

"Questions?" Elsie guessed.

"Yes," Iyanka admitted, keeping her voice too low for the others to overhear. "I don't understand why…why does Cook hate Victorin?"

"It's bitterness mostly," Elsie sighed, confirming one of Iyanka's suspicions. "Her son, Claude, was one of King Ignacio's personal guards. He was killed when the barons attacked, and she blames the king and his family. She believes we wouldn't have been attacked if the royal family had acted differently."

Iyanka took a while to think that over. She had a point, Iyanka supposed. If the rulers of Siersh and Eisadel had lived differently, if they'd lived more peacefully, would the barons have considered them such a threat? But that brought in generations of history, decades of conflict.

"But why blame Victorin?" Iyanka asked. "He was trying to *fix* what his father did."

"From your side, perhaps," Elsie said, with a sad smile. "But *we* saw a prince raised in the footsteps of his father, far more powerful but just as cunning."

Iyanka looked down at her hands. "I...didn't know that."

"We didn't realize how different Victorin is from Ignacio until...well, watching his determination to keep you safe."

Iyanka looked up, but not at Elsie. Her eyes searched out Victorin, sitting confidently as he rode in the midst of the group. He didn't talk with anyone. In the fading light, she could see him keeping watch on the land around them, always vigilant. She could feel Elsie's gaze on her.

"You lived in Siersh before the attack?" Iyanka asked, wanting to break that moment, that silence.

"Yes," she said. "My family lived near the coast."

"What happened to them?"

"I don't know, actually. I didn't see them often...they didn't approve of my marriage to Claude."

"Oh." Iyanka turned toward Elsie, chest aching for her friend, for the far-off sorrow filling her eyes as she stared at the sky. It explained so much...

Elsie shrugged, glancing at Iyanka. "I stayed with Cook and Gretta…afterward. To keep them safe, keep hunters away from them…that sort of thing."

"I'm sorry," Iyanka said in the following silence, at a loss for what else to say.

"It's alright," Elsie said, glancing over again to give Iyanka a smile that didn't reach her eyes. "It was a long time ago."

But not long enough. Not long enough to erase the pain. Iyanka knew that all too well.

Neither of them spoke the rest of the ride to the homestead. They'd fallen behind, and by the time they reached the group, Egan and Victorin had dismounted and were talking to a couple standing outside the house. Zef was running around with a boy around his age while Lynn watched closely. Kale was caught holding the horses again, and Gretta was having a whispered conversation with Cook that looked like an argument.

Iyanka and Elsie dismounted near Kale. Elsie took Iyanka's reins, nodding toward Victorin when Iyanka started to protest. The smile Elsie gave her was more like herself, and so Iyanka gave in with an eyeroll.

Victorin saw her coming, taking her arm and drawing her to his side.

"Jack, Emmy. This is Iyanka, Milek's sister."

Iyanka nodded to the couple, jumping a little when Jack bowed from the waist.

"It's an honor to meet you, Princess," Jack said.

"Just…just Iyanka, please," she stuttered. "It's an honor to meet you too."

166

"It's good to see you alive and well," Emmy said, her green-brown eyes sparkling with good humor. "We all worried about you, when those wretched hunters attacked the palace."

"All?" Iyanka asked, glancing up at Victorin.

"All of us citizens," Jack explained. "The ones the hunters left alone. We heard of Queen Visha's passing, and Prince Milek leading the survivors, but we heard nothing of you."

"All true citizens worried about our Northern Lily," Emmy added before Iyanka could respond. "Wielders or not, we're loyal to you and your family."

"Thank you," Iyanka managed to choke out, overwhelmed. Loyalty? Who was she to deserve loyalty? She'd abandoned them. She tightened her grip on Victorin's arm, fighting to hold their eyes. "I'm sorry I was gone for so long."

"Don't worry about that," Emmy said. "You're home now, Your Highness."

Iyanka nodded, but she didn't have any more words…

"You'll head into the forest in the morning?" Jack asked, his attention back on Victorin.

"Yes," Victorin said. "The hunters won't give up looking for us. We don't want to put you in any more danger than we have to."

"I'll get some provisions together for you to take," Emmy said, shuffling toward the open door behind her.

"Henry!" she called. "Don't bother the chickens."

"Sorry, Ma," the boy called out. Iyanka turned toward that voice, finding a young teenaged boy with a tanned face under a layer of dust, his light brown hair unruly and his eyes like his mother's. He met her gaze, and for a moment Iyanka thought she heard the gentle rustling of leaves in the forest. He quickly turned away, breaking Iyanka from that strange moment as he led Zef in a new direction.

"I'll show your man where to put the horses," Jack said, an amused spark to his eyes as he watched Kale struggling. Kale was all too happy to hand over a few of the horses. Jack led them toward the barn, Elsie winking at Iyanka as she passed with the last two mounts. Gretta and Cook's argument broke, Gretta stalking off with her face twisted in anger. Cook followed after a slight hesitation. Lynn had followed Emmy to help inside, and Egan exchanged a few hushed words with Victorin before also disappearing. Soon Iyanka and Victorin were left alone in the yard, muffled voices the only sign of their companions.

"Victorin," Iyanka whispered, turning toward him.

He twisted so they faced each other, brushing a piece of hair from her face as he gazed down at her, his face questioning.

"Are we putting this family in danger by staying here?"

His expression darkened, softened, and he sighed. "They're always in danger, Iya. They know how to handle themselves."

"But…I don't…" Iyanka fought to swallow the lump in her throat. "I don't want that boy to be hurt because of us."

Victorin's expression shifted again, but before Iyanka could read it he was pulling her into his arms, against his chest. "I don't either."

"This is…*wrong*. Kids like Zef shouldn't have to fear for their lives. They should run, and play, and *laugh*, and…and not have to worry if they'll be killed the next day."

Her words were barely coherent by then, marred by the tears streaming down her face. Victorin continued to hold her, one hand stroking her hair.

"I know," he murmured, his voice gruff. "That's what we're fighting for."

Iyanka turned her face into his chest and didn't say anything more. Victorin stayed silent too, gently holding her as she brought her tears under control. The sun set behind one of the hills surrounding them, leaving the small valley in dusty twilight.

"Ma, Da!" Henry shouted, skidding around the corner of the house with Zef on his heels. Both boys' chests heaved, like they'd run for a good distance, and Zef's eyes were wide. Victorin and Iyanka stepped apart, turning toward the boys.

Emmy appeared in the doorway, Lynn following her.

"What is it?" Emmy asked.

"I was showing Zef the forest where I've made it grow, and we went up Bunkor hill to get a good view…"

"Henry, you know you're not supposed to go that far out this close to dark," Emmy scolded.

"I know," he said. "But Ma, there're soldiers camped out there, between Bunkor Hill and Raven Pass. Hundreds of them."

The blood drained from Iyanka's face, and she grabbed Victorin's arm to keep herself steady. *Hundreds of soldiers…* What were they doing here?

"Is this because of us?" Iyanka asked, looking up at Victorin. His jaw was set, his face grim.

"Not directly," he said. He turned to Zef and Henry. "Were you seen?"

"No," Henry said. "We weren't up there long, and we stayed in the tall grass."

"Where is Bunkor Hill?"

"I'll show you," Henry said, taking a step backward.

Emmy stepped forward, mouth opening, but Victorin spoke before she could.

"I won't let him go all the way. I just need to know what hill it is."

Emmy sighed, nodding. "Alright."

"I'll tell the others," Zef said.

"Will you tell Egan to follow us?" Victorin asked.

Zef nodded and took off toward the barn. Iyanka reluctantly released Victorin, stepping back.

"Be careful," she said.

His fingers brushed her cheek, his eyes softening for just a second. "Don't worry."

With that, he followed Henry around the corner of the house. Iyanka followed just far enough to watch them jog through the fields beyond, toward the close edge of the valley. She wrapped her arms around her middle, fighting down the panic stirring in the pit of her stomach. *Please let him stay safe,* she prayed.

It wasn't long before Egan passed her, and she heard other members of their group emerge and gather behind her. She kept her eyes on those figures disappearing in the dim light. Iyanka flinched when Elsie rested a hand on her shoulder, meeting Elsie's eyes sheepishly. Elsie just smiled, squeezing Iyanka's shoulder. Iyanka tried smiling back, grateful for the comfort, but the effort was pitiful. She turned her gaze back to the hills. The light was fading. Soon stars would wink into view…Victorin wouldn't be seen, right?

"Come inside," Emmy said. "There's no use standing in the open."

Footsteps marked the others following Emmy. After a moment Elsie tugged on Iyanka, drawing her back toward the door. Iyanka allowed herself to be led, until she reached the doorway. Until the fire in her chest blazed to life.

"No," she breathed.

Iyanka twisted, pushing past Elsie into the open air. She skidded, catching herself on the corner of the house as she turned toward the hills Victorin had gone to. Someone behind her called her name, asking what was wrong. She didn't bother to answer. *I have to find him.* Fire raged again. She looked up to find flames licking the sky, marking the hill where he stood. Someone caught her arm.

"Iyanka," Kale gasped. "Wait."

"He's in trouble," Iyanka said, fighting to pull away. She never took her eyes from that fire. There was no doubt he'd be seen...

"Just wait a second."

Iyanka kept fighting him, writhing and kicking. It took another blaze in her chest for her to come to her senses, to take a moment and pour snow into the flames. The fire on the hill flashed blue. Iyanka took a deep breath, forcing her chaotic ice storm into that little candle, that tiny channel connecting her to Victorin. Too little. It was too little...

She'd stopped fighting Kale, her attention elsewhere. He'd relaxed, his hands gripping her bare wrists. With another deep breath, she sent ice across his skin. He released her with a hiss, and Iyanka ran.

"Wait," he called, his fingers grazing her back as she leaped away.

He wouldn't stop her this time. Iyanka pushed ice through her bare feet, a slippery path to mark her footsteps, and silently apologized to Jack and Emmy for the damage to their pasture. Kale didn't catch her again.

She didn't pause at the bottom of the hill, leaping up and climbing the steep incline, grasping at grass and brush to help her go faster. Before long she was gasping for breath, pushed on by the blue fames above her. She didn't stop, didn't catch her breath. That fire still roared, and she continued pouring in as much ice and snow as that narrow path would allow.

Near the top a hand on her arm made her jerk away. She lost her balance, tipping backward...but the hand grabbed her again and pulled her against the hill. This time she saw the young form hunched near the ground.

"Princess," Henry whispered. "Take these."

He pressed a handful of small pods into her hands. "What…"

"They're seeds," he said. "When you're up there, throw them on the ground."

His eyes glinted in the light of the fire, and for a breath she could only stare into his dark gaze. There was no fear on his young face, only determination.

"Be careful," she said.

"I should say the same to you, Princess," he replied, his voice wry. "Now go."

Iyanka followed that order, climbing more slowly now because of the hand full of seeds curled against her chest. She glanced back once and thought she saw Henry climbing toward the other side of the hill. She whispered a prayer for his safety and kept moving.

Nearing the top, she stayed low to the ground, searching for Victorin amid the flames. Five or six tall figures were silhouetted by the flame, standing between her and Victorin's flames. Their blades glinted in the light. She thought she spotted two figures kneeling in the midst of the blaze, but couldn't be sure without getting closer.

Iyanka took a deep breath, shifting her feet so she could stand, ready to run. But she hesitated. A thousand gruesome possibilities flashed through her mind. Those glinting blades piercing her flesh, spilling her blood onto the grass, Victorin's cry…. Her knees shook. She collapsed against the ground with a half-choked sob. Her eyes stayed locked on the fire, on the hunters between her and Victorin. *What do I do?* How could she reach him without the hunters seeing her?

More figures in armor topped the hill, their weapons drawn as they surrounded Victorin. How long until the entire hillside was covered with soldiers? How long until one of them found her huddled in the grass? Every part of her screamed, begged her to run. Run back to the farm, tell the others what she'd seen. They could do more, they could help.

But she didn't move. She couldn't take her eyes from where Victorin knelt, trapped in a circle of flames that would eventually go out. *If I had half of Zef or Henry's courage, I wouldn't hesitate.* Why did this always happen? Why did her fear rule her? And why couldn't she *get up from this cursed ground?*

She wobbled, biting back a sob, and reached to the ground to steady herself. And she remembered the seedpods in her hand. That...that she could do.

Looking again at the fire, making sure no one was looking her way, she rose on her knees and threw the seeds as hard as she could. They spread in an arc between here and the fire. She fell to the ground again, catching her breath, waiting for someone to shout that they'd seen her. Instead, a deep groan split the air, interrupting the crackle of the fire.

A dozen trees sprouted from the hillside, and Iyanka thought she glimpsed a dozen more on the other side of the fire. They shot into the air: growing twenty feet in the course of a minute, stretching tall and wide, spreading limbs to shadow the entire hillside. Shouts of panic rose above the groaning trees. At least one man tripped and tumbled down the hill, toward the camp on the other side. The rest backed away from the trees, pulling out of reach of branches that seemed to grasp at them.

Their growth slowed. Leaves shriveled on the branches, the trees once again filling the air with cracking and groaning as one by one they died. Iyanka watched the great show of power in awe, unable to help searching for the boy hidden somewhere on the hill. *Gardener indeed.*

A deep breath, and Iyanka edged forward, toward the nearest tree. The better shelter made her erratic heartbeat calm somewhat, especially since the soldiers were still staying away from the trees now covering the hilltop. She watched the fire, the soldiers retaking their place around it…and still couldn't force herself forward. *I'm sorry.* Iyanka hunched over, eyes on the ground. And after two silent breaths, she buried her hand in that soil. *I won't do* nothing*!*

She stole a tendril of ice from the blizzard she still forced into Victorin's fire, pressing it into the ground instead. Ice formed a silent path across the top of the hill, stretching far to either side of her. And when it was complete, Iyanka connected it to Victorin's circle of flames.

Flame raged, devouring the ice, spreading the length of Iyanka's path in a breath. Again, the soldiers fell back, and Iyanka ducked further behind the tree.

Her hand was still on the ice path, sending more frost and cold along its length and into Victorin's circle.

But the storm in her heart was fading, nearly spent. Her throat was dry, her fingers trembling, her face too warm. Victorin's fire was flickering. If they didn't do *something*, if they didn't escape soon...

But then a sudden wind tore across the hillside. Flames twisted, bowed, and caught on the dead trees towering above her. Iyanka dove onto her ice flame path to escape the new blaze, natural fire the hunters would be powerless to stop ice or no ice. Smoke surrounded her, choking her, and she raised her sleeve to her nose. She rose on her knees, searching for Victorin. Two silhouettes were leaving the fire circle, one supporting another figure who stumbled several times on his way to the hill's edge. Iyanka raced toward them.

Victorin looked up as she neared, their eyes meeting. She wondered if relief shown from her gaze like it did from his. She skidded to a stop a few steps away, her eyes turning to Egan. Victorin was half carrying him, while the older man breathed heavily through gritted teeth. But he was alive. She looked back to Victorin. *Will he make it?*

An enraged shout brought her attention back to the present, and she spun to find a soldier running toward them, sword bared. Iyanka screamed and flinched back, into Victorin's side, but his arc was interrupted by Kale jumping between them, his own sword flashing. The blades clashed as the men fought, and the hunter let out a sickening gasp as Kale sank his sword into the man's gut. Kale withdrew his stained blade as the hunter fell, turning to search for other hunters. Iyanka couldn't take her eyes from the man's body, her heartbeat throbbing in her head.

Other people materialized out of the dark, familiar figures even in the dark. Jack took over supporting Egan, while Zef and Henry took up posts on either side of Victorin. Kale slew another hunter trying to sneak up on them, and beyond Iyanka thought she saw Lynn with wind whipping around her. Gretta grabbed Iyanka and pulled her down the hillside.

"Come on," Gretta growled, tugging Iyanka's arm when she was slow to follow. "We have to get out of here."

Iyanka allowed Gretta to lead her down the hill. Her feet were like frozen blocks, her hearing still muffled. She glanced back at the fire-covered hillside when she hit level ground, but somehow she was detached from the scene.

They finally reached the house, where Emmy and Cook were waiting with water and supplies. Jack lowered Egan into a kitchen chair, where Cook descended on him with water and bandages, peeling his blood-soaked shirt from the wound on his shoulder. Emmy tried to get Victorin to sit, but he went straight for Iyanka, opening his arms. She leaned into him without hesitation, taking deep breaths and focusing on his steadier heartbeat. Behind them, Egan cursed, and Cook scolded him, her gentle voice belaying her words.

"The horses are ready," Elsie announced, bursting through the door.

"Good," Victorin said, his chin brushing Iyanka's hair. "We'll leave immediately."

Victorin turned away, but kept Iyanka tucked against his side. She pressed into that safety and surveyed the chaotic scene. The small kitchen wasn't built for so many people, and there was barely room to move.

"Egan, can you ride?" Victorin asked, his voice colored with worry.

"Get me on a horse, and I'll ride fine." He winced as Cook bandaged his shoulder.

"Henry," Jack said. "You're going with them."

"But…" the boy's eyes were wide, panicked. "What about you?"

"We'll be fine," Jack said gently. "But the hunters will know you're nearby, now. You'll be safer in Prince Milek's city."

"You'd be safer there, as well," Victorin added.

Jack shook his head. "Too suspicious. If we leave, this place will be lost to us."

Iyanka couldn't take her eyes from Henry. His eyes were closed, his head shaking.

"I don't want to leave you," he said, voice wavering. A tear escaped onto his cheek, and he wiped it away.

Emmy wrapped her arms around Henry, pulling him to her chest. Her eyes were shining with tears as she kissed his head.

"We don't want you to leave," she said. "But it'll keep you safe."

Iyanka shifted on her feet, suddenly aware that she was intruding on a private moment. She forced her eyes to the wall, where shadows flickered, bending and twisting like clawed beasts. Emmy whispered something to Henry, as Jack moved to join the embrace. A glance around confirmed that she wasn't the only one wishing she could give the family more privacy.

"They'll take care of you," Jack said. "And you can help them."

"And if something happens to you?"

"Nothing will happen to us."

Victorin cleared his throat. "We should leave now, before the fires die."

That thought spurred everyone into motion. Most of the group filed outside to the waiting horses, leaving Victorin and Iyanka with the family that had sheltered them at so much cost. Emmy was wiping her eyes, grabbing bags from the table to carry outside. Henry helped her, staying close to her side, while Jack approached Iyanka and Victorin.

"Take care of him," he said, staring hard at Victorin. "He's more special than you'd ever guess."

"You know I will," Victorin promised, resting his hand on the other man's shoulder.

"Good," he said, sniffing and straightening. "Now let's get you out of here."

They left the house, and Iyanka stayed close to Victorin. The horses were gathered in the open yard, the full darkness of night shielding most of their group where they sat, already mounted. Victorin helped

Iyanka mount the horse she'd ridden earlier. It snorted, but held steady.

"Henry, can you ride with Egan?" Victorin asked.

"Of course, sir," he replied, his voice still unsteady, but determined.

"Good."

Victorin helped him onto the horse behind Egan, where Henry gingerly gripped the older man's shirt to hold on. Egan didn't speak or acknowledge Henry's presence behind him; even in the dim light Iyanka could see his jaw set, eyes narrowed. *How much pain is he in?* Iyanka met Victorin's gaze and saw her own concern mirrored there. She realized the wisdom of asking Henry to ride with Egan: the teenager would help him stay alert, and he could take over guiding the horse if necessary.

Victorin mounted his own horse, turning it in a half circle to survey their group. He nodded to Jack and Emmy, who stood in the doorway, and rode toward the west. The sky there still showed the last remnants of sunset.

Iyanka followed closely, afraid of falling behind in the darkness. When they left the shelter of the trees surrounding the homestead, the flames covering Bunkor hill lit up half the night. Iyanka watched, seeing a few scattered figures, dwarfed by the flames. It would be a while before the fire died. Iyanka hoped now that it stayed away from the fields, away from the forest. The prospect of rest seemed so far away, now…now that this new threat had erupted in their path.

Her horse stumbled in the dark, jerking her attention back to her immediate surroundings. She patted her mount's shoulder in comfort and turned her gaze to the dim figures surrounding her. Their slow pace was a necessity in the dark, but it grated on her. There were no trees to cover them, no hills to shield them. Only the darkness concealed them, and it seemed like a thin veil indeed with the fire blazing so near them. How many were descending the hills even now? How soon until they came to Jack and Emmy's house: searching, accusing. How soon until… *No.* She wouldn't think of it. She couldn't freeze up again.

They reached the edge of the fields and started up a low hill, the horses scrambling for footing. Iyanka leaned low on her horse's neck, his mane brushing against her face. She heard a gasp from Egan, and when she turned Henry had taken the reins.

When they reached the top of the hill, Iyanka spotted the river glinting silver in the emerging moonlight less than a mile away. Beyond it, a dark mass rose up into the sky…the forest. Once they crossed the river they would be in Frieda's Refuge and, according to the ancient treaty between all the citizens of Elnar, safe from pursuit. But that supposed safety hadn't been a reality since the barons took over. Now the trees were the real haven, where Victorin would lead them through the depths. Where, somewhere, her brother waited.

But even the shelter of the forest didn't banish the dread in the pit of her stomach. Before they were fleeing a group of hunters set on their trail. Now they were fleeing an *army*. Iyanka wasn't convinced a forest, even one as treacherous as this, would stop them.

From Malchomy's forest, it seemed like once they reached the northern forest and Milek she'd be safe, but would she? What if she and Victorin were bringing danger to this haven? Together they could hold off a few dozen hunters, but they had no chance of defeating an army. The conflict that night proved how limited they were. Iyanka's hope of living without fear, without dread, was quickly fading. Every part of her was exhausted: tired of fighting, tired of running, tired of being hunted down like an animal. Would she ever be allowed to rest?

Chapter X

Iyanka looked up, gazing at the towering trees engulfing her. They'd crossed the river and ridden for several hours before stopping to rest, which was over in what felt like a blink of an eye. Then they'd continued their journey.

Dawn had arrived several hours ago, turning the forest from eerie shadows and patches of moonlight to a dim gray that was less creepy, but did nothing to improve anyone's mood. The air felt damp and subtly charged. Iyanka guessed that if she could see the sky, it would be overcast. As it was, all she saw above her was branches, leaves, random bits of muted light.

She turned her eyes back to Victorin, forcing them to stay open. Everyone in their group rode slumped and silent, exhausted but unwilling to stop. Unwilling to chance the soldiers and chaos they'd left behind them catching up. If they *could* catch up in this place.

As they rode through the forest, Iyanka understood why the hunters hadn't found Milek and the others. Already, they'd had to ride out of their way for several miles to avoid a steep ravine, and the ground contained so many rock outcroppings and canyons that it was impossible to travel in any semblance of a straight line. Iyanka had lost all sense of direction shortly after entering the trees, and their surroundings all looked too similar for her to even try to regain it.

She kept her horse close to Victorin's and hoped he had a better idea of where they were.

He seemed to. He never faltered when choosing a direction, but Iyanka had no idea how he did it. Now, he stopped and dismounted.

Iyanka watched perplexedly as he walked over to Egan and Henry to help them to the ground.

"There's an outpost nearby, but we have to lead our horses there," Victorin explained, supporting Egan as he lowered himself to the ground with a grimace.

"Where is it?" Iyanka asked.

She dismounted her mount, wobbling when she hit the ground. Her horse grunted when she leaned against his flank, waiting for the spinning to stop. A hand on her shoulder made her look up. Victorin was watching her, forehead creased with worry.

"I'm fine," she said. "Just tired."

He nodded and squeezed her shoulder. He didn't pull away as he turned, gesturing ahead of them with his free hand. "The outpost is between those rock faces, built into the stone."

Iyanka looked where he pointed, but couldn't see anything different than the forest they'd been riding through all night.

"Is anyone there?"

"Yes. They've seen us, but they don't approach visitors."

With the rest of their group safely, if not happily, on the ground, they approached the narrow canyon. Iyanka and Victorin led the group, but Iyanka didn't have the energy even to turn and ensure the others were following. It was all she could do to keep setting one bare foot in front of the other.

"They don't approach even *you*?" Iyanka asked.

Victorin glanced down at her. "They approach no one. They can't afford the risk. This outpost is vital."

Iyanka turned her eyes to the leaves at her feet. What would happen if they rode in with hunters on their trail? Would they still not approach, even to save someone's life? Even to save their prince's life?

They reached the entrance, rock rising as silent sentinels on either side of their path. Old leaves lay thick on the ground. Water hadn't flowed through this canyon in a long time.

As they walked, the canyon narrowed above their heads, forming a partial tunnel that explained why they couldn't ride. Iyanka watched the sliver of light between rock faces and wondered what it looked like from above. Was it even noticeable among the leaves and rocks? And where was this outpost? Iyanka saw no sign of a structure, no sign of any shaping to the rocks save the wearing of time. Until they rounded a bend, and Victorin stopped.

Iyanka looked up, her head heavy. "Oh."

They'd emerged in a wider section of canyon, still mostly concealed by rock above. To their left an over-hang had been enlarged and a wall of stones and limbs blocked off the front, forming a paddock. Ahead of them the canyon was blocked by a large boulder, which nearly concealed the entrance to a cave in the rock face on its right.

A short man dressed in rough green clothes appeared from behind the rock. His thick beard and weathered face made Iyanka think of a bear, and his gaze was sharp as he studied them. But Iyanka thought she saw a smile beneath his untrimmed beard.

"Commander," the man greeted Victorin, executing a shallow bow as he approached. He glanced at Iyanka where she stood, half behind Victorin. She edged further behind him, nodding to the stranger. His gaze turned beyond her, and he clucked his tongue.

"What trouble did you meet, Egan?"

"The wrong end of a hunter's blade," Egan replied, voice tight. He stepped forward to stand beside Victorin and Iyanka, shoulders hunched and weary. Iyanka's forehead creased as she studied him, noting the dried blood staining his bandage.

The man whistled, making her jump.

"Get inside, before you tip over." His gaze took in the rest of the group. "My name's Gunther for those who don't know me. Your horses can go in the paddock. Inside there's stew over the fire, and room to rest."

There were murmured thank-yous and the jingle of bridles as everyone led their horses to the overhang. Elsie took Iyanka's reins again, and Iyanka thanked her with a smile. Victorin let Kale take his horse with a nod, and turned back to Gunther, his hand catching Iyanka's.

"Where's Lara?"

"Up keeping watch."

"I need her to take a message to Milek at Agera immediately."

"She's coming down in an hour or so," Gunther said, glancing toward the sky. "You could rest for a bit…"

"This can't wait," Victorin said. "We met a battalion between the forest's edge and Raven Pass. I doubt they're the only forces the barons have mobilized."

Gunther whistled again, and this time he nodded. "I'll get her, then. You all head inside."

Victorin sighed. "Thank you."

Gunther nodded again, then turned and leaped onto the cliff, scaling the rock as easily as a paved path. Iyanka watched in awe until Cook came up, shooing Egan inside with insults that lacked bite. Lynn and Elsie followed with Zef and Henry in tow, the boys whispering to each other as they entered the cave. Victorin followed them, and Iyanka was close behind until a commotion made her look back.

"Would you *stop* that?" Gretta growled, shoving Kale's arm away from her. Kale said something, his hands held out in supplication, but Gretta drowned it out.

"My heart is engaged elsewhere, and you need to leave me *alone*." Her voice was hard, her eyes shining with tears. She turned away from Kale. Iyanka studied her face and saw little more than exhaustion and sadness.

"I didn't know," Kale said, face red, an edge to his voice Iyanka had never heard. "You've never paid preference to any of the men…"

"That you *saw*," Gretta growled, whirling to glare at Kale. "Now I'm telling you: leave. Me. Alone."

This time when she turned toward the cave, she practically ran toward it. Her eyes met Iyanka's only briefly before focusing on the ground. Iyanka burned with embarrassment. She shouldn't have listened, but now... She reached out and caught Gretta's shoulder. She stopped, but didn't turn, and Iyanka followed her deeper into the cave entrance, out of sight of Kale.

"I don't want to talk about it," Gretta growled, wiping tears from her eyes.

"You don't have to," Iyanka said, trying to catch her eye. She squeezed Gretta's shoulder and leaned in to embrace her. Gretta's stiff, hot posture eased. Iyanka heard her choke back a sob before she pulled away.

"Thanks," she muttered, ducking into the cave.

Iyanka didn't try to stop her again. She waited for a breath, letting Gretta retreat, before following. And then her frayed attention was stolen once again, as she took in the room that surrounded her.

It wasn't as dark as she'd expected: a fire to her left and rays of light near the back gave the cave a dim glow, enough to illuminate the room's occupants. The floor, walls, and ceiling were all rough-hewn rock with a few wooden supports. Fur covered areas of the floor, and a low table dominated the center of the room. Everyone was already sprawled on the floor all around the room, which had more than enough space for all of them, but no one was asleep yet. Cook and Elsie were changing Egan's bandage, to his vocal chagrin, and Lynn served up bowls of stew to Zef and Henry. It took Iyanka longer to find Gretta, huddled against the back wall beside a few baskets.

"Get some rest," Victorin whispered, startling Iyanka by appearing at her shoulder.

"What about you?" she asked.

"I'll sleep as soon as Lara's riding for Milek. There's no reason for you to wait up."

I should protest. But she was swaying on her feet, and as Victorin steadied her he gave her a wry smile that stole her words.

"Sleep," he said.

"Alright," she said.

Victorin squeezed her shoulders and backed away, leaving Iyanka to weave her way toward the back of the room. She found a bearskin rug. Pulling a blanket from and nearby stack, she laid down on the warm fur. She didn't even remember closing her eyes.

OO0

Iyanka woke up to hushed voices and a warmth pressed against her side. She opened her eyes, blinking slowly to clear her blurry vision, and tried to understand why she saw dancing shadows on stone above her. Slowly, her location came back to her: the outpost in the forest. Her tongue felt like sandpaper, and her mouth *tasted* like sand. *How long did I sleep?* The warmth at her side was explained when she looked down and saw Henry's mop of brown hair on her shoulder. He was half-curled against her side, his breathing slow and even. *He looks so much younger asleep.* Iyanka's heart squeezed, a lump filling her throat. She held still as she could as she continued to search out her surroundings.

The voices continued, but she couldn't discern *who* was speaking. Turning her head to peer over Henry, she spotted Victorin sleeping a few steps away. Most of their group was still asleep, scattered in nests around the room.

Did she hear Egan's voice near the fire? She only caught snippets of what they were saying, something about hunters and fire. Not exactly a surprising topic. One of the speakers clucked his tongue and drifted into silence.

Iyanka held still, trying to align her thoughts. By now she was fully awake, and not inclined to go back to sleep. But she also didn't feel like moving, though her muscles were stiff.

Something crashed against the stone floor, and someone cursed. Iyanka tensed at the sound, but Henry shifted without waking. On his other side, Victorin slowly sat up and looked around. When his eyes found Iyanka he smiled, making her stomach flutter. He turned in the direction the sound originated from.

"We've slept too long," he murmured. "It's nearly morning again."

"That long?"

They'd slept through the day *and* another night? No wonder she was stiff.

Iyanka slowly extracted her arm from beneath Henry, shifting his head onto the blanket. He barely stirred. Free to move, Iyanka sat up, wincing as she flexed her arm to return the blood flow. Others were stirring around her, looking blearily around the room or stretching.

Egan and Gunther sat beside the fire, along with a woman and a dark-skinned man Iyanka didn't recognize. The doorway was open, and Iyanka could just see the gray of pre-dawn.

Victorin rocked to his feet, stretching his arms above his head and pressing his palms against the ceiling. Then he reached out to help Iyanka to her feet. The sudden shift made darkness crowd at the edges of her vision, but she ignored the dizziness and followed Victorin to the group by the fire.

"The dead are raised," Gunther said.

"You should've woken me," Victorin replied, lowering himself to the floor with his legs crossed in front of him. Iyanka sat beside him, so their knees touched.

Gunther grunted. "You're no good to anyone half-dead."

"Milek received your report," the woman said, her voice high pitched but quiet. "He's beginning preparations and awaits your arrival."

"Any information from his front?" Victorin asked, allowing the change of subject.

"None of consequence, but he wanted you to know that he sent scouts to the plains and western border. If other forces are coming, we should know by tomorrow."

"Good. Thank you, Lara."

Of course, Commander," she replied, bowing her head.

"Princess Iyanka?"

Iyanka turned automatically at the sound of her name, meeting the burning gaze of the other stranger at the fire.

"Yes," she said, feeling her face heat and resisting the urge to duck her head. *I need to get used to this again. I don't have to fear being known anymore.*

"I wondered if it was you, Highness," Gunther said. "You and your brother both have your father's eyes."

"Thank you," Iyanka said slowly. "How…"

"We should leave soon," Egan interrupted. "Daylight's fast approaching."

Iyanka let the subject drop, but she still pondered Gunther's observation. Eisadel hadn't received any official visitors from Siersh in Iyanka's lifetime until after her father's assassination. Gunther should never have seen her father, let alone know the color of his eyes. And while the assassins responsible for her father's death had been caught and executed, their accomplices had escaped. Was it possible? Could this caring man have helped plan her father's death?

No. He was loyal to Victorin, and Victorin…he'd assured Iyanka's mother that he'd had no part in the King's death. He'd said he was ashamed of his father's actions, that he wanted to do things differently. Surely, he wouldn't…

She'd think on this later. And when she was alone, she'd ask Victorin. Right now, she had other matters to worry about.

It took a while for everyone to wake up and get ready, but when they left the outpost the sunlight was barely beginning to shine through the trees. For the first part of the morning they rode in silence, and it seemed that despite their long rest, no one had the energy to keep up conversation. Or maybe it was the silence of the forest, looming and dark all around them.

Iyanka didn't feel *tired*, exactly. She certainly didn't want to sleep. For the first time in days, she was alert, ready to face what lay before them. Ice and snow swirled in her chest, her miniature winter as vibrant and potent as ever. But still, she didn't speak. Didn't engage with anyone for that first stretch of ancient forest.

The terrain varied as they traveled, forcing them to ride around thickets of undergrowth, lacey drapes of vines, steep canyons, and rocky outcroppings. Without exhaustion weighing down her eyes, Iyanka studied their surroundings more closely as they passed. The land here was different from the areas they'd traveled through on their path north, different too from Eisadel.

Pine mingled with oak, beech, and maple. Their massive trunks dotted the landscape like pillars of a strange cathedral, holding up that filigree ceiling of mingled leaves and sunlight. Creaks and groans surrounded them, high branches tossing in a breeze that didn't touch Iyanka on the ground. She could feel the weight of centuries pressing around her, the presence of this ancient and ominous place. And though she *knew* these trees were not wielders, still she felt eyes following her.

But still birds sang in the branches, unbothered by their ancient presence as they flitted from tree to tree in sudden bursts of movement and color. Deer drank from the streams, startling at the passing of Iyanka's companions. Life abounded around them, beneath the shelter of those trees. And she let herself relax.

Zef eventually broke the silence, asking Henry a slew of questions about the forest and the plants they rode past. Henry responded readily. Most of the trees he knew by name, knew their seeds, their lifespan, the soil they needed to grow well. He knew which plants were useful for food, for medicine, and which were poisonous. The information he spouted was overwhelming, and Iyanka knew she wouldn't remember it. But she listened closely, fascinated regardless. And though Zef was the only one who asked questions, Iyanka didn't doubt that everyone was listening to Henry's answers. Iyanka couldn't help but wonder how Henry knew so much. Had someone taught him, or was this another skill of gardeners?

Eventually Henry and Zef ran out of plant life to discuss, and silence creeped back in. Her own thoughts crowded that space, demanding attention. And again, the question of Gunther, and the knowledge he shouldn't have, plagued her. No matter how much she tried to explain it away, the doubts remained. She glanced at Victorin, riding close by with his eyes ahead. Victorin, who had done nothing but shield her.

"Victorin?" she asked, casting her voice too low for the others to understand.

"Yes?" he replied, glancing over at her.

"How does Gunther know what my father looked like?"

Victorin didn't respond immediately, and as that silence grew so did the sickening dread swirling amid the cold within her. *Please no.* Victorin sighed, not looking at her.

"He was assigned to watch your family."

"Did he help kill my father?"

"No."

Iyanka swallowed, her eyes on her horse's ears. "Then what was he doing in Eisadel?"

"He was gathering information. Most of which my father never received."

Iyanka nodded, but her heard still pounded. Her dread hadn't cleared. Her breaths came shallow, words echoing in her head that she didn't want to speak. But she had to…she had to know.

"Did you know what your father was planning?" Her voice was strangled, too quiet. But Victorin heard.

"Yes."

Iyanka squeezed her eyes shut, tears burning. Leather creaked as Victorin reached for her. She turned her head away. She'd always assumed he hadn't known, that he hadn't been involved.

"Iya," he breathed. "Iya, I tried to stop him."

"You did?" her voice cracked.

"I tried…He was a good man. He didn't deserve that death."

Iyanka kept her eyes closed, not bothering to wipe away the tears shed for that old grief, that sharp sorrow that never disappeared. The first true sorrow she'd known… But that wound wasn't Victorin's fault. He'd always…he'd always showed regret at her father's death, and *his* father's part in it. Iyanka opened her eyes, blinking away the tears that blurred her vision. And her mind replayed her first glimpse of the fire prince, at her father's funeral. She'd wanted to despise him then.

"I never understood why you came to his funeral…every person there wanted to kill you."

"I know," Victorin said. "But I wanted…I *needed* your family to know that I didn't stand with my father. He was wrong."

Iyanka dragged in a shaky breath…and turned to Victorin. Her smile was broken and watery, but it was genuine.

"Thank you for trying."

Victorin reached out again, and Iyanka bridged the gap to grasp his hand. His grip was gentle, warm. He held her hand in silence. For long moments they rode like that, hands linked. *He tried to save the King of his enemies. He risked his life to stand with us against his family.* Slowly that throbbing pain eased, sinking back to the depths where it remained, beside grief for her mother, for her people. And that poisonous, skulking dread steadily crumbled away. *I won't doubt him because of this. I won't hold it against him…he did what he could.*

They continued their ride through the unchanging forest, eventually letting their hands fall to their side to ride more easily. Other murmured conversations drifted behind her; birds continued to sing above them. More time passed, and it was late morning when Iyanka saw Victorin straighten, saw his eyes take in their surroundings with recognition.

"Are we close?" Zef asked.

Victorin nodded. "We should reach the sentries in a few minutes, and the city a mile or so after that."

"City?" Iyanka asked.

Victorin slowed his horse, riding closer to her side. "An ancient one, from before Siersh and Eisadel existed."

"You called it Agera?"

She'd taken note of the name when he'd mentioned it but had forgotten to ask. Agera was a name of legend, the capitol of a great kingdom that existed centuries before Eisadel's capitol city was even built. Iyanka had gone to sleep as a child listening to stories of Agera's valiant warriors and terrible kings.

Victorin smiled. "We don't know for sure. But the name fits."

"How much of the city is left?"

"Enough to be defensible. Most of the outer wall is intact, but the structures inside vary. It looks like the city was burned."

"That fits with the stories," Iyanka said, mind turning to stories of Agera's fall.

She's always hoped the legends were true, but she'd never considered that the city might still stand. The stories told of dragons and wielders attacking the city, burning the royal palace before the king surrendered.

A whistle, too shrill to be a bird, sounded from the trees above. Iyanka jerked her head up, searching the branches. But she never found the sentry, even when he whistled again, this time low and varying, and another a series of quick bursts. The same series of sounds repeated ahead of them, and again even further, sounding their way to the city.

"They're notifying Agera of our arrival," Victorin explained, drawing Iyanka's gaze back to him. "The first and second were telling the size of our group, and the direction that we're approaching from. The third let them know that we're friends."

"No signal for you?"

"Word will probably travel ahead." Victorin glanced toward her, his gaze suddenly wary, and Iyanka sat straighter. "You should also probably know…most of the city knows I vowed not to return without you at my side."

"You *what*?"

"I wasn't leaving you there," he murmured, staring at his hands. "And it was the only way to keep Milek from running off to rescue you."

Oh, Milek…

"Then how does the whole city know?" Iyanka asked.

"A few of Milek's advisors aren't as quiet as they should be."

Iyanka took that in, again searching among the trees for the sentries she knew watched them. Already, her heartbeat had quickened. She'd thought they'd slip through the streets unknown, that only Milek would be there to recognize her.

"What should I expect?" she asked.

"Probably whatever you'd expect if you were returning to Eisadel."

Not that, surely. Iyanka's heart ached as she thought back to those days, where people would gather in the streets with lilies to welcome her home. She hadn't traveled from home often, but her handful of returns were memorable…it had seemed like too much even then, before the world fell apart.

Victorin must've seen the disbelief on her face. His face turned wry. "They've been waiting for you."

He probably meant it as encouragement, but the words cut. They shouldn't be waiting for her. They shouldn't be waiting because she should already *be* here, standing with her brother. They shouldn't be waiting because now, after how long she'd hid, she wasn't worthy of it. But it was too late to do anything about it now…too late even to ask Victorin if there was a less conspicuous way inside.

Between the trees emerged a tall stone wall, nearly hidden by vines and moss. Trees grew right up to its edge; in some places, ferns grew out of wall itself. To their left was a gate, the ancient portcullis intact and raised. A stone bridge stretched over what once was likely a moat, but now was filled with trees and blackberry vines.

Children were scattered in moat picking berries, and they stared at Iyanka's group as they passed. One girl, no more than fourteen, stared hard at Iyanka, her forehead scrunched in thought. Iyanka managed to give her a timid smile and waved. Children waved back, but that one girl continued to stare, her gaze moving between Iyanka and Victorin. Then her expression cleared, recognition dawned and she scrambled up the edge of the moat toward the gate.

"Commander Victorin is back," she shouted, passing the gate guards as if they were no more than stones. "He brought Princess Iyanka! The Northern Lily has returned!"

Chapter XI

Iyanka's heart pounded, ice racing along her veins, pressing against her skin. *I'm not sure I can do this.* Her horse entered the bridge beside Victorin's, hooves clacking on the stone. The guards at the gate bowed in unison as she and Victorin passed. She barely remembered to nod to each of them, as she was taught to do for Eisadel's guard. It had been a long time...and yet they felt so close today, those memories. Too close.

She closed her eyes and took a steadying breath, pushing back against the frost creeping onto her skin: a visible witness to her nerves. *Keep it together. You owe them that much.*

Zef whispered to Henry, a comment on the city. And Iyanka opened her eyes only to lose her breath in awe. *How was this place lost?*

They rode on a large cobblestone lane stretching to the heart of the city, lined with what once must've been shops and mansions. Stone walls and worn buildings surrounded her: some were crumbling to nothing, while others stood so intact Iyanka expected to see their original owners watching her from the windows. The forest didn't stop at the wall, and instead trees intermingled with the buildings. Roots pulled up cobblestones, leaves and branches created ceilings for collapsing homes. Vines spread across walls, covered windows, screening the inside from view.

In some places Iyanka could see wood and canvas forming ceilings and walls, tendrils of smoke rising from makeshift homes. Stacks of loose stone marked walls rebuilt, stumps showed the origin of the wood. But largely the city seemed to be undisturbed, a testament to the passage of time.

But more than all this were the *people*: hundreds of faces lined the streets on either side, watching. A mosaic of eyes, minds, stories, all staring up at her. Some with worry, others with stoicism, and far too many with radiant smiles. Iyanka's heart clenched, ashamed at the sight of their thin faces so delighted at her overdue return. The girl who'd heralded their arrival stood near the front, beside a man Iyanka recognized as one of the landscapers from the palace. She met his eyes and fought for a smile, to hide how overwhelmed she was.

This was so different from her memories…because no matter how much they smiled, no matter how warmly they welcomed her to this haven, she couldn't forget. She couldn't forget that she was an exile princess returning to a broken people. She couldn't forget that they were all being hunted as animals, as monsters. None of these people owed her loyalty anymore, and yet they smiled. They welcomed her to Agera as if she were still the beloved princess. And every moment of that ride made her want to collapse before them and beg their forgiveness. But she rode on, she smiled, and she begged forgiveness in silence.

The encouragement in Victorin's gaze every time she glanced his way helped her keep going, as they slowly climbed that twisting street that hid their destination. It seemed to stretch on forever…surely it had been hours since they entered the city.

At last, they rounded the final bend. They passed a decrepit wall covered in ivy, which guarded a large courtyard shaded by a dozen tall birch. The center of this courtyard was clear, opening a path to a set of steps leading to a great doorway without a door. And in that doorway was a group of people, one standing a head above the others, with white-blond hair…

The blond head turned, and broke into a run, skipping steps as he bounded toward them. Iyanka dropped her reins and leaped to the ground, breaking into a run as soon as her bare feet hit stone. And then Milek caught her in his arms, lifting her from the ground and spinning her around.

"Milek," she whispered, tightening her arms around his neck. "You're alive!"

"Of course, I am," he laughed. "*You're* alive! You're *here*!"

Iyanka let out a sound that was half-laughter half-sobbing as Milek set her on her feet. And he stepped back, hands on her shoulders, and looked her over. She did the same.

He was so much *taller* than she remembered. His hair was the same unruly mop unfit for dignified royalty, his eyes the same pale blue of the clearest ice. But gone was the gangly boy she remembered. He bore her scrutiny with a careless grin, raising his eyebrows when her gaze met his.

"You're taller," she remarked.

"You have more freckles," he replied.

She flicked his jaw. "So do you."

"But at least I look like a proper ice wielder, Raspberry."

He accompanied this statement with a tug on her ratty red braid, an action that once would've made her growl with annoyance. Now Iyanka only batted his hand away so she could hug him again, tears freezing in crystalline patterns across her face. *He's really here.* She took a deep shuddering breath. His returning squeeze brought more tears, because he never would've done that before. He never would've accepted a hug like this. *So much has changed.* But he was here, they were together. That was what mattered.

This time when she pulled back, she furiously wiped at her face to rid her skin of the tell-tale frost. It likely didn't do any good, but it gave her something to do, an excuse to avoid meeting anyone's eyes for a moment. And when she did look up, it was to see the rest of her companions watching her with Milek. Her face heated, and she searched for Victorin, standing only a few steps away.

Milek followed her gaze and stepped toward him. The two men grasped arms in greeting. It was strange for Iyanka to see her little brother tower over Victorin. Stranger still to note the vast respect in Milek's eyes as he greeted him.

"I'll never be able to thank you enough," Milek said softly.

"You know I don't need thanks."

"I do." Milek shrugged, but his gaze was solemn. "But you still have it."

Milek waited until Victorin nodded before breaking the moment, turning toward the rest of the road-weary group that watched him.

"Welcome to Agera," he said, casting his voice over the courtyard. "Egan I recognize, but I don't think I've met the rest of you."

Kale stepped forward, one arm trailing behind due to the horse reins he grasped, and knelt with his free hand over his heart.

"Kale Shinagel. I am a former member of Baron Malchomy's guard, but my loyalties lie with you and Prince Victorin, Your Highness."

Iyanka glanced up at Milek, watching for his reaction to this somewhat dramatic pronouncement. His eyes were on Victorin, and when he nodded Milek turned back to the kneeling figure with a smile.

"Well met, Kale Shinagel. We appreciate any and all loyalty we can find."

Iyanka glanced again at Milek, one eyebrow raised. *When did* he *become so eloquent?* He saw her look and winked, then turned back to the others. Iyanka followed his gaze. Gretta was rolling her eyes at Kale, her hands crossed over her chest. Lynn stood with her gaze lowered, a firm hand on Zef and Henry's shoulders. While Zef gazed around the courtyard with wide eyes, Henry assessed it calmly but intently. When Milek looked at them they both bowed, Zef a little too quickly and Henry with stiff respect. Cook stood beside Egan, watching him with concern, but when no one spoke she met Milek's gaze boldly.

"Martha Vawdry, Your Highness. Iyanka worked in my kitchen at Malchomy's fortress." She gestured to Gretta and Elsie in turn. "My niece, Gretta, and my daughter-in-law, Elsie."

"A pleasure to meet you," Milek replied, glancing at Iyanka as he bowed his head. "I applaud your patience. My sister isn't exactly the kitchen type."

Iyanka rolled her eyes where he could see but couldn't hide her smile. She'd missed this...*so* much. He shook his head and moved on.

"I'm Zef, Your Highness," Zef declared, his voice as bright as ever. "This is my sister Lynn, and this is Henry."

Lynn dipped into a quick curtsey when Milek looked at her and didn't say anything. Henry bowed again, his brown-green eyes meeting Milek's gaze without hesitation.

"Thank you all for the part you played in keeping my sister safe," Milek said, sidestepping so he could place a hand on Iyanka's shoulder. "It's an honor to have you in Agera."

"Thank you, Your Highness," Elsie said, "but the honor is ours. Iyanka is like a sister to us."

Elsie looked to Iyanka as she spoke, and Iyanka returned her smile, her heart full.

"Call me Milek," he said, with another glance over their group. "I'll have someone see to your horses, and George can show you to rooms where you can rest."

He gestured behind to the group still standing on the steps.

"Thank you, Your Highness," Egan said. "But we've already slept for more than a day and are likely more rested than you."

Milek's laugh was drowned out by Cook saying fiercely, "*You* are going to rest regardless."

As Egan protested, Victorin stepped closer to Milek and Iyanka. "When can we discuss the barons' forces?"

"Everyone's already gathered in the great study," Milek answered, casting his voice low. He looked back to the group and raised his voice. "I'm sorry to leave so soon, but Victorin and I have some business to catch up on."

Iyanka's companions acknowledged that at turns, and Milek stepped back. Iyanka followed.

"I'm coming," she said.

Milek looked down at her in mild surprise, but Victorin nodded as if it were the most normal statement in the world.

"Alright," Milek said, but his eyes seemed to ask when Iyanka had taken an interest in governance. She didn't doubt he'd ask her about it later. But for now, the three of them turned toward the steps.

Iyanka glanced over her shoulder as they left, for one more glimpse of her companions. Zef grinned and waved, Elsie catching her gaze and waving on. Iyanka waved back and turned back to catch up to Milek and Victorin. In a few strides she was at Victorin's side.

As they climbed the steps together, she dared to reach out, her fingers brushing Victorin's hand. He captured her hand before she could pull away, threading his fingers through hers. She grinned and stared ahead as they walked, every nerve and line of her being thrumming with *life*.

Milek paused briefly at the top of the steps to introduce the group of people waiting for them. There were three men, two of whom had advised her mother and father during their reign. They both bowed deeply to Iyanka and murmured greetings. The third man wasn't familiar, but the marked respect with which he greeted Victorin made her guess he was from Siersh. Like the others from Agera, he addressed Victorin as Commander, not Prince. Victorin had already explained that, while Victorin commanded their forces and scouts, Milek was the sole acting ruler of the wielders. She hadn't had time to ask why that was.

The last member of the group was a woman a dozen or so years older than Iyanka, with wind-blown hair and honey brown eyes. Milek introduced her as Captain Astrid Waleys, and Iyanka wondered if she was one of the famous wind wielder captains. The wind wielders were notorious for their fast ships and sailing prowess. They practically ruled the seas surrounding Elnar even after the barons' takeover, though she'd heard they leaned more toward piracy in recent years. The woman gave Iyanka a shallow bow, her greeting polite but her eyes hard and suspicious. Iyanka tried not to take it personally.

After introductions were finished, Milek led them all through the halls of the crumbling palace. Iyanka examined the space as well as she could at the quick pace Milek set, wishing she could stop and look more closely.

The palace was in worse shape than many of the buildings Iyanka had seen on their ride through the city. In many places, the roof and the floor of the second story were broken and open to the sunlight above, creating patches of light that dimly lit the halls they navigated. Some of the walls were blackened from fire, in others only scraps of plaster clung to the stone to hint at the former splendor. No trees grew inside, but branches stretched through open windows and gaps, and leaves littered the floors. Ivy and other vines creeped in through holes as well, covering walls and draping down from the ceiling. *I wonder what Henry thinks of this place*. It all looked like a gardener's haven.

Milek turned left and led them into a darker area of the palace, where there were fewer windows and the roof remained mostly intact. Another few turns led them to a room with a thick curtain covering the doorway, which Milek ducked through. Victorin pulled the curtain aside, gesturing Iyanka through first. Iyanka smiled in thanks and stepped inside, taking in the room as she creeped further in.

The ceiling here remained intact above them, though one wall had several windows that let in light and several creeping branches. Canvas sheets were fixed above these windows, providing a cover for bad weather, but they were currently pulled out of the way.

A large table dominated the room, with several smaller tables, bookshelves, and chairs lining the walls. Maps were fixed to the surface of the main table, with globs of wax marking specific locations. Five or six other people were already gathered around those maps, talking in hushed tones that fell silent at the entrance of Milek.

"Welcome back, Commander," a middle-aged man with gray hair and a large belly greeted.

"Thank you, Thomas," Victorin replied. "Any reports from the borders yet?"

Another, younger, man with a hawk-like nose and a shockingly deep voice answered. "Horice and Gilbert scouted the plains around Solling. Around five-hundred soldiers are gathered three miles from the forest's edge bearing the crests of Joktan and Malchomy. More are approaching from the southwest from Leon and Richard."

Iyanka shivered, taking in the wax globs with new horror. Over five hundred already gathered? And more were coming? That wasn't even counting the forces they'd met near the river. The only reason for such a number would be if the barons expected a battle…or a slaughter.

"What about the east?" Victorin said, planting his fists on the table. "If they're taking forces from Eisadel, they'll bring some from Siersh as well."

"Gisele and Tara haven't returned yet, but we're expecting similar numbers, maybe more," the hawk-nosed man said.

Thomas shook his head. "Baron Torock dispatched two-hundred of his men to Siersh six months ago to settle a revolt, and before that he stationed another company at the coast to deal with the pirates. We'll be lucky if there are fewer than eight-hundred coming from the east."

"As far as we know, they're still there," Captain Waleys countered, her voice surprising Iyanka with its rough quality. "My people still have ten ships patrolling the coast, giving Coyne's ships a good chase."

Victorin shifted, tapping the edge of the map. "Torock knows ground forces are no use there. If they've found us, they'll send all the forces they can spare without risking a coup."

The conversation continued around the table, discussing the numbers they could expect from the other barons, and how soon the forces would likely strike. Iyanka listened with mingled interest and horror, doing her best to store away all that she learned. She knew little of battle strategy, but to her untrained eye...she couldn't see how they stood a chance. If every soldier bore an enchanted weapon, the forces already gathered outside the forest could easily slaughter what Iyanka had seen of the city.

But the men around the table didn't speak as though their situation was hopeless. She didn't know if that was determination to fight to the last, or knowledge beyond Iyanka's. Either way, listening to their discussion brought up questions. She stored them away to ask Milek and Victorin when they were alone, unwilling to interrupt the conversation with so many strangers to listen in.

"Did you find that weapon you were searching for?" Thomas asked.

The question jarred Iyanka from her private musings. All eyes around the table were fixed on Victorin, now, and Iyanka turned to join them.

"I did," Victorin said, locking eyes with Milek for the briefest moment. "We tested it against the enchanted weapons during our escape, and it proved effective."

Iyanka looked from Victorin to Milek. *What was that look about?* She didn't understand the careful vagueness of Victorin's answer. *Why hide our bond? Why not explain what we can do together?*

The others had moved on, accepting Victorin's answer without question. But Iyanka kept her eyes on Victorin as they discussed defenses, waiting for him to look at her. When he finally did turn to her, she tilted her head in a silent question. He leaned down, his breath warm on her ear.

"I'll explain later."

She shivered and nodded, dragging her eyes back to the worn map before them. The meeting lasted at least another hour, as the gathered advisors discussed improvements to Agera's defenses and strategies the barons might take. Victorin stayed silent except when asked a question, and it seemed to Iyanka that he was already familiar with all that they discussed.

Milek also contributed little, and the untrained eye might think he was ignoring the discussion entirely.

He wandered the edge of the room, staring out the windows, never glancing at the maps the others referenced. But Iyanka knew better...he'd perfected this art with their tutors. He'd remember every word said, every detail related... it drove their teachers *crazy*, which of course meant Milek had practiced this skill often. But why was he feigning disinterest *now*? Who was it in this room that they didn't trust?

When the meeting finally came to an end, Captain Waleys was the first to sail from the room with mutterings of correspondence. The one other woman in the room, tall and a few years older than Victorin, left in silence soon after. The men, by contrast, seemed to be in no hurry, stretching and talking and approaching Victorin to ask more questions. Few of them acknowledged Iyanka beyond greetings, though they watched her. She was looking for an escape when Milek sauntered up, throwing his arm around her shoulders.

"If you'll excuse me, I'm going to steal my sister away."

The men talking to Victorin only nodded and returned to their discussion. Victorin's acknowledgement lasted longer, his eyes intent on Milek. It seemed a message passed between them, one Iyanka couldn't decipher. And then Victorin's eyes turned to her, searing her. Her breath caught as Milek tugged her backward. She didn't look away until the curtain fell into place, blocking her view. When she turned, Milek wore a knowing look, a smirk curling the edges of his lips.

"Why are you giving me that look?" Iyanka asked, her face heating.

Milek shrugged. "He doesn't waste any time."

"What's that supposed to mean?"

He grabbed her arm, leading her down the hallway. And Iyanka's heart panged at how much she had to tilt her head to meet his eyes. They'd been nearly the same height…before.

"If you don't know, I'm not saying."

"That's not fair." She shoved his arm.

He pushed back, knocking her off balance and then yanking her back upright by her arm. She squawked in protest. Iyanka winced, glancing around the empty hallway.

"Still afraid of people hearing you?" Milek asked, tugging her down a narrower hall.

"Only when I'm loud," Iyanka said, easily falling into the old argument.

Milek turned down *another* hallway, stepping into a doorway leading to a descending staircase.

"Because it would be the end of the world if anyone heard you talk at a normal volume."

"I talk normally," Iyanka insisted, examining the darkened stairwell. "Where are we going?"

"Somewhere more private. But we have to wait here for Victorin. I forgot to light the torch earlier."

"Why didn't he leave with us?" Iyanka asked.

"Appearances."

"And who is it you're maintaining appearances for?" She pulled back to better see Milek and raised her eyebrows.

"We'll explain when we're downstairs." Milek turned toward her, shadows falling across his face and making him look older. "While we wait, I have a question for you."

Iyanka's heard sped up, tossing flurries in her chest. She swallowed hard and waited.

"Did they hurt you, at Malchomy's castle?"

Iyanka's breath caught. *That's* what he wanted to know? No "why did you run"? No "where were you when I needed you"? *I don't deserve you.*

"No," Iyanka whispered. "I stayed out of sight, and they ignored me."

"Good."

Milek didn't ask anything else, turning to glance down the hall. Iyanka stared at him, willing herself to speak. *I'm sorry! I'm so sorry that I ran. I'm a coward, and I should've stayed. I should've been beside you all this time…I'm sorry for abandoning you.* But though she fought to speak those words, even opening her mouth to cast them out, they refused to come. And before she could find the will to make a sound, a flame sparked to life beside her, matched by one in her chest.

"Need some light?" Victorin asked, flame dancing in his eyes.

"Yes, thanks," Milek said, holding out a torch to Victorin.

Victorin held his flame-coated hand to the torch, which quickly caught fire and illuminated the narrow space. Victorin led the way down the stairs, holding the torch to cast the flames behind, to light the way for Milek and Iyanka. Iyanka was sandwiched between the two men and saw little of their surroundings until they reached the bottom of the stairs, which let out into a wider hall devoid of light. Victorin kept walking, and Iyanka rushed to catch up after staring at a root weaving its way along the edge of the floor. Milek chuckled at that.

They passed a few rotting doors and darkened halls before Victorin turned into a room. Iyanka followed, jumping as Milek shut the ancient door. Its hinges didn't creak as she would've expected, making Iyanka wonder how often Milek and Victorin came down here.

The room was small. She doubted Milek could stretch to his full length along any of the walls. The torch lit most of the narrow space, with its low ceiling and rough stone floor. A glance was enough for Iyanka to take it all in, and she turned back to Victorin and Milek.

"Why are we down here?" she asked.

"Oh, nothing much," Milek said, leaning his shoulder against the wall. "Just avoiding the traitor."

Chapter XII

"A traitor?" Iyanka repeated, throat dry, her mind on the new faces she'd just spent over an hour among. "Do you know who?"

"We have a good idea," Milek said, glancing at Victorin. "I still say we should lock him up."

"If we do that, we lose what advantage we have." Victorin's voice was steady, as if he'd repeated this many times. "Whoever's controlling him will only send someone else."

"At this point, does it even matter? We're days away from a confrontation regardless."

"Who is it?" Iyanka asked.

"It's best if you don't know," Victorin said apologetically.

Iyanka wanted to argue. She wanted to know who it was, who she should guard herself against him. But she refrained. *If I know, I'll give it away. I've never been good at hiding my thoughts.*

"So," Milek said. "That archaic binding works?"

"It works," Victorin said.

"Care to show me?"

Victorin turned to Iyanka, eyes lit with mischief that drew a smile out of her. She held up her hand, palm facing him, and he pressed his hand to hers. Her ice *lunged* at the contact. Frost spread from her fingertips along their hands, sealing them together and crawling along their skin. Victorin's fire flared to leave with as much fervor as her ice, engulfing her ice with a flash that drowned out the torch with its brilliance.

Milek choked out a single word that Iyanka would tease him for later. She met his wide eyes and grinned, laughing at his shock. Then she turned back to Victorin, and his eyes captured her. Their mingled power reflected in his gaze, blue flame against fathomless black.

Milek cleared his throat, and Iyanka broke away. The knowing look Milek cast her made her blush, and she turned away to face the room at large.

"It works like you thought?" Milek asked.

"Almost."

Victorin twisted his hand, lowering his arm so their entwined hands hung loose at their sides. Fire and ice still mingled on their skin, brightening the room with its cool light.

"My ice fuels Victorin's fire," Iyanka explained. "When they're combined, the hunters can't approach."

"Defense or offense?" Milek asked, still warily eyeing Iyanka and Victorin's flaming hands.

"So far we've used it as a defense, but has potential as a weapon," Victorin said.

"It would be more effective if I had your sort of power, Milek," Iyanka added. "Storms of fire and ice would be more useful against an army."

"Your strength is perfect," Victorin countered. "Your precision is invaluable."

"Thank you," she murmured, her heart nevertheless sinking at the prospect of using her ice as a weapon. They spoke of battle as a certainty. With so many forces gathering against them, she supposed it was.

"I take it from your *harried* arrival that the barons know?"

Victorin nodded. "Our first test was escaping the barons."

"Is that why they're gathering against us now?" Iyanka asked.

"Partly," Victorin said, squeezing her hand. "But they've been planning this for months. We merely...forced their hand."

Milek nodded, and Iyanka stared at both of them for another heartbeat.

"How do you know?" she asked.

Milek grinned, the expression suddenly dark, twisted. "We have spies of our own."

"Not that we should rely on them," Victorin said. "They might have second thoughts, with armies on the move."

Milek snorted. "It wouldn't surprise me. I've always thought it strange that they'd turn around from slaughtering us and offer to help."

"They might regret what the barons did," Iyanka said, voice small. "Perhaps they don't want a part in future violence."

"That would mean they're capable of feeling regret," Milek glared, glaring at the wall. "After what they've done, I doubt it."

Iyanka blinked, frowning as she took in her brother once again. Such bitterness... Milek had tended to hold grudges when they were younger, but never this far. *What have you faced in these years?* She glanced at Victorin, wondering if he could explain Milek's cynicism, but she found Milek's expression mirrored there. *Victorin too?* Then was she wrong to think the barons' servants might turn? Were they beyond hope?

"Anyway," Milek said, seeming to shake off that resentment. "What's our next move?"

"Any news from Cron or Waneroth?" Victorin asked.

"Nothing good. Both continents are still oblivious to Ecleath's activities, and they aren't willing to help us."

"How did you contact Cron and Waneroth?" Iyanka asked.

"Captain Waleys and her husband, Admiral Gordon Waleys, keep in contact with other wind wielders," Victorin explained. "They've carried our messages to other lands, but finding alliances has been…unfruitful."

"And Ecleath?"

Iyanka bit back a wince at the country's name. It had become tantamount to a curse over the years, though once, it was said, the kingdom's name had been held in awe. But that was before they'd turned to darkness.

"They supply the barons with their enchanted weapons," Milek said.

"Oh."

She should've guessed that. Where else would the barons get enough magicked weapons to attack two kingdoms? But she hadn't guessed the barons would…

her father had avoided trade with Ecleath. She'd only heard of Ecleathian ships landing on Elnar once, when a storm drove them into a port in Eisadel. She'd been on a tour of the land with her father, and she'd seen glimpses of them. They'd seemed normal enough, but they'd caused trouble in the port trying to sell mag-icked baubles, fighting back when guards put a stop to it. She'd been whisked out of the city in the dead of night while her father had gone to end the fighting and send the Ecleathians out of Elnar. But of course, she knew now that the barons had less qualms regarding magic.

"Are they still involved?" Iyanka asked. *Will we be facing sorcerers alongside the baron's forces?*

"They're still equipping hunters with spelled weapons, but they aren't sending troops," Milek said. "More shipments are coming in. The wind fleet sank one, but two others made it to port."

"Did they find any correspondence?"

Milek shook his head. "They're still sinking them from afar. They don't want a repeat of what happened last year."

Iyanka waited a moment for them to explain, then gave up. "What happened last year?"

"Ecleathian sailors took one of their ships," Victo-rin said. "They...weren't merciful."

Iyanka didn't ask for anything more. She could imagine all too well what that would mean for the wind wielders.

"I understand their reluctance," Victorin said, leaning against the wall with a huff. "But if we could find *any* word on Ecleath's relations with the barons..." he sighed and shook his head.

"Doesn't matter much, now," Milek said.

Because the barons are here. It didn't take much effort to finish Milek's thought. She took in Milek and Victorin's grave expressions, heart sinking.

"Do we have any hope of defeating them?"

Victorin rubbed his forehead, not looking at her. "Not if they catch us unaware in Agera. But if we meet them on our own terms, we have enough hope."

"And if we fail, at least we buy time for the non-combatants to get out," Milek added.

The flickering torchlight only made Milek and Victorin look more grim. It didn't seem to Iyanka that they had much hope, but still they were determined.

"And if we teach others to use their elements as Victorin and I can?" she asked. "Surely that will give us a better chance."

"That's harder than you'd think," Victorin said. "Not everyone can use their elements as we can."

He spoke almost hesitantly, glancing at Milek from the corner of his eyes. Iyanka followed that glance, only to see Milek *glaring* at Victorin. She shifted on her feet. *Once again, there's something they're not telling me.* Rather than asking, she did her best to break the tension.

"What's next on the agenda, then?"

It worked. Milek turned away from Victorin, stepping away from the wall. "Next, you and Vic should get some food. I'm sure you're tired of trail rations by now."

"Very," Victorin grunted, shoulders relaxing. "I'm sure I have a mountain of reports to sift through, after that."

"You do." Milek glanced again at Victorin, his eyes colder than usual. "I'll meet you in your office, to discuss more of our...plan."

Victorin met that gaze steadily, nodding. But neither said anything to Iyanka, and she wasn't brave enough to push for answers.

Milek led the way out of the cramped room with the torch, Victorin tugging Iyanka along by their clasped hands. They were silent as they wound their way back upstairs, remnants of tension trailing between the two men. But by the time they reached window-lined halls, Milek's smile was genuine.

"I have work I've been putting off," he said, pulling Iyanka into a fierce hug that squeezed the breath out of her. "I'll find you later. Don't run off, alright?"

His lighthearted teasing plunged through Iyanka's heart, an unintended dagger twisting in her chest.

"I won't," she promised earnestly.

He released her to ruffle her hair, nodding to Victorin before sauntering up the hall. His long stride quickly took him out of sight, and Iyanka turned to Victorin. He was already watching her.

"Ready?" he asked.

She nodded, and Victorin took them down another crumbling, vine infested hall. They walked in silence, but a comfortable one. There were armies gathering, enchantments to battle, death to overcome. But for now, Iyanka appreciated that moment of peace.

Victorin led Iyanka to an informal mess hall set up in what once was likely an elegant great hall. Glimpses of faded murals decorated what stucco remained on the stone walls, faces and fragments of places Iyanka didn't recognize. She studied them as Victorin pulled her deeper in the room, where most of their group sat gathered at a roughhewn table.

Elsie and Lynn nodded to Iyanka as she sat, but didn't interrupt Cook's rant about the state of the kitchens and the food. Gretta picked at a piece of bread, occasionally rolling her eyes but otherwise not engaging with the other occupants of the table. Kale was carefully *not* watching Gretta from across the table, shifting to make more room for Victorin and Iyanka. Laughter echoed off the walls, drawing Iyanka's gaze to where Zef and Henry ran through the empty space.

Cook's rampage ran down soon after Iyanka sat, and for a few moments silence reigned. But soon that void was too much, and Victorin cleared his throat.

"I'm sure those in the kitchen would appreciate your expertise," he said.

She snorted. "I'd hope so."

But she was staring at her lap now, and Iyanka wondered if her anger was more *worry* than anything.

"Any news on the barons?" Kale asked, eyes intent on Victorin.

Victorin hesitated. "Forces are approaching along the south and west, gathering at the edge of the forest near Solling."

"What's the plan?" Lynn asked. "Do we run?"

Gretta snorted. "Run where? The Valkis mountains? I'm sure the dragons and ghouls and Creator *knows* what else would love to torment us up there."

"Our next action is still being determined," Victorin replied, swinging his legs over the bench to stand. "And in fact, I have work to see to regarding our defenses. I'll see you all later."

He squeezed Iyanka's shoulder, nodded to the rest, and left the long room with a confident stride. Iyanka watched him go before turning to the plate of food Lynn had pushed her way. The stew of meat and root vegetables was a wonderful change from the travel fare they'd been surviving on, though Iyanka understood some of Cook's rant as she ate the bland meal.

The table was quiet, tense. When Iyanka looked around the table she saw her companions looking anywhere but at each other. *Exhaustion? Or did something happen that I've missed?* She debated breaking that silence as she ate, but ultimately couldn't think of what to say.

Zef and Henry ran up, skidding to a stop at the end of the table.

"Iyanka," Zef said. "This place is amazing. Is it really Agera? Why do they call your brother the prince if he's ruling? Have you seen the gardens yet? There's this one spot..."

Zef continued spewing questions without waiting for answers, filling the tense air and lightening the mood. Iyanka's wasn't the only smile to appear around the table as Zef's enthusiasm washed over them. The boy finally had to pause for breath, and Henry rolled his eyes and stepped forward.

"What we were wondering, Princess, is if you'd come to the garden with us. We found something we want to show you."

"When did you go to the gardens?" Lynn asked, eyes narrowing even as she smiled.

"When you and Elsie and Cook were helping Egan," Zef answered, twisting to look at his sister. "We just went exploring."

Lynn's concern didn't lessen at this assurance, but she didn't say anything more. Zef turned back to Iyanka, his eyes pleading.

"Will you come with us?"

"Of course."

"Great!" Zef grabbed her hand, tugging her away from the table as soon as she stood. She glanced back at her companions to share a smile with Elsie and Lynn before turning her attention back to Zef's chatter and Henry's occasional additions.

Henry grabbed her other hand as they left the room. Together, the boys led her through halls and outside through a small side door. Just outside was a large kitchen garden, filled with all sorts of vegetables and fruit trees. She recognized most of the plants from Malchomy's kitchen, but she'd never seen any plants so large and vibrant. Her inspection was cut short by Henry and Zef pulling her onward.

Apples and tomato plants gave way to overgrown hedges and towering trees that blocked out much of the sun. Vines dotted with fading flowers crept over trees and stone pillars that might once have been statues. She thought she could see faded faces amidst the leaves, but still Henry and Zef didn't slow. She promised to return to study it all more later and forced her attention back on the boys leading her through maze-like paths weaving among trees and weathered stone. *How do they make sense of it all?*

Finally, Zef and Henry stopped before a veritable wall of vegetation. Trees stretched far to either side in a ring of columns, barely a hand width between some of the trunks. Shrubs and vines filled in the remaining gaps, effectively blocking off whatever was on the other side.

"Through here, Princess," Henry said, kneeling on the ground. He pulled back a few current branches to reveal a cleared tunnel between two trees.

Iyanka examined that hole with a little trepidation, unsure how easily she'd fit, but another glance at Henry and Zef's faces prompted her to sink to her knees and crawl through. The ground was littered with dead leaves and twigs, but below that the soil was soft and dark. It released a pungent, loamy scent that reminded her of the southern forest.

Iyanka crawled at least a horse-length before emerging from the tunnel, standing and ignoring the dirt on her skirts to study her surroundings. Her eyes roved the clearing before her, once a courtyard: stone benches overtaken with vines or pushed over by encroaching trees dotted the edges, weathered cobblestones covered with years of fallen leaves made up the

floor. The wall of trees and hedges completely surrounded the space, making the courtyard feel close and
secret.

Zef and Henry joined her as she examined the ancient haven, taking in the trees overtaking the sky
above and the vine-covered mass marking the center.

"What is this place?" she asked.

"We don't know," Henry said, voice hushed.

"Henry thinks it's a memorial for the king who
built the palace."

"That's just a guess," Henry said. "I haven't read
all of the inscription yet."

"Inscription?" Iyanka asked, staring at what
Iyanka was beginning to think was a statue of a man.

"Over here," Henry said, grabbing her hand again
to tug her toward that vine enshrouded monument.

They circled to the other side, where vines had
been pulled from the stone at the base. She knelt to
study that cleared space, the boys kneeling with her,
and ran her fingers over the faint carvings. The figures
were in some dialect she'd never seen before. What she
could make out was archaic at best.

"Can you read this?" she asked, turning from the
stone to Henry. His dark eyes, so like the mingled bark
and leaves above her, stared back at her steadily. The
intensity of his gaze was a disconcerting sight on his
young face.

"Yes, Princess. I can read it."

She opened her lips, intending to ask him
how…how did a farmer's son know an ancient script

like this? Iyanka, in all her studies, had never seen anything like this. But as she met his eyes, for the briefest moment she thought she saw the glint of sunlight on leaves... and she pushed that question and all its implications to join the others she'd been gathering regarding this quiet boy.

"What does it say?" she asked instead.

Henry turned toward the statue, squinting at the markings. "It's talking about King Jasper and his fight against the Agoloths, and how they won their freedom at great cost. Thanks to the power of the Shacar warriors, the Agoloths were forced out of Elnar. That's all that I've uncovered."

Henry edged his way around the statue, pulling away more of the leafy vine hiding the statue. Leaves shriveled at his touch and crumbled away, the branches snapping easily under his hands. The inscription circled the base of the statue, and Henry examined it silently for several long moments before speaking.

"What does it say?" Zef asked, unable to contain himself any longer. "Does it explain what Shacar are?"

"Not exactly, but I think I know."

He pointed to a line of faded script, and Iyanka shifted to examine them. They made little sense to her.

"It's something about a binding ceremony," Henry explained. "Between King Jasper and his new queen, Evalia. It mentions the marriage of fire and wind, and that many of the Shacar were there to welcome the rulers to their order."

"The Shacar were wielders," Iyanka murmured, staring at the incomprehensible stone. "They used their elements like Victorin and I."

"But they had some sort of ceremony for it," Zef said, turning to look at Iyanka. "Did you and Victorin do that?"

Iyanka shook her head. "No, no ceremony. We just…mix them as we use them. Does it say anything else?"

"Just about King Jasper's reign here, in Agera."

The three of them were silent. Iyanka stared at the stone, scanning the inscription again, wishing she could read the words herself. Wishing they said more. She ripped her eyes away to study the rest of the court-yard again.

Zef stood and began pulling vines, most already shriveled, off the rest of the statue. Henry joined him. Part of Iyanka's mind whispered that she should help them, but she stayed where she was, kneeling on leaves and stone with her hands limp in her lap. Kneeling in *Agera*.

There were others like Victorin and me, and entire order…where did they go? Why have we never heard of them? If they had known…if they had known mingling powers was possible, could they have defended themselves against the barons? Could they have saved all those lives lost to hunter blades? *Or would Ecleath have given them a stronger enchantment?*

Zef and Henry clambered all over the statue, which stretched high above Iyanka's head, and worked together to pull away the last of the enshrouding vines.

Their efforts revealed a weather-beaten man with a crown, hand outstretched and wreathed in flame and swirling patterns. *Wind?* His eyes were blank, staring ahead at empty air. Free of greenery, he loomed over the courtyard, an ancient and regal presence. Iyanka pushed to her feet so she could back away, over-whelmed by that figure.

"Is this what you wanted to show me?" she asked.

"Part of it," Zef said. "But we didn't know about the Shacar thing."

"What's the rest of it?" She turned around to search out the courtyard, unsure of what she was look-ing for. At this point, she wouldn't be surprised if they'd found tunnels to the sea or a dragon's nest.

"The trees," Henry said, still clinging to the statue's head as he leaned back to gaze at the branches above them. "They're almost awake."

Iyanka turned back to Henry.

"*Almost awake?*" Her voice wavered, but she didn't bother to hide it. "You don't mean..."

"They're not wielders," Henry said. "But some gardener was here and grew them. Someone gave them orders, and they've been fulfilling them for gen-erations."

"What orders?"

"To guard this place."

Iyanka glanced at the trees. Were they closer than before? "Why?"

"Don't know," Zef said. "That's why we brought you."

"We were hoping you'd know more about Agera," Henry added. "And we were wondering how the trees would react to another wielder being here."

Iyanka turned to the two boys, raising an eyebrow. Zef suddenly looked *far* too innocent. Henry met her gaze steadily.

"You and Zef are wielders," she said.

"I'm a gardener," Henry said. "The trees see me as one of their own."

Zef jumped to the ground. "And trees don't care about wind."

"Frost on the other hand…" Henry shrugged, looking down at her from his perch.

"You said they were ordered to guard this place," Iyanka said, waiting for both boys to nod. "What happens if they think I'm a threat?"

Henry jumped down from the statue, landing a few steps in front of her.

"If they try to attack, I'll stop it before you get hurt."

Iyanka stared at him, protests running through her head. Provoking ancient trees that were *almost awake* seemed fraught with danger, particularly in this place. But… curse her curiosity. She wanted to know likely as much as Zef and Henry did.

"You're *sure* you can control them?" Iyanka asked, eyes on Henry.

"Yes," he said without hesitation. "Zef and I will protect you, Princess."

She nodded. "Alright."

She stepped up to the nearest tree and laid her hand on its trunk. She didn't sense any deeper presence, nothing like the forest beyond Malchomy's fortress. And yet…there was a faint thrumming beneath her hand, too quick to be her own pulse. She took a deep breath and, before she could talk herself out of it, collected a tendril of ice. Frost spread across the bark in precise swirls.

Deep groaning. It echoed through the courtyard, thrumming in the ground beneath Iyanka's feet. Then the tree began to *move* beneath her hand.

Iyanka yelped and leaped backward, tripping over a cobblestone. She fell to the ground, eyes locked on that shifting tree. Zef and Henry were at her side in moments, Zef helping her to her feet while Henry took a protective stance between her and the tree she'd offended.

But the tree wasn't *attacking*. Instead, it was shifting away, pushing aside stone and soil to form a gap in the wall. A glance around confirmed that the other trees were doing the same: bushes receded, trees shifted their place, branches intertwined above them to form delicate arches and a domed ceiling open to the sky.

"They're welcoming you," Henry said softly, awe edging his voice.

"Why?" Iyanka asked, rubbing the bruises aching at the base of her palms. Her gaze danced between the still-shifting trees and Henry, until Henry turned to look at her.

"They recognize you as a Shacar. They were guarding this place for *you*."

Chapter XIII

Milek and Victorin stared up at the trees and their woven architecture from the midst of the courtyard while Iyanka watched *them*. It had taken a while for Iyanka and the boys to find Milek and Victorin. Late afternoon sun filtered through the leaves and bathed the place in warm light and scattered shadows. Victorin turned to gaze up at the statue, its worn features more severe in the deeper shadows.

"I never knew this place was here," Milek said, kicking at the loose dirt the trees churned up with their movement.

"I didn't either," Victorin said. He turned his eyes to the two boys standing beside Iyanka. "How did you find this place?"

"The trees felt different," Henry said. "They were guarding something, and Zef and I wanted to know what."

"And then we wanted to show Iyanka, because we didn't know what they were guarding it *from*."

"And you used Iyanka to trigger their defenses."

Victorin's tone was disapproving, but neither of the boys shrank away. Iyanka fought to copy them when his eyes turned to her.

"That was the idea," Zef said. "But something else happened."

"The trees recognized what Princess Iyanka is, and her presence activated a second set of orders," Henry explained.

"What she is?" Milek asked.

"The trees see her as the return of the Shacar."

"How do you know that title?" Victorin asked, his voice suddenly harder, flames flickering in the gaze he turned on Henry.

"The inscription on the statue," Iyanka explained. "Do you know it?"

Victorin glanced up at her. The flames didn't dissipate.

"The source I studied about combining elements mentioned them. Where's this inscription?"

Zef was the first to reach the statue, gesturing to the runes surrounding the base. Victorin knelt to examine them as the rest gathered around him. After a few moments of quiet he leaned back on his heels and looked up at Iyanka.

"Can you read this?"

Iyanka shook her head. "I've never seen a dialect like it."

"Henry?" Victorin turned toward the boy at Iyanka's shoulder. "Did you translate it?"

"Yes, sir. I can read it."

Instead of questioning Henry, as Iyanka expected, Victorin merely nodded. "What does it say about the Shacar?"

"They fought with King Jasper, and they were present at a binding ceremony to welcome King Jasper and Queen Evalia to their ranks."

"Is that all?"

Henry shrugged. "It also recounts King Jasper establishing Agera as the capitol city and building this palace."

"So this is Agera," Victorin murmured, one side of his mouth twisting up.

"I told you it was," Milek said. "There's never been any other city in this area even half this size."

"That we know of," Victorin countered, standing. "We're obviously missing a lot of Elnar's history in our records."

Milek rolled his eyes and shrugged, overly dramatic as usual. "I was still right."

Iyanka smiled at Milek before returning her attention to Victorin. "What do you know about the Shacar? Other than that they joined elements."

"Not much," Victorin said, stepping closer to Iyanka. "We know at their height they were an entire society. Not just warriors but craftsmen, explorers, farmers, traders. And the records I searched mentioned wielders of stone, animals, lightning…things I've never heard of."

"Henry, Zef," Milek said. "There's another statue on the other side of the gardens that might have an inscription like this one. Care to help me look?"

Though he was talking to the boys, Milek fixed his gaze on Victorin in a vaguely challenging way. Iyanka frowned. Henry and Zef joined Milek as he turned toward one of the arches that now led out of the courtyard.

"What does the statue look like?" Zef asked. "Is it another king? A queen? A dragon?"

Henry added a question of his own to Zef's long string, making Milek chuckle. They soon disappeared amid the thick greenery, and Iyanka turned to look up at Victorin. His gaze was cautious as he watched her.

"What was that about?" she asked.

"He's pushing me to keep my word."

There was an exasperated edge to his words, and Iyanka tilted her head.

"About what?"

"There's something I haven't told you…about the Shacar."

A slush-filled pit of dread started up its familiar churning at Victorin's hesitation, the way he kept glancing away.

"What is it?"

"The Shacar were all…married couples."

Iyanka's eyes flicked to the stray vine Victorin was blackening with his nervous touch. *I should know what that means.* But the connection danced along the edges of her mind, just out of reach.

"And that means?" she asked.

"Only wielders promised to each other or bound in marriage can use their elements together."

Oh. Iyanka exhaled, but she couldn't seem to draw breath back in. Ice was already creeping over her dress, the leaves beneath her feet… She took a step back, turning her back on Victorin. She needed to think, to compose herself…

"So, our elements work together because…"

"Our betrothal is binding in the eyes of the Creator. And mine."

He spoke those last two words so quietly, Iyanka almost didn't hear them. She stood still, breathing shallow. *I hadn't dared to hope...* why was the only emotion in her chest right now *terror*?

"Iya?" Victorin said hesitantly. "What are you thinking?"

"I...I don't know."

What *was* she thinking? Their betrothal was binding... In all the weeks they'd traveled together, Iyanka had wished there was a way, but now, now she didn't know what to think. She didn't know how she felt. She thought somewhere in her heart was relief, wonder, but it was all overshadowed.

A hand touched her shoulder. Iyanka flinched, sending frost across Victorin's hand. But he didn't pull away. Iyanka turned to face him, unable to raise her gaze above the neckline of his shirt. *What do I say?* Victorin placed his hand under her chin and tilted her face back until she had no choice but meet his eyes. His gaze was gentle, cautious.

"Iya, do you...not want to marry me?"

"I...I do," she stuttered, struggling to form coherent thoughts while staring at his dark eyes. So familiar, so dear...were they always this intense? "I just...I need to think."

His brows furrowed, carving deep wrinkles between his eyes. "Alright."

"I...I need to think...by myself." Iyanka stepped back, breaking free from his grasp. "I'm sorry."

Iyanka spun away, sprinting for the nearest path out of the courtyard. She had no idea where it led, she didn't care. Away, that was all that mattered. She raced down the overgrown paths, taking turns at random, greenery blurring as her eyes filled with tears. Her breath was ragged. Her head pounded with the need to escape, to be alone, out of sight.

She turned a corner and found herself in a dead end, a small area surrounded by hedges and climbing roses obscuring what was once probably an arch. Instead of turning to find a different path, Iyanka collapsed to the ground in a heap and leaned her head against her knee. *Breathe in, breathe out. I'm alive. I'm alright.* As the mindless need to flee eased, other thoughts entered.

She was betrothed to Victorin. Still, after four years, the Creator saw them as promised only to each other. *That* was why her frost and his flame mingled without destroying one another, why they were able to fight the hunters. *He knew…he knew from the beginning, but he didn't tell me.* All the agonizing over whether he'd ever want her, useless.

But he does *want me.* Even though she ran, even though she'd abandoned them, even though their kingdoms had been torn apart, *Victorin* saw their betrothal as binding. Why? Why did he want her, after all that he knew about her? *Why did I run?*

"Iyanka?" called a young voice Iyanka knew.

Iyanka looked around, but she didn't see Zef anywhere. Muffled sound came from beyond the rosebushes, but when she looked all she saw was thorn covered branches and fading leaves.

"Can you get through?" Zef asked in a loud whisper.

Henry's voice replied, "Yeah, but it might take a while. Rosebushes are stubborn."

"I'll get Prince Milek." Footsteps sounded beyond the hedge, quickly fading into nothing.

Iyanka took one more steadying breath before forcing herself to her feet, taking a few steps toward the rose wall as she wiped tears from her face.

"Henry?"

"Yes, Princess. You should probably stand back. The roses might snap back."

"What are you two doing here?"

"Exploring," came the reply in a tone that said the answer was obvious. "Somebody found Prince Milek and needed to talk to him. Zef and I got bored standing around. What are *you* doing here? Where's Prince Victorin?"

"He's...back at the courtyard."

Iyanka tried to keep her voice from wobbling and failed. She stared at the rose vines as they moved, uncurling from each other and pulling back from the opening of the arch. Some of the branches *did* snap away from their place, whipping back with a force that made Iyanka jump.

"Are you alright, Princess?"

"I'm fine, Henry."

"You don't sound fine."

"How do you know how to do this?" Iyanka asked, a desperate attempt to steer his focus away from her.

"Some of it I know from practice."

"And the rest?"

Silence emanated from the other side of the rose bushes for several long breaths. "The rest I learned from…my family."

"I thought your parents weren't wielders."

"Ma and Da aren't my birth parents."

Not his… Iyanka said the first thought that came to mind. "But…your eyes look exactly like your mother's."

"Yeah…that's one of the reasons Prince Victorin left me with them after he found me. We look enough alike that no one would question it. And they were happy to take me in."

"When Victorin *found* you?"

Vines continued to twist away from the arch, the larger branches moving reluctantly. Enough were out of the way that she could see Henry through the leaves, but she couldn't make out his expression.

"My story is a long and strange one, Princess. I'm not sure now is the best time to tell it."

"Of course," Iyanka said. "I'm sorry."

"No need to say sorry, Princess."

"You can call me Iyanka, you know," Iyanka offered, unnerved by his use of her title. He didn't say it like a gesture of respect…more like an emperor addressing a vassal king. Not in an arrogant way, but utterly confident. She didn't know what to make of it.

"Thank you, Princess."

Iyanka shook her head, but a small smile pulled at her lips in spite of her confusion and heartache. The last vines pulled away, unblocking the gateway between her and Henry just as Zef turned a corner, Milek in tow.

"Iyanka," Milek said, ducking under the arch. "Are you alright?"

Iyanka nodded, then promptly burst into tears. Milek was at her side in moments, wrapping his arms around her shoulders.

"I take it he told you," he said wryly.

"You knew?" Iyanka asked through the snot and tears.

"Of course, I knew. Why do you think I left you two alone?"

"You wanted him to tell me."

"Yes." He squeezed her. "Didn't think it would make you cry. What happened?"

"I…I ran."

Milek pulled back to look at her. "Why?"

"I don't know."

Milek raised his eyebrows. "Afraid he'd sprout wings and breathe fire?"

"Milek," Iyanka groaned.

"No, listen. Were you scared?"

Iyanka looked down. "Yes."

"Why?"

Iyanka glanced up to see Milek's face devoid of humor.

"Do you wish you and Victorin *weren't* betrothed?" he asked.

"No. I mean, that's not it."

"Then what is it? What made you scared?"

Iyanka shook her head. She didn't know why, why she was terrified or why she'd run.

"You love him, don't you?"

"What?" Iyanka looked up, face heating. "You can't..."

"Save it, Yanka," Milek interrupted softly. "You've never been good a bluffing. You love him. So what scares you?"

Iyanka looked at the hedge on her left. "What if he changes his mind?"

"He won't."

"You can't know that."

"Yanka, come on. He loved you before you were even engaged."

Iyanka jerked her head up to meet Milek's gaze, her mouth opening and closing several times before she could make any sound come out.

"That can't be true."

Milek shrugged. "It is. Why do you think I hated him so much? I didn't want him to steal *you* away after he already spent so much time with Mother."

"I didn't know any of that," Iyanka whispered. "Why didn't you tell me?"

Milek shrugged. "It doesn't matter. It's all changed now."

They were silent for a few moments. Iyanka sighed and leaned her head against Milek's shoulder.

"What am I going to do?"

"Have you considered *talking* to him? I've heard that tends to work."

Iyanka looked up at him with one eyebrow raised. His voice *dripped* sarcasm. He stared down at her, smirking, and elbowed her.

"Unless you'd like to live here with the roses."

Iyanka rolled her eyes, smiling, even as every beat of her heart threatened to send frost across the stones underneath her feet. She took a deep breath.

"I'll talk to him."

"Good." Milek stepped away. "I'll leave you alone, then."

"What?"

Ice skipped out from her feet, making her slip as she whipped around. Victorin stood in the other entrance to the little clearing, one foot inside and one foot out as if he wasn't sure if he should come closer. But his eyes met hers readily, making her heart skitter. Vaguely, she heard Milek and the boys retreat, but she didn't take her attention from Victorin. He took a step closer.

How much had he heard? What should she do? What should she *say*? Iyanka stood, literally frozen in place as more frost spread across her toes, as Victorin slowly approached. She wanted to smile, to say *something*, but she couldn't.

He stopped an arm's length away from her, close enough she could close the distance easily. It was farther than he usually stood from her. That one, tiny gesture sent a spasm through her chest, a single icicle lodging in her heart.

"I'm sorry I ran," she whispered, glancing down at the cobblestones so she didn't have to meet his eyes.

"You're scared," he said softly. "Scared I'll stop loving you."

Iyanka kept her lips pressed tightly together. Admitting it felt like confessing a flaw in herself. Maybe it was. She didn't know.

Victorin took a shuffling step closer to her, bending his head to meet her eyes.

"Iya, that won't happen."

Iyanka squeezed her eyes shut, still not saying anything. *How can you know?*

"Did your mother tell you that I was…reluctant to agree to our betrothal at first?"

Another icicle pierced her chest.

"No," she said, a breathless whisper. *This isn't making me feel better.*

"Iya," he said, cupping her cheek in his hand. She shivered at the warmth. "I didn't want you to marry me because of some treaty. I wanted…I wanted you to *choose* me."

A light flickered to life, frail amidst her blizzard, so like the flame that burned in her chest even now. She forced her eyes open, meeting his gaze.

"But *why*? Why would you want *me*?"

He tilted his head, just slightly. "I watched you interact with your family, the servants, citizens in Eisadel... I saw your tenderness, your love and compassion..."

"My cowardice?" she added, voice choked. "My naivete? My impatience? I'm not perfect, Victorin."

"Neither am I," he half laughed, before turning serious once again, soft brown eyes boring into her. "You don't have to be perfect to be loved, Iya."

"And you love me?" A strange, lightheaded feeling was steadily overtaking the remnants of her panic as she stared into Victorin's eyes.

"I love you," he said. "You're the woman I want to live at my side."

Iyanka breathed that in, willing herself to believe it.

"And you?" he prompted, suddenly uncertain.

"I..." Did she? "Yes. I love you."

She loved him, not as the mysterious fire prince her mother spoke highly of, or the bright possibility of having a marriage like that of her parents'...after weeks of watching him fight to protect, to lead, to guard not only her but people who were bitter and distrustful of him...she loved *him*. She wanted to stand at his side.

Victorin's grin could light up the night. He leaned down so their foreheads touched, his hands barely touching either side of her face.

"Will you forgive me for not telling you about the Shacar earlier? It was wrong."

"I forgive you," she murmured.

"And will you, Princess Iyanka of Eisadel, be my wife?"

She lifted a trembling hand, wrestling within herself, brushing a strand of his too-long hair from his face.

"Yes, I will."

Chapter XIV

"It's about time!" Elsie crowed, leaning back with a grin that split her face in half.

She and Iyanka were sitting cross legged on a makeshift bed of layered blankets in the room they were sharing, while Gretta and Lynn tried to hang curtains over the open windows. Iyanka blushed at Elsie's words, looking down at her hands and smiling in spite of herself.

Iyanka and Victorin had stayed in the garden a while more after Victorin's proposal, talking and hiding. As soon as they'd returned to the palace, Victorin was dragged away by scouts needing to report to him. And Iyanka had searched for the girls to help with whatever they were doing.

Somehow, they'd already heard about what had happened in the garden—Iyanka suspected it was Zef's doing—and they'd whisked her off to the room and insisted on hearing every detail. Every one of them had smiled as Iyanka recounted, with halting words and a heated face, everything that had happened.

Not that she told them *every* detail. Some things...some of what Victorin said she wasn't willing to share. Some moments she wanted to secretly treasure.

"So, when's the date?" Elsie asked.

Iyanka stuttered for a second before Gretta jumped to the floor and rolled her eyes.

"We have an army marching to annihilate us, and you expect her to pick a wedding date?"

"It's not entirely unlikely," Lynn said, "that they would want to get married before."

"We haven't talked about it," Iyanka said, trying to ignore the sinking dread that accompanied the reminder about the barons. So much had changed…but they still faced impossible odds.

"You should," Elsie said, eyes glittering. "After all, you've been betrothed for *four years*. I'd say you've waited long enough."

"*Elsie*," Iyanka groaned.

"It's true," Elsie laughed. "Four years is a *long* engagement."

"Not if you're royalty," Gretta argued. "I've heard some engagements last for ten years or more. Of course, that's expected when your parents choose your spouse when you're *five*."

"My mother and father were engaged for fourteen years before they were married," Iyanka added quietly.

Mentioning her parents felt awkward. She didn't expect it now that they knew who she was and had obviously accepted it pretty well. But talking about her parents, a king and queen, in front of servants and merchants' daughters…she didn't want them to think that she felt superior to them. She didn't want them to distance themselves.

"How old were they when they were married?" Lynn asked. She tugged a corner of the curtains to settle it better and jumped to the floor beside Gretta.

"Father was twenty-three, and Mother was seventeen."

"So, your mother was engaged when she was *three* to a prince who was *nine*," Gretta said, voice dead. She shook her head. "Royals."

"Yes," Iyanka said. "But they grew up together. My mother was raised in Eisadel's capitol, and their parents made sure they spent a lot of time together."

"Were they in love when they got married?" Elsie asked.

"Yes," Iyanka said, a bittersweet smile spreading across her face. "They even convinced their parents to let them marry two years earlier than planned."

"That's sweet," Elsie said.

"Why didn't your parents set up an engagement like that for you?" Gretta asked.

"Gretta," Elsie scolded, grabbing a dust rag to throw at her.

"What?" she asked, ducking the rag. "I'm only curious."

The rag ended up hitting Lynn in the face, but she only pulled it off and neatly folded it. Then she sank to the floor between Elsie and Iyanka, rag in hand. Iyanka watched them and picked at a loose thread on her dress, hoping Gretta's question would slip away. But all three girls turned toward her, waiting for her answer. Iyanka sighed.

"They tried. It didn't work out well." Iyanka turned her eyes to the floor to avoid their sympathetic gazes.

"What happened?" Gretta asked. Lynn handed Elsie the rag, and Gretta added, "If you don't mind talking about it."

Iyanka shrugged, still picking at that loose thread. "He sailed over for my twelfth birthday. When he found out Milek would inherit the throne, he broke off our engagement."

"Ouch," Gretta said.

Elsie reached out to touch Iyanka's knee. "That must've been hard."

Iyanka managed a smile, glancing around at her companions. "It wasn't too bad. We'd exchanged a few letters before that, and…I don't think we would've gotten along well."

"If he left you because he wouldn't get a shiny crown as your dowry, you're better off without him," Gretta said.

"Yes," Elsie said, wriggling her eyebrows. "Especially with the *vastly* superior fiancé you have now…"

"Oh, stop it," Iyanka said, lobbing a pillow at her.

She caught it and laughed. "You better get used to it, miss Northern Lily."

"Caught that, did you?" Iyanka asked, still smiling despite the pang the title sent through her.

"Do you not like it?" Lynn asked.

"No," Iyanka said slowly. "It's just strange hearing my *friends* call me that…"

Footsteps pounded in the hallway, interrupting Elsie's reply. Henry and Zef burst through the doorway, skidding to a halt just short of their makeshift bed.

"There's a strange lady in the city," Zef panted. "With a spruce branch and white poppies."

"They think she's a sorceress from Ecleath," Henry added. "The Princes sent us to bring you to the entrance."

Iyanka sat frozen for a stuttering heartbeat. Then she scrambled to her feet, following Henry and Zef back down the hallway at a run. The girls followed her. As Iyanka ran her mind spun in a thousand directions, none of them making sense. They'd only arrived that morning...now there was an Ecleathian? *Here*? Bearing the signs of peace, no less. What did she *want*? Their surrender? Their allegiance? *What will she do if we refuse?*

Outside, they stopped at the top of the steps, where Milek and Victorin were already waiting. Iyanka stepped up between them, while the others stayed in the shadows of the palace beside others already gathering to watch. The sun had already set behind the trees, casting the courtyard in the eerie half-light of dusk.

"What happened?" she asked.

"She approached the city gates and requested an audience with us," Milek said. "All she said is that she has a proposition for us."

"What does that mean?"

"Nothing good," Victorin said.

He tugged Iyanka forward just slightly, so she stood even with him and Milek. His hand snagged hers, holding tight. Together they stood close, the three of them waiting in silence for the mysterious visitor to arrive. They didn't have to wait for long.

The suspected sorceress rode into the courtyard on a small donkey that was white as moonlight, her cloaked form a black mass on its back. She dismounted at the bottom of the steps, smoothly gliding up with her cloak billowing behind her. Her hood was tilted up, like she was watching them, but all Iyanka could see of her face was her pointed chin. At the top of the stairs she stopped, dipping into a low bow.

"My princes," she purred. Her head tilted to the side, just slightly. "And princess, I see."

"Why have you come here?" Victorin asked, voice hard.

"My dear fire prince, is this how you welcome guests? I've heard word of your people's warm hearths and great hospitality. But perhaps that has cooled in recent years…"

Iyanka listened to the woman's silky voice with unease, frost tracing paths just beneath her skin. She was too smooth, too welcoming…as treacherous as a frozen river in the spring thaw. At some point, the chasm would open beneath their feet.

"It's hard to keep a hearth warm when it's used as a target to slaughter you," Victorin replied.

"True," she murmured. "Pity that they have all the power, isn't it?"

"Their only power is what *your* people supplied," Milek countered, tone as hard and imperious as Victorin's.

"Only for a price, young ice prince," the woman said, seemingly unbothered by that harsh tone. "But we are willing to take it away…for a price."

"Why are you here?" Victorin asked again.

"I was hoping to discuss this with my lords out of the open air."

Victorin and Milek hesitated for a moment, glancing at each other, before Milek replied.

"Fine. Follow us. One of our men will see to your mount."

"Very courteous," she said. "Lead the way, princes."

Victorin turned toward the palace, pulling Iyanka in front of him to place himself between her and the sorceress. He kept a hand on her back as they walked through the hallways. Iyanka glanced back and found Milek walking just behind her as well, offering her a reassuring smile. But Iyanka's eyes also found the sorceress smiling cruelly further back. Her eyes were still shadowed, but Iyanka felt her gaze on her. Iyanka turned forward and didn't look back again.

Victorin didn't lead them to the study with the maps they'd gone to that morning, but instead entered a smaller, windowless room devoid of furniture save a rough table and two chairs. Three lamps hung from the walls, which Victorin lit easily. Milek closed the door behind the sorceress, who swept over to the one of the chairs and sat, looking completely at ease. Iyanka shivered.

Victorin, Milek, and Iyanka gathered across the table from their guest, all of them ignoring the open chair in favor of the wall at their backs. This time Victorin stood at the center, Iyanka just behind his elbow. Was it her imagination that the sorceress was studying them, silently prodding? Searching for weaknesses? *Creator, help us.*

"We're in private," Milek said. "Now speak."

"The girl can leave," the woman said. "I have nothing to discuss with her."

"That *girl* is my sister, Princess Iyanka of Eisadel. She stays," Milek said.

Iyanka's heart swelled at his words, despite the unease that still plagued her at this sorceress's words. She seemed less than impressed.

"I know who she is," she said. "I still want her out."

"She stays," Victorin said, his voice brooking no argument. "Speak or leave."

"Perhaps you should let the lady decide for herself."

Her voice was back to deceptively smooth tones, chilling Iyanka's skin as her ice swirled, readying itself for whatever threat this woman posed. Anxiety tingled there among the frost, whispered that she should leave. She shouldn't be here.

But she couldn't abandon Milek and Victorin. She *couldn't* leave them alone with this *sorceress*, especially if she wanted Iyanka gone so badly.

"I'll stay," Iyanka said, voice rough but audible.

The woman's smile cracked, just for a moment, before she recovered. "Very well."

The sorceress raised both hands to throw back her hood, revealing a delicate face with an olive skin tone, framed by thick black hair brushing her shoulders. Her eyes were black-brown and didn't reflect the lamplight, didn't show anything except darkness.

Beside that she looked…normal. When she smiled again Iyanka noticed her teeth were slightly crooked. She didn't look like a magic practitioner. She didn't look dangerous. Iyanka whispered another prayer to the Creator for safety.

"Let's go straight to the point, shall we?" She glanced between Victorin and Milek until Victorin nodded.

"Excellent," she said. "I'm sure you know of the armies moving against you. I heard you had a bit of a skirmish with their eastern forces a few days ago."

"We know about them," Victorin said, his jaw tight. Iyanka slipped her hand onto his arm, trying to offer subtle support. The sorceress's eyes flicked to Iyanka before turning back to the princes.

"And you know that two Ecleathian ships made it to port not two weeks ago, their cargo distributed among the barons' forces. You're outnumbered three to one, and facing enchanted weapons your powers are useless."

"Have you come to gloat, then?" Milek asked.

"Patience. I was merely offering a reminder."

"Reminder received," Victorin said. "Now what's your 'proposition'?"

"Power," she purred. "I offer you charms to render their weapons useless, enchantments to enhance your own power, even reinforcements."

Iyanka shifted on her feet, fighting to keep frost from spilling into the air. She was offering dark magic, the same power that had destroyed them. Now this sorceress wanted them to use magic to save themselves? *Why? Why the change of heart?*

Victorin had the same thought. "I imagine the barons aren't pleased that you're offering this kind of *assistance*."

"They don't know I'm here," she replied, laughter bubbling in her voice. "They have no right to know. They sought our help, and we gave it. But you…to you we *offer* our aid."

The sorceress let that statement hang in the air, her promise so tempting: the power to defeat the barons without a massacre. The power to save their people, to take back what was stolen from them. They'd searched for allies and found none…now here was a land offering their help…

But what she offered was *darkness*. Iyanka couldn't forget where Ecleath's magic came from, couldn't forget that it would lead to ruin in the end. She couldn't forget. She glanced up at Milek and Victorin to see their faces mirror images of stone, glaring down at the sorceress.

"Why?" Milek asked. "You didn't care about us when the barons slaughtered our people. Why help now?"

"The barons paid a good price," the woman said with a delicate shrug. "But my leaders are disappointed with how they've held up their side of our bargain. Ecleath is looking for powerful allies in the years ahead, and your people are far more promising."

"We're not interested in any alliance with Ecleath," Victorin said. "Now or in the years to come."

The woman's lips twisted into a smile that seemed too bitter to be genuine. She drummed her fingers on the table, that rhythmic tapping the only sound in the room.

"Your people are strong," she said, voice low and beckoning. "They have a will to live. And you, Princes, are strong leaders. But even if you win the battle ahead of you, can you imagine the cost? So few of you will survive…so few of your people will live to see the day you're fighting for. You know how many of them will die, slaughtered by the barons' armies. They will cut down your soldiers like cattle, kill your women and children with no pity. Your people will be *lost* to this world. Such a needless waste of life."

As she spoke, something tugged on Iyanka's mind, a faint strain of music she couldn't quite capture. Ice faded from her limbs as those words, that music, lulled her, convinced her. Finished with her speech, the woman smiled, her eyes fixed on Victorin with an intensity Iyanka didn't understand.

"If you want to save your people," the sorceress murmured. "You need our help."

For a breath, there was silence. Easy, lulling silence.

"What are your terms?" Victorin asked.

His words broke Iyanka from the trance. *What?* They didn't want Ecleath's help...they *couldn't* take what she was offering.

Iyanka glanced to Milek, wondering if he knew what Victorin was doing, but his gaze was also fixed on the woman at the table. Iyanka examined the witch, heart pounding, and noted her cat-like smile as she continued to tap her fingers on the table. What kind of magic was she using? Iyanka could still feel it fighting to draw her in, tempting her focus with that faint music. But now that she recognized it, she was able to resist the draw. So how had Milek and Victorin been taken in?

"The terms are simple, my prince," the woman said, her gaze barely flicking to Iyanka as she spoke. Iyanka stiffened. "The charms and weapons necessary for you to defeat the barons, in exchange for future service to Ecleath."

"What kind of service?" Milek asked. Iyanka was relieved to hear the suspicion in his voice.

"Whatever Ecleath needs."

"That's a steep price."

"But isn't *any* price worth saving your people?"

The woman barely glanced at Milek, but in that instant Iyanka thought the sorceress's expression changed, turned harsh and forbidding. Iyanka glanced at Milek and saw him staring at the floor, his jaw tight. *What did she do?*

Iyanka returned her eyes to Victorin, same as the sorceress. She searched for any sign that he was seeing what she saw, any hint that he was planning to get rid of this woman. But his eyes were fixed on the sorceress, his expression torn. Iyanka slipped her hand onto his clenched fist, but he didn't grasp her hand in return. Pressure continued to build within Iyanka's chest, panic and ice swirling...*what is this sorceress* doing? *How do I stop it?*

"I need an answer, my princes," the woman said.

The air in the room turned oppressive as Victorin and Milek stood in silence. Iyanka squeezed his hand, tried to catch his eye, tried to do *something* that would shake him loose from...whatever this was. He opened his mouth to speak...

"We need a few minutes," Iyanka blurted, turning to face the sorceress, fighting to keep her ice within. "To think it over."

The look the sorceress aimed at her was enough to make Iyanka shrink back, yet her voice remained congenial. "I believe the fire prince has already decided."

Iyanka glanced back at Victorin, saw him nod. His attention solely on the sorceress, not even a glance toward Iyanka. Fear turned to anger, as her ice took on a harder edge.

"Victorin isn't the only one who has to decide," Iyanka said. She was pleased that her voice didn't waver, that it was loud enough to be heard clearly.

Victorin *finally* looked down at her, surprised and confused. Iyanka turned away from him, forcing herself to glare at the sorceress sitting only a few steps away, her skin prickling at the darkness in the woman's gaze. The sorceress's smile was poisonous as she glared at Iyanka.

"We're going to discuss this. Alone."

Not bothering to wait for the sorceress's response, she grabbed Victorin's arm and tugged him toward the door. She glanced back enough to ensure Milek was following, right on their heels.

"Remember," the sorceress called as they walked through the door. "If you refuse our help, your people *will* die."

Victorin shuddered. Iyanka kept tugging him forward. Out in the hall, Iyanka stopped as Milek closed the door behind them. But once that was done, Milek grabbed her arm and Victorin's and tugged them further, not stopping until they'd nearly reached the end of that darkened passage. He released both of them, eyes wild as he turned back to Iyanka and Victorin.

"She's more powerful than we guessed," he said.

Iyanka turned to Victorin. Away from the sorceress's poisonous gaze, tears stung Iyanka's eyes. They froze before they could even spill onto her cheeks.

"Victorin," she said, forcing a warning into her voice. "You're not considering this."

Victorin shook his head, but Iyanka's hope was quickly dashed.

"Maybe we should consider it," he said.

"You don't know what you're saying, Vic," Milek said, stepping closer so the three of them formed a tight circle. "Whatever manipulation magic she's using is serious. She had me convinced for a minute."

"I know," Victorin said, speaking slowly. "But she's right. If we face the barons, there *will* be a slaughter."

"You don't know that," Iyanka said. "There's still hope."

"What hope? You and I can't destroy and entire *army*."

"Then we teach others what you and Yanka can do," Milek said. "But this deal with Ecleath…it's not good. There's more going on, here."

Iyanka's voice turned pleading. "We *can't* accept this offer. She's offering us the same power the barons used to destroy us in the first place."

"But this time it would be wielded for good," Victorin said.

"And that makes it *right*?" Iyanka cried. "Evil turns to good when it's used on our enemies?"

"Wouldn't it be worse to have the chance to save our people and refuse it?"

Iyanka ripped her gaze away from Victorin's glazed eyes, taking a step back. When she looked to Milek, his worry matched her own. This wasn't Victorin, it couldn't be…but how did they break whatever the sorceress had done to him? How did they make him wake up?

"What about this price she talked about?" Milek asked, his voice cautious. "Sounds like allying ourselves to Ecleath will subject our people to slavery. They could ask us for anything."

"But they would be alive," Victorin countered, with an edge Iyanka had only heard him aim at his enemies.

"Some things are worse than death."

Victorin shook his head. "You're not listening."

"No, *you're* not listening," Iyanka said. "You shouldn't be considering this. You shouldn't have let that sorceress step inside this building."

"I'm trying to find a way to save us," Victorin said. "So we won't have to hide in the shadows, so you don't have to live in terror."

"Well, stop it!" Iyanka cried. "Some lines shouldn't be crossed, Victorin. Not for safety, not for life…using that sorceress's darkness would *condemn us*."

"Iyanka…" Milek jerked his chin toward the door down the hall. "Maybe we should keep it down a little…"

"I won't be quiet!" Iyanka shouted. Ice leaked from her pores, dropping the temperature around them several degrees. "I'm tired of cowering. *Let her hear*."

"Iya," Victorin said, his voice now cautious. Iyanka turned to him.

"*You*…you know better than this. You've watched what their enchantments do, you *know* they're wrong.

And if it takes that kind of power to survive, then I'll accept death!"

"Iya, you need to calm down," Victorin said.

He moved to put his hand on her shoulder, ignoring the fierce cold radiating from her skin. But she smacked his hand away, taking another step back.

"Don't touch me," she snarled. "Not with her poison clouding your eyes."

Confusion entered Victorin's eyes, confusion and hurt. Iyanka seized that glimmer of an opening, snatching the hand that still hovered near her shoulder. Frost poured across his skin at the contact.

"Fire, now," she said.

Victorin stared at her for a heartbeat before flame flickered to life, igniting the frost that had already spread down their forearms. She took a deep breath and met his eyes.

"*This* is what we will use to fight the hunters. We will defeat them using the power bestowed on us by the Creator of Agon, or we will fall. There is no other option."

She searched his face for any sign that she was getting through, any hope that he was *hearing* her. Victorin's gaze turned to their glowing hands, to the frost and flame curling its way up their arms. And something in his expression softened. When he looked up, his eyes had cleared.

"You're right," he said, voice cracking. He closed his eyes, brows drawing together. Iyanka held her breath.

"Vic?" Milek said. "You back?"

"I'm back."

"And if we go back in there?" Iyanka asked. "Will she twist your mind again?"

"She'll try," Victorin said, opening his eyes to meet her gaze. "But now that I know…she tricked us into inviting her in. Now that I know, I'll guard myself better."

"Victorin…"

"It won't happen again." He lightly touched her cheek with his free hand. "Don't worry."

Iyanka took a deep breath. Whatever boldness had overtaken her had now fled, leaving her knees weak. But she forced her voice to be hard as she spoke.

"You didn't think it was going to happen the first time."

"She has a point," Milek said. "The sorceress knows Iyanka didn't fall for it. She's going to be fierce when we go in there again."

Victorin sighed deeply and stared at the ceiling for a moment. When he lowered his gaze again, he looked reluctant.

"If it happens again, take over negotiations. If she's using the same spell, we should keep enough sense to stay quiet."

More dread washed through Iyanka's core at that prospect, speaking to that woman with Victorin and Milek stiff and silent on either side of her.

"It'll be fine," Milek said. "We'll protect you, dark spells or no."

Iyanka took a deep breath trying to calm her mind. Victorin tugged on her hand, stepping back toward the room where a sorceress awaited them. Iyanka followed.

Victorin released Iyanka's hand soon after, leaving enough time for the frost to melt before the entered the room. The frosted flame had spread all the way to their shoulders, but Iyanka hardly took note as they approached the door that seemed to lead to their doom.

The woman was sitting at the table just as they'd left her, her probing eyes following them as they reentered the room. Iyanka tried to hide her fear, tried to stand tall. One glance from the woman convinced Iyanka that she didn't believe the act.

"I take it you've made your decision?" she asked.

"We have," Victorin said, glancing down at Iyanka. "We will fight this battle on our own."

"Are you sure you want to do that? Fighting on your own, you will fail."

Her voice was still cloying, still reaching for Iyanka's mind. But her stance was stiff, her hands too tightly clasped to fit within the serene image she'd been trying to project. *What changed?*

"Perhaps," Milek said, edging a little closer to Victorin and Iyanka. "But we're willing to take the risk."

"Refuse now, and the price will be heavy should you seek our help in the future."

"That won't be a problem," Victorin said.

The sorceress sat still for several long moments, eyes flicking between the three of them standing before her. She bowed her head. "I see. Then I'll leave, now."

"We'll walk you out," Milek said.

The woman stood and turned, cloak swirling around her legs, and swept down the hall. Victorin, Milek, and Iyanka followed close behind her, not taking their eyes from the sorceress. The only sound in the halls were their muffled footsteps. Iyanka didn't dare break that silence, even as it seemed to suffocate her.

The woman led them to the courtyard without falter, sweeping down the stairs without even a glance back at them. Her donkey was waiting there, a young man backing swiftly away from it as the sorceress approached. Once she was mounted, she finally turned back to the face them, her raised hood once again shadowing all but her mouth.

"Do not expect mercy from us," she said. "You've chosen your own destruction."

Iyanka shivered, but Victorin spoke, his voice hardened.

"Leave swiftly. The forest is treacherous in the dark."

She smiled, teeth white in the darkness. "Nothing in these woods poses a danger to *me*."

With that, she turned her steed around and urged it into a trot that quickly took her out of the courtyard. Iyanka watched the road long after her donkey's white coat had faded out of view, needing to assure herself the sorceress was truly gone.

"Make sure she leaves, but keep your distance," Victorin ordered a few guards.

"Yes, Commander," the guards saluted.

Milek let out his breath in a woosh of whitened air, his own nerves finally revealed by the frost crawling around his feet. "Well, I wouldn't repeat *that* experience in a hundred years. Why do you suppose she left so easily?"

"I don't know," Victorin said. "I'll be more at ease when she's fully gone."

Victorin reached over to take Iyanka's hand, but she pulled it from his grasp. She kept her eyes on the road, but from the corner of her eyes she could see Victorin watch her.

"We need to talk," she said. "Alone."

Chapter XV

"Garden or cellars?" Victorin asked cautiously.

"The cellars."

She didn't want to be outside right now, with the sorceress still so close. Where the night air shrouded their surroundings.

"Let's go, then," Victorin said, turning back toward the palace. Iyanka followed closely, trying to smile reassuringly at Milek as she passed him. She and Victorin were silent as he led her through the darkened halls, down to the narrow underground room. Iyanka entered first, pressing her back against the nearest wall. Victorin shut out the darkness of the hall and put the torch on the wall, slow to turn toward her.

"You're angry," he said, quiet and even.

"Yes," Iyanka whispered.

"That I considered allying with Ecleath, or that I fell under her enchantment?"

Iyanka took a deep breath, but her voice still wavered. "How much of it was the enchantment?"

"Iya..." Victorin stepped toward her.

"How much?"

He sighed. "I don't know."

"How can you not know?"

"The magic she was using," Victorin said. "Once you let it in, it takes existing fears and magnifies them, twists them to her purpose."

Iyanka huffed, glaring at the wall. "Explains why I didn't notice."

She'd noticed the fear, of course, but it was hardly unusual. She met Victorin's gaze, saw the pity there and looked away.

"She used your fear of failure," Iyanka said. "Your fear that they'll die needlessly."

"And I played right into her hands."

Iyanka nodded, eyes on the wall as she thought that through. She'd already known Victorin shouldered more responsibility than necessary, that he took every failure as his burden as well. It shouldn't have shocked her that a sorceress could use that to her advantage. But Iyanka's mind still wasn't at ease.

"Have you considered allying with Ecleath before her...influence?"

"I've sought alliances, but not with Ecleath."

She couldn't doubt the earnestness in his voice, the apology that lingered behind his every word. So why this betrayal stinging her heart? Had she expected Victorin to be invincible? *No,* she thought. *Just stronger than me.*

"Iyanka, I'm sorry," Victorin whispered, taking another step toward her. "I should've guarded myself better. I should have..."

"You're not invincible, Victorin. You just..." Iyanka's voice broke, and she had to swallow before continuing. "You scared me. I didn't think...I never expected to *see* you like that."

Victorin took another step, and Iyanka closed the distance to lay her head on his chest. His warm arms surrounded her, as she inhaled his smokey scent and tried not to cry. The ache hadn't faded completely, but she could breathe past it. They stood together in silence for a while, but as much as Iyanka wanted to stay that way, she had one more question she had to ask.

"Is there really so little hope?"

Victorin sighed, holding her tighter.

"The barons' forces outnumber us three to one," he said. "And the reports I've received say at least half of them have enchanted weapons."

Iyanka's heart plummeted again, dread turning to slush in her stomach. So many people wanted to kill them...she still didn't understand *why*.

"Is there a chance we could teach others to use their elements as we do?"

"Some. But I don't know how many would come. They have to be couples bearing different elements, and they have to be truly bound."

"But you'll ask?"

"I'll send a request out to the city."

"And how long do we have?"

Again, Victorin hesitated, and Iyanka pulled back to look at him.

"A few days at most," he said.

Iyanka took a deep breath through her nose, willing her nerves to calm. She should've expected that. The army was already half gathered. They couldn't take the chance the barons would attack them *here*, so of course they'd have little time. *Will I lose everything again? I just got Milek back...*

"Come," Victorin said. "You need rest."

Rest. That one word and she suddenly realized how she her legs trembled, how heavy her eyelids were. This day had seen so much…

"Alright," she said, allowing Victorin pull her out of the room and along the dark path leading to the rest of the palace. The halls that were dim in the day were now filled with a blackness the torch didn't seem to fully penetrate. The flickering light illuminated a small sphere around them but left flickering shadows and dark doorways around them. Iyanka was relieved when they reached the door to her shared room.

"Sleep well," Victorin said, reaching out to stroke her cheek.

She automatically leaned into his touch, her heart calming. She finally met his gaze, and the relief she saw there banished the last awkward remnants of her anger.

"Goodnight," she said, smiling as best she could. He smiled in return before backing away, eventually turning away toward his own quarters.

Iyanka turned toward her door, edging it open quietly in case the others were asleep. She needn't have bothered. All of them were sitting up, turning toward her as soon as she emerged through the door.

"What happened?" Gretta asked. "What did she want?"

Lynn scooted over so there was room for Iyanka in the circle they formed on the floor, and Iyanka lowered herself to the blankets.

"She came to offer us Ecleath's help."

"Creator save us," Cook said, standing near the window. "You didn't take it, did you?"

"No, we didn't." And silently, Iyanka vowed to keep the details of their meeting to herself.

"Good," Gretta said. "It's *their* power that got us into this mess in the first place."

"I'm guessing she wasn't happy to be refused," Lynn said.

"She wasn't," Iyanka said.

Elsie's brows drew together. "Do you think she'll seek retribution?"

That was a disturbing possibility that Iyanka hadn't considered.

"I hope not."

"Those two princes better keep an eye out," Cook said. "You too. From what I've heard, Ecleathians are a vengeful lot."

"We will," Iyanka promised.

Gretta stretched her arms in the air and laid back, yawning as she spoke. "I don't see how it matters much. You'd think seeing us slaughtered with their own spells would be enough revenge for them."

"Gretta," Elsie groaned. "Why do you have to say things like that?"

"It's called being realistic," Gretta said, rolling to avoid Elsie's attempt to slap her arm.

Lynn ducked Gretta's flailing feet. "There's realistic and there's pessimistic. You tend toward the latter. A lot."

"So what?" Gretta asked, sitting up, her eyes flashing. "Assume the worst, and I won't be broken by whatever comes. It's called surviving."

"That's not a good way to live," Cook snorted.

"Why not? You seem to do fine living that way," Gretta replied harshly.

Dismay overtook her features as soon as the words were out of her lips. She turned toward Cook, who was staring out the window.

"Yes," Cook said quietly. "But I'm living to regret it, aren't I?"

"I'm sorry, I didn't mean…" Gretta trailed off, biting her lip.

It's fine," Cook said, back to her usual gruffness. "It's true, and there's no use pretending otherwise. Just don't make my mistakes."

Uncomfortable silence overtook the room, and it took several long moments for anyone to break it.

"How's Egan?" Lynn asked.

"Last I saw him, you were trying to convince him to rest," Iyanka added, earning a grateful look from Lynn.

"He'd be better if he'd sit still," Cook said. "Old goat."

Iyanka tilted her head as she watched Cook, wondering about the worry that seemed to plague her regarding Egan. They'd hardly spoken to each other for most of the trip, and when they did it was to argue. Yet Cook obviously loved him, almost like…almost like they were siblings.

Iyanka sat up straighter, studying Cook in the lantern light. For the first time, she noticed how she and Egan shared the same colored eyes, the same chin and brown hair amid gray. *Why didn't I notice it before?* It explained how they knew each other, and why Cook was so concerned for him despite how much she and Egan seemed to disagree.

"You girls get to sleep," Cook rumbled, lowering herself to her own mound of blankets across the room. "I doubt tomorrow will be any less hectic than today was."

Iyanka and the others obeyed without argument, settling into the nest of blankets beside each other. When everyone was laying down, Lynn sent a breeze around the room that blew out the lanterns, sending the room into darkness.

Iyanka closed her eyes, focusing on the breathing of the people around her and tried to match her breath to theirs. Tried to keep calm. And she prayed that she'd fall asleep before the events of the day returned to torment her.

0O0

Iyanka awoke to light flickering across her eyes as a chill breeze blew the makeshift curtains aside. It was the still the gray-light of predawn, but once awake Iyanka knew she wasn't going to find any more rest. She sat up, blinking as she looked around the room. Cook and Gretta were already gone, but Lynn and Elsie were still sound asleep. Only their faces peeked out of the blankets, and both girls had their legs curled up close to their chests. *Is it really that cold?*

Iyanka rocked to her feet and moved to the window, lifting the edge of one curtain to peek outside. Delicate frost decorated the world outside, covering everything in a fine layer of white. Columns of smoke rose from the kitchens, and Iyanka thought she saw more toward the city. Off toward the gardens, she spotted tendrils of steam snaking through the trees from some hidden source. Was there a pond in the gardens?

Another breeze pushed past the curtain, brushing against Iyanka's skin. She closed her eyes and breathed in the crisp air. The taste of winter in the air made her restless: she couldn't stay inside when such a wonderful world waited outside.

Stepping lightly so she didn't wake anyone, pausing to throw her blanket across Elsie and Lynn, Iyanka left the room. She took the first door she found that led outside, which took her to a part of the gardens she hadn't seen yet. She took a moment to gaze around her, smiling at the chill that overtook her skin. Then she searched for the rising fog and took the closest path leading that direction.

The frost-covered cobblestones were soothing beneath her bare feet, and Iyanka allowed the ice rising to the surface to spread along the ground as she walked. Frost spread across her arms as well, stirred by the chilled breeze.

Iyanka hadn't experienced a morning like this since Eisadel fell. Even in winter, the southern half of Elnar didn't have these silent mornings of a world encased in frost. It was always soulless wind bringing in storms of sleet and rain, never the crystalline beauty before her now. It made her ache for her old home, and at the same time satisfied a longing she hadn't consciously realized was plaguing her.

As she searched for the source of the steam, she examined the gardens around her: walls and statues covered in vines, hidden from view by shrubs and trees gone wild. Every leaf covered in thorny vines of scrollwork frost. So delicate, so easily destroyed by the brush of a hand or a warm breath.

Wandering the paths was enough to set her at ease, to satisfy that *need* to be outside, but she was still glad when the path opened up at the edge of a small pond. It wasn't much, just a stone edged pool half filled with cattails. Tendrils of steam wafted from its surface, adding mystery to what later in the day wouldn't be anything spectacular.

Iyanka stood on the edge of that pond, breathing deeply and watching the slowly moving mist. It took her too long to realize there was a cloaked figure standing on the other side. The thought that it might be Milek was dashed when she realized how small the person was, too slight to be Victorin either. *Who?*

Just as Iyanka began to think it was another statue, the figure moved, floating around the edge of the pond toward her. Iyanka took a step back, wondering if she should run. But the figure moved more quickly than Iyanka expected, blocking her escape before Iyanka could take another step back. The person lifted their hands, and Iyanka flinched. But they only tossed back their hood, revealing black hair and crooked teeth. The sorceress. *Creator, protect me.*

"You said you would leave," Iyanka blurted, breath abandoning her.

"I didn't, actually."

She stalked around Iyanka, until she had her back to the pond. Mist swirled around the bottom of the sorceress's cloak, clinging to the fabric like grasping hands. Iyanka forced her gaze to the woman's face, heart pounding.

"What do you want?" Iyanka croaked.

"You're scared of me," the woman mused. "You should be."

Iyanka shivered, clenching her fists as she tried to steady her breathing. "What do you want?"

The woman clucked her tongue. "So filled with terror. Yet you resisted me last night. I want to know how."

She searched for escape, finding none. Iyanka already knew she couldn't outrun the sorceress, and she knew better than to fight her. The woman's eyes dared her to try, darkness gathered around her form. That left talking to her, praying she'd leave Iyanka alive.

"I don't know," Iyanka whispered.

"I know you don't," the woman said soothingly. "Luckily, I have ways of finding out for myself."

Something passed over the woman's face, a veil of shadow, and Iyanka was hit with a wave of terror. No reason, no cause, just raw panic. Like the anxiety that struck in the night and sent chills of deadness through her body, making every breath a struggle.

Iyanka gasped and wrapped her arms around herself, tears already streaming down her face. Everything hurt: her head, her arms, her legs, her heart... Daggers of a dead cold ripped through her chest. Another wave, and Iyanka fell to her knees, hunched over herself, barely seeing the hoarfrost surrounding her as her world collapsed in on itself.

"That's interesting," the woman purred, walking circles around Iyanka. "You should be begging for mercy by now."

Iyanka clenched her teeth against the agonized wail that fought to emerge. She'd never felt fear like this, never had this crippling despair pressing down on her. But she was no stranger to this feeling of weakness. She wouldn't give this woman the satisfaction of hearing her scream. *Creator help me.*

Another dagger struck, formed in shame and regret. Everything Iyanka had ever done wrong in her life, pressing out from the depths of her memory to cut and burn. Running away, failing Milek, not saving her father...

Iyanka gasped, her grating breath harsh in that air.

"That's it." The sorceress crouched to be at Iyanka's level. "Feel the pain, the terror, the shame. Let it consume you. Do you want my help now?"

Iyanka was too busy sending frantic prayers to the Creator to reply, too broken to say a word. But she managed to lift her head, to meet the woman's black gaze. Iyanka knew she looked beaten. Maybe she was. *Please save me. Creator, Theohyios, please...*

"Still no give." Through the cloud suffocating her, Iyanka heard the sorceress's frustration. "Let's see how you do with sorrow added to the mix…"

Iyanka did her best to brace for another onslaught, gritting her teeth against the scream that would come. But it never came. Instead, a ripping sound rumbled the ground, followed by the rustling of leaves.

Vines exploded from the cracks in the cobblestones. They wrapped around the sorceress's legs as she screamed and ripped at them. The vines continued without pause.

Iyanka scrambled away on her hands and knees, her shattered mind not making sense of the scene before her.

"Princess," a voice whispered, followed by a gentle hand on her arm.

Iyanka still flinched, but she managed to hold in the frost threatening to overtake Henry's hand. She looked up and found his brown eyes flickering green, staring down at her in gentleness. His jaw was set, his brows in an angry slant that looked out of place beside the gentleness she found in his eyes.

"You should stand," he whispered. "I'll help you."

Iyanka nodded and laid her hand flat on the ground to push herself up. Her legs wobbled, but Henry kept her steady. Once Iyanka was on her feet, Henry turned to glare at the bound sorceress, and Iyanka followed his gaze. The woman was bound in thick vines from her waist down, arms captured at her sides. One vine wrapped around her neck to gag her, but her eyes were uncovered and spitting malice.

Henry flicked a hand, and the vine silencing the woman withdrew. But Henry spoke before she finished spitting leaves out of her mouth.

"What is your name?"

"I don't answer to forest brats," she spat, a bit of leaf still stuck to her lips. Her expression turned pained as the vines tightened.

"Your name."

Iyanka turned back to Henry in raw, broken shock. His normally sweet voice had turned hard, commanding. There was no sign of the quiet gentleness Iyanka was used to. Henry bore the air of an executioner.

"Gamir," the woman snarled, drawing Iyanka's attention back to her.

"Sorceress Gamir," Henry said, his voice taking on an accent Iyanka hadn't heard before. "Attack another person in these lands, aid these barons seeking destruction, and you'll learn the potency of my wrath. I won't extend mercy again."

The woman's eyes widened, her jaw going slack. And she spoke something in a heavy, cloying tongue Iyanka assumed was Ecleathian. Iyanka's own jaw went slack when Henry replied in the same language, the words he formed elegant, and knife edged.

Whatever he said upset the sorceress, causing her to thrash in the vines. Henry watched her dispassionately, and the vine returned to gag her.

"Princess," Henry said, hard edges gone as he turned toward her. "We should find Prince Victorin now."

It took longer than it should have for Iyanka to find her words, to force her mouth open to speak them. Henry waited patiently.

"What if she escapes?" Iyanka asked.

"She won't. The ivy is too strong."

With one last look at the trapped sorceress, Iyanka allowed Henry to lead her away from the pond and toward the palace. She shook even with Henry's hand holding hers, giving her a solid connection to the world that still felt insubstantial around her. The chill was no longer pleasant, the silence no longer comforting. Her body felt like fractured ice, on the edge of falling to pieces. And her mind spun and twisted, showing her images, replaying words without making sense of them. The sorceress had returned for *her*. Henry had defeated her, and spoken *Ecleathian*. Those moments screamed their importance at Iyanka without forming a coherent picture.

Footsteps thundered down the path, and Iyanka stopped, stiff all over. But it was Victorin who appeared, and her heart slowed. He paused when he spotted Iyanka, and whatever he saw caused a moment of panic to overtake his eyes. He bounded forward, reaching Iyanka's side in an instant.

"What happened?" he asked, opening his arms as Iyanka leaned into him.

"The Ecleathian sorceress lured her into the garden," Henry said. "She was torturing Princess Iyanka when I found them."

Torture? Iyanka supposed that was an appropriate word for it. She shivered, and Victorin's arms tightened around her: bound up all her broken pieces.

"Where is she now?" Victorin growled.

"Tied up at the pond. You won't be able to move her until I remove the vines."

"That's good, Henry. Thank you."

"You're welcome, sir."

Victorin released Iyanka, shifting his hands to her arms and gazing down at her.

"Will you be alright if I leave you for a bit?"

"I think so," Iyanka whispered. Her mind was beginning to clear, the world no longer an oppressive weight around her.

"The sorceress used strong emotional manipulation on her," Henry said. "She shouldn't be left alone for a while, just in case."

Victorin nodded to Henry. "Alright. I sent Zef to find Milek. Will you take her to him? I'll come as soon as I'm finished with the sorceress."

"I'll be fine, Victorin."

Victorin looked unconvinced, but when Henry nodded, he seemed satisfied. He released Iyanka, turning down the path Henry and Iyanka had just left. Henry only waited a few moments before taking Iyanka's hand again and leading her toward the palace.

The dark hallways inside reignited some of that curling, seizing fear, and Iyanka was grateful for Henry's hand anchoring her. And it wasn't long before they entered a cheerfully lit study, a fire banishing the delicious chill while also chasing away the shadows.

Henry led her to the other side of the room, where an empty chair stood. Iyanka sat without protest and watched as Henry lowered himself to the floor. He examined their surroundings carefully, on guard even as he sat cross-legged with his chin in his hand. He still looked so young…and yet the look in his eye wasn't young at all. How hadn't she noticed that before?

"Henry," Iyanka said. "That was Ecleathian you were speaking, wasn't it?"

He hesitated. "Yes."

"How…" Iyanka trailed off, unsure what to ask.

Henry stared back at her, a pained sort of understanding in his gaze. It made Iyanka's heart ache to see it.

"My story shouldn't be told in pieces."

"Will you tell me someday? Your story, I mean."

Henry stared at her, and in the flickering torchlight it seemed memory and sorrow hung from him like a cloak. "Yes, Princess. I'll tell you my story."

Iyanka held his gaze for another heartbeat before breaking away, unnerved by all his eyes contained.

"She was right, you know," Henry said.

"About what?"

"You shouldn't have held up so well under that kind of onslaught."

Iyanka was silent, trying to think of a proper response to that, recalling the far-too-recent memory of that dark pain invading her body.

"I didn't hold up well," she whispered.

"Iyanka," Henry said, and the shock of hearing her name from him made Iyanka meet his eyes again. "The magic she cast is used to break the minds of hardened warriors. The fact that you're *talking* to me is astounding."

Iyanka blinked, unsure what to say to that. He couldn't be right…could he? She wasn't that strong.

But how did Henry even know this? It couldn't be personal experience…could it?

Henry watched her, silent and steady. Like he knew the questions that she was asking. And his words echoed in Iyanka's mind: *My story shouldn't be told in pieces.* If she asked, he wouldn't answer. Not yet.

The door opened, making her jump, and Milek marched in. Zef and Cook followed close behind, but Iyanka didn't take her eyes from her brother. Her eyes filled with tears again. *I've failed him…so many times.*

"Yanka," he said, wrapping her in a hug. "What happened?"

"The sorceress trapped her in the garden and was torturing her," Henry answered.

"*Torturing*? What did she do, Iyanka? Where are you hurt?"

At his panic, Iyanka managed to swallow back the tears to answer.

"I'll be fine. It was only emotional pain."

"Only? How bad?"

Iyanka tried to shrug it off, but Henry's eyes caught her, disapproving.

"It was…bad," she admitted.

Milek nodded, still worried.

"Prince Milek," Henry said. "I should go. Prince Victorin needs my help with the sorceress in the garden."

"I'll go with you," Milek said, a sudden simmering anger in his eyes.

Henry shook his head. "Someone should stay with Princess Iyanka."

"I'll be fine," Iyanka said, just as Cook announced, "I'll stay with her."

"Thank you," Milek said, ignoring Iyanka's assurance. He squeezed her tight one more time before stepping back. Even then, he stared at her a long moment, searching her gaze with reluctance. Iyanka smiled brokenly.

"I'll be alright, Milek. It's not like I haven't felt fear before."

"I'll be back soon," he promised. "Stay out of trouble while I'm gone."

He said the words lightly, but his eyes were still strained with worry.

"I will."

"Good." He turned to Henry. "Lead out."

Henry nodded, glancing back at Iyanka once more as he walked toward the door. Iyanka did her best to smile, but his young face didn't relax. Was something else troubling him? *Nothing he would tell me, I imagine.*

When both of them were out of the room, Cook wrapped an arm around Iyanka's shoulders and drew her toward the door.

"Come, lass. Some hot tea will do you good."

Hot tea probably *wouldn't* do her good, but Iyanka didn't say anything. She'd rather cool it herself when Cook wasn't watching than argue with her. Iyanka didn't think she could take sharp words now, even if there was a warm heart behind them.

To Iyanka's surprise, Zef had stayed with them instead of going with Milek and Henry. He sprang to his feet, bounding to Iyanka's side as they neared the exit.

"No questions, you hear?" Cook told him, a hint of her usual fire in her tone.

"I'll be quiet," Zef promised, taking hold of Iyanka's hand. Iyanka accepted the contact gratefully, and Cook didn't argue any more.

Iyanka wondered as they walked what she looked like. Was the turmoil and agony visible on her face? They were treating her like glass, even energetic Zef. He didn't ask a single question on their way toward the kitchen, didn't say a single word. And though she wanted to insist that she was fine, that she didn't need coddling, she kept her silence. Because her mind and heart were still ragged, and she didn't know what would push her into falling apart again. So she held tight to Zef's hand, closing her eyes against the shadows.

Chapter XVI

Iyanka sat on a kitchen stool with her hands wrapped around a tepid cup of tea, watching the people around her work. She'd offered to help, but Cook had ordered her to stay where she was, and no one was willing to cross her. It seemed Cook had managed to make an impression already on the occupants of Agera.

So Iyanka sat with her tea, the guilt of being useless tempered by her still-shattered emotions that were glad not to have to navigate anything more complicated than answering Elsie and Lynn when they spoke to her. Gretta stayed at the far end of the kitchen, not talking to anyone, but Iyanka didn't have it in her to ask why. Not right now.

"Princess," a voice sounded behind her. Iyanka turned to face Henry, frowning when she took in his drawn, weary look.

"Henry," Iyanka said. "Are you alright?"

"Faced more of a challenge than I was prepared for," he said, shrugging.

Iyanka's brows furrowed as she tried to decipher that. *What challenge? What happened?*

"The princes sent me to bring you to them."

"Where are they?"

"Gathering the others," he said, looking around the kitchen and nodding at their companions. "I'm supposed to bring them, too."

Henry stepped toward Cook, tapping her elbow, whispering something that made her set down her work. He did the same to the girls, and soon they were following him through the palace, to the same study where Victorin and Milek met with their advisors the day before.

The same group of people were gathered within, including the rest of their companions from the journey here. While Egan and Kale stood to one edge with practiced bland expressions, Zef's eyes were bright with excitement. Lynn went straight for her brother, and their rest of their group followed.

Iyanka hesitated, glancing between Victorin and Milek at the head of the table, and the rest of their group gathered along the wall. She wished they would all stand together…but after another moment of hesitation, she stepped toward Victorin and Milek. *I'm not choosing a side.* They wouldn't judge her for standing with Victorin and Milek, no matter what her battered mind whispered to her. It seemed the sorceress's work hadn't evaporated completely.

"How are you?" Victorin asked as she stopped at his side.

"Better. I think."

"Good."

"Where's the sorceress?"

"Dead," Milek answered without turning from the map he was examining.

"What?" She winced at the volume of that word, but a glance around showed no one watching her.

Victorin shifted on his feet "She tried to escape. If she'd reached the barons, it would've been disastrous."

"It's no more than what she deserved," Milek muttered.

Victorin nodded, and Iyanka stared at them both with mounting horror. Had they killed the sorceress because of what she'd done to *Iyanka*? She didn't want that kind of weight on her. She didn't want to be responsible for someone's death, for blood on the hands of her family...*but I'm still relieved she's gone.* That felt wrong. But she was kept from dwelling on it more when Thomas spoke, leaning on the edge of the table.

"Prince Milek, Commander," he greeted. "What's the purpose of this impromptu meeting?"

Milek straightened, taking on the regal bearing Iyanka had glimpsed the day before. "Last night, an Ecleathian sorceress came to offer us aid in our fight against the barons. We refused."

Grumbling and hissed whispers overtook the room. Some looked unnerved, perhaps at the concept of a sorceress in their haven. Other looked annoyed, even affronted. *Probably that they weren't consulted.*

"This morning," Milek continued. "That same sorceress attacked Princess Iyanka in the gardens."

More murmurs, and a dozen sets of eyes turned to examine her in concern and curiosity. She flinched, fighting to stand tall under so many gazes. She sincerely hoped the anger she saw in some of them wasn't aimed at her.

"Where is this fiend?" Barek, one of her father's former advisors, demanded. "Has she been punished?"

"She has," Milek assured. "She was apprehended and questioned, then killed in an escape attempt."

"We called you here to discuss the information she divulged," Victorin said.

And with that, the room fell silent, every eye on their leaders at the head of the table. Iyanka was no exception. *What did she know? What information would make them call this meeting?*

Milek was the first to speak.

"As you know, the barons' forces have been gathering at the southern edge of the forest. We stand against well over four-thousand men, over half bearing hunters' weapons."

"More soldiers are coming from the southern provinces," Victorin said. "They should be here within a week."

"How many?" Thomas asked, hands folded over his gut and his expression grim.

"We don't have exact numbers," Victorin said. "But at least a thousand."

Iyanka watched closely as expressions of dismay and fear overtook those filling the room. But with that dismay also came a spark, a fierce light Iyanka couldn't name. But it wasn't hopelessness, she knew that.

"We already knew this, to some degree," Milek said. "But we now know that a ship carrying five Ecleathian sorcerers docked in Glaren two months ago. One is the woman we apprehended this morning. The others will be here in under two weeks."

"That soon," a man whispered.

"And they will fight with the barons?" Barek asked.

"Yes," Milek said. "Now that we've rejected their offer, all Ecleathian involvement will favor the barons."

"The witch told you this?" a hawkish man asked. When Milek nodded, his eyes narrowed. "How can we know that it's true?"

"My men are trained in interrogation, Achan," Victorin said. "She wasn't lying."

Interrogation? *Does he mean torture?* Iyanka shuddered at the thought of even that twisted, cruel sorceress facing the kind of pain she imagined Victorin's men could inflict. But was it justifiable? Iyanka couldn't decide.

Captain Waleys stepped from the shadows, eyes fixed on Victorin and Milek. "Two of my captains sighted an Ecleathian ship docked in that area. At last report, it was still there."

"Then what course is left to us?" Berak asked. "We can't fight armies *and* sorcerers, especially with enchanted weapons blocking our only advantage."

"We flee to the north," Thomas said. "From there, flee to Cron."

His words were met with silence as people turned to him. Some seemed to consider his words, while others shook their heads.

"Are you out of your mind?" Achan asked. "If winter didn't trap us in the mountains, the dragons will kill us for invading their territory."

"Sailing to Cron in winter would not be wise," Captain Waleys added.

"We can't even be sure Cron would accept us," a quieter voice said. "They've refused to aid us so far."

The debate continued, more voices joining in the flurry of argument in favor and against fleeing north. Thomas defended his proposal without much visible conviction, still at ease in his seat.

"We can't run," Victorin announced, cutting through the babble. "Abandoning Elnar now would doom everyone who remains to a rule of terror."

"Then what do you propose?" a woman asked.

"We fight them."

"That's suicide," Thomas said. "Even if the numbers were even, we don't stand a chance against the hunters' weapons."

"We've trained to fight without our elements," Achan mused. "We might stand a chance."

"Not against so many," another voice said, still quiet compared to the rest. "You forget that it only takes a small cut for those weapons to kill us."

"Not always," Egan called. "I have the wounded shoulder to prove it."

"Not all of us are as strong as you, my friend."

"We have a way to fight back," Milek said.

This time, the room didn't quiet. More people inserted themselves into a debate that was growing more heated by the moment. Noise filled the room, pressing in on Iyanka with an oppressive weight. Milek turned toward Victorin and Iyanka.

"Looks like I'll need some help getting their attention," he said, winking.

"You didn't put much effort into it," Victorin said, eyebrow raised.

"No, but can you blame me?"

Victorin only shook his head.

"We're going to show off our elements," Iyanka said.

"How'd you guess?" Milek asked.

"I know you," Iyanka said flatly, unable to resist answering Milek's grin. "Anything specific you have in mind?"

"Something to break them from their argument," Victorin said.

"What about that prank on Lord Regga when I was ten?" Milek asked.

Iyanka shook her head. "Too many people."

"You're too cautious. What about the trick from the winter solstice?"

Iyanka shook her head again, but the memory gave her an idea. "You want it to be dramatic?"

Victorin shrugged. "Might as well."

"I know what to do, then."

Iyanka cupped her hands together, dripping ice from her fingertips and stretching it as it grew. She formed a rod as long as her arm, then set to work forming the details: adding a cross-guard, shaping and lengthening the blade, and adding a pattern of frost shaped into flames across the surface. Finished, she held the sword out to Victorin.

"That's a useful skill," Victorin said, wrapping his hand around the grip. His fingers overlapped with hers, already warming.

Iyanka shrugged. She doubted her parlor trick could be used for anything other than show. But it should accomplish its purpose. A few were already watching them.

Victorin's hand warmed almost unbearably, and the ice sword erupted in blue flames. Ice cracked as fire consumed it, but Iyanka sent more ice to replenish the blade. Frost and fire crawled up Iyanka's fingers, sealing her hand to Victorin's. And when Iyanka dared to look up, she found a room silenced in awe and terror.

"As I was saying," Milek said, his smile smug. "We have a way to fight against the hunters' weapons."

Victorin raised the sword, Iyanka's hand still beside his own, and brandished it at the group.

"Half a year ago, I traveled south in search of a weapon unaffected by the enchantments the hunters carry. This is the weapon I found."

Berak tore his gaze from the flaming ice and locked his eyes on Iyanka. "Your ice is…*feeding* his fire. How?"

Iyanka glanced at the sword as she spoke, speaking slowly so she wouldn't say anything wrong.

"The way I understand it, our betrothal binds Victorin and I in a way that allows us to meld our elements.

"And the hunters' weapons are ineffective against our elements when combined," Victorin added.

"You've tested this?" Achan asked.

Victorin lowered the sword and took his hand away, extinguishing the flames. The ice sword hung heavy from Iyanka's hand, pointing toward the floor.

"We used our combined fire and ice against the hunters several times during our escape."

Iyanka glanced around the room as Victorin answered more questions about what they had just witnessed. They all watched Victorin, and many faces now bore a spark of hope. Anger and frustration had drawn back, at least for the moment.

Her eyes wandered to her companions toward the back, and she received nods and smiles from several of them. Zef even waved. She returned their smiles before moving on, her eyes catching on Thomas. He watched Iyanka and Victorin with a new intensity, a sort of hunger in his eyes. She quickly looked away.

"Can this power you possess be reproduced?" a younger man asked, rubbing his wrist nervously as if he didn't like speaking up.

"Yes," Victorin said. "Any couple with differing elements who are bound in the eyes of the Creator are able to use their elements together."

"But will it be enough?" Thomas mused, drawing eyes to him. "Two wielders can take on four, perhaps five soldiers? But that leaves most of our people still defenseless."

"Not defenseless," Milek said. "With Victorin and Iyanka, and any others willing to bind their elements, we're hoping to create a widespread effect that will take down the size of their army to something we can face."

"That's putting a lot of responsibility on two people," Berak said reluctantly.

"I agree," Thomas said. "Putting the outcome of a battle on the backs of two people isn't wise. But if we flee, Prince Victorin and Princess Iyanka could use their powers to guard our backs."

"That would also be placing two much responsibility on two people," Achan said.

"But they'd be more likely to succeed."

Milek interrupted Achan's reply. "We've already established that running isn't an option. It's never been an option."

An echo of the pain of that morning, the crushing shame, made Iyanka flinch. *Running has never been an option.* But she'd run. And it made everything so much worse.

"But should we rule it out?" Thomas asked. "Perhaps it would be better to risk winter than wait for slaughter."

"We're not waiting for them to find us," Milek said with forced patience.

This conversation is going in circles. The same proposals, the same reasoning, the same arguments. How could they stand it? How could they sit and talk and do nothing but cite the impossible? The words droned on and on, each statement beating against her mind, still ragged from the morning's torture.

"We've already established that we can't wait that long…"

"We'd never make it to the sea…"

"…but if we fought from the forest…"

Iyanka closed her eyes and tried to block it out. It didn't work. Was *anything* being accomplished?

Milek's and Victorin's voices stood out from the rest, as they inserted counters and proposals to the rest of the room. As far as Iyanka could tell, it did nothing. Even their voices were repetitive and grating.

Iyanka needed out. She needed silence, peace…something other than this droning, crushing debate. Iyanka glanced at the sword slowly dripping onto the floor. Her fingers went slack, the sword shattered on the stone floor. The noise didn't even falter. Must *everything* be overly dramatic to draw their attention?

Sighing, Iyanka gathered up the ice and snow in her chest. It had already built to a blinding storm in her chest, pressing against her skin with the panicky need to be free. She pushed away her natural grimace at drawing attention, taking a deep breath. And as she breathed out, she pushed all that ice through her skin and into the air itself, dropping the air to near freezing and sending tiny ice crystals floating through the room. The cacophony ceased.

Iyanka looked up to find every gaze on her. For a panicked moment she couldn't remember what she'd planned to say, frozen under all those eyes. But with another breath, it came back.

"Talking about what is impossible isn't going to get us anywhere," she began. She waited for a response, an argument, but none came. They only stared, shivering. She searched blindly for Victorin's hand, heart easing as his fingers threaded between hers. She dared to meet a few of those gazes as she spoke again.

"You all continue talking about the same matters over and over without moving forward. The same ideas, problems, impossibilities. It's getting us nowhere."

"Then what do you propose we do?" the younger man asked, still rubbing his wrist. "How can we accomplish anything without communication?"

"Talking in circles isn't communication," Iyanka said, growing louder in her exasperation. "You're so busy pointing out what we *can't* do that you haven't given any attention to what we *can*."

"Then tell us, Princess," Thomas said. "What *can* we do?"

His eyes seared her, pushing her to back down. Making her wonder why she'd spoken up in the first place. But Victorin squeezed her hand, and that familiar pressure encouraged her to keep going.

"I don't know much about fighting or leading," she admitted. "I'm no warrior. But I'm *sick* of doing nothing. It's all I've done: cowering in Malchomy's shadows, holding so tight to survival that I never lived."

She glanced around the room, taking in all those faces. "At least if we fight, we'll know we *tried*. We have a *chance* of proving our right to live."

Iyanka knew it was no noble speech, no rousing words to turn hearts and minds. Her hands shook, her voice so quiet it was barely audible. But it had an impact. For several long breaths, the silence she'd created continued unbroken, the occupants of the room staring at Iyanka or turning their eyes to the ground.

The younger man cleared his throat, gaze darting around the room as people turned to him. His eyes eventually locked on Victorin and Iyanka.

"I'm a fire wielder," he said. "And my wife wields wind. We'd be honored if you'd teach us how to combine our elements."

"Thank you," Victorin said, inclining his head toward the man. "Do you know any other couples who might be willing to learn?"

"A few. I'll speak to them this afternoon."

"Come to the palace at sunset, and Iyanka and I will teach you."

The man nodded, glancing around the room again, now with a hint of challenge. A question of what they would say. And after a moment, Achan stepped forward, leaning over the table as he pointed to an area on the map.

"Most of the forces are gathering here. Taking the battle to them, we might be able to use the trees to mask our numbers. Keep a few tricks up our sleeves to guard our retreat."

Milek pressed both hands against the surface of the table, leaning forward. "How much can we set up in a day? The latest we can afford to make our move is day after tomorrow. We can't risk the enchanters arriving early."

"Can we gather our forces in that little time?"

"They're already gathering," Victorin said. "All border scouts are traveling to Agera as we speak. I sent word to most of our forces to begin preparations as soon as I returned."

"What of those who cannot fight?" a woman asked. "Do we leave them defenseless?"

Thomas spoke, voice bitter. "If the hunters reach Agera, no protection will be enough."

"We'll ensure they're as safe as we can make them," Milek said, shooting a reproving glare in Thomas's direction.

The discussion continued in a more productive stream, planning details and battle strategies. Not all strife and argument had disappeared from the conversation, but it didn't overtake the room again. The meeting stretched on for hours and the only real issue came when they discussed where to place the Shacar during the battle. Victorin didn't want them to be on the front lines, or at least he didn't want Iyanka there, but the others argued that at the front is where they'd be the most effective.

Iyanka didn't contribute much to either side. Her knowledge was too limited, and she saw truth in what each side argued. But she also knew how useless she would be on the front lines. She'd already run once, already proved her cowardice. She barely knew how to fight, could barely defend herself. If was placed in the center of a battle, how much of a liability would she become?

But how would she use her ice effectively from so far?

oOo

That evening, as the sun filtered through the trees at an angle that cast long shadows, Iyanka and Victorin gathered the couples who'd come into a garden courtyard near the front of the palace. There were twelve couples, most only a few years older than Iyanka. Represented among them were wielders of fire, ice, wind, and even plant life. There was only one gardener, but even that was a surprise. Iyanka had spent her entire life knowing of no gardener save the trees, and now she'd met two.

"Thank you for coming," Victorin began. "What we're going to teach you is an ancient skill developed by a society known as the Shacar. These wielders bound their elements together to use for the protection of Elnar. We need that protection again, and today we hope to usher in the return of the Shacar."

A wind wielder from the back spoke up, his arm tight around his wife. "If we learn this skill, do we have to join the battle?"

Victorin hesitated. Silently, Iyanka begged him to say no. They didn't have the right to hoard this ability. They didn't have the right to demand these people fight, to say their reason for holding back wasn't enough. *The Shacar weren't only warriors.*

"No, you don't," Victorin said. "But if you stay back, I do ask that you remain in Agera to protect those who cannot fight."

"What do we do?" A fire wielder asked.

Victorin and Iyanka turned to face one another, each raising their hand to press their palms together.

Frost rushed through her arm to the tips of her fingers, seeking the familiar warmth of Victorin's hand. It seemed each time they did this, fire and ice drew closer together. Iyanka struggled to hold it back, waiting for Victorin's cue.

"Place your hands together like this and push your element into your partner's hand at the same time."

Iyanka felt when Victorin activated his flame and allowed her ice to rush to the surface, beginning the path of flaming frost spreading over their skin. She looked over those gathered before them, watched them copy her and Victorin's stance. As she watched, fire flared to life, flames flared blue, or danced wildly in a sudden wind. The others weren't so obvious at first glance. More than one person jerked back when their spouse's element first brushed their hand, but they all kept trying. And within minutes each couple had succeeded, wild forces working together like they were created for that purpose.

"That's good," Victorin said, turning to face them again. Iyanka copied him, holding tight to his hand even as they lowered their arms.

"With us, Iyanka's ice fuels my fire, making it more volatile," Victorin continued. "Your own elements should work together in different ways, depending on their natures."

Iyanka watched closely as the couples gathered before her practiced, experimenting and she suspected playing with how their elements melded together. She was surprised at the ease with which these powers that by nature destroyed each other now combined. When

Victorin first showed her, shock had overridden any other thought. But now she wondered…had the bond already been in place, waiting to be sealed? Was it only present in couples of differing elements? Or might all married wielders bear this secret strength?

But as she stayed close to Victorin, wandering among the couples to lend a hand or answer questions, this wasn't the only realization she came to. She held onto it, dread closing her throat. But as they retreated to overlook the new Shacar, she couldn't hold it in.

"Victorin," she whispered, looking up at him.

"Yes?"

"You have to be with them on the front lines."

He squeezed her hand. "I know."

Iyanka's heart pounded in her throat as she struggled to frame her next words, fought to make them emerge.

"I have to be with you."

He looked away, but Iyanka didn't miss the way his face twisted in pain.

"I know."

Chapter XVII

Iyanka tugged on her arm guard, unused to the feel of the leather armor Captain Waleys had lent her. Then she adjusted the way her new knife hung from her belt. She stood in the front courtyard, watching the frenzy of activity around her as people called out to each other and loaded horses with supplies. It had only been a day since the sorceress attacked her in the garden, yet already they prepared to ride toward an army gathered to destroy them.

"Ready?" Milek asked as she stepped up to her side.

Iyanka looked up at him, doing her best to smile. "I think so."

"Good." He looked her over, eyes taking in the leather bodice and arm guards, the hunter green dress stopping at midcalf, the high leather boots guarding the rest of her legs.

"You look ready for battle," he said.

"Very funny," she grumbled, discreetly adjusting the bodice. "I feel ridiculous."

"You don't look ridiculous. How do you like the shoes?"

Iyanka looked toward her feet. "They aren't terrible. They don't pinch my toes, at least."

"Promise me you won't take them off in the middle of the fight." Milek was smirking.

"I will do no such thing."

Egan rode toward them, mounted on the charger he'd stolen from the hunters. "If you two are finished talking, the plan is to get started *before* nightfall."

"It's barely dawn, Egan," Milek said, still smirking.

"Soon it won't be, if you keep chattering."

"We're on our way."

"Where's Victorin?" Iyanka asked.

"Giving some last instructions to the ones staying here," Egan said. "He told me to get everyone on their horses."

"Iyanka!" Elsie called. Iyanka turned and found her waving from a doorway.

"I'll be back," Iyanka said, running toward Elsie.

"Everything alright?" Iyanka asked.

Elsie's smile wavered. "I'm...I'm staying here."

"Oh."

"I can't fight, and I'm more help here..." Elsie trailed off

Iyanka nodded, not sure what to say. But she opened her arms, and Elsie was quick to grab her in a bone-cracking hug.

"May the Creator protect you," she whispered in Iyanka's ear.

"And you," Iyanka replied.

Elsie took a deep breath before pulling back, fixing Iyanka with a serious look.

"Now show those barons what you're made of."

"I'll try."

She squeezed Iyanka's arms once more before letting go, gesturing toward Milek. "You better go."

Iyanka nodded, backing away before forcing herself to turn toward Milek and run back to where he waited, holding the reins of two horses. One was the war horse she'd ridden to Agera. He waited for her mount and handed her the reins.

"Interesting horse you have," he said as he mounted his own steed.

"I, uh…stole it from a hunter."

Milek laughed, shaking his head. "I *never* would've expected those words to come from your mouth. Life certainly changes."

"Yes, it does."

Victorin rode up on Iyanka's other side, smiling as he watched the siblings. "What's so funny?"

Milek gestured to Iyanka. "You've turned my sister into a horse thief."

Victorin shrugged. "It wasn't all my fault."

"When she was under my care, she wouldn't even raid the kitchen."

"I imagine you did that enough for the both of you."

"Are you really arguing over who corrupted me?" Iyanka asked over Milek's insulted sputtering, trying not to laugh.

"It's a valid question," Milek said.

They continued the conversation as they left the courtyard, leading the long procession out of the city. At first, Iyanka wondered how Victorin and Milek could discuss something so meaningless at a time like this, but as she saw how people watched them she thought she understood. If their leaders could talk and laugh on their way to battle, there must be hope. Victorin and Milek were *giving* them hope.

The conversation fizzled out by the time they reached the crumbling city gate, and Iyanka and the two Princes nodded to the men guarding that entrance. The men on either side bowed deeply to the passing royalty, maintaining that stance until they were well outside the gate. And a cold lump rose in Iyanka's throat at that show of loyalty, of respect. These men knew...they knew they were likely seeing their princes for the last time.

Outside the city, Victorin's captains were waiting with the majority of those who'd chosen to fight. The men parted to allow a path through the middle of their ranks, then fell in behind Milek, Victorin, and Iyanka. The presence of so many people at her back made Iyanka want to squirm, but she squashed the thought and kept her horse between Milek and Victorin.

She knew that somewhere behind her rode Egan, Cook, Gretta, Zef, Henry...all of their band save Elsie. Behind her was the majority of the wielders who'd taken shelter in the crumbling city they were leaving. They all rode toward the very people who'd caused them to flee here, the people who'd stolen away their loved ones and the lives they'd known. Yet they all moved forward, no one turning back or running away. They rode to their possible doom willingly. The least Iyanka could do was ride before them.

Beside her, Milek began humming a familiar tune. It was a song they'd sung as children when they played in the garden, a silly rhyme about the flies that filled the air in the summers. Soon he broke out into song, and it only took a few moments for Iyanka to join in.

"You see them here, you see them there. They fly in your ear, they fly in your hair…"

Soon others joined in, until the end of the song Iyanka's voice was drowned out by dozens of others. There were a few laughs at the end of the song, the singer gagging as he swallows one of the flies. A few heartbeats of near silence, and someone began another song. More joined in, and the pattern continued. They were all silly songs, children's rhymes or ballads designed to amuse and lift peoples' spirits.

Iyanka sang along to as many as she knew and laughed at the rest. Normally the thought of singing where others could hear would mortify her. But for this moment she refused to let that stop her. She sang and sang and grinned when Victorin laughed at her. She wouldn't think about where they were going, about what they would face when they arrived. She'd ride beside her brother and her betrothed like she hadn't a single care. This was her way to offer hope. She only wished it would work for herself.

oOo

An owl hooted in the trees, and Iyanka jerked her head toward the sound. After that initial reaction, her cheeks burned, and she turned her eyes to the fire without meeting the eyes of any of her companions. An arm wrapped around her shoulders, and she leaned into Victorin's side.

"We're safe here," he whispered, his breath on her ear. "We're in thick forest, miles from the edge."

"They have no idea we're here?"

Victorin's jaw brushed her hair. "No. Their camp is quiet."

"And there's no chance the traitor could escape and tell them?"

"I have men assigned to watch him all night. He's not going anywhere."

"Good."

"You should rest," Victorin whispered.

Iyanka shook her head, though her body ached with fatigue. "I won't be able to sleep tonight."

"Try. Please."

"If I close my eyes, everything we're about to face will hit me at once."

Victorin sighed. "Alright."

Iyanka stayed huddled under Victorin's arm, looking around at the spots of light among the trees that marked other fires. Most people had already gone to sleep, but others still spoke to each other in hushed tones as the forest creaked and groaned around them. A few of the people around their own fire still talked, too, but Iyanka didn't listen.

Her eyes drifted closed, and she forced them back open and stared hard at the fire. She didn't want the nightmares that would come with sleep. She'd rather stay awake until dawn. But they drifted closed again, and soon Iyanka couldn't find the will to open them again. Somehow, Victorin's shoulder felt like the softest pillow in the world, and she was powerless as sleep took her.

0O0

A cool breeze drifted through the camp, stirring the last embers of the fire. Iyanka sighed in contentment at the brush of the wind and snuggled deeper into the fabric that smelled like soap and smoke. But something was missing. Where was the warmth that came with that scent?

Iyanka forced her eyes open and lifted herself up on her elbow. She blinked, taking in her dim surroundings. The forest was the gray and back of pre-dawn, with barely enough light to see her surroundings. *Where's Victorin?* He wasn't beside her, though it was his cloak covering her.

She sat up further and searched for any sign of him, her eyes finally latching onto his sleeping form on the other side of the dying fire. Iyanka smiled and pushed her hair from her face. After a moment, she stood and tiptoed around the fire, slowly draping the cloak over him. He barely stirred.

"That's a good man you have," a voice behind her said.

Iyanka whipped around, but relaxed when she saw the older man with smile lines approaching her. He wore a rough medallion around his neck that bore the Creator's symbol, identifying him as a shepherd: a servant of the Creator who guided people in how to follow Theohyios, the Creator's Son.

"Thank you, sir," Iyanka replied.

The shepherd smiled. "You may call me Caleb, Your Highness."

"Only if you call me Iyanka."

"As you wish," he said, inclining his head.

"You know Victorin?"

Iyanka shifted under Caleb's gentle but piercing gaze.

"I do," he said. "I live a few miles south of the forest. Many wielders fleeing to Agera stop at my house for rest and aid, including Prince Victorin."

"Even with the hunters gathering?"

"Are you surprised?" he asked, his expression amused.

"No…no," Iyanka stuttered. "I just, I didn't know so many were willing to go against them…"

"You'll find there are many who see the wrongs of the barons and their hunters, Iyanka. Just because we don't speak out does not mean we don't help."

"I know," Iyanka whispered. "…and thank you."

He bowed his head. "If you have anything you'd like to talk about, I'll be around until you break camp."

"Alright."

Caleb turned away, walking toward another fire where three men were already awake and rekindling the flames.

"You've met Caleb," Victorin said, voice heavy with sleep.

Iyanka turned toward him. He was sitting up and running a hand through his hair, which accomplished nothing but making it messier.

"I did. He's kind."

"One of the kindest men I've met. And one of the bravest."

Iyanka watched Caleb as he went from fire to fire, speaking to people and quietly laughing with them. And an idea sprouted in her mind, a faint whisper that grew the more she considered it. The very thought of voicing it made her shrink back, but she couldn't dismiss it. The idea lodged in the front of her mind and continued to grow there, slowly taking shape.

"What's that look about?" Victorin asked. He was kneeling beside the fire, where the now-blazing embers danced.

"Nothing." Iyanka looked away.

Victorin stood, stepping around the fire to take her hands. "What're you thinking?"

Iyanka bit her lip, warring with herself. Should she say it? *Could* she say it? Part of her wanted to brush it off, pretend the thought had never occurred to her. The other part of her wouldn't let the idea die. She looked down at their entwined hands so she wouldn't have to watch his reaction.

"I was thinking that, with Caleb here…"

Forget it. She couldn't say it.

"Yes?" Victorin prompted.

"I was thinking we…we could get married."

That last bit came out all at once, along with what was left of Iyanka's breath. She kept her eyes firmly on her pale, freckled hands held by Victorin's ruddy ones.

"Iya…"

Iyanka squeezed her eyes shut, willing back the tears. "It's a stupid idea."

"It's not stupid."

But his voice was too gentle, too cautious, for her to believe him.

"Forget I said anything," she whispered.

"Not likely."

Iyanka shook her head. Victorin placed two fingers beneath her chin, tilting her face up so she had to look at him. She considered closing her eyes, but it felt too childish, too cowardly. His dark eyes were soft and warm, but she was worried she saw pity there along with the affection.

"It's not that I don't want to marry you today," he said. "Heavens, I'd love to. But I don't want to take that step out of fear of the future."

The day's battle had been at the back of her mind, but now all that fear and dread roared to life. She did her best to push back thoughts of the fight ahead and focus on Victorin.

"That's not why," she whispered.

Victorin's brow furrowed. "Then tell me why...please."

"Because it's never been possible before," she said, voice cracking. "The barons attacked, I ran away, we had to escape, we had to plan...this is the first time in four years that we've had the option. I don't want to wait any longer."

Victorin was silent for several long moments, and Iyanka worried that he thought her reasoning *was* foolish. She did her best to hold his gaze, but her eyes kept flicking away, afraid of what she'd see.

"Are you sure you want this?"

Iyanka pulled her eyes back to his. *Am I sure?* "Yes."

Victorin's lips spread in a slow smile, low flames flickering in his eyes. "Then let's do it."

Iyanka's heart pounded, ice slipping through her veins, but for once it was excitement making her tremble. Victorin took her hand and they found Caleb, pulling him aside to ask if he'd marry them. The older man listened closely with the occasional nod, then broke into a smile and said he'd be delighted.

That taken care of, Iyanka went in search of Milek and Cook and the rest of their group while Victorin talked to a few others. Iyanka barely managed to explain everything to Milek, her face bright red, but when he laughed with an "It's about time," she relaxed enough to tell the others without as much stumbling.

All throughout, her heart fluttered like a strange bird, with every beat asking herself: was she really doing this? Was she really going to marry Victorin like this, at the edge of fight for their lives? Was she going to wake up beside the fire and realize she'd dreamed it all?

Within an hour, Iyanka stood facing Victorin under the gaze of nearly the entire camp. Somehow the news had spread like wildfire — Iyanka suspected it was Zef's doing — and all of them wanted to watch their commander and princess marry. Iyanka could hardly bear to look at the crowd, but as she sneaked glances she was astonished at the joy and excitement she found there. Maybe this, too, offered them hope:

the joining of two souls, the assurance that life would continue beyond this day.

Looking elsewhere was easier: Milek stood behind Victorin, and Cook, Gretta, and Lynn were nearby as well. Iyanka missed Elsie, wishing her face was among them. Henry and Zef were right at the front: Zef grinning and bounding in his exuberant way, Henry smiling and looking on with approval in a way that warmed Iyanka's heart.

Caleb lifted his arms to silence the already-quiet crowd and began speaking. Iyanka knew what he was saying from the other marriage ceremonies she'd witnessed, but she couldn't hear well over the pounding in her ears. Was this really happening? The feeling of being in a waking dream was starting to wear off, and in its place was panic. She was marrying Victorin. She was making a decision she could never take back. Was she ready for this? She didn't feel ready...

The time came to repeat vows...vows that would seal them together irrevocably in the eyes of the Creator and all else. *Lord, help me.* Could she do this? She locked her eyes on Victorin and concentrated on not hyperventilating.

Victorin's voice came out confident as he recited the ancient vows to love Iyanka above himself, to lead her and protect her. Iyanka continued to send silent prayers to the Creator to give her strength, and when her time came to say the vows a strange peace overtook her, and she recited them with a steady confidence.

When she finished, she took a shaky breath and looked up at Victorin. The ceremony wasn't finished yet. Caleb tied a length of cloth around their wrists, reminiscent of the betrothal ceremony they'd gone through four years earlier. This time, though, the words had changed. Iyanka didn't need to repeat after Caleb this time.

Iyanka and Victorin locked gazes as they spoke in unison.

"Before the Creator and all the eyes of His creation, we are one. Let no man, no will, no power separate what the Lord of All has joined."

Before the last word had faded from Iyanka's lips, searing light enveloped their bound hands. Frosted fire ignited their skin, traveling toward their hearts. And before Iyanka had a chance to react it was in her chest with another blinding flash and stab of pain. She gasped, sent off balance by the sudden shift in her heart. And she looked up at Victorin, his eyes mirroring her own wonder.

Victorin slipped his unbound hand to the back of Iyanka's head, closing the distance between them. Her eyes flickered closed as his lips met hers in a searing heat that she welcomed.

Vaguely, she heard the cheers of the crowd. But her attention was elsewhere. On Victorin, and on the strange sensation dominating her heart. Heat and flame sat in her chest, not in a small chasm sealed away but *everywhere*, mixing impossibly with the cold and snow. At last, she and Victorin were fully and truly bound to one another. Forever.

Chapter XVIII

Iyanka sucked in a ragged breath as she and Victorin emerged from the trees. They'd been in place for over an hour while traps were set and final plans reviewed, but this was her first glimpse of what waited for them outside the forest. It wasn't what she'd expected.

There was no shambled camp, no soldiers going about their morning business unaware. The field beyond the trees was a shimmering sea of armor and pulsing darkness. Strange shadow enveloped them, almost as if the enchantments they bore stole away the light. Ten of the sixteen barons stood at the forefront of the army, elite guards and hunters surrounding them. *Did they know we were coming? Why didn't they attack, then?*

"There's so many," Iyanka whispered.

Victorin squeezed her hand in comfort but didn't reply. Iyanka looked up to see the expression of grim concentration carved on his face. Was he scared, too? Knowing the number of men they fought was one thing; seeing them gathered against them was entirely different. Or was he merely assessing the situation, adjusting plans to their best advantage?

Behind Iyanka, whispers and shifting feet echoed down the people gathering at the uneven line that marked the end of the forest. Bridles jingled as horses shifted, picking up on the fear and nerves surrounding them. Most of their forces were mounted, giving them an edge on the foot soldiers that made up the majority of the barons' armies. Victorin and Iyanka, as well as the rest of the new Shacar, needed to be on the ground to fight best. Iyanka glanced down the line either side of her, finding the couples at regular intervals, facing the barons in the same stance as Victorin and Iyanka.

Iyanka heard low cursing behind her and turned to shoot Milek a disapproving look. He didn't notice: his eyes were fixed on the army facing them.

"They knew we were here," he said, his voice too dead for Iyanka's comfort.

"Yes," Victorin said, his tone matching Milek's. "Thomas escaped to warn them this morning."

"He did?" Milek shook his head, muttering something Iyanka didn't catch. "I knew we should've locked him up in Agera."

Victorin grunted his agreement. "I underestimated his determination."

Iyanka listened in silence, picturing Thomas's hard eyes. She's suspected it was him. But she'd dismissed the notion, assuming someone betraying their own people to ruin would at least be more subtle about it. Apparently, she'd been wrong.

"What's done is done," Victorin said, but the edge in his voice told Iyanka it still bothered him.

"Everyone is ready," Egan announced from behind them.

The old warrior still had a bandage around his shoulder, but he was mounted with a sword in his hand and a scorching glare ready for anyone who suggested he stay back from the fight.

"Give the signal," Milek said.

Egan sounded a three-toned whistle that was repeated down the line. Within a breath, everyone was stepping forward, marching into the field until only the last few lines of their fighters were within the trees. Iyanka and Victorin remained at the front.

It took everything Iyanka had to keep stepping forward, to not shrink back. Her breath was ragged and shallow by the time they stopped, little bits of frost escaping onto the grass and covering her shoes.

The army facing them didn't move right away, though Iyanka could see Malchomy speaking to Wulfguard and the other mounted knights riding near him. Wulfguard glanced Iyanka's way once, and her knees shook. *How can we face this? How can so many people want us dead?* The old voice in her head demanded that she run, told her she couldn't do anything in this place. She should save herself. *But I can't do that.*

Iya," Victorin said, turning toward her. Agony shone in his eyes, agony and deadly resolve. "Stay by my side. No matter what happens, don't let them separate us."

Iyanka nodded, placing all her focus on his words, on his eyes. She couldn't allow fear to control her, not this time. So much more was at stake beyond her own life. *Creator help me,* she prayed. *Give me courage to fight. Please don't let me fail them.*

"I love you," Victorin said, bending down so their foreheads touched. Iyanka ignored the stares from the army across the field and twisted her head up, stealing one more kiss from her husband.

"I love you too."

Victorin grinned, but he didn't have time to say anything.

"They're starting to move," Milek said.

Iyanka looked up in time to see the mounted knights leave the barons and take up positions along the line of foot soldiers. Wulfguard stayed at Malchomy's side, joining his master in staring out over the wielders with contempt.

"Are you ready?" Victorin asked.

No. Iyanka took a deep breath. "Yes."

Victorin held tight to her hand, calling on his flame. Iyanka felt the fire respond, roaring in her chest, separated from her own blizzard by a thin, easily penetrated barrier. She marveled at that fierce heat as she drew from her frost and ice, filling her heart with numbing cold. The contrasting elements licked at that thin barrier, and with a nod from Victorin she pushed through. She couldn't help her small gasp as that wall evaporated, snow rushing to meet molten fire, frozen flame blazing in her veins. Victorin's grip on her hand tightened.

The melded elements concentrated where their skin met, and she didn't have to look down to know that frost and flame were coating their skin, blazing with a pure light bright enough for the barons and their army to see.

In front of them, soldiers shifted and leaned to whisper among themselves. Some even took a stuttering step back as Iyanka and Victorin set their elements blazing. Apparently, the barons hadn't told their armies what they'd be facing. Perhaps there was hope that they'd stand down. Perhaps Victorin's proposal wouldn't just be for show.

Victorin and Iyanka stepped forward, walking across the field side by side, their hands intertwined and their steps effortlessly synchronized. As they approached their enemies, Iyanka searched the faces before her, gauging their reactions. She didn't find the disgust she feared.

Ald stood next to the barons, watching Iyanka with an indecipherable expression. Iyanka quickly looked away as his dark gaze caused the pool of dread in her stomach to spread, threatening to smother the lively flames.

She focused instead on the feel of Victorin at her side, his hand holding hers, his fire swirling within her. She concentrated on that miracle of fire and ice, forces that only the Creator held under total control, bound together and answering their command. Not by dark powers drawn from evil, not by coercion, but entrusted to them. And that dread slowly receded as they stopped halfway between the barons and their own people behind them.

"Come to surrender?" Malchomy called mockingly.

"Would you let us live if we had?" Victorin asked.

A few barons sneered, others wore masks of indifference. Malchomy scratched his chin, appearing to consider it. "No. But I might give you a less painful death."

Those who had sneered laughed or glared, but Iyanka watched as those indifferent masks cracked, as the men who wore them winced or looked away. And a flicker of hope whispered that maybe those barons weren't as hardened against the wielders as it seemed.

"We've come to ask you to consider what you're doing," Victorin called, his voice spreading over the entire army before them.

"We've come to rid Elnar of an abomination," Baron Leon answered.

"You call us abominations, but our power is given by the Creator Himself. Yours is taken by bloodshed and darkness, given to you by servants of evil."

"If you're seeking mercy for your people, you're failing fire prince," Malchomy growled.

"I don't seek mercy because I know you'd give none," Victorin replied, a fierce edge to his voice as their hands flared. "You're gathered as if to face an army, but you will be killing desperate people defending their lives. You'll fight warriors, but also farmers, merchants, servants, and families. *You* seek power, we fight only for the right to live in peace."

Victorin's voice reverberated with righteous fury, making Iyanka stand taller, daring to meet the eyes of the men watching them. Malchomy's face twisted in anger and arrogance.

"You paint your people as bleeding lambs, but too many of our people have died in your petulant squabbles. None of these men will turn back as long as the lives of their families are at stake."

Though phrased as a righteous defense, Malchomy growled that last sentence as a threat. Iyanka didn't need Victorin to explain the double meaning: Iyanka could see the pain and fear on the soldiers' faces. *How many? How many of these men are here only because Malchomy holds their families to coerce them?*

She turned her eyes to Malchomy. He met her gaze with a smirk, but for once it didn't fill her with fear. Now she was angry. *Is there no line you won't cross? Is there no life you won't take for your own selfish goals?*

A whistle echoed across the field, signaling that the last of their militia was in place. The distraction had served its purpose; it was time to begin the fight. And a wash of panic overtook Iyanka's fury. *We can't fight yet...we can't fight without giving these men another choice.* They had to show them that they didn't *have* to bow to evil.

"Victorin, wait," she whispered, turning toward him and grabbing his other wrist.

"What is it?"

"If Malchomy is threatening their families, that means not all of them want to fight us. What if they will fight *with* us?"

"Iya, they wouldn't be here if they didn't want to fight."

Iyanka shook her head. *You don't know…you don't know how completely fear can rule.*

"Victorin, please."

He stared at her for the briefest moment before nodding. She smiled her thanks and turned back to the army, keeping her eyes on the soldiers rather than the barons. It was them she needed to address.

"I know what it's like," she called. Her voice was quieter than Victorin, but she took a breath and tried again. "I know what it's like to be ruled by fear. I know what it is to live every day wondering if it's your last, to serve the very men who would end your life."

"Don't listen to this vixen," Wulfguard ordered.

"I'm proof that you have another choice!" Iyanka shouted, drowning out Wulfguard's orders. "Take a coward's testimony: you *can* choose to stand, to fight for what's *right.* There's *freedom* in fighting for right, even if you die."

Iyanka's voice broke on that final word, the pounding of her heart accepting that this might be her final hour. But determination stood alongside the dread that plagued her. Live or die, she wouldn't give into these men. Not today. Not ever again.

Iyanka watched and waited as silence engulfed the field. Shifting armor, a lonely cough, were the only sounds. No one moved, though they all stared. *Am I wrong, then?* She saw Victorin raise his arm to give the final signal, and she didn't try to stop him.

But before he could, Ald and his horse lunged forward, toward Victorin and Iyanka. He drew his sword as he rode, his face grim. Victorin stepped in front of

Iyanka with his own sword drawn, but as the hunter neared them he wheeled his horse around and stopped, his *back* to Victorin and Iyanka.

"I will stand with them," Ald, shouted, tossing his enchanted weapon to the ground, drawing a second blade from his saddle.

While everyone stared at Ald in varying levels of shock and fury, over two dozen men broke from the ranks as well. They backed toward Iyanka and Victorin, tossing their enchanted weapons on the ground.

"Traitors," Malchomy snarled. "Any who try joining them will find a knife in their back."

"Prepare to attack," another knight shouted. The soldiers drew their weapons, shifting their stance.

"Get behind us," Victorin ordered.

Thankfully, their new allies listened, running toward the rest of the wielder army.

The foot soldiers began their charge. A zing of fear and thrill shot through her at the fact that they were headed for *her*. But rather than shrink back, she channeled that dread into the frozen fire that had been building within her throughout their conversation, drawing thick ropes of it and directing the rush through her fingertips. Still holding Victorin's hand, she crouched and pressed her hand to the soil, pushing frosted fire into earth, rock, and grass. Victorin was already throwing shards of flaming ice at the approaching soldiers when Iyanka's efforts revealed itself.

Spikes of ice rose from the ground all along the battle line, igniting with lethal flame as soon as ice touched air. The spikes grew as tall as Victorin as

Iyanka fed them beneath the soil, freezing the ground to use as a channel. The spires weren't close enough to stop the soldiers from coming through, but it certainly slowed them down. The soldiers soon discovered that, rather than dying away, the blue flame *leaped* at anyone bearing an enchanted weapon. More than one cast their weapon to the ground to avoid those grasping flames.

The barrier in place, Iyanka and Victorin backed toward the trees, their makeshift army surging forward to meet them. The Shacar were assembled a few steps ahead of everyone else, already putting their power to use. Those who made it through the barrier were met with fire, wind, ice, and tree roots attacking them with the same fury as the frozen flames they'd just escaped.

But there were too many for the Shacar to stop them all. Soon the air was filled with the sounds of battle: clanging metal, shouts, screams of pain… Iyanka was surrounded by pure chaos. She tried to create a path to the barrier of ice spikes, but someone attacked them too often for Iyanka to keep her connection stable. Victorin stood before her, sword covered in flaming ice, not hesitating to cut down any man who attacked them. Bodies fell around her, screams ringing through the air, blood crystallized in crimson frost covering the ground. The smell of death made her gag.

Victorin slit a man's throat and his body fell toward her. Iyanka shrieked and leaped aside, breaking her connection with the wall and exposing herself to the enemy.

Victorin was already in another fight, so the next soldier approached Iyanka freely. She scrambled backwards. His two daggers bled darkness, his movements too calculated for the foot soldiers who'd rushed them so far. *A hunter.*

Iyanka rose to her feet and drew her dagger, her hands shaking so badly she nearly dropped the blade. Frost and blue flames coated the blade without conscious effort, but the hunter barely blinked at her strange weapon. He leaped toward her, slashing at her chest. Iyanka avoided the attack by leaping back, but then he attacked with the other knife. She parried with her own knife. As the dark alloy met her blade, the fire leapt and pushed the weapon aside. But the hunter remained unaffected. Another joint attack, this time toward her other side. Iyanka jumped back again, tripping over a body and crashing to the earth. Iyanka threw her arm across her face, unable to watch his final attack.

But Victorin jumped between them, stabbing the hunter in the gut. The man's hand seemed frozen in the air as his face contorted, and Victorin shoved him to the ground. He turned to face yet another soldier, as Iyanka stared at the hunter's body as frost crawled across his prone form.

"Iya," Victorin shouted, pushing back a young man who'd rushed him. "Stay behind me."

Iyanka rushed to his side, but it was obvious that staying behind him wasn't enough. The barons' forces had penetrated their lines far beyond where Iyanka and Victorin stood. There was fighting all around them, men attacking them from all directions. And for the first time since the battle began, Iyanka's mind cleared enough to assess herself: the pool in her chest was smaller, coming more reluctantly and less potently. If they kept expending power like this, how long until they ran out? Did they have a choice?

"The wall!"

Iyanka turned in time to see the columns topple under an unseen force: weakened ice shattering, flames extinguishing. Malchomy stood on the other side, his hand raised and his lips stretched in a smug grin. Iyanka watched as he pulled his hand into a fist, and another blast of unseen power rushed across the field. Slick darkness and anger coated her like oil. She choked and fell to her knees, people all around her succumbing as well. Victorin managed to stay standing, but he staggered, barely deflecting the next attack.

Iyanka screamed as the hunter's blade found Victorin, opening a slice on his shoulder. But the wound barely slowed Victorin as he brought his blade up, knocking the soldier's sword from his hand. The soldier soon laid among the bodies surrounding them, and Iyanka ran to Victorin's side. She forced ice and fire through her boots and feet, creating a small circle of protection for them both. But when she grabbed his arm to see how bad he was injured, all she found was slit cloth and red-tinged frost spreading from a thin line. Ice had sealed the wound.

"Malchomy's a sorcerer," Victorin said, breathing haggard.

Iyanka looked up, finding Malchomy as he stalked across the battlefield. Any wielder who tried to fight him was sent to their knees with a flick of his hand, left for the men following him to kill. His gaze never left her and Victorin.

"He's coming for us," she said.

"I know."

Victorin straightened, lifting his sword again and grabbing Iyanka's hand. "I'll keep his attention on me, and you trap his feet."

Iyanka nodded and clung to Victorin's hand. Rather than wait, Victorin stepped toward Malchomy, and Iyanka followed close to his side. They stopped a few dozen steps away, but Malchomy kept coming, and Iyanka's pounding heart dulled the noise surrounding her. She reached into the well of ice and fire, dragging up as much as she could at a time as Malchomy stopped.

"You aren't the only one seeking arcane powers," he said, looking at his hand.

Why is he talking? What's he stalling for? But she didn't call his bluff. It gave them more time. If only she didn't have these smothering boots on!

"Ours won't destroy us," Victorin replied. He also drew on their shared power, reigniting his sword. Malchomy barely glanced at the weapon.

"We'll see," he said.

He lashed out.

A great weight fell on Iyanka. She was pushed to her knees, one hand pressed to the ground to steady herself. But she couldn't take advantage of it, couldn't reach her ice to push into the earth. She managed to turn her head and see Victorin in a similar position, his head up as he glared at Malchomy. Iyanka reached out and snagged his hand. Their power flared at the contact, and the weight began to lift. They rose to their feet together.

Malchomy only watched, a calculating look to his eyes. *Why didn't he attack? Is he testing us?*

The force hit them again, pushing them apart. Iyanka braced herself and only fell to one knee. Victorin managed to stay standing, just barely. They were too far apart to touch, but with a flare in their chest the weight again lifted. She stood.

"How interesting," Malchomy said, starting to circle them. Iyanka watched with dread, waiting for his next attack. *Why is he toying with us?*

"Is there a point to this?" Victorin asked. "Or are you stalling?"

Malchomy's mouth curled into a sneer. "I don't fear you, *Prince Victorin*. I killed your father. You think I can't kill you?"

Iyanka glanced to Victorin, finding his face closed off with concentration. Had he known? He must have. *Oh, Victorin…*

She finally remembered what she was supposed to be doing and began sending ice into the ground. What ice she had left struggled to penetrate the leather of her shoes, frost gathering on the surface instead of pushing into the ground like she wanted. She needed to *touch* the ground, bare skin against the earth.

"I am not my father," Victorin said. He took a step toward Malchomy, putting himself between the baron and Iyanka.

"No, you're softer. An easy target."

Another blast of that oppressive weight over-whelmed her, but this time it surrounded her, pressing her arms to her sides, rendering her motionless. The same happened to Victorin, but he broke free...just in time to deflect an attack from Wulfguard on his right. Wulfguard pulled back and snarled, attacking Victorin again.

Meanwhile, Malchomy slowly stalked toward Iyanka like a cat toying with its prey. Iyanka broke free from the invisible bonds, but she couldn't reach for the ground now. Bending down would practically be an invitation to kill her.

Instead, Iyanka pulled her leg up and tugged on the leather boot, hopping around ridiculously to keep her balance. Malchomy took advantage of her distrac-tion and lunged forward, sword poised to run her through. But Iyanka dodged in time to avoid him. He turned and came for her again, and Iyanka threw her boot in his face. She scrambled to the side as he roared his fury.

With one foot bare against the ground, Iyanka went to work while she danced to avoid Malchomy's exceptionally deadly looking sword. Sending ice to-ward him while constantly shifting her feet was nearly impossible, but she didn't give up. She couldn't give up now. Malchomy hadn't taken the boot to the face well, and he was more frustrated in his attacks than she would've expected. But she was shaking so hard, her blood surging with adrenaline, that she couldn't take advantage of it. All she could do was stay out of reach.

Achan appeared suddenly, darting in after one of Malchomy's sweeping attacks to slice through the baron's arm. Malchomy roared in rage and attacked Achan, giving Iyanka the chance to run…but Victorin was still battling Wulfguard, and she knew…she knew Achan couldn't defeat Malchomy. He was already wounded, blood seeping from his side between the fingers he pressed there. As she wavered, Malchomy swept his sword, sending Achan's blade flying. Achan backed away a step, but he made no attempt to flee. Malchomy raised his sword…

Iyanka jumped forward with her dagger raised, aiming for Malchomy's exposed side, his back, anything that would stop his strike. But a wave of power knocked her to the ground. She looked up only to see Malchomy run Achan through. A choked cry made it past her frozen lips as Achan slumped, eyes glazed with mindless pain.

Malchomy turned toward Iyanka, sword dripping red. She pushed up, trying to scramble away. He was on her in an instant. He grabbed her by the hair and yanked her to her feet, dropping his sword in favor of a dagger he placed at her throat.

The dagger's dark magic pressed against her, threatening to choke her. But with horror she realized that same suppressive darkness emanated from Malchomy. The same force imbued in the weapon had just tossed her to the ground like a doll. Malchomy was no sorcerer.

"You had the Ecleathians enchant *you*," she choked out.

"Clever, isn't it?" Malchomy said. "They warned about…side effects. But I'm finding it's worth it."

He pressed the dagger closer to her throat as he spoke, shifting his grip from her hair to her neck. With that grip, he forced her to turn where to watch Victorin, still fighting Wulfguard. Both men showed the strain of the drawn-out fight, as they circled each other with weary eyes. Victorin was limping, and blood dripped into Wulfguard's eyes from a nasty looking cut.

"Let's watch, shall we?" Malchomy whispered, making her shudder.

Wulfguard lashed out at Victorin. Victorin blocked the attack, but he didn't recover quickly enough. Wulfguard followed the attack with a kick to Victorin's knee, sending him to the ground. Wulfguard was poised to attack again. A scream rose to Iyanka's lips, choked back by the dagger's pressure.

Ald jumped into the fray, slashing at Wulfguard's back between pieces of armor. The knight howled and spun, a wild swing of his sword forcing Ald to leap back. But he leaped forward again to attack Wulfguard, his movements fast despite the cuts and scrapes covering him.

"Traitor," Wulfguard snarled, slashing at Ald.

"Then prove me wrong," Ald replied, blocking the attack. He backed away from Victorin, and Wulfguard followed with rage in his eyes.

Ald's distraction had bought Victorin enough time. He stood, turning to face Malchomy. He found Iyanka and froze, the light dying from his eyes.

"Attack, and she dies," Malchomy said. "Surrender, and she'll live. At least for a while."

"Don't even *think*—" Iyanka's words were cut off when Malchomy pressed the dagger closer to her skin. Victorin stared at her, tortured. His eyes never left hers. He lowered his sword.

"*No*," Iyanka choked out. He couldn't surrender. Not for her. She tried to plead silently, to beg him not to give in. But he shook his head. Her heart plummeted.

Victorin dropped his weapon, raising both his hands, shoulders slumped in defeat. He turned his gaze to Malchomy. And as he moved, Iyanka glimpsed the slashed fabric on his sleeve, the wound still sealed together with ice.

"You win," Victorin said. "Let her go."

The knife on Iyanka's throat only pressed closer.

"Call your men to surrender, first."

Ideas spun in Iyanka's mind: too fast, too panicked. They couldn't lose. Not because of her. The knife, the dark power, the ice sealing the cut…

Iyanka reached deep in her heart, praying as she dragged up what ice and flame was left at her disposal, forcing it through her veins. She saw Victorin's horror just as she dug her fingernails into Malchomy's arm.

She sent all her power into his skin, deep into flesh and bone. Ice froze his veins, flame ignited his skin, traveling through his arm, neck, chest. He stiffened in silent agony, causing a line of smothering darkness to slice across her neck as she froze his heart.

Chapter XIX

Iyanka pushed at Malchomy's arm, fighting to force the knife as far from her throat as she could even as his body slumped to the ground, taking her with. The pain in her neck was fierce. The ice in her veins escaped with her blood, sealing the cut closed, stopping the blood flow even as the pain sharpened.

"Iya," Victorin cried.

Before Iyanka could disentangle herself from Malchomy's body, he was there, pulling her into his arms.

"I'm alright," she croaked, grabbing his hand as he tried to cover what should've been a bleeding wound.

"You're not," he said, voice strangled as he took in the frost-covered wound.

"The cut isn't deep."

She tried to stand, failing when Victorin refused to let go of her. For a moment she held still, pressing into the warmth of his trembling arms. Allowing herself the comfort of his safety after such a close brush with death. But the sounds of battle still surrounded them.

"We can't stay here like this," she said.

Reluctantly, Victorin stood, helping Iyanka to her feet. He supported most of her weight, one arm still tight around her as he took up his sword again.

"We need to get you away from the fighting," Victorin said.

A soldier rushed toward them. Victorin raised his sword, shielding Iyanka, but the man never reached them. Roots exploded from the ground, encasing the man in a single breath. The man screamed as the roots tightened, and Iyanka looked away as Victorin led her toward the forest.

"You two shouldn't be here," Victorin growled.

Zef and Henry ran up to them, the boys flanking Victorin and Iyanka as they moved toward the trees.

"You needed help," Zef said. "We couldn't stay in the trees and do *nothing*."

"He was trying to kill Princess Iyanka," Henry said, as if that explained everything.

They continued through the chaos toward the trees, weaving around fallen men from both sides and dodging fights. Few enemies tried attacking, and those who did were quickly taken out by Henry and his tree roots. Turning her head pulled at her wound, making it throb, but Iyanka did her best to take in what was happening in the battle.

The ground was littered with bodies of men and horses, the grass trampled and burned. The wielders were holding their own in the fight, but exhaustion lined every face she saw and the soldiers kept coming. Four of the Shacar were surrounding Baron Leon on his horse. He fought against them frantically, his sword slashing across a woman's chest. Iyanka spotted Ald still fighting, with *Gretta*, of all people, at his side. Everywhere she looked was blood, her ears rang with the screams and moans of agony, her nose assaulted with the smell of sweat and blood and death...

Why wasn't it stopping? Malchomy was dead…wasn't he the overall leader of their forces? Why was everyone still fighting?

Iyanka stopped, forcing Victorin to stop beside her. Zef and Henry paused as well, looking up at Iyanka with confusion.

"It's not stopping," she said, looking to Victorin.

"Princess, we need to get you away from here," Henry urged as Zef grabbed her hand and tried to lead her toward the trees. She kept her feet planted and stared at Victorin. He met her gaze steadily, his expression pained.

"The battle isn't over yet," he said.

"Then why are we going to the trees?"

What am I saying? The chaos, the death all around her sickened her. Her body screamed for her to escape, to get away from this horror-scape. *But we're not finished yet.*

"You're hurt," Victorin said.

"So are you."

"Iya…"

Seeing the pain in his eyes, she nearly gave in. But she shook her head.

"I'm not running away. We're going to fight together until we end this."

Victorin wanted to argue, Iyanka could *feel* it. But he didn't. Instead, he pulled two knives from his belt and handed one to her.

"Henry, Zef," he said. "Either get back to cover or stay close to us."

"Yes, sir," both boys chorused as they took up a position on Iyanka's left.

"Wait," Iyanka said when Victorin started forward. She unwrapped her arm from around him long enough to tug off her other boot so both her feet were bare. Walking barefoot across the battlefield was likely foolish, but it would give her closer access to the ground. And she wouldn't be hopping awkwardly in one shoe.

"I thought I told you to keep your shoes on!" Milek shouted as he ran toward them, hair flopping in his face. His clothes and arms were covered in dirt and blood, sweat made tracks down his face, but he moved unhindered.

"I said I made no promises," Iyanka replied, taking in his uninjured appearance with a silent thanks to the Creator.

Milek stopped in front of them, his eyes instantly finding the frosted cut on Iyanka's throat.

"You're injured?" he asked, glancing to Victorin.

"It's nothing," Iyanka said, but she was drowned out by Victorin.

"Malchomy's doing, while she froze him solid."

Milek whistled, looking back to Iyanka with pride and mingled concern. "Nice, Raspberry. How bad is it?"

"I'm fine."

Milek looked over her once more as Henry captured another assailant in a cage of roots behind them. Milek didn't acknowledge the man's screams, turning to Victorin.

"Leon, Saxony, and Richard are dead. Torock and Bartram are nowhere to be found."

"That makes six gone with Malchomy dead. What about the other four?"

"Still fighting over there," Milek gestured to their left, where four barons were fighting atop their horses, guards all around them. "But they're acting scared. Some of their forces have started running."

Victorin looked to Iyanka. "Are you strong enough to surround them?"

Iyanka nodded, wincing at the sting it caused.

"Good. Let's go."

The five of them made their way toward the last of the barons. Few soldiers attacked them on their way, and those who did were taken down or scared off by Milek and Victorin. Henry and Zef stayed at Iyanka's side and watched for attackers, though none of them came. Most of the barons' forces still alive seemed to be gathering to their leaders or fleeing.

The reached the thick of the fighting, where a perimeter of wielders fought the soldiers surrounding the remaining barons and guards. At the edge of the fighting they stopped. Milek, Henry, and Zef warded off would-be attackers as Iyanka and Victorin joined hands. Victorin raised their joined hands, their frosted fire serving as a beacon, as Iyanka sent ice and flame through her feet to ignite the ground. Men jumped back as the path spread to surround the majority of the remaining soldiers. It was no wall of ice spikes, but their enemies were wary of the flame nonetheless.

"Baron Malchomy is dead," Milek shouted. "Blood from both our peoples stains the ground. Surrender now, and we'll let you return to your lands in peace."

The soldiers continued to back away from the blue flame, defeat lining each of their faces. They separated as the barons rode toward the edge of the circle to face Milek, Victorin, and Iyanka. Baron Joktan led them.

"What are your terms?" Joktan asked, voice heavy.

"Relinquish all weapons and enchanted items, and order your men to stand down while we negotiate."

Joktan glanced back at the others, but they said nothing. And slowly, Joktan dismounted his horse and drew his weapon, dropping it to the ground in front of him. Iyanka watched as the other barons followed suit, and soon the air was ringing with the sound of weapons being cast to the ground by the remaining soldiers.

She and Victorin maintained the wall of flame until all of them had surrendered, though Iyanka swayed on her feet by the end. By the time the frost melted from the grass, the soldiers were being marched away toward their camp, where they'd be kept prisoner until negotiations were finished. Iyanka's silent question of what they'd do with their wounded went unanswered, as they left the battlefield with hardly a backward glance.

Milek and Victorin, accompanied by as many unwounded wielders as they could spare, followed the captive army. But Victorin didn't let Iyanka come, insisting she stay and rest. She wanted to object, but knew better. She'd be a liability to him right now, tired as she was. So she watched Victorin and Milek as long as she could, as Zef and Henry pulled her to where more of their people, including Cook and Lynn, were already tending to the wounded just inside the trees.

Cook rushed over and started clucking over her, scolding Iyanka for getting herself hurt.

"What happened to you?" Cook asked, tilting Iyanka's head back to get a better look at the cut. Iyanka couldn't answer with Cook's hand on her chin, so she waited until Cook released her and raised her eyebrows, waiting for an answer.

"Malchomy had a knife to my throat," Iyanka said. "When he died, he fell and the knife cut me."

"You're lucky, girl. Much deeper and you would've bled out."

"Cook," Lynn called. "I need help."

Iyanka and Cook turned toward Lynn holding a blood-soaked cloth to a young man's side. Cook whipped around and pointed at Iyanka.

"Don't do anything to open that wound, you hear?"

"I won't," Iyanka promised.

Cook nodded and rushed over to Lynn. Iyanka looked around at the people surrounding them. Too many had gruesome injures that she could hardly bear to look at, all of their faces twisted in pain. The few un-injured fighters who didn't accompany Milek and Victorin were searching the battlefield for survivors, but Iyanka could see they didn't even look at the fallen soldiers. There were no men from the other side searching, either.

"How're you doing, Iyanka?" Zef asked, appearing at her side from nowhere.

"Better than most," Iyanka answered, eyes still on the bloodstained field. "Zef, is there anyone searching for survivors among the barons' soldiers?"

"I don't think so," he answered cautiously. "They're the reason everyone here is hurt. I don't think anyone feels like helping them."

Henry appeared at her other side, shoving an unfamiliar pair of shoes toward her hands.

"Put these on," he ordered.

"Where…"

"Don't think about it. Just put them on."

Iyanka was too tired to argue. She slipped the shoes on her feet, taking in with a resigned sigh that they were too tight across her toes.

When she looked up again, Iyanka spotted one man in a hunter's armor struggling to stand, one arm hanging limp from a shoulder wound. None of his compatriots were in sight to help him, and all the wielders were keeping their distance. *He'll try to kill me.* Iyanka stood.

"Henry, Zef, will you help me with something?

"You want to help that hunter," Zef guessed.

"Yes."

"That's not a good idea, Princess," Henry said. "He's not on our side."

"I still want to help him."

Henry and Zef looked at each other, then nodded as they came to a silent agreement.

"We'll help you," Zef said.

"Only stay behind us, Princess," Henry said. "So we can protect you."

Iyanka placed a hand on each boy's shoulder. "I'm not letting either of you get hurt for me."

"We won't get hurt," Zef said, already walking toward the soldier. "We just want you to be careful."

Iyanka rushed to catch up to Zef, Henry staying by her side. They walked side by side toward the hunter. They were only a few steps away when the hunter saw them. He drew a knife from his belt and brandished it at them, his face ashen as blood continued to drip from his shoulder. Iyanka stopped.

"Come to finish me off, witch?" the man asked, his voice weak despite his harsh words.

"Don't call her a witch," Zef said, taking a small step forward.

Iyanka grabbed Zef's arm to stop him, afraid the hunter would attack. She didn't want any of them within his reach. Each beat of her heart made her head pound, and too late she realized she was too weak to summon enough ice to save them should this man attack. *This was a bad idea.* But she couldn't leave him now.

"We've come to help you," Iyanka said softly. Strange how what bravery she'd found during the battle was brushed away by a single injured man.

"You're *helping* me?" he scoffed. "I hunted your people like beasts."

"You're losing too much blood to make it to your camp," Henry said, voice steady and matter of fact. "If you want to live, you'll take her offer."

The hunter stared at them, arm shaking as he continued pointing the knife at them. His stance was aggressive, but Iyanka could see the fear in his eyes. *Is he afraid of* me?

"I can't hurt you," Iyanka said. She held up her hand and tried drawing up ice. What frost she could summon to her palm melted in seconds.

"See?" Iyanka said, turning her gaze back to the hunter, trying to ignore how stupid she was being. "I couldn't even frost your clothes. I just want to help."

"Would I be your prisoner?"

Iyanka bit her lip. She didn't know what Victorin and Milek would do with him.

"I don't know," she admitted.

The man nodded, looking down at his knife. "I don't have much choice, do I?"

Before Iyanka could respond, he'd tossed his knife away and raised his good hand. His other arm remained at his side; Iyanka wasn't sure if he *could* move it.

Henry stepped forward, swinging the man's uninjured arm over his shoulder to take some of the man's weight. The man sagged, head hanging as Henry led him toward Iyanka.

"You should go ahead and explain," Henry said. "Zef and I will help get him there."

Iyanka hesitated. The hunter didn't look like he had another way to hurt them, but Iyanka didn't like the idea of leaving the two boys alone with a hunter. Then again, what could *she* do if the man did attack? She shouldn't have gotten the boys involved. What was she even doing, helping a man who'd killed her people?

Because he's a person too. Because I know the fear in his eyes. Iyanka turned and ran toward the makeshift infirmary before she could second guess herself.

"Cook," she called, searching for the older woman among the busyness around her.

"What is it? Cook asked, striding toward her as she wiped her hands clean of blood. "Did you hurt yourself?"

"No, I'm fine," Iyanka said, wincing as she searched for a way to explain. "I…I found someone who needs help."

Get him over here and I'll see what I can do."

"He's coming."

Iyanka gestured to where Henry and Zef were helping the hunter across the field. Even from this distance Iyanka could see that Henry was supporting most of the man's weight as they stumbled toward the trees.

"What are you thinking?" Cook hissed. "He's one of them."

"He's too weak to hurt anyone," Iyanka said. "He can barely stand."

"And when he's stronger? Do you want him to slaughter us in our sleep?"

"Please," Iyanka pleaded. "He's losing too much blood. He'll die without help."

Cook's faced softened for an instant as her eyes went back to the hunter, but her voice stayed hard. "He's better off dead. For all our sakes."

Iyanka started to protest, but Cook turned away and went back to the others. Iyanka glanced between her retreating back and the hunter, at a loss.

"I'll help him," Gretta said, pushing away from where she leaned against a tree. Her face was paler than usual, and she had a bandage around her left arm, but her expression was as fierce as ever. Iyanka stared at her a moment, shocked she'd be willing to help where Cook refused. But she didn't question.

"Thank you," Iyanka said as the two woman walked to meet Henry and Zef with the hunter.

When they reached the trio, Gretta instructed Henry and Zef and set him down against a tree. She knelt at his side, digging through a pack of medical supplies Iyanka hadn't noticed.

"Who are you?" the hunter groaned, wincing as she pulled the fabric of his shirt back from his wound.

"My name is Gretta," she said, not taking her eyes from her work.

"I assume you're a friend of the princess."

"Yes."

Gretta didn't offer up any more information, and the hunter didn't ask any more questions. His eyes flicked all around, looking anywhere but at the blood coating his right side.

"What's your name?" Iyanka asked.

"Peyton Aldrige," he said, gasping as Gretta pressed a clean cloth to his shoulder to stop the bleeding.

Gretta leaned back, still pressing the bandage to his shoulder.

"You're kidding me. *You're* Peyton Aldrige?"

The man nodded, his eyes guarded. Iyanka watched the interaction in confusion. The name sounded familiar, but she had no idea why it was significant.

"I don't understand," Iyanka whispered, glancing at Henry and Zef. Henry shrugged, but Zef was staring at the hunter with a thoughtful expression.

"Aren't you the commander of Baron Algheny's soldiers?"

The man nodded as Gretta snorted.

"And the leader of his hunters," she added. "Not to mention his nephew and heir."

Iyanka stared at the man in horror. Of all the hunters she could've helped, he was perhaps the most dangerous in all of Elnar. A ghost of a smile crept across Peyton's face as he took in Iyanka's expression.

"You didn't know?" he asked.

Iyanka shook her head. That seemed to amuse him even more.

"I assumed it was why you approached me."

"I just saw that you needed help," Iyanka said, choked.

Peyton nodded, turning to look over the field of fallen. People still searched among them, but they brought fewer back. Some looked like they were beyond hope.

Gretta shifted the bandage, leaning back.

"It isn't slowing. I need to cauterize it. Do you have a knife on you?"

Iyanka reached to the dagger Victorin had given her, but before she could draw it Peyton had pulled a small knife from his boot. Gretta took it with raised eyebrows.

"You didn't think to *disarm* the hunter?" she asked, already heating the metal in her hand.

Iyanka stared at the small knife. She hadn't considered that he would have other weapons. She met Peyton's eyes and realized he was smiling again.

"Your innocence is why I decided to trust you."

"Thank the Creator you didn't take advantage of it," Gretta muttered. She pulled a stick from her bag and handed it to Peyton. "Bite down on this."

"Wait," Peyton said, his eyes still on Iyanka. "Are you willing to help the other men out there?"

"Of course."

Peyton pulled something from his uniform and held it out.

"Show this to anyone you find and mention my name. They should come with you after that."

Iyanka reached to take it, but he didn't let go.

"Take others with you," he said. "Not all of them will come peacefully."

"I don't know who I would take," Iyanka admitted.

Gretta sighed, pointing to a group of trees as she turned to Iyanka. "Ald is back there resting. He'll help you."

"Ald?" Iyanka repeated, glancing toward the trees in trepidation. "I don't know…"

"He's not who you think. You'll be fine." Gretta turned back to Peyton. "Now bite down on that so I can stop the bleeding *before* you pass out."

This time Peyton obeyed. Iyanka was quick to turn away so she didn't have to watch Gretta work. She paused at the edge of the trees Gretta had indicated, hands in fists as she warred with herself. Ald had fought *with* them. He'd saved Victorin from Wulfguard. Gretta *knew* him...so why did the idea of facing him still make her tremble?

"Princess?" Henry asked, resting his hand on her arm. "What's wrong?"

"Ald is the hunter who found out Iyanka is the ice princess," Zef explained.

"But today he fought on our side," Henry said. "Why would he betray you to the barons if his allegiance is with us?"

"I don't know," Iyanka said.

"Are we sure he can be trusted?" Henry asked.

"I trust Gretta. And he helped Victorin."

Zef grabbed Iyanka's hand. "Then we'll ask for his help and be careful."

Henry was already on her other side, and the boys flanked her like guards.

"We won't let anything happen to you," Henry said gravely.

Iyanka smiled at his assurance, grateful for their encouragement. Grateful for their presence at her side. They stayed close to her as they entered the forest, Iyanka sweeping her eyes across the landscape to find

Ald sitting beneath a tree. He heard their approach, straightening as he saw them.

"We need your help," Iyanka said quietly, thankfully without her voice shaking.

"Alright," he said slowly. "Help with what?"

"Getting help for the wounded hunters and soldiers."

He stood gingerly, and Iyanka glimpsed a bloodied bandage beneath his shirt.

"Shallow cut," he explained. "What do you need me to do?"

"We need someone to protect Princess Iyanka while we search for wounded soldiers," Zef said, voice too bright and innocent to match the assessing gleam in his eyes.

"Peyton Aldrige gave us this to convince them to come willingly," Iyanka held up the badge. "But we don't want to take chances."

Ald took one look at the badge and nodded. "I'll help. Lead the way."

Iyanka hesitated. Turning her back on Ald, even now, was…difficult. Ald noticed her reluctance, offering her a smile tinged with sadness.

"Or I'll go ahead, if you'd like."

"Yes," Iyanka said, stepping back to let him pass.

Ald strode past her without another word, careful not to come within arm's reach of Iyanka. She stayed a few steps behind him as they walked, only drawing closer when they neared the field. Zef stayed at her side, while Henry fell back a step. Guarding their backs?

They searched the area, finding far too many bodies that were pale and lifeless. Iyanka tried not to examine their faces too much, terrified she'd find some she knew. She'd already watched Achan die, already seen far too many lives taken that day. If she found a friend in that bloodied field of dead…it might be too much.

Most of the soldiers they came across were hostile at first. One called Ald a traitor and tried to attack him, collapsing to the ground when he put weight on his injured leg. But most accepted their help in the end. Ald made sure to strip them of all their weapons, making Iyanka truly grateful that he was with them. She'd had no idea how many places knives could be hidden.

They'd brought half a dozen men back to Gretta and Peyton before others began to help them. Lynn joined Gretta in tending their injuries, while others helped search the field for hunters. They brought far too many men for Gretta and Lynn to handle alone, but when Cook was finished helping the wielders she gave in and saw to the wounded soldiers as well. And if she was sharper to them, no one mentioned it.

Iyanka helped where she could, but she reached a point where it was all too much. The blood, the suffering, the weariness… she walked away, just to catch her breath. *So much suffering.*

Victorin found her like that a few hours later, her back pressed to a tree as she stared at the unblemished forest around her. Trying to forget the sight behind her, where the wounded rested and people were already gathering the dead for a mass burial. At Iyanka's request, the dead of both sides were gathered together.

"I thought I told you to rest," Victorin side, appearing so silently that Iyanka jumped.

"I couldn't," Iyanka said, leaning into him. "Not with so many people needing help."

Victorin had changed into clean clothes, and Iyanka pressed into his warmth gratefully.

"I know," he said, resting his chin on her head. For a few moments they stayed that way, taking in the silence of the forest.

"What do we do now?" Iyanka asked.

"We try to avoid another battle when the rest of the barons arrive."

Iyanka tilted her head back to look up at him. "Aren't their armies already here?"

Victorin's eyebrows drew together. "No. Why do you ask?"

"The commander of Baron Algheny's hunters is over there," Iyanka said, gesturing to where Peyton still sat.

Earlier, he'd slept, but now he was awake and taking in the activity around him.

"I need to talk to him." Victorin took his arm from her shoulders, stepping toward. Iyanka grabbed his hand as she followed him.

"I'll go with you."

Peyton saw them coming, his face turning grim. He seemed to brace himself as they approached, his eyes guarded as he stared up at Victorin.

"Your highness," he greeted as Victorin and Iyanka stopped before him.

"Commander," Victorin replied, kneeling to be at eye level with Peyton. "I'd like to speak to you on a few matters."

There was no room for refusal in Victorin's tone, and Peyton seemed to know it. He gestured for Victorin to continue. His right arm still hung limp.

"Do you know when the forces under your command will arrive?"

"Two days at the latest," Peyton said. "Any men from the southern barons will be with them."

"Will they attack?"

"That depends," Peyton replied cautiously. "If I command them to stand down, they will."

Victorin nodded. The look in his eyes made Iyanka uncomfortable. It was hard, and far more unyielding than she was used to. *What's he going to do?*

"What do you want in order to avoid another battle?"

"I don't *want* anything other than our lives and homes," Peyton replied, measuring his words as he spoke. "My uncle and the barons of the south were hesitant to follow Malchomy's lead. With what's transpired today, they should be willing to withdraw their forces to their own lands."

"Why?" Iyanka asked, ducking her head when she realized she spoke aloud. Still, Peyton answered her.

"You aren't power-hungry tyrants as we were led to believe." His eyes fixed on Iyanka, suddenly earnest.

"As you and Prince Victorin said, you are only defending your right to live."

Peyton turned to the camp, gesturing to the wounded surrounding them, to Gretta and Lynn still wandering among them seeing to any need they could.

"This alone proves Malchomy wrong."

Iyanka took a deep breath, as the three of them assessed each other in silence. When Victorin spoke again, his voice was warmer.

"Would your uncle and the southern barons be willing to negotiate a treaty with us?"

"Yes," Peyton answered with little hesitation. "Especially with Malchomy's hold on Elnar broken."

"Good," Victorin said, only a hint of his relief evident as the lines around his eyes eased. "I'll let you rest."

Victorin stood, pulling Iyanka up with him.

"Your Highness," Peyton called, making Iyanka and Victorin turn back to him.

"Thank you for your mercy," he said. "I know it's undeserved."

"I wouldn't have given it," Victorin said. "Thank Iyanka."

Peyton took Victorin's frank statement in stride. His gaze turned to Iyanka, and he bowed his head. "Thank you, Princess Iyanka."

"Of course," she murmured, ducking her head and unsure how else to respond. Her heart still pounded. Victorin pulled her close, tucking her against his side, and drew her away from the gathered people.

"It's time to rest," he said, leading her toward the camp that was already set up.

Iyanka didn't protest. The pain and horror of the day had kept her mind wide awake, but her body was on the verge of collapse. Victorin stopped beside a quiet tree, within sight of one of the fires being started, and helped her sit on the ground. They both sat at the base of that tree, Iyanka tucked under Victorin's arm. She closed her eyes and listened to his heartbeat, thanking the Creator that they were both alive.

Chapter XX

The southern barons and their armies arrived the next day. Though their meeting was tense, with Peyton's help negotiations began. Iyanka sat between Victorin and Milek for every moment of it, determined to do her part to find a new peace. The process was tedious and tense: not every baron was willing to accept the wielders back into Elnar's society, or to give back the land they'd taken. Iyanka feared fights would break out over several of the matters they discussed. It was at these times Iyanka spoke the most, struggling to calm the ragged tempers around her. The negotiations continued.

After the fifth day, a treaty was drafted and signed by the twelve remaining barons and the three remaining royals of Siersh and Eisadel. All land held by wielders prior to the conquest of Siersh and Eisadel was returned to them. The wielders would stay within their borders unless invited elsewhere, while the barons vowed to dissolve the hunters' ranks and destroy all enchanted weapons. Finally, the treaty of Frieda's Refuge was reestablished.

It was less than Iyanka hoped for, but it was a beginning. It would take more years of healing before they could reach an easy peace, but at least they had hope. At least they'd have a place where wielders would be safe.

On the sixth day, the barons and their forces departed for their own lands. A few stayed, either too injured to be moved so far or choosing to remain among the wielders. Many of those who'd fought with the wielders chose to go to Agera. Among them was Ald. He'd kept his distance from Iyanka since the day of the battle, but he stayed near Gretta. No one was surprised when he announced his intention of returning with them to Agera.

Most of the wielders had already returned to the ancient city, including the wounded. But Milek and Victorin chose a few to stay with them and wait for the expected Ecleathians. On the seventh day, they arrived.

It was a frosty morning, mist swirling close to the ground. Iyanka was curled against Victorin's side trying to wake up when one of their sentries announced visitors approaching from the plains.

That banished the weariness from her mind. Iyanka stood with Victorin, heart crashing against her breastbone. Milek had been resting, but he rocked to his feet at the signal, smoothing his hair back as he blinked.

"Are you ready?" Victorin asked.

"Yes," Milek said, lowering his hands to his belt as he stood tall.

Iyanka didn't trust herself to speak, but she nodded to Victorin and Milek when they looked to her.

"Good," Victorin said. "We'll meet them at the edge of the trees. There's no reason to let them wander into our camp."

"Prince Victorin," Henry said, standing and looking more awake than the rest. "Please let me accompany you."

"Me too," Zef said, his eyes half closed as he stumbled to his feet.

"That's not a good idea," Milek said. "You're only here in the first place because you hid from Lynn and Cook."

"There was a reason we hid," Henry said, turning his steady eyes on Milek. "I need to be there."

Iyanka watched Henry, as memories played in her mind. Memories of Henry facing the sorceress, speaking to her in Ecleathian. *My story shouldn't be told in pieces.* While Zef tried to convince Milek and Victorin that he should go, Henry turned to Iyanka. He nodded, as if confirming her silent suspicions.

"Henry should come," Iyanka said.

Milek and Victorin turned toward her. Milek's face was painted in surprise, confusion. But not Victorin's. She took that in, deciding to talk to him later.

"Alright," Victorin said hesitantly. "Henry, you'll come with us."

What about me?" Zef asked.

"The fewer people they see, the better," Egan said, laying a hand on Zef's shoulder. "You'll stay here with me."

Zef's disappointment was obvious, but he didn't argue. Henry patted his back in apology as he passed, but he didn't argue either. Iyanka suspected he understood the danger of these sorcerers better than any of them.

"Let's go," Milek said. "Before they get any closer."

They walked toward the field together, Milek and Victorin leading as they stepped onto the soil where they'd fought only a week before. The bodies of the fallen were buried in mass graves nearby, but the morning mist hid the trampled ground. The scattered trees and open field looked peaceful in that early morning light. Until her eyes found the four cloaked figures waiting for them only a few dozen steps from the edge of the trees.

There were two men and two women. A short man with slicked back hair and a gold ring in his ear held the hand of a woman slightly taller than him, with light freckled skin and gray eyes. The other pair were taller, with skin the color of the earth and eyes that watched Iyanka and her companions with eerie focus. They all had the hoods thrown back, but their billowing cloaks hid the rest of their forms.

Victorin and Milek continued to approach until they were a few steps away, close enough to converse easily. Close enough for them to attack easily, if they so chose. Iyanka stood between Victorin and Milek, Henry right behind them. For a moment the two groups stared at each other, assessing.

"Greetings," Milek said, stiff with formality.

The short man turned his head to the side, eyes glittering. "Prince Milek, Prince Victorin, Princess Iyanka. It seems we've missed much."

"Our disagreement with the barons is already resolved," Milek said. "Your allies are already returning to their own lands."

"Allies is a strong word," the taller woman answered, her voice more abrupt than Iyanka expected. "Our association continues only as long as it benefits us, as I'm sure you know."

"Your associate told us as much," Victorin said.

"Indeed," the shorter man said. "Do you know where we could find her? She never returned to us, and we're *very* concerned for her safety."

Iyanka glanced up at Victorin and Milek, wondering what their reactions would be. They hadn't discussed this, what to say if the Ecleathians asked about Gamir. They risked the Ecleathians' wrath with any response Iyanka could think of.

"She left out city when we refused her proposal," Milek said.

"And returned to speak with Princess Iyanka, last we knew," the freckled woman said. Her eyes turned on Iyanka, making her stiffen.

"Speak to her," Victorin repeated, his voice nearly a growl. "An interesting way to describe it."

Iyanka winced, recognizing what Victorin had given away. All four Ecleathians *intensified*: their postures stiffer, more hostile, all gazes on Victorin.

"Then you know what happened to her," the short man said. "Enlighten us to her fate."

"She attacked Princess Iyanka and was imprisoned," Milek said.

"Is she still imprisoned?"

"No," Milek admitted, jaw tight.

"She's dead," Henry said, stepping forward.

Milek reached toward him as if to hold him back, but Henry ignored him. His focus was on the Ecleathi- ans. He had that same intensity in his eyes, that same edge that dared anyone to cross him. Iyanka wouldn't have challenged him, no matter his age. At the same time, she longed to hide him from the four pairs of eyes that now swiveled to him.

"Thank you for your honesty—"

"I killed her."

Iyanka stared at Henry, wondering if she'd heard correctly. She flicked her eyes to Victorin, and he nod- ded, face grim. Iyanka's breath caught as she turned back to Henry, now the center of attention.

"*You* killed Gamir?" the previously silent man hissed.

"Yes," Henry said, and when he opened his mouth again it was Ecleathian he spoke, low and threatening. The Ecleathians listened closely: eyes narrowed, trying unsuccessfully to hide their shock. Milek and Victorin watched the exchange with expressions that were sud- denly guarded, as Iyanka gauged their reactions and prayed for a peaceful end to this standoff.

The short man replied to whatever Henry had said, and a short conversation ensued. Not knowing what words were exchanged, not able to guess what would happen next, was disconcerting. But even more disconcerting was when the Ecleathians backed down. Their shoulders hunched, their eyes darted away, while Henry stared them down with the confidence of a king. The shorter man was the first to remember Iyanka, Victorin, and Milek were there and turned to face them.

"It seems our presence is unnecessary," he said. "We'll leave swiftly."

"Take care that you do," Victorin answered.

The four of them bowed their heads and backed away, disappearing in the mist too soon to be natural. Iyanka stared at the place where they'd been, waiting for them to return, to attack. They stood alone for several long moments before Victorin turned to Henry.

"Are they gone?"

Henry nodded. "They will leave as they said."

"What did you *tell* them?" Milek asked.

"I told them Elnar was well protected, and to tell their king their plans are futile."

"Is that all?" Victorin asked, and Iyanka couldn't tell if he was sarcastic or not.

"They also asked who I am." Henry shrugged, but that look of wary expectation was back in his eyes.

"I'd like to know the answer to that, myself," Milek said, staring down at him with one eyebrow raised.

Iyanka didn't bother trying to defend Henry, too relieved that Victorin and Milek's response to Henry's actions seemed to be mild, measured. Henry could apparently handle himself, anyway.

"Someday, I will explain," Henry promised, glancing at Iyanka as he did. "But I don't think now is the time."

Milek nodded, satisfied at least for the moment. But Victorin didn't move.

"Henry," he said. "Will they return?"

Henry's eyes were too weary, too mature for his young face as he answered. "Yes. But not soon. They won't come back until they're sure they can win."

"They're not sure they can win now?" Milek scoffed. "How would we fight them if they attacked?"

"Cron and Waneroth are still ignorant of Ecleath's influence," Victorin said. "It appears they want to keep it that way. For now."

"That gives us time to prepare," Iyanka offered, ignoring the dread conjured by the idea of Ecleath returning, of fighting them personally.

Milek chuckled humorlessly. "Let's hope they underestimate us."

As they talked, they'd all turned back toward the forest, meandering toward their camp. Milek walked close to Henry, asking him questions Henry answered respectfully but vaguely. Iyanka and Victorin hung back, walking slowly. Victorin had his arm around Iyanka's shoulders, and she leaned into him.

"What happens now?" Iyanka asked quietly.

"We rebuild our lives," Victorin answered.

"Will we stay in Agera?"

"At least for now. There are too few of us to spread out now, even with a peace treaty in place."

"Ruling two kingdoms from one city," Iyanka mused. "I wonder if it's been done before."

"One kingdom."

Iyanka stopped, pulling back so she could look at Victorin properly. "What?"

"Our people are already united," Victorin said. "There's no reason to separate them again. Milek will rule over both lands."

"You're alright with giving up your family's throne?"

Iyanka spoke slowly, watching Victorin closely.

"Yes. Your brother is already a better king than I'd ever be."

There was pain in his voice, and Iyanka stepped closer.

"You'd be a good king, Victorin."

He shook his head. "I'm a commander, not a ruler. I'm satisfied with my position. I'm glad to support Milek."

Iyanka stared at him another moment, searching for any sign that his words were less than genuine, that there was pain or bitterness in this decision. She found none.

"Alright," she said, stepping forward again. They walked in silence for a few moments.

"What are you thinking?" Victorin asked. "Are you upset?"

"No," she said, and it was true.

She hadn't expected Victorin to withdraw from his place as leader of the fire wielders, hadn't expected him to give up his family's crown. But with what she knew of King Ignacio, she thought she understood it. She respected Victorin's decision. And secretly, she was grateful for it. She'd never relished the idea of being queen.

Worry still marked his eyes, though, so she smiled up at him.

"I'm wondering though…what does that make us?"

He returned her smile, weight lifting from his shoulders.

"Most call me Commander, and I imagine you're still a princess. Although…" His eyes brightened with mischief. "I'm sure Milek could give you an honorary title. *Defender of the realm*, for instance."

Iyanka shuddered. "No, thank you."

Victorin laughed, and the sound of it loosened something deep in Iyanka's soul. It was the first time he'd laughed since the battle, the first *joyful* sound Iyanka had heard from him in days. *We can come back from this.*

They continued their meandering path toward the camp, taking their time. Ahead of them, Iyanka could hear Zef asking his fast-paced questions about what he'd missed, and Milek laughing as he answered. Henry's steady voice was there too, when Zef aimed more questions at him.

"What do you know of Henry's past?" Iyanka asked, too quiet for anyone to overhear.

"Not much," Victorin said, turning so they walked around the camp instead of toward it. "I found him alone in the southern forest, a few months after the barons attacked. He never explained how he got there. He has no family, no home…"

"Do you think…is it possible he was one of the trapped gardeners?"

Even suggesting it felt ridiculous, but Victorin didn't dismiss it. And it would explain so much…

"I've wondered that," Victorin said. "But he won't say. Every time I've asked, he says his story—"

"Shouldn't be told in pieces," Iyanka finished. "He's said that to me, too."

She glanced back at the camp, finding Henry among her friends.

"He promised to tell me his story, someday," she said.

"I hope he'll let me listen in."

"I think he will. It's not that he wants to hide it, it's…" Iyanka trailed off, seeing the weary understanding, the hidden pain of Henry's gaze. "Something about his past…it's difficult for him."

"That's not surprising. Few in Elnar know how to speak Ecleathian."

"True," Iyanka said. "But whatever his story, he protected us."

"I have no doubt about Henry's loyalties," Victorin said, his voice soothing. "Though I wish his intervention was enough to keep Ecleath away permanently."

"You think they'll return?"

"They said they were seeking allies for the years ahead. They must have larger plans. We haven't heard the last of Ecleath, whether they return to Elnar or not."

Iyanka knew he was right. Just as she knew, with bone deep certainty, that Henry had a role to play when Ecleath came again. She prayed he'd be prepared. That he'd survive. *He won't stand alone.*

"We'll be ready," Iyanka whispered.

"We'll be ready," Victorin echoed. He grabbed Iyanka's hand and held up their gasp, hints of frost and flame flickering around their joined hands. "We've barely scratched the surface of what the Shacar are capable of. The Creator gave us a power able to withstand magic. We'll seek His guidance in how to use it."

Iyanka smiled and rested her head on Victorin's shoulder. He was right.

They would rebuild. They would learn. They would face the future without fear. And if Ecleath returned, they'd find the wielders of Elnar prepared to face them. They would find *Iyanka* ready to face them, no matter what power they brought with them.

The Creator had seen them through death and darkness already. No matter what came, Iyanka would trust Him to see them through it again.

If you enjoyed Frosted Fire, please consider leaving a review.
And read on for a glimpse of Henry's story in

Born in Darkness

Book two in the Agonizomai Series

Frosted Fire

A Story Owed

Henry settled on the ground a few feet from the campfire, staring into its flames rather than the faces watching him.

Victorin wasn't so bad. He'd nodded to Henry as he sat, and then turned his attention to Iyanka at his side. But Milek stared at him from across the flames with ill-concealed curiosity, and Iyanka's eyes held a worry she was trying to hide. Enough years had passed that Henry couldn't really remember his mother's face, but he knew she'd often held the same expression Iyanka did now.

And with that reminder, the past came flooding back, along with all its guilt and pain. The lies he'd believed, the violence he'd caused, the losses he'd mourned…all of it called from the depths of his mind far more quickly than he liked. He'd promised Iyanka he would tell her his story. If it had been anyone else, he wouldn't have followed through.

Henry looked up to Iyanka, he saw himself reflected back in her eyes. She saw him as a boy, as a child to protect. He'd almost started to see himself that way.

For four years he'd lived as the child he'd never gotten to be under his father's guidance. And while it wasn't long enough to forget, it had been long enough to change, to wish that he *could* be the carefree boy Jack and Emmy had encouraged him to be. But that wasn't who he was. And now, with Iyanka, Victorin, and Milek all waiting for him to speak, he knew it was time to move on. He wasn't carefree, he wasn't from Elnar, and in many ways, he was no longer a boy.

Ecleath will return to Elnar. They need to be ready. Henry continued to watch the flames of the campfire. Above him, branches and leaves quaked in a wind that didn't touch him on the ground. Within that sound, so common and familiar, were a thousand memories he'd wanted to forget. He closed his eyes.

"My full title is Eero Henry, second son of King Duna and Queen Acacia of Ecleath. I was born over two centuries ago, in the ninth year after Ecleath was shut off from the rest of the continent. I was known as the most accomplished sorcerer of my generation."

Chapter I

Soldiers marched down a narrow street, their armor gathering shadows instead of sunlight. They didn't notice the old blind woman leading the boy across the street.

Bairka crossed into a trash-littered alleyway with practiced confidence, tracing her hand over the graffiti carved into the wall as she hobbled down the alley. Henry watched closely, surprised at how well the old woman navigated the world around her with such terrible eyesight.

"Here," Bairka whispered, stopping before a door and tapping on the wood. The pattern was different from the last safehouse Henry had visited.

The doors opened, and Bairka reached back to grab Henry by his hood.

"Come child, before they see us."

Henry allowed himself to be tugged inside, keeping his head down until the door was closed. Bairka released him then, and Henry turned around to survey the room. It wasn't much. It looked like the back room of a shop, turned into a gathering place. Two dozen people milled about, men and women of all ages, talking and gathering the remnants of a meal. Henry didn't recognize any of the faces. His father would be disappointed.

"Eero," whispered a voice. "Bairka, what've you done?"

Henry turned at the sound of his title to see a young woman staring at him.

"But he's just a child…"

Bairka turned toward Henry and squinted at him, her eyes widening in horror when she finally recognized him.

Henry threw back his hood and glanced around the room. For three heartbeats, everyone was still. Henry gathered power within him, ignoring the weight in his chest as he waited for someone to run.

The young woman was the first to move. She leaped into action, and Henry threw magic outward, setting guards on the doors and windows. But instead of running toward the door like he expected, the woman dashed toward the mats near the back of the room. The men in the room converged to hide her from sight as the other woman pulled the children in the same direction, toward the back wall.

Henry thought he heard the creaking of hinges. He advanced on the men, who withdrew but didn't break ranks. Their faces were grim, full of fear. *Easily defeated.*

Henry flicked his hand, sending magic to knock them aside with ease. A few women huddled behind them, pressed into the corner, their arms wrapped around each other as they watched Henry approach.

He stopped. There were fewer here than he'd seen when he entered. Bairka and the woman who'd recognized him were there, but the children and two of the older women had disappeared. He could knock them aside as easily as he had the men…but he hesitated.

"Move aside," Henry ordered. None of them obeyed.

Behind him, the door splintered. Henry removed the guards from the door, allowing the soldiers to enter the safe house, but his attention stayed on the women before him. Shouts and fighting filled the room as the soldiers captured the men, but still the women didn't move. Henry advanced, grabbing Bairka by the arm and pulling her away from the others. Her companions tried holding onto her, but eventually they released the blind woman in favor of keeping their place. An older woman stepped in front of the others, spreading her arms out as if to shield them.

Futile, Henry thought as he forced her out of the way as well. And as the other women shrank back from Henry's gaze, he spotted the edge of a door in the floor beneath them. He didn't need to ask where it led.

He motioned to two soldiers, who surged forward and forced the women from their place. Henry ignored their cries as he strode up to the door and grasped the iron ring. It didn't budge.

"Allow me, Eero," one of the soldiers said.

Henry moved to the side, fists clenching as the soldier opened the trap door with ease. But he kept his face a disinterested mask as the soldier moved aside and let Henry drop into the tunnel first.

Inside, the sewer was dark and damp. The canal running down the center was filled with greasy water and pieces of trash, and the walkways on either side were hardly better. The two soldiers climbed in after him, and one made a gagging sound as the smell assaulted him. Henry smirked, resisting his own gag reflex.

Holding his breath, he listened, fighting to isolate the sounds in the dark tunnel. Water dripped from the ceiling, rats skittering across stone. Somewhere ahead, Henry heard a rock skid across the floor and the sound of one person shushing another.

"This way," Henry said, surging ahead. He had to step over tree roots that had found their way into the sewer. Those could be helpful, if Henry could use them without collapsing the walls.

Two dozen steps ahead, the tunnel curved toward the right and intersected with another canal. As he rounded the corner, he saw a glimpse of a skirt pulling out of view. The soldiers on either side of Henry surged ahead, Henry close behind. Rounding another bend, half a dozen women and children came into view. They screamed and scrambled, dodging into side tunnels and throwing themselves into the putrid water in attempts to escape.

One girl darted down a narrow tunnel and Henry followed, leaving behind the soldiers busy capturing the others. She didn't make it a dozen steps down the tunnel before she tripped, roots wrapping around her ankles and snaking their way up to capture her wrists. She screamed and writhed. Her thrashing hands grabbing one of the roots and sent frost across its surface, and Henry raised his eyebrows in surprise. But he didn't stop. She'd frozen one root, but there were plenty of others to use. She quickly gave up and curled in on herself, quivering as she watched Henry approach.

"Please don't," she whispered.

Henry stopped. She was a few years younger than him, ten at the oldest. Her ice blue eyes were filled with an innocent sort of fear that silently pleaded with him. No one had ever looked at him like that before. Why was there hope in her eyes? *Does she really think I'll let her go?*

Henry made the roots retreat, holding his hand out to her. Gingerly, hesitantly, she grabbed hold. And as her skin touched his, dark ropes that sparked energy coiled around her arm, capturing her other hand and cinching them together. She screamed and tried to pull away, but the magic held. Henry ground his teeth together at the tight burning in his chest, determined not to give in to weakness. He could manage this much until they reached the rest of the squadron.

Henry pulled her to her feet and turned to rejoin the others, trying to ignore the muffled sobs behind him. Back on the street, the girl's cries were drowned out by the noise of her companions' pleas and useless prayers. Henry took his place at the front of the group and refused to look back.

Within the palace complex, Henry split off from the group, winding through halls and stairways to his father's study. King Duna demanded reports on raids before dealing with the prisoners, especially those Henry assisted in. And he wasn't patient about delays.

When he reached the tall oak door that led into the study, though, he was stopped by the guard beside it.

"King Duna's meeting will not be disturbed," the guard, Elas, said.

Henry swallowed back his annoyance, knowing better than to argue. "How long will I have to wait?"

"Shouldn't be long."

Henry nodded and stepped to the other side of the door, hands clasped behind his back as he mirrored Elas's stance. Staring at the wall opposite him, Henry flexed his hands and rubbed at his wrists. His veins were stinging. It was harder to ignore when he had nothing to distract himself with.

A few minutes later, the door opened and two of his father's personally trained guard strode out. They paused long enough to rest three fingers to their chin in deference to him, then continued down the hall. Henry waited a few seconds before entering his father's study and stepping up to the front of the desk. He bowed his head and raised a fist to his lips, the deference of prince to king, then raised his head.

"Henry," King Duna greeted. "Was your mission successful?"

"No, sir. The leaders of the Theophiloi still elude us."

"But you captured the members of the group you infiltrated?"

"All present, Father."

The king's face finally softened as he leaned forward in his chair. "Well done. Sooner or later, we will stamp out this cult."

Henry did his best to keep his expression neutral, but his father's brow wrinkled anyway.

"You disagree?" he asked.

"No, Father."

Except he did. They would never weed out all of them at this rate, not when so many were still being added to their ranks. Safe houses kept springing up from the ashes of those destroyed. Many of their leaders still eluded capture, somehow continuing to interact with the rest of their members while on the run. The Theophiloi were growing, not shrinking.

"Speak, Henry," the Kind Duna said, softening the order by adding, "I want your thoughts."

"Many of the people still sympathize with them," Henry explained. "They are reluctant to accuse members, or even give us information."

The king nodded and stood, turning to face the window overlooking the city. "That *is* a problem. They do not understand how dangerous this sect is to our well-being, to the survival of our kingdom."

Henry waited silently for his father's next order. King Duna looked out over the city for several breaths, then turned back to Henry.

"You are finished for the day. I'll have Hallan help me with the prisoners."

Raising his fist to his lips again, Henry bowed his head and turned to go.

"You might visit your mother," King Duna called out, causing Henry to turn.

"She was asking after you this morning," his father explained. His gaze was softer, less commanding.

And Henry recognized this as a suggestion, not an order.

"Did you tell her what I was doing?"

"Of course not. No need to worry her."

Worrying her didn't concern him as much, but it didn't matter. As long as Father had told her nothing, everything was fine.

Henry knew his mother sympathized with the Theophiloi, even considered herself one of them. She'd be disappointed if she knew Henry was taking part in eliminating them.

"Thank you, Father," Henry said.

His father nodded, but he was already staring out the window again. Henry left the study as silently as possible, nodding to Elas as he turned toward his mother's rooms.

The lady in waiting standing outside her chambers let Henry through without a word. He barely acknowledged her as he strode into his mother's parlor, the plant-filled room easing the tension that always came with a raid.

He stopped in the middle of that space, closing his eyes for a moment to stand in the silence. He took a deep breath, letting the day drain away before he saw his mother. She didn't know what Father had him doing, any of it. As far as she knew, Henry's training kept him to the castle grounds, practicing with soldiers. He wanted to keep it that way.

But as he took one last breath to clear his mind, Henry frowned. The plants that lined every wall, climbing high to the ceiling and spilling out of the large windows...they weren't as healthy as they should've been. Opening his eyes, Henry looked to the ceiling. The vines clinging to the rafters were hanging limp, flowers that yesterday had been in their prime faded and falling to the floor. The others were the same.

Crossing the room in a few bounds, Henry pushed open the door to his mother's room and searched for her. He found her in her bed, her head laid back against the pillows, eyes opening at his entrance. Henry approached her bedside as she pushed herself into a sitting position.

"I'm sorry I woke you, Momma," Henry said, glancing from the way her arms shook to her tired gaze.

"Don't apologize," she said, giving him a soft smile.

"How are you?"

Her smile faltered, but in less than a heartbeat it was back. "Well enough. A bit tired is all."

Henry scratched at his wrist as he continued watching her, not sure what to say.

"You don't believe me?" she asked. Her voice was coaxing, almost teasing, and it made Henry smile against his will. But he still shook his head.

"No, I suppose you don't," she sighed. "You've always been too observant for your own good."

"Father says I got that from you," Henry replied.

"Yes." She looked away, her smile fading. Henry waited, and after a few moments she turned back to him. "But enough about me. How was your day?"

"Difficult," Henry decided after a moment of thought.

"Your father isn't pushing you too hard, is he?"

"No," he was quick to reply. She didn't look convinced. Her lips were pursed in the concerned expression Henry tried to avoid.

"Henry," she said, her voice quiet, "let me see your arm."

Henry considered arguing, but he knew that she wouldn't let it go until he obeyed. Arguing would only tire her more. Holding his breath, he held his arm out for her inspection, and she pulled the sleeve of his shirt to his elbow. Black lines traced his veins, stopping a few inches above his wrist. They burned in the light, and Henry grit his teeth to keep from pulling his hand back so he could cover up the marks again.

"Henry," his mother sighed. Something about her voice made his face burn, settled a stone in his gut.

"It's nothing, Momma," he said. She released her grip on his wrist, and he reclaimed his arm. The burning eased once he had his sleeve pulled down again.

"It's not nothing," she replied, her eyes glittering with unshed tears. "Using that power will destroy you. You should use the gifts the Creator gave you, not that darkness your father embraces."

"I do." To prove his point, Henry turned to the normally lush plant growing beside his mother's bed. Focusing on its life, Henry sent a spark of energy into it, causing the wilted leaves to perk up. Seeing the renewed plant made Momma smile, but Henry didn't match it. It wasn't like her to let them falter.

"You're weaker," Henry said, turning back to her.

His mother smiled sadly and cupped her hand around his cheek. "I'm fine."

He didn't believe her, but as always, he had nothing he could say. He couldn't make it better. *Helplessness.* He hated the feeling, especially when it came to his mother. She stared at him for a few moments, the tears spilling over as she stroked his cheek.

"You're my miracle, my gift from the Creator," she whispered. "You know that, right?"

"Yes," Henry said, hesitant. She'd always called him that, but this time the words sounded different. More than a pet name or an empty belief. The sound of it tightened his chest, made his own eyes burn.

"And I love you more than life itself," she continued.

"I love you too..." Henry paused, searching her eyes. The answer he found there wasn't encouraging. There was sorrow there, and *acceptance*. But faced with Henry's inspection, she smiled again.

"Never forget," she said.

"I won't forget," Henry said, compelled to give his promise even as his mouth soured with the taste of goodbye in the words.

She wasn't that weak, was she? Father would've said something if she was, unless... *He told me to visit her. Was that his warning?*

"Momma?" Henry asked. The crack in his voice bothered him, but he ignored it, keeping his focus on his mother. "How are you really?"

The smile slipped from her face, and that sorrow overtook her eyes. All of a sudden, Henry could see how gaunt her face was, how her hand trembled as she held it to his face.

"I fear my time is coming," she admitted. Her voice was thick with tears, and Henry's own eyes continued to burn.

"What can I do to help you?"

There had to be something. He couldn't be helpless, not in this. *I won't let weakness stop me. There has to be something I can do.*

"Nothing, son." Her hand slipped from his face, and she let it fall to the bed. "I will go when the Creator calls. No one can change that."

"Why?" The question he'd silently asked for years, ever since she got sick, slipped from his lips. "If He's good like you say, why would he let you die? If He loves His people, why does He let Father kill them?"

"We don't always know the Creator's whole plan, but we can trust…"

"Why do you trust in a God who either can't save you or doesn't care?"

"Don't," Mother said, her voice the strongest Henry had heard in months. Her eyes flashed with fear, even anger. "Don't speak of the Creator like that Henry."

As quickly as the passion had come, it faded. She sagged against her pillows, her breathing shallow, but she kept her eyes on Henry.

"I don't have all the answers," she said. "But He is good, Henry, and He has the power. Never doubt that."

"I'm sorry."

Sorry for exciting her, at least. But his question remained. *Why?*

A knock sounded at the door, and when Henry turned his mother's lady in waiting was curtseying at the doorway.

"Sorry to disturb you, my Queen, Eero. King Duna requests Henry's presence in the courtyard."

Henry waited until the maidservant had retreated to turn back to his mother.

"You should go," she whispered.

Henry nodded, but he didn't turn away. After a moment's hesitation, Henry climbed onto the edge of the bed and wrapped his arms around his mother's neck. He was too old for this kind of display, but he didn't care. She returned the hug and Henry stayed carefully still. If only he could return to years ago, when his mother held him this way every night, telling him stories before he went to sleep. When she ran and laughed with him, when her eyes weren't telling him goodbye. She couldn't leave him. *I won't let you die.*

Father would be angry if Henry kept him waiting. Finally, that thought pulled him away from his mother. Even then, he moved slowly.

"I love you," he whispered as he slipped off the bed and backed away.

"I love you too," she said, smiling. "Now go. You shouldn't keep him waiting."

Henry backed away until he reached the door, where he was forced to turn away from her. He healed the plants in her parlor on his way out in case she was well enough to sit up in the afternoon. And he ignored the nagging, twisting fear that told him not to leave. That told him this was his last chance…his last chance to see his mother alive. He wouldn't bow to that fear. It was *wrong.* He'd find a way to make her strong again. He wouldn't let anyone take her from him, God or not.

As he marched toward the courtyard where his father waited, his thoughts hardened in resolve. He'd ask his father and tutors for ideas. He'd search the dusty tomes of the library. His mother would live.

His attention deep within his thoughts, the screams startled him. He jumped, flexing his hands as he took in the courtyard. *Of course.* It was one of the prisoners, a man older than Father. The guards were already dragging him away when Henry reached his father's side.

"Henry," King Duna rumbled. "Good of you to come."

Henry bowed his head at the slight rebuke, then met King Duna's eyes.

"What do you require of me?"

"*That* is how a prince should respond to his king," Duna said, glancing at Hallan behind him.

Hallan stood at attention, his hands behind his back and his face impassive, but he was redder than usual. Henry couldn't tell if it was from anger or embarrassment. Maybe both.

"Your *brother* doesn't have the stomach to interrogate these criminals," King Duna continued, turning back to Henry. "I want you to show him how it's done."

Henry glanced at Hallan, but his brother refused to look at him. So Henry turned to face where the king was gesturing. The guards had finished returning the man to his cell and were bringing forward another prisoner. When the guards stopped, their girl lifted her head, and her vibrant blue eyes met his gaze.

Not her.

Henry wasn't sure where the thought came from, where the clenching panic emerged from. But rather than aloof duty, protectiveness flooded his chest, and only willpower kept him in his place. Only practice kept his expression impassive. He glanced up at his father and found the King watching him.

This is a test, he realized. *To see if I'm strong enough. If I can do what's needed.*

Henry turned back to the girl, shoving aside whatever weakness recoiled at what his father was asking. *It's only because I've been spending time with Momma. It's her I need to protect, not this girl.*

"Father, she's just a child," Hallan spoke up. "Surely you won't punish her like the others."

"Henry at twelve is old enough to choose," King Duna said. "So is this girl. Proceed, Henry."

The girl was staring at the frost that spread around her, her lips moving though no sound came out. *Praying to her God?* Henry wondered. Not that it would do any good. There was hope for her, though. She was weak, he could see it. She'd break easily and her life would be spared. *Maybe I can save her...*

"Are you one of the Theophiloi, worshiper of the Creator and the man Theohyios?"

"Yes," she said.

"The penalty for belonging to this seditious cult is death. Deny your God and you will be spared."

"I will not deny my King and Savior," the girl said, her voice high pitched with fear.

Henry clenched his fist, pulling strands of power and sending it into the girl. She flinched, and her legs started shaking. But she didn't make a sound.

"Your death will be a thousand times more painful than this if you do not renounce Theohyios."

Her voice was quiet, but her voice was surprisingly steady as she replied. "Theohyios is my Savior, my Lord, one with the Creator of this world. I will not deny Him."

Dread crept into Henry's gut. *What if she doesn't break?* Fear strengthened the magic twining around his fingers, and this time he sent it straight to her heart. She screamed. Her legs gave out, and the guards let her fall to the hard ground, where a jagged circle of ice spread from her huddled form as Henry continued to pour power into her blood. His own chest burned from the effort. He flinched at her screams. When he let up, the girl's arms trembled as she pushed herself up on her elbows.

"Deny Theohyios," Henry ordered.

She finally met his gaze, her face lined with pain, somehow lit with a hope Henry couldn't understand.

"I will not."

Regret washed through Henry. *I failed.* But his heart numbed, and he cleared his throat, finishing the sentence with voice as dead as the stone beneath his feet.

"Three times you have refused to turn from your ways. You are therefore bound to your word and charged with sedition, for which the penalty is death by cleansing."

Terror flashed through her eyes as the guards grabbed her arms and pulled her back to the holding cells at the other end of the small courtyard. Henry watched, nearly flinching again when he felt a hand on his shoulder.

"Well done, son," King Duna said.

Henry didn't respond, missing the words to say. Instead, he turned and met Hallan's gaze. Henry couldn't tell if the disgust in his brother's gaze was aimed at him or Father. Henry hoped his own feelings weren't so obvious. Henry glanced back toward the prison gates, that same burning question echoing though his mind. *Why do you trust in a God who lets you die?*

Frosted Fire

Want free stories?

Sign up for my newsletter on my website! You'll receive a collection of short stories, including…

- A journey into the mind of a storyteller with too many stories to tell...
- The story of the Blood-born Champion and the Stuttering Songbird who follows him...
- And an Ashton Legacies short story following the events of *Aderes in Karkhana*

My newsletter is a quarterly email that will give you updates on my books, recommendations from my bookshelf, and glimpses of the wonder saturating the world around us.

.

ABOUT THE AUTHOR

Maegan M. Simpson accepts many titles, including Daydreamer, Mountain Girl, and Indie Author of 9 books. She believes that God created our world full of beauty and wonder, even in the broken pieces, and endeavors to capture that wonder in her writing.

Maegan's life so far has been full of adventures, whether it's finishing college, taming dragons (alright, they're cats), or devouring every book she can get her hands on. When she's not exploring fantasy lands or searching for faeries in the shadows, Maegan lives in rural New Mexico with her family. There, she enjoys gardening, painting, and exploring the mountains she calls home.

You can find Maegan on Instagram, Facebook, or on her website, https://maeganmsimpson.com/

Frosted Fire

Other books by Maegan M. Simpson

The Agonizomai Series:
Frosted Fire
Born in Darkness
Broken Healer
Menacing Whispers

Ashton Legacies
Aderes in Karkhana

Secrets of the National Parks Series:
Shadow of Memory
Dragon's Flight
Midnight's Wings

Stand Alone:
Stone Heart

Made in the USA
Columbia, SC
05 July 2025